EVERMORE

"Evermore" by Douglas Clark. ISBN 978-1-60264-130-3 (softcover); 978-1-60264-138-9 (hardcover); 978-1-60264-141-9 (electronic).

Library of Congress Control Number: 2011912425.

Manufactured in the United States of America.

Also by Douglas Clark

SHELL GAME

BELFAST, A NOVEL OF THE TROUBLES

TAKE FIVE, SHORT STORIES

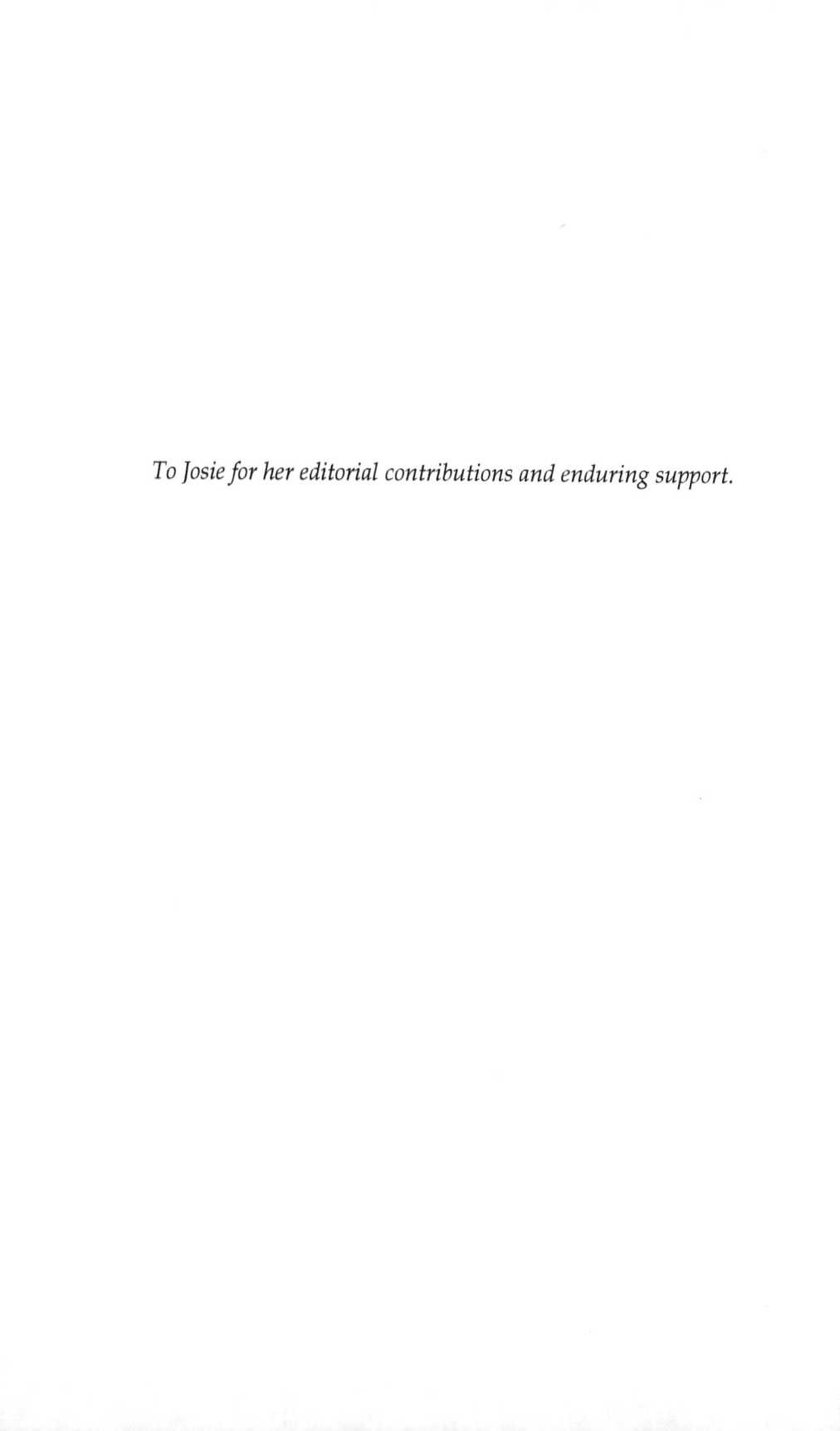

To Josie for her editorial contributions and enduring support.

Douglas Clark

EVERMORE

A Novel

Thy soul shall find itself alone
'Mid dark thoughts of the grey tomb-stone;
Not one, of all the crowd, to pry
Into thine hour of secrecy

Be silent in that solitude,
Which is not loneliness-for then
The spirits of the dead, who stand
In life before thee, are again
In death around thee, and their will
Shall overshadow thee; be still.

The night, though clear, shall frown,
And the stars shall not look down
From their high thrones in the Heaven
With light like hope to mortals given,
But their red orbs, without beam,
To thy weariness shall seem
As a burning and a fever
Which could cling to thee forever.

Now are thoughts thou shalt not banish,
Now are visions ne'er to vanish;
From thy spirit shall they pass
No more, like dew-drop from the grass.

The breeze, the breath of God, is still,
And the mist upon the hill
Shadowy, shadowy, yet unbroken,
Is a symbol and a token.
How it hangs upon the trees,
A mystery of mysteries!

Edgar Allen Poe, *Spirits of the Dead*, 1827

CHAPTER 1

PROVENCE, FRANCE – 2009

It was October. There was a light chill in the air as the middle-aged man and a younger woman sat on a patio in the south of France sharing a bottle of wine. The large early nineteenth century stone farmhouse was located outside the quaint wine town of Châteauneuf-du-Pape in Provence. It sat back off a secondary road surrounded by trees with views of vineyards and olive groves spreading out in all directions. The Rhone River was two miles in the distance. The leaves on the grapevines had turned hews of yellows and reds.

"All right, Elliot, are you going to tell me why you insisted I fly here to see you?" Allison Kryszka said. She was an attractive woman probably not yet forty, dressed impeccably in a fashionable silk blouse, tailored slacks, and expensive heels. New York accent. She had arrived just a few hours ago by the high-speed train from Paris to Avignon after flying in from New York.

Elliot Gaston looked to be around sixty. Fit and tanned. Good head of gray hair. Average height and build. Dressed in casual attire of a blue cotton shirt and chinos, the sleeves of a sweater draped over his shoulders, he looked typically Provencal.

"Certainly, Allison. I'm sorry that I've been so cloak and dagger about why I wanted you to come here all the way from New York. Let me first say that you are more than my literary agent. You're my most trusted friend. No, you're more than a friend. More like family really."

He reached over and took her hand. "Part of what I'm about to tell you will dismay you. As for the rest, you also will not believe me, at least at first. Hopefully I can convince you. That's why I needed to talk to you here. Somewhat captive. But is it not magnificent?" He said sweeping his hand to the surrounding view.

"Yes it is, Elliot, but now you have me worried. Tell me what this is about."

Still holding her hand he said, "Allison …. I've been diagnosed with terminal cancer, leukemia actually."

She grabbed his hand with both of her hands and started to cry. "God, no. Are they sure? It's not treatable?"

Gaston gently touched her cheek and attempted to wipe her tears with a handkerchief. "I'm afraid not, Allison. I've been to the best oncologists in Paris. It's known as acute myelogenous leukemia. It has an 85% mortality rate. I've been receiving chemo -therapy for a couple of months. Unfortunately, the therapy has not put the cancer in remission, and the side effects are dreadful. It's been a couple of weeks since my last treatment that's why I look normal. But I didn't bring you all this way just to tell you about my impending mortality. There's something more I must explain."

"Damnit, Elliot, you're too talented to die. You're too young. What are you, sixty?" Allison said.

Elliot Gaston paused for several moments and looked into her eyes. "No, I'm not sixty. That's what's at issue here. That's what I need to explain. I'm much older. You won't believe what I'm about to tell you, but that's why I wanted you here, so I can attempt to convince you."

"What do you mean? So you're sixty-five? More?"

Elliot sighed and answered, "Much more than that I'm afraid. Allison, I was born in 1873."

Allison Kryszka stared at him for several moments, before responding. "What the hell's that supposed to mean, Elliot?" She pulled her hands away from his.

"Well I don't know how to say it any other way. I assure you that I'm not deranged. I know it's not seemingly possible, but it is true, Allison. I've lived every minute of those years. Here, this will help with the details."

Elliot placed a three-inch thick manuscript on the table. "It's a first draft. Needs more work before it's ready for publication. It's the story of my life. I want it to be more than a just a journal or a memoir. I want anyone reading it to see my unusual journey. It's a hell of story, Allison. Considering my situation, I wanted you to see it and start the process of believing."

Allison shook her head slowly and stood up. "I don't know what you're trying to do, Elliot, but it's pretty shitty to drag me all this way to France to play whatever game this is."

She was angry and paced about with her hands on her hips.

"It's not a game, Allison. I would never do that to you."

"I don't know what to say, Elliot. I've always thought you to be this erudite man of the world. A Frenchman that writes in English. Now this comes out of the blue. You seem rational, but you're asking me to dispel common sense. First you tell me you have a terminal disease then you tell me you're over a hundred years old. What makes *you* think that you are not just imagining this?" There was still anger in her voice.

"Listen, Allison, all I ask is that you spend a couple of days here to let me try to convince you. Right now, let's go inside and I'll prepare us some dinner. I've become a passable cook these last years. Limited repertoire, but what I can do is pretty good."

Elliot seated Allison at the kitchen table and refilled her wine glass. He then lit a fire in the massive fireplace in the adjacent family room. While Elliot busied himself preparing dinner, Allison moved the conversation away from talk of mortality and this disturbing assertion about his age.

The house was quite magnificent. The walls were of great stones. Twelve-inch thick exposed beams supported the weighty slate roof. The walls were decorated with paintings and old photographs. The effect added to the feeling that one had stepped back in time.

Elliot told her that it was built around 1820. He spent a couple of years renovating and modernizing the plumbing and kitchen. Between keeping an eye on dinner, he would guide her around the rooms explaining the house's linage and the details of its construction. The conversation was light as Elliot talked about living and writing in Provence, drawing in Allison to talk about the contrasts with her living in New York.

"This is an absolutely charming house, Elliot. Too clean for a bachelor. How do you manage?"

"I have a wonderful couple of housekeepers, two old-maid sisters, Antoinette and Pauline," Elliot said. "They've adopted me. The day they come in to clean every other week, that evening they prepare dinner and the three of us enjoy a couple bottles of wine. I'm sure that it's a special part of their social life. I tease them that there must be a local rumor about our being a threesome."

Elliot opened another bottle of wine and sat down at the table. "Where to start?" he said as much to himself as to his longtime literary agent. "I don't want to discuss the cancer. That's secondary right now, Allison."

Allison sat silently, disoriented by all that her favorite client had told her. She both admired his work and held a special affection for him. These bizarre assertions troubled her on a personal level. Her initial anger had abated but she still didn't know how to reconcile Elliot's wild claim to absurd longevity with the man she had known for many years.

Elliot said, "Have you ever wondered how I've been so successful with my novels of the early part of the twentieth century? Why the critics say that I am able to evoke an uncanny sense of feeling for the time?"

"You're talented," Allison said. "You have an astounding knowledge of history and an extraordinary gift for painting a feeling for those times. Others have had success writing fiction about previous periods."

"Not many. Any come to mind? The good literature was mostly written by those of that time. Most writings about earlier times are biographical or more historical in concept. Novels are even rarer. Mine are more about the people. What the times were like. What shaped the thoughts and aspirations of people. How they lived and felt. *Why* they felt the way they did. To show, not to tell the reader what it was like during those earlier times. To give them a sense of the complex factors effecting events, not the simplifications presented as history.

"My unusually long life spanned a special period. A time that has shaped so much of what is part of today's world. It was a time of such great change, great hope. Technology advances and social change exploded. The democratic process in the United States exerted its influence for the first time. Women's suffrage and the organized labor movement advanced to the forefront.

"Maybe because it was all so sudden, there was a counter reaction with the unleashing of mankind's ugly side. The old clashed with new philosophies. The early twentieth century was a time of warfare and exploitation. The ugliest type of warfare to the extent that it transcended anything that came before. Conflicts of cultural ambitions inflicted horrors from the middle ages. Then as the World birthed itself into the modern age, once again it descended into chaos, seemingly bent on its own destruction."

"So you're saying it's because you lived those times you were able to write of them so powerfully? That you're somehow immortal?"

"Not immortal, Allison. Remember, I have a terminal disease. I've had broken bones. I bleed. I get sick. I just don't age at the same rate everyone else does."

"Every woman would hope for that," Allison said. She smiled and then said more seriously, "I'll admit that for the thirty years or so I have known you, you don't really look much older."

Elliot pulled his French passport from his pocket and handed it to her. "Take a look at the birth date, Allison."

She looked at the passport, and then looked back to Elliot with a puzzled look. "It says you were born in 1926. That makes you over eighty. Absurd enough since you look at least twenty years younger, but I thought you said you were born in 1873?"

"I was. But with my *problem* I had to acquire a new identity at some point. I'll expand on those details later. As you can imagine, even now I'm experiencing some problems of incredulity if anyone checks my date of birth when I need to show ID. Take a look at these." Elliot handed Allison an envelope.

She opened the envelope and spilled out a dozen photographs. All were black and white. Many were clearly of an older type of photography. They were cracked and dog-eared.

"Recognize me?" Elliot said as Allison looked at each photograph.

"Maybe. Hard to say with old pictures. I guess there's a resemblance. The young boy could be you. The others do appear to be you. They're old photos, or at least they look old."

"Come on, Allison. Do you think I'd fake these? Try to deceive you? That would make me raving mad or a charlatan. Look at them again. Look at the photographer's imprints on the back of several of them."

She turned the photographs over and stared at the dates. Somewhat subdued, she asked, "Why are you telling me this, Elliot? What is it you want me to do?"

"Just listen to my story. I want to tell you about the major events that shaped my life. And about times that shaped our world today. About a philosophical perspective that could only come from my unique longevity. Along the way, I hope to give you enough evidence for you to believe what I say is true. Enough for you to get this work published. And to publish it as non-fiction if that is possible."

And so began the first part of Elliot Gaston's story.

CHAPTER 2

From *Time Travels* by Dillan Murphy
EASTERN PENNSYLVANIA – 1885

My real name is Dillan Murphy. I was born March 31, 1873. I was of Irish ancestry. My grandfather immigrated to America in 1846, from County Mayo in the west of Ireland with my grandmother and my father. That was the first disastrous year of the Great Potato Famine in Ireland, killing or driving out enormous numbers of the poor threatened with starvation or disease. My grandfather took a job in the coalmines in Pennsylvania. With little other opportunities, my father eventually followed him into the anthracite coal mines at age seventeen.

We lived in Schuylkill County, Pennsylvania. Our house was better than most miner families. It wasn't a company-owned house but it still wasn't much. The roof sagged and leaked in the rain. There were three small rooms. The exterior was weathered unpainted clapboard siding. Of course there was no running water. We had a good well however. Outhouse for a toilet. My father still took pride in our little house since it was his. For this he had to walk three miles to the mine. It was only until I left home that I realized how desperately poor we were.

My mother died when I was three, probably from cancer, but back in that time it wasn't as easily diagnosed. According to my father, once she fell ill and took to her bed, she passed on in a matter of months.

My father told me some years later that he would never have gone on after her death if it hadn't been for me. He had married comparatively late in life for back then. Wanting a better life for his future family than his fellow miners, he saved as much money as possible before courting my mother. When they married, he presented his bride with the small house set on a couple of acres. He was in his late thirties and she was in her early twenties. They were both devoted to each other as much from intellectual attachment as from the emotional bond. A year later I was born. I was to be their only child.

Father was strict about my education. Unlike many others my age from miner families, he saw to it that I always attended school. Although uneducated himself, he could read and he loved books. When I was around ten years old, I remember him saying to me, probably because I was not being as serious as I should with my studies. "Dillan, you ever wonder why there are so few boys at school?"

"Yes, Sir," I said. I saw them everyday walking back from the mines. Boys as young as ten, covered in black soot carrying their lunch pails just like the older men. "Most are workin' in the mines."

"That's right. And I made a promise to your mother just before she passed on. I promised her that you'd never go into the mines. Not as a child, not as a man. It's a terrible life. It killed your granddad, and it'll be killin' me 'fore long. You work in the dark and damp. You're breathin' dust that will shorten your life, that's if you don't get killed in some accident first. I've got the black lung myself. Don't know how many more years I have."

I remember that conversation because I was jarred by his revelation of his own impending mortality. He went on to tell me, "And the only way out for you, Son is to get an education. That means hard work at your studies. And I don't mean just secondary school. I mean going on to university. We live tightly because I always put away as much as I can towards your education. When you're of age in a few years, there'll be enough to get you started."

I didn't even know of anyone that attended a university other than the village doctor. Getting an education at a university became both of our focus. We talked every evening about the future. My father and I discussed history, philosophy, and science. I wondered what he might have done had he not been trapped in poverty.

My father became my best friend. We shared things beyond the interest or understanding of my schoolmates. He opened a world for me that I would otherwise never have considered. He told me he came late to his appreciation of books and the world of knowledge. It was only after he met my mother. She was not educated either but loved books.

Through my father I learned to appreciate the elegance of language through Shakespeare and Shelley's poetry. I read history and the great epic stories of Homer's Iliad and Odyssey. There was Plato and Aristotle. To my father, these classics expressed the real soul of man. He was less inclined to give the same weight to the Bible.

In retrospect I do not remember my father explaining how he acquired these books. This was before the lending library. The books were well worn, the spines damaged on many to the point of falling apart. They were still my father's treasured possessions.

My father was one of those that commanded respect instinctively. He was never loud but always spoke with confidence. At work he had risen to the position of foreman. Not a management position, just a job with enough responsibility to get a higher wage and not have to swing a pick. He descended everyday into the mines with the other men. It was his task to supervise a group of about twenty miners and keep up the production output. He was also responsible for individual performance of each of his miners.

This brought on a continual internal battle within my father. Management had no incentive to cultivate their human resources. It was solely a matter of optimizing profits. Health and safety were simply added costs. Manpower was a commodity that could be replaced more cheaply than investing in improved working conditions. My father did what he could to help his men but in the end he had little influence. If they became sick or injured there was no way he could protect their jobs. At the most he could only influence the safety of the operations he supervised. Accidents not only killed miners but cost the owners profits.

At night he passionately discussed the terrible plight of those working in the mines. It was understandable why he became strongly pro-union. It seemed the only way to force better conditions in the mines. He likened the Pennsylvania mine owners to English and Scottish landholders in Ireland, making their wealth in agriculture on the backs of poor tenant farmers. They had turned their backs on the plight of their starving serfs during the Great Potato Famine. In like kind, the mine owners held the workforce in economic bondage with the *company store* concept, and then forced them into unsafe mines.

There was many a night that he was out late. With no mother, I was home alone. I remember being terribly worried and unable to sleep until his return. The usual reason given was some need to help a family of one of his fellow miners.

I remember one night my father had gathered all manner of food in a flour sack. I was probably twelve at the time. He was particularly angry. I asked him where he was going.

"I need to take some food to the family of Patrick Burke. I believe they're in a bad way."

"Who's Patrick Burke, Papa?"

"A miner."

"One of your men?"

"No. But he works at my mine."

"Why do you need to help him?"

My father looked at me with such an expression of anger that I expected a tongue lashing. But his eyes quickly softened.

"Because I can. Because others are afraid to. Because it's the right thing to do."

"Why are others afraid to help?"

Before answering I could almost see him composing himself. I guess he must have been thinking how he could explain the circumstances to a twelve year old.

"Patrick Burke is a man for the unions. Rumor is he was doing what they call organizing. That means trying to get miners to sign to be part of the Union. What isn't a rumor is that it was the Pinkerton goons that beat him. Happened a few days ago. He's in a bad way I'm told. Broken arms and other injuries. He won't be working for some time. Has a wife and four kids."

"Who are the Pinkertons, Papa?"

"They're hired muscle, thugs. Hired by mine management. They say for security, but it's also for keeping out a union. So they're used to intimidating the miners."

"Will it be dangerous for you to help, Papa?"

Of course it was, but my father would not admit that to me. "No. I'm a foreman. The Pinkerton's won't be bothering me."

Because of his politics, I asked my father once if he was a member of the secret organization, the Molly Maguires. Everyone knew of the Molly Maguire's. They were a violent group of Irish immigrants in Schuylkill County that pitted themselves against the mine owners in the early days of labor union organization. The Mollies were either terrorists or freedom fighters depending on whether you were pro-coal mine management or a

miner. To the miserable miner families, there was a romantic aura in the Molly Maguire's' resistance to the powerful mine owners.

"The Molly Maguires are no more, son. They hanged the
leaders in '78. You were too little to remember. I'm for the Unions though, just not for the murderin' ways of the likes of the
Mollies. They were no different than the greedy bastards that
own the collieries. They only make it tougher on us Irish."

Even so, he knew a surprising lot about the Molly Maguires,
perhaps too much I speculated. The other boys at school still
talked about the Molly Maguires as Robin Hood-like heroes.
Violent acts against the mines still occurred.

Other miners frequently came to talk to my father. Most often it was a couple or more men at one time. I could tell that he
was held in some esteem. He always made sure I was not able to
hear their conversations. Then there was his being out late at
night so often. I suspected it might not always be to help those in
need. Miners needed their rest and my father was sometimes out
all night. His explanations were not convincing. Maybe the Molly Maguires were still active.

The background for my novel, *Color Me Black,* was largely
autobiographical coming from listening and watching my father
and his fellow miners. The Molly Maguire protagonist came
straight out of the environment I knew. History is fuzzy on the
impact or even the existence of the Molly Maguires during that
time. But I can tell you from firsthand experience they did exist.
It was common knowledge among us Irish.

My later research for the book suggested the Molly Maguires
might not have been as bad a lot as the Government painted
them. The evidence against those leaders was almost solely from
a single Pinkerton Detective. The struggle of the mine workers
for a living wage and safer working conditions was part of my
early life. It was not an abstraction. The brutal means exercised
by the mine owners to maintain control gave me my first expe-

rience of social injustice.

I came from very humble beginnings, but rich in my father's love, and rich in intellectual stimulation. It was a singularly unique life, totally at odds with my environment. By the time I was in secondary school, my teachers recognized me as a student very different from his peers. My peers recognized that also. Since I was *different*, there were a lot of fights. I was not that big so I got the worst of many of those until a fellow miner friend of my father's taught me how to box.

Charles Fergus was a small young miner who augmented his income through wagers with pick-up, bare-knuckle fights. He got takers because of his slight stature, and there were always new miners coming into the area to provide him fresh opportunities.

"Boxin' is all in your head, Lad. If you've good reflexes, you can learn to handle yourself, at least good enough not to get the shit beat out of you," he said. "I'll teach you some moves and how to *read* the other guy. Boxin' is one thing, but street fightin' is another. I'll teach you some of that too."

Charles Fergus did just that. In exchange for my father teaching him to read, he taught me how to fight. He did a good job and I was a good pupil. Fergus' principal admonition was to protect your own nose first, then go for the other guy's. A shot to the nose was the quickest way to end a fight according to Fergus.

After inflicting a couple of broken noses among several tormentors, it wasn't long before no one was picking on me. I got to the point where I was getting pretty cocky. Instead of avoiding confrontation, I provoked it. That was until I picked on someone I thought was a big dumb farm boy. He turned out not to be as slow as I thought. After the terrible bruising of that lesson, I reserved my pugilistic skills for defense only.

CHAPTER 3

PROVENCE, FRANCE – 2009

"You're leaving out a lot of detail about your early life, Elliot, or is it Dillan?" Allison asked. She had decided to listen to Elliot's story and see where this was going. The premise was nonsense. What was he up to? Although professionally associated for thirty years, she really didn't know Elliot Gaston that well.

"Either name works. I've lived a long time as both. What other details do you mean?"

"Are you religious? Being Irish you grew up Catholic I assume?"

"As a matter of fact I didn't grow up Catholic even though I was baptized as such. We never went to Mass."

"So your father was not religious?"

Elliot smiled. "Hardly. Antagonistic against the Church I would say. Probably only allowed my baptism because of my mother. One incident stands out in my memory. It's in the manuscript but I'll tell you about it.

"All the kids I knew were Irish and all were church-going

Catholics. At least their parents made them go to mass. They all told me the worst part was going to confession. I'd probably questioned my father before this incident but I don't recall any specifics.

"I was probably nine or ten when the parish priest came one night to our house. My father opened the door but did not invite the priest in."

"I'm Father O'Farrell. I haven't seen you or your boy at Mass, Mister Murphy."

"And you won't, Father. We have no need of your Church."

"Everyone has need of the Church, Mister Murphy. I'm sure....."

"I'm sure we don't."

"Might I ask why that is?" the priest asked.

"I'm sure you're a good man, Father. I have no wish to offend. Let's just leave it that my boy and I will not be coming to your Mass."

After the priest left I remember asking my father why we do not attend church.

"If you're of a mind to lad I won't be stopping you. As for me I have harsh feelings about the Church. In the Old Country during the time of the great famine the Church did little to help the poor survive. They gave them Mass instead of bread. I listened to my father, your granddad, often condemning the Church. Its great land holdings, its wealth, yet doing nothing for its starving followers. It seems much the same here. The people clinging to the Church out of habit and desperation."

"Do you believe in God, Papa?" I asked.

My father took a moment before answering. "No. I see no evidence of a God, at least the God the Church preaches about. The Bible is just literature written by mortal men. If there is a God he has no regard for his people. The charitable view might be a God that simply set everything in motion then stepped aside. Or God may simply be another tyrant that inflicts all manner of deprivations upon people and then demands they worship him. God is man's invention."

What about you, Elliot? What do you believe?" Allison asked.

"Well I don't believe in the God of the Roman Catholic Church, or any other religion for that matter. Belief in a deity is not necessary for mankind to live in societies that are just and productive. My own father proves that. Organized religion has not prevented war and cruelty. To the contrary, it has often been the principle contributor. I have softened my antagonisms as I have matured but I find no emotional need to embrace faith in the form of some organized superstition."

Elliot suggested a walk. The day was sunny. The vineyards had been harvested a couple weeks ago. The leaves of the vines were starting to change colors.

"So we've covered your religious upbringing, or lack thereof. What about girls, your first romance? You were pretty handsome it seems by these old photographs. How'd you escape not falling in love?"

Elliot smiled. "I didn't escape falling in love. I just escaped marriage. That allowed escape from the difficult environment I was born into. It's all in the manuscript."

"I'll read it. But I'd like you to tell me about it. That's what you brought me here for isn't it?"

"Ok. When I left Pennsylvania there was no one left behind. But as they say, I did come of age. Not some tragic romance, but rather a fond memory of an extraordinary woman."

CHAPTER 4

From *Time Travels* by Dillan Murphy
EASTERN PENNSYLVANIA, 1876-1890

I had the same sexual cravings as all young men. Those Victorian times did not change basic biology. The difference during that time and a hundred years later is only a change in societal constraints. In the late nineteenth century it was simply difficult to be alone with a girl. If caught in some compromising sexual activity it might mean a forced marriage. Or in the poor rural mining society of Schuylkill County it could mean being shot by the girl's father or brother. The customs of the old country still prevailed.

My father was surprisingly candid about sex. He gave me a fairly broad sex education. Later in my life I reflected that he and my mother must have enjoyed their intimacy since he was not embarrassed to describe things that made me blush at the time. Along with that education was his fervent harping on avoiding involvement with any girl that would lead to marriage. Early marriage would ruin my prospects, ruin my life. Getting a girl pregnant was an even greater disaster.

I got the message but my father never offered an alternative as to how to satisfy those teenage longings. But since I was a pretty good looking lad, smarter than most, maybe luckier than most, I found a solution. Or I should say the solution found me. That solution was in the form of Miss Emily Ferguson.

Emily Ferguson was my schoolteacher. She was unmarried in her early thirties. I thought her the most beautiful woman I had ever seen. Perhaps that was youthful infatuation, but even years later I could look at a picture she gave me and still regard her as beautiful as any in New York.

You didn't get a look at a woman's legs with the clothing of the era, but you got a real assessment of the torso. The shirtwaist blouses of the time fit snuggly to the woman's contours. If the woman had a narrow waist and well developed breasts it displayed more than it concealed. What Miss Ferguson displayed would arouse any man young or old. I thought she was a goddess.

I learned Miss Ferguson was a divorcee. Everyone in the community thought she was a widow. She took up teaching after her husband, a purchasing agent for one of the railroads was caught taking kickbacks and fired. They lost everything. The husband lost Emily. Social pressure made it easier for her to leave Pottsville. Her only job prospect was teaching school in our rural community. I only learned the truth because she confided in me. But I get ahead of myself.

She never said, but I thought she must be in her early thirties. She taught all grades at our one-room school. The other two boys my age were dullards that would have preferred to be elsewhere than school. They were in school rather than the mines because their fathers were in mine management positions.

I on the other hand was bright and intellectually inquisitive. That made me appear more mature in addition to my good looks. The truth was Miss Ferguson had few prospects for male companionship in our community. She wasn't the type to go for a miner or farmer. The few shop owners were married, as were most of the mine management men at the mines. Adultery would have been more taboo than a liaison with a male student. I'd like to think she saw me as someone special. In reality I was probably just her best available sexual opportunity. But it worked for both of our needs. So much of life seems to be a convergence of such factors.

Our first encounter was in the fall of 1889. I was sixteen, the oldest boy in her class. As Miss Ferguson dismissed the class, she asked that I stay behind. I was still seated in my desk.

"By next year, Dillan, you will be done with this school. You are clearly the brightest student I have. What is it you plan to do?"

"I'll be going away to university," I answered.

Miss Ferguson acted surprised but in a pleasant way. "That's marvelous, Dillan. But you know that costs a lot of money. Is that possible for you?"

"Yes, Mam. My father and I talk of it all the time. He's planned it. Saved money for years. He's determined I should make something of myself."

Miss Ferguson had been leaning against her desk. She unfastened the top two buttons to her high-collared blouse. My eyes were fixed on her exposed neck. She walked over to me and touched my face with her hand. "Of course, Dillan. You're a very smart young man. Great opportunities await you."

I was still seated. Miss Ferguson bent down and kissed me lightly on the mouth. "Come here, Dillan," she said and then grabbing my arm to gently pull me up out of seat.

She placed my right hand on her breast. The sensation sent a shock to my loins. I may have even gasped audibly.

"Have you ever made love to a woman, Dillan?"

She was inches from me. I could smell her sweat breath. Her arms held my shoulders. I could feel my arousal being so close to her. I answered meekly, "No."

"Do you want to make love to me?"

My eyes must have bulged wide. I swallowed and said, "Yes."

She led me to the back storage room of the schoolhouse. Emily Ferguson initiated my right of passage into manhood in a profound way. Even during that first encounter she held my adolescent ardor under control. The experience made an indelible impact.

She was remarkably experienced. I dared not ask how or with whom she learned such things, but somehow I think it was mostly just innate to her personality. Unlike the public repression of sexuality of these Victorian times, Emily Ferguson was totally uninhibited. She taught me techniques of how to pleasure a woman and how a man could enjoy that giving for his own gratification. These were things never to be learned from the rough talk of exaggerated sexual adventures from the men I overheard.

Besides the joys of sex, Emily also expanded my intellectual horizons. She was a passionate teacher and took great interest in that part of my education as well. After lovemaking in the schoolhouse backroom, we typically discussed literature, history, or philosophy. Apart from the physical intimacy, the intellectual exchanges were an equal part of our relationship. It also served as a perfect cover for spending extra hours after the normal school day.

Where my father had steeped me in the great classics, Emily introduced a whole new world of more modern literature. These were the great novelists of the nineteenth century. Where the old classics were often hard slogging, these modern novels carried me off into untold adventurers. I read them all. All the European novelists like Flaubert, Balzac, Thomas Hardy, and Victor Hugo. The Americans writers, Melville, Cooper, Hawthorne, and Poe. How I admired the ability for these authors to create these worlds populated with fascinating characters. Maybe someday I would write such fiction.

My father did not share my enthusiasm for this new style of writing called the novel. He felt it was not serious literature. The grand ideas belonged to the ancients. Not sure I ever totally convinced him of the merit of the nineteenth century novel, but I did persuade him to read a couple. Grudgingly he did admit that Nathaniel Hawthorne's stories were interesting.

A year later I was off to university in the big city. Apart from my father, leaving Emily Ferguson was almost as difficult. Thanks to both of them, I was intellectually prepared. My lowly circumstances made me a fighter. Emily made me a man. Even though I was a rural bumpkin, I arrived in New York City better prepared for life than most seventeen year olds.

CHAPTER 5

From *Time Travels* by Dillan Murphy
MANHATTAN, NEW YORK CITY - 1890-1898

I was seventeen when I went off to study at Columbia University in New York City. In 1890 it was known as Columbia College. At that time it was located on 49th Street and Madison. My father insisted I should attend one of the best schools. Harvard and Yale were in Massachusetts and Connecticut, but Columbia was in New York City. I pushed for that. New York seemed as much of a difference as possible from the rural coalfields of Pennsylvania.

My father wanted me to study law. It was a good foundation for politics. That was the place where I could make a name for myself he said. I wasn't sold on that as my career path. However, I studied history and political science during my first couple of years at Columbia as a foundation for a law degree. I also took a journalism course. The professor was passionate about the field. He argued forcefully that a free press was the singular institution that made the United States the most effective government in the world. No matter the scoundrels and the corruption that we had just as other countries, always probing to discover wrongdoing was the American press that could stir the public to bring them down.

I was smitten. With my love of the written word, it clearly was what I wanted to do. My father was initially disappointed but I swayed him with my arguments. Perhaps naïve, I told him that I didn't want to be involved with all the corruption that seemed such a part of politics. I wanted to be on the side of right. It was the objective of journalism to expose wrongdoing.

It turned out that I had a real talent for writing. My father came around to my ambition when I showed him a letter of praise from that same journalism professor that first inspired me.

So I changed my focus to journalism, receiving my degree in 1894. First-rate professors provided an invaluable academic background. Some years later the prestigious School of Journalism was created at Columbia with a bequest from the great publisher Joseph Pulitzer. On a personal note, I received free tuition my last two years through a scholarship fund endowed by Pulitzer. Without that, my father's hard earned funds would not have sustained my college expenses those last two years.

At college, I learned firsthand about class distinction based upon wealth. I was the poor kid from the rural working class. There was no shortage of snobbery among my fellow classmates. I recall no real friends, probably because of my defensiveness. Hard work at my studies developed an intellectual arrogance to counter my lack of means. Regardless of the real or perceived intolerance of some of my fellow classmates, I'm sure I was not approachable. My recollections were probably skewed but I do not recall the time fondly.

Life was tough in the coalfields of Pennsylvania before the turn of the century, but New York City was an equally hostile environment. This was especially true of a newcomer, a rural bumpkin. Even though English was the language, it sounded foreign here to the typical brogue of my native Pennsylvania.

Then of course there were actual foreign languages that were commonplace throughout the City.

It was the time of heightened immigration to the United States. Ellis Island held out the hope of opportunity that too often turned to a numbing despair of life in the tenements. New York City probably has never been an easy place to survive for anyone. I was not too much different than the foreign immigrant. The money my father had saved went for tuition and books. I had to make my own way to provide food and shelter. I was just another poor working class kid. I worked nights at a restaurant cleaning tables and washing dishes to support myself. I was paid almost nothing but the job afforded meals and a small room upstairs.

I was just as much an outsider as the Irish or East European immigrant. I had no contacts to land a job in some office. My Irish accent marked me as lower class. So I was forced to compete for unskilled work against immigrants. At least I spoke very good English.

With studies and work there was virtually no time for girls for the first couple of years. There were times of sexual desperation where I might have even considered a prostitute had I ever had enough money. My only female companionship was during Christmas when I returned home to visit my father and was able to sneak some time with Emily Ferguson. I missed her terribly the rest of the year.

My hard work paid off. With recommendations from professors, I was able to secure an internship my last two summers with the *New York Herald* newspaper. Those summer internships lead to a full time position working in the pressroom my last year at Columbia. Since newspapers are printed at night it was an ideal arrangement. It wasn't journalism but at least I had a foot in the door.

Upon my graduation I was able to secure an entry level reporting job with the Newspaper. My summer internship assignments had provided some influential internal contacts at the Newspaper. They also afforded opportunity to show off my writing skills.

The *New York Herald* was James Gordon Bennett's newspaper. He was the flamboyant publisher who had sent Henry Morton Stanley to find the famous Dr. David Livingston in the unexplored regions of East Africa in the 1870's. Every aspiring journalist hoped for such a great opportunity as Bennett had given to Stanley.

I spent the next two years learning about the newspaper business and reporting. My assignment those first years was the crime beat. I would spend most of my days at various precinct houses getting facts on crimes committed during the previous night, or follow-ups on major crime stories. I learned quickly that good writing had nothing to do with job success as a reporter. It had everything to do with giving editors what they wanted - newsworthy copy by deadlines. I quickly learned that was best accomplished by making relationships among the police.

The police of the time did not communicate with their colleagues in other precincts. It was as if each crime was the singular investigative responsibility of just a couple of cops. I kept well organized notes in a journal I carried at all times. Since I moved about over a wide range of precincts, I often passed on useful information to another precinct. That and getting police officers names in the newspaper lead to frequently being given *unofficial* front page information before my competitors.

In 1898 one of my assignments was to cover the story of Theodore Roosevelt's efforts to raise a regiment of volunteers to fight the Spanish in Cuba. I knew of Roosevelt from my association with the police. Just prior to my starting crime reporting, he was the President of the Board of Police Commissioners for New York. Most recently, Roosevelt had been Assistant Secretary of the Navy before resigning his office to take the lieutenant colonelcy of a newly forming volunteer cavalry regiment.

A chance encounter led to my first journalistic adventure outside New York. After giving an interview to a group of reporters, I followed Roosevelt out of the hotel whereupon I asked him, "How does one join up with your regiment, Mister Roosevelt?" It was a spontaneous impulse as I had not given it that much thought.

Roosevelt stopped and looked at me with his fabled intensity, "I know you. You're one of Bennett's reporters?"

"Yes, Sir. Been reporting for the *Herald* for several years."

"Well what skills do you have young man? This is a cavalry regiment you know. Can you ride? Can you shoot?"

Neither, I thought to myself, but answered, "Well, I can write and I can box. I can lick any man with my fists in your regiment, Sir." I wasn't at all sure that was true.

Roosevelt responded, "Well bully for you, young man. I know something of those endeavors as well. And your name, Sir?"

"Murphy, Dillan Murphy."

"Yes, of course. I've read your bylines, Murphy. First class reporting. I shall request that Mr. Bennett make you a war correspondent and attach you to my regiment. Might take a little pressure because your publisher is a notorious tightwad and he probably has already assigned a reporter to accompany our adventure. Since the *Herald* is focused only on New York City, I shall tell him that you are particularly qualified to report on the forthcoming war from the perspective of New York City's interests."

That's the origin of how I followed the First United States Volunteer Cavalry Regiment to Cuba in the Spanish-American War. Because the regiment's composition was largely of western rough adventurers, they soon became known as the *Rough Riders*.

CHAPTER 6

PROVENCE, FRANCE – 2009

Elliot interrupted his narrative. They had finished the bottle of wine "It's time for dinner." He rose and retreated to the cellar for another bottle of wine.

Upon his return Allison said, "What you are saying is that you knew Teddy Roosevelt? That would be around the turn of the century?"

"1898, to be exact."

"So you were in New York in the 1890's?" She shook her head at the thought. "Tell me what it was like back then." Her intonation suggesting she was patronizing him, not yet buying into this longevity story.

Elliot was pleased that she was testing him rather than just dismissing him as unhinged.

"Obviously, the lack of automobiles was the most striking difference then to now. Horses pulled the freight and moved people. But what I remember most vividly of New York at the turn of the last century were the bad smells. Garbage, horse waste on the streets, the sewers, unwashed bodies. Pungent smells assaulted one incessantly a hundred years ago."

"Describe places I would recognize today, Elliot," she said.

"Very good, I shall tell you a little about New York back in those days, but only after dinner. We are having gnocchi, with a typical Provencal *daube de sanglier,* that's wild boar stew. Boars abound in the area. It's a lean meat with only a slight gamy flavor. I do like my French stews."

After dinner he cleared the dishes and settled with Allison in front of the fireplace. Coffee and a fire countered the slight chill coming from the autumn night. "So what do you want to know about New York of a hundred years ago?" Elliot asked knowing Allison was quizzing him still trying to understand what this was all about.

"What about Midtown Manhattan, around Times Square?"

"I've not been back to New York since the first time I came to your agency. And that was the only time since before the Great War. World War One to you. So I know little of modern, twentieth century New York other than from pictures and movies. But the memories are vivid from my early years in the City.

"As I was saying, if you were to go back in time to the 1890's, the first thing to strike you about New York would be an assault of pungent smells. Most of them bad. You had the sewers. This was before modern sewage treatment facilities. You had coal being used for heating so the winter air was permeated with soot and a cloying odor. You had the elevated railroads spewing all manner of their own coal soot as well as noise from fifty feet up. But at the street level, you had the garbage and the horse dung.

"You see, the first subway route wouldn't happen until well after the turn of the century. What you had for public transit were horse-drawn trolleys and horse drawn omnibuses. All over town you had continuous piles of fetid horse dung. It would make your eyes water in the summer heat. In winter, steam rose from the piles of fresh droppings.

"As for Midtown, what is today's Times Square was a great barnyard that housed the majority of these horses used for public transportation. It was actually located on the southern half of the bow-tie *islands* created by Broadway and Seventh Avenue. And it smelled like a stock yard.

"The area didn't become Times Square until the *New York Times* built a new building on the site of those old horse yards about the same time that the first subway was constructed. Around the turn of the century, Forty-Second Street was the northern boundary of the City's business district at the time."

"So was Central Park like it is today?" Allison asked.

"Pretty much from what I see in pictures. I think it was constructed about the time of the Civil War."

Allison stifled a yawn.

"I agree, my Dear. It's been a long day for you and I also confess to the effects of so much wine. Let's get a good night's sleep. I'll continue my story in the morning after our coffee."

He showed her up stairs to the quest bedroom.

"Should be everything you need. You have your own bathroom. Extra blankets are in the armoire. Sleep well, Allison."

Allison looked at him. "I hope I will, Elliot. I can't imagine dreaming a more bizarre dream than what you've told me." She touched his cheek. She wanted to say something but just shook her head. "Good night, Elliot."

The next morning was warm and the hills suffused with bright sunshine. It was an idyllic setting on the patio. The old stone house set in perfect composition with the surrounding countryside of an olive grove and distant vineyards. Elliot had prepared coffee and croissants.

"I don't want to recite my whole life's story or I'd be talking for weeks, Allison. What I want to tell you is about my life. The strangest tale you have ever heard. Most of all, I want to try to convince you it's true. Inexplicable, but nonetheless real. I want you to see how I matured from the innocence of youth to the burden that comes from life's experiences. My experiences having been broader than most, simply because I have lived for so long. My personal experiences are a microcosm of the twentieth century."

CHAPTER 7

From *Time Travels* by Dillan Murphy
CUBA – 1898

This commentary is not intended as a history lesson, but I do need to put America's early adventurism into context. Why would we invade Cuba?

At the turn of the twentieth century, the United States had defined the forty-eight contiguous states by buying or coercing the western areas from France, Spain, and Mexico, during the previous century. The U.S. was becoming a major industrial power and there was a clear national mood to expand its influence. The concept of Manifest Destiny that espoused the inherit right of the United States to expand its boundaries from the Atlantic to the Pacific now took on an outward view to include the entire western hemisphere. This nationalistic fervor became directed at Cuba just ninety miles off the coast of Florida. A populace insurgency against the repressive colonial rule of the Spanish proved to be a rallying cry for the United States own imperialistic expression.

The U.S. battleship *Maine* was dispatched to Havana harbor

as a show of U.S. force. She sank after a mysterious explosion, killing 250 American sailors. The disaster probably resulted from an accident, but public outcry in America blamed the Spanish for an act of sabotage. Sixty days later, the U.S. Congress gave President McKinley a declaration of war.

And so it was that young men from all walks of life flocked to join the military ranks. Prospective enlistees for Roosevelt's First United States Volunteer Cavalry Regiment were ten times more than the allotted regimental strength. Even educated men were eager to join the ranks. I was no different. This was a great adventure. Individual aspirations were inseparable from the Nation's ambitions.

I joined the Regiment in Tampa, Florida just two weeks before disembarkation for Cuba. They were a curious collection of hard men from the West and Eastern aristocrats. They were a glorious group of men, each with a reason for going to war.

I fit the same mold. This was to be a great personal adventure. After several years reporting on crime and politics in New York City, the lure of armed conflict in the exotic Caribbean was heady stuff.

My written story is hopefully enriched with the details and names of some of the wonderful and interesting characters associated with the Regiment. That was the good part. My first experience of combat was anything but good. It was brutal and ugly. I had seen the violent underbelly of New York City, but it did not prepare me for combat. There were those that found the experience exciting in a positive way. Certainly Teddy Roosevelt did. Some of the troopers were ex-lawmen, ex-gunfighters from the Old West who had faced death many times before. For them it was maybe different, perhaps just an extension of what they did for a living. For most of us though, the experience was terrifying. It was only exhilarating in retrospect.

Our regiment engaged in some minor skirmishing with the Spanish before we moved to the major engagement of taking the city of Santiago. My first taste of real battle was the Regiment's participation in the assault on San Juan Hill, or what we called Kettle Hill. Not much of a hill even by eastern Pennsylvania standards, but the Spanish were well entrenched in defensive positions on its higher ground.

It was frightfully hot with a repressive humidity that made every breath an effort. My shirt and trousers were soaked with sweat. My feet sloshed in liquid inside my boots. Too hot even for the mosquitoes, but they would be back in force at nighttime to expand the torment of this terrible place. I attached myself to a Sergeant Fuller who seemed to be in command of at least his own survival in this tropical pesthole.

"Tell me Sergeant, why'd you join up for this?" I asked as the troop rested. The regiment was dismounted except for the officers. It seemed an odd use of cavalry to me.

"You're a New York feller I hear. A reporter. Why'd you come, Mister Murphy?"

"Bored with the big city. Adventure in an exotic place. A warm place," I said, smiling with the irony.

He scratched the stubble on his jaw. "Guess it's the same with me. Been a soldier, been a lawman, been a farmer. Farming was boring and it didn't work out, so I'm back soldierin'."

We had that brief chat about an hour before I saw Sam Fuller take a bullet through the eye and fall dead next to me. We had been taking fire from the Spanish defenses for several minutes as we advanced through trees and tall grass. The Spanish Regulars fired their Mausers in volleys, the rounds making a buzzing noise because of their great number.

"We'll be fucked this day," a trooper by the name of O'Neil said as he passed and looked down at Sergeant Fuller.

Not everyone was fucked that day, but Trooper O'Neil did foretell his own fate. I was hunkered down with him in the tall grass, which was the only cover we had. Later I determined that T.R. was credited with moving troops from various regiments out of the exposed areas where we were taking fire from the Spanish firing down on us from trenches on the hill.

Our captain rallied the men forward from atop his horse. From fifty yards away I saw an artillery shell burst above him and the shrapnel tear off his left arm. I remember the horror on his face as he looked at the blood squirting out of the severed stub, probably realizing it foretold his death as well.

As the troop rose up to advance, O'Neil was hit in the lower abdomen. It was an ugly wound, not the clean type of wound usually made by the steel-jacketed Mauser round. O'Neil was literally holding his intestines in his hands. I knelt beside him.

"Well I'm truly fucked good. Will ya do me a favor, Murphy?"

Of course I said I would as I tucked his bedroll under his head.

"Write my ma and pa. Las Cruces, New Mexico. Tell 'em I did my duty. Tell 'em I died well."

I don't know what O'Neil meant about dying well from such a painful wound that probably took hours to extinguish his life. I returned to his body after the battle ceased. I sat with dead Billy O'Neil awhile and wrote of this day in my journal.

The taking of San Juan Hill was no great thing as most battles go, but there were a lot of Rough Riders that fell that day. Death in war is still death no matter the battle. I had come to know many of these fine men as my friends. I still ponder on their reasons for joining in this fight to risk life and limb in such a contrived war. But then again, my own reasons to risk my life in pursuit of a story might seem just as curious to them.

The war was a one sided affair lasting only four months. I admit to falling into the trap of reveling in the success of the United States. I was too young to see the puffing out of America's chest at it bullied its way to seize the crumbling colonial empire of Spain. Along with Cuba, the United States acquired Puerto Rico in the Caribbean and Guam and the Philippines in the South Pacific. The United States now had its own colonies but we didn't see it that way. We called ourselves liberators. Later in my life I would involve myself in other colonial conflicts and see them for what they were.

I was not unrealistic about what war was like however. My brief exposure to combat removed any romantic view of war. I would see more warfare in my lifetime but it would forever remain a monumentally ugly thing to me. There was no glory in men being killed and maimed.

CHAPTER 8

"Let's take a walk. It's a beautiful morning. Then we'll drive into town to have lunch," Elliot said to Allison as he rose from his chair on the patio to stretch.

As they strolled next to an olive grove, Allison asked, "You skipped a lot about your personal life. You say you were born in 1873. So you were twenty-five when you were in Cuba. Was there a wife? A girlfriend?"

"Not exactly, Allison. There were a lot of girls, but no one that I fell in love with. I was arrogant and too full of myself at the time. Regretfully I admit to being what during the times would have been called a despoiler of young women. Although in retrospect, most were already 'spoiled' when I had my liaisons."

Allison smiled. "Now that sounds intriguing. You hear about the sexual repression of the Victorian Era. Was that really the case?"

"Only in the degree to which people discussed sex, which they didn't very often. As far as actual sexual relations, my personal experiences suggested it wasn't much different than to-day."

"So who were these girls that you seduced? Or did some seduce you? Were they *good* girls?" Allison asked.

"You're asking an old man to talk about his youthful conquests?"

"You opened up the subject, Elliot."

"Fair enough. There were all sorts of girls in New York City. As a reporter I interacted with women in all walks of life. But if you mean were they *loose* women, I'd say not. Most just followed their desires and ignored the conventions of the time. Like anything else that society prohibits, its value is raised by that prohibition."

"So where did you meet girls a hundred years ago?" Allison asked with a smile. It was a genuine question but she realized what an absurdity. Was she buying into this fantastic fable?

"Single women didn't frequent bars during that era so you had to be creative to find opportunities other than the workplace. There were a few women that worked at the Newspaper, but church picnics were the best."

"Church picnics? You mean you would go to church picnics for the express purpose of picking up girls?" Allison laughed.

"Listen, I told you I was no saint. The other area of opportunity was gatherings of the women's suffrage movement. I had the perfect entry being a reporter. My foraging, I guess you'd call it that, gravitated to those young women aspiring to higher education, especially those associated with the suffrage movement. They were the independent thinkers, which I liked. They were also the ones to reject the sexual repression of the times, which proved convenient. My experiences with the intelligent and confident Emily Ferguson made a lasting impression.

"You must remember this was a time that women did not even have the vote. Many women, particularly those at university, were feeling rebellious. Perhaps as part of that rebellion, they were more persuasive to sexual adventure."

She was still smiling at Elliot's slight embarrassment. "So how about comparing sexual practices of a hundred years ago?"

Elliot grinned. "My narrative is not for the purpose of discussing the titillating details of sexual practices during the early part of the twentieth century."

"And why not, Elliot? If I'm to embrace your story I need details, I need to understand the times. But I'd rather you told me more about your lovers from that time. Was there someone special?"

Elliot was quiet for several moments and looked down. "Yes there was. After returning from Cuba, I took up reporting again in New York. The next several years were spent advancing my career as a reporter. I became quite good at what later became known as investigative reporting. I was one hell of a muckraker."

"You never wrote about that though," Allison said

"Oh yes. Much later, in 1930. My novel titled *Mean Streets*. Of course that was as Dillan Murphy. I tried to give a sense of organized crime and corruption in that early part of the century. Political corruption was more than a problem back then. It was the way things were done. At the top of the scale, every municipal contract involved bribes and kickbacks. At the lower levels, most cops were on the take. I became very good at exposing all manner of official corruption. Had a knack for putting the pieces together and mining information from those with a grudge. My success was measured by the number of enemies I made."

Allison interrupted, "Tell me about this first love of your life."

"Very well. Her name was Eleanor, Eleanor Kilpatrick. Irish. Maybe not a classical beauty but she was special. Fiery eyes, sharp tongue, an outsized intellect. And yes she had red hair.

"And how'd you meet her?"

"At the morgue," Elliot answered.

"The morgue?"

"You see Eleanor was studying medicine and worked nights at the morgue. I was following up on a murder. It involved dismemberment and I was going to try to bribe my way in with a photographer to get photos. The first person I saw was this woman in a particularly bloody apron. After my clumsy attempt to get entry, Eleanor berated me with her acid tongue for my antics."

Allison chuckled and Elliot continued, brightened by the memory. "Well I was pretty glib, so I was not only able to appease her, but to my surprise I also got her to agree to lunch the next day."

Elliot filled the next hour telling Allison all the remembrances of his romance with Eleanor Kilpatrick, even titillating her with some of their sexual adventurism, bold for the time. Eleanor cared nothing for convention. She also had a healthy sexual appetite.

"But it ended. I guess no different than what happens to so many people. A misunderstanding. At least I thought that to be the reason. It had to do with a certain prostitute."

"A prostitute? You mean Eleanor had a *misunderstanding* about you and a prostitute? You'd better explain that one, Elliot."

"Well you see I was very good at digging out dirt on politicians and other shady characters because I played one low-life against another. I passed out my share of money to get information, but my best results came from playing on rivalries and hatreds. I'd learn something then put it together with other information. I could then use it to barter for even better information, something that I could write about in the Newspaper."

"Some of my best sources were prostitutes. I was amazed by the level of either their compassion or their hatred for many of their customers. I'd help them out when I could. Route them to doctors I knew who would perform abortions. Trade information they could use to get vengeance against an abusive john. That sort of thing."

"So what happened that caused you to lose Eleanor? Didn't she know what kind of work you did?"

"She knew I was a newspaper reporter covering crime and politics. I never told her about the danger and the kinds of people I interacted with. At any rate, there was this prostitute by the name of Francis Healy. One of my best sources. She hated cops and politicians and had a fair number of them as regulars. So one night I'm working this bar trying to get this guy drunk who's a clerk at some city contractor's office so he can do a little spying for me, when in comes Francis.

"Francis is disheveled, dress is torn. She goes to the bar and orders a whiskey. A few minutes later this fat guy barges in and yells, 'Where's that fucking whore?' He's raging drunk and some bigger guy, obviously a lackey, is with him.

"I recognized him as the local ward boss for the district since I knew all the local politicians. The guy saw Francis and moved toward her, grabbed her by the arm, then backhanded her across the face. 'You fucking whore, I'm goin' to kick the shit out of you so bad nobody'll be fucking you for weeks.'

"Francis was on the floor as I stepped between her and the ward boss. 'Who the fuck are you?' the guy snarled. I hit him with a right to the face, square on the nose, followed by a left to his midsection. He went down hard on his knees gushing blood and holding his face, then vomiting up booze and the greasy digestion of a recent meal.

"His goon was a big ugly guy that looked like he'd taken a few too many hits to the head. Ex-boxer most likely with the damaged nose and scars around the eyes. The guy took a swing that I blocked with my left forearm. He took a hard blow to his chin as my right connected solidly. As he staggered, I battered him with repeated jabs to the face. He went down cold with blood flowing from his badly broken nose. Because I was enraged, I kicked the ward boss in the jaw knocking him unconscious."

Elliot paused a moment to let the emotion of the memory subside. "To shorten the rest of the story, I took Francis back to my place. She was frightened for her life. Rightly so, since this ward boss was well connected with both police and organized crime. A couple of hours later, Eleanor shows up. She has a key to my flat and walks in and sees Francis in my bed. There's an ugly scene with her angry at what she thinks is going on, and my indignation at being falsely accused. She wants nothing of my explanation. That angers me. The situation escalates. Lots of shouting. Lots of things said by both of us that are tough to forget. At any rate, it's never reconciled between us. Probably both our egos. So our relationship ends."

"Did you ever see her again?"

"No."

Allison could feel this was still an emotional wound after one hundred years. Even thinking of it in those terms made her shake her head slightly. "How about we have some lunch, Elliot?"

They drove into the small town of Châteauneuf-du-Pape and settled in a small café off the main street. Elliot ordered a bottle of the excellent local Rhone wine while he interpreted the menu for Allison.

"And your father? What became of him?" Allison asked.

Elliot reflected for a few moments and his eyes moistened slightly. "After I returned from Cuba, my father took ill and had to quit the mines. Like most miners he had black lung. I brought him to New York and he lived with me for two years before he died. He was only fifty-three. I grieved deeply. I loved that man who was a giant of a father as well as a mother to me. It was an enormous act of love that he sacrificed so much so that I would not face a life in the mines."

Allison was finding herself immersed progressively deeper

into Elliot's story. He was truly *reliving* these events, or at least thought he was. It was clearly not acting. If she didn't think about the chronology it was easy to accept Elliot's version of these events as real.

Lunch arrived. They were seated outside at a small café. Elliot delighted in Allison's obvious savoring of her *bouillabaisse*, the signature Provencal fish soup. Elliot was a frequent customer and the owner made a fuss over Allison. She was sure to be the talk of the town with everyone wondering about the beautiful young woman visiting Monsieur Gaston.

Declining dessert but taking a few cheeses and coffee, Allison said, "Go on with your story, Elliot."

"Well. I prospered as a journalist. With a better offer, I went over to the *New York Times* in 1904. I was becoming a scourge to the politically corrupt. I elevated my targets from the street level low-lifes to the real bosses. There were times that I made my editor and even the publisher nervous. To their credit, they resisted a lot of political pressure to rein me in. I had articles published in McClure's, kind of the exposé magazine of the times. You can check that out, Allison. Byline was *Dillan Murphy*."

"Wasn't going after official corruption a dangerous business during those times?" Allison asked.

"Yes it was dangerous. But I was full of myself. Not stupid about what I was doing, but not fully realizing what the bad guys might try to do to quiet me. I took basic precautions; no walking down dark streets, always checking out those in my vicinity. What military types call situational awareness. But there was one time. A time that still haunts me.

"I was at a bar with a friend. T.E. Fitzgerald's on Sixth Avenue and West Forty-Fourth. My friend Graham Flynn was a young civil engineer working for the Interborough Rapid Transit Company, the subway company. Bright guy. He was destined for a great career with the success of the new subway system that had opened just a couple of years earlier. Quiet. Soft-spoken. Loved classical music. Got me interested in fine music.

"Anyway, we were having a couple of drinks at Fitzgerald's. He was telling me about his recent engagement to a secretary at the IRT. Two guys came into the bar. Tough looking guys with overcoats. My instincts perked up as they clearly were looking around for someone. I grabbed Graham and pulled him out of his chair and moving us toward the back of the bar hoping to get to a rear door. I wasn't quick enough though. Graham took two bullets in the back meant for me. I would have been killed too except the bartender shot one guy with a sawed-off shotgun he kept behind the bar. The other guy took off."

Elliot stopped his narrative and finished his coffee.

Allison interrupted the silence after a few moments, "Well?"

"Nothing more to say. I felt guilty, but didn't know how deeply until at the funeral his fiancé accused me of causing his death, then slapped my face. The experience of Graham Flynn's murder changed me. Hard to explain how, but I saw the world with a different perspective after that. I was no longer as arrogantly confident. I couldn't manipulate everything around me without considering the consequences.

"Beyond the emotional loss of my friend, more troubles were ahead. My intrigues among the underbelly of turn-of-the-century New York City to gather news were catching up with me. I had more than a few enemies. Among them was the prostitute, Francis Healy's fat ward boss client with the now misaligned nose."

CHAPTER 9

From *Time Travels* by Dillan Murphy
MANHATTAN, NEW YORK CITY – 1915

Tammany Hall was the shadow government of New York City. Ostensibly, it was the political machine for the Democratic Party but that was because it must be aligned with a major political party. Tammany marched to its own drum, dominating New York politics for most of the nineteenth century and well into the twentieth. If you were not backed by Tammany, you didn't even get to run for office, much less get elected.

The ward boss was their local enforcer. He got out the vote and made sure it was a Democratic vote. He accomplished this by dolling out patronage, and muscle, whichever worked. While the ward boss corrupted at the grass roots level, his bosses corrupted at the higher levels. The Mayor's office, the police, judges, even the state government in Albany, all benefited from and owed Tammany Hall.

Tammany Hall knew me. I had given them some minor black eyes with my stories. My stories irritated Tammany but rarely lead to any changes. So I was an enemy, albeit a fairly minor one.

Until the incident when Francis Healy pissed off this particular john.

Terrence Keane was the typical New York City ward boss. Big Irishman. Immigrant. He was a former stevedore until he found the better pay and the easier work of muscling people instead of cargo. The big bosses wouldn't ordinarily make anything out of one of their lower-level guys getting the shit beat out of him. But Terry had an uncle high up in the Tammany organization.

I knew Frank Keane, or I should say I knew a lot about him. He was featured in several of my stories. Frank Keane was officially the Borough President for Manhattan. Unofficially he was in charge of Tammany Hall's muscle for all the boroughs. When it suited the politics or his own personal gain, Frank could cause labor strife with as much violence as necessary by seeding a crowd with his own provocateurs. Or it might mean bringing some union organizer into line. He was a corrupt, nasty piece of work. So I knew I'd probably be hearing from Frank Keane.

A week after I broke Terry Keane's nose, I looked out the window of my third floor flat on Bleecker Street to check on the weather that morning. I damned near dropped my cup of coffee. Terry Keane was standing across the street in front of the grocery with his nose still bandaged. My guess was that it might be some sort of ambush. He would be the spotter to recognize me. Keane would have others lurking close by.

I'm not sure what the smart thing to do was, but a direct confrontation with Keane and his thugs probably was not the best alternative. Still the best defense was often offense. Besides, Terry Keane was a piece of shit. For what he represented and personally for his abuse inflicted upon people like Francis Healy. Seeing his ugly face taking up surveillance of my flat just triggered a rage. Checking first that there was no one watching, I slipped out the back door of my building.

I made my way north a block then cut back west to Second

Avenue. I calculated where the rear of the grocery store would be. A small hand lettered sign indicated its rear delivery entrance.

"Hey! Who are you?" the young box boy in the rear of the store said.

I ignored him and proceeded through the store past the startled grocer behind the counter. Once to the front, I could see Terrance Keane's back through the window. My blood was up. I reached into my jacket pocket for the straight razor I always carried for protection.

"Terry, what is it you think you're doing you fat fuck?" I said after I had come up behind him and put the blade of the razor to his neck.

"What the hell you doin'!" he said and started to turn his head until he felt the edge of the razor on the side of his neck.

"Well I'm fixin' to slit your jugular vein if you move, Terry. Now tell me where the others are."

"Don't know what you're talkin' about."

I drew the razor across the meaty part of his neck about a half an inch, cutting deep enough to hurt and draw blood. Not enough to do serious damage but it made my point. Keane let out a muffled groan.

"Terry. I'll ask you just one more time then I'll really cut you. Where are they?"

Keane's shirt collar was soaking with blood. I'd cut him pretty good.

"Two guys down there to the right. Two more around the corner over there."

"So what are we to do about all this, Terry?"

"What do ya want?"

"Want? I should be asking you that question."

I reached around with my left hand and patted Keane down to see if he had any weapons. Sure enough he was carrying a .38 revolver tucked into his rear pants pocket.

As I extracted the weapon, Keane swung around, his arm catching me in the head. The blow sent me back against the store window. Keane lunged at me grabbing me around the neck with his powerful hands.

"You fucking prick, you cut me!"

Keane was intent upon choking me. He didn't realize I still had the razor in my right hand and his pistol in my left. I opted not to kill him. Instead I drove my knee into his groin. He released his hands from my throat.

He doubled over before slowly collapsed to his knees on the sidewalk. I held the gun ready but he didn't have any fight left in him.

"I'll fucking kill you, Murphy!" It came out as more of a raspy loud whisper. The nausea from the blow to his genitals caused him to vomit. He was making a habit out of messing himself in front of me.

From both directions, Keane's henchmen came running. My only escape was back through the grocery store and out the back. I could hear the rear door to the grocery slam as my pursuers took chase. Fortunately I had a good enough lead. After a couple of blocks I was soaked in sweat but safe. At least for the moment.

I dumped Keane's .38 in the Hudson River along with the straight razor. Didn't want to be holding that evidence in case the police paid me a visit. I proceeded to my office downtown. I told my boss, the managing editor, Charlie Kendrick, what happened.

"Jesus Christ, Murphy. You know there'll be hell to pay for this. Frank Keane can't let it pass. Even If he regards his nephew as a stupid clod, what you did will still look like a challenge against him personally. Especially with that material you dug up on the painting scam last year. You caused Frank Keane to sacrifice one of his senior aides."

The Borough of Manhattan contracted for the painting of city owned iron objects such as street light posts and the elevated train structures. A whistleblower terminated from the contracting firm contacted me directly having read my byline. The painting contractor used diluted paint. The inferior paint would require re-painting within a year. It was a variation on an old Tammany Hall scheme from decades earlier. Much of the exaggerated profits were channeled back to Frank Keane's borough offices in the form of kickbacks.

"That wasn't such a big deal. Frank Keane has much bigger things going on. You know as well as I do, Charlie, that every municipal contract in the City of New York probably involves kickbacks or some sort of corruption. In Manhattan, that means Frank Keane. I've got a couple of things I've been working on."

"I hope so. You may need it to bargain with. The cops are in Keane's pocket. You can probably expect a visit very soon. So I want you to go see Jonathan Winslow right now, today. Just in case you need some legal help."

Winslow was the general counsel for the Newspaper. He was closely connected to anti-Tammany politicians in Albany. He was a confidant of Franklin Roosevelt who lost a Democratic primary bid for the U.S. Senate to a Tammany Hall-backed candidate in 1914. All of that meant that Winslow had his own considerable political clout.

It turned out that I did need it.

I approached my apartment building cautiously that evening. Instead of thugs I recognized two Manhattan detectives. They were standing beside their car, a half a block from my door, smoking. I couldn't avoid what was coming but no point in making it easy. More than that, I might be taken for a ride to be delivered to Terry Keane. Now there was a frightening thought. If they wanted to arrest me, they could do it at the Newspaper offices with lots of witnesses.

I spent the night at a hotel. At nine o'clock the next morning, the same two detectives came to the Newspaper. Jonathan Winslow was there. So was a photographer.

Once in the police car, the detectives took out some of their frustration. One elbowed me hard into the chest.

"You're a stupid sonofabitch, Murphy. Not satisfied with just writin' your stories you have to go pissing off Frank Keane by cuttin' up his nephew. What'd you think was going to happen?"

I said nothing. Couldn't really since the wind was still knocked out of me.

The other detective said, "We're arresting you for assault with a deadly weapon, Murphy. You cut-up Terry Keane. We've even got two witnesses."

After going through the booking process, I was placed in a room that smelled like sweat and cigarettes. Thinking this was the place that police beat out confessions, I expected some rough going from the detectives. That never happened. I was there only twenty minutes by myself when the precinct captain walked in with the attorney Jonathan Winslow.

"You're free to go, Murphy, at least for right now," the captain said. "Assault charges are still pending. When the DA reviews your case, I suspect a warrant will be issued for your arrest. So we'll be seeing you back here soon."

I shook hands with Winslow as we left the police station.

"Thank you, Mister Winslow. I didn't relish spending too much time with the detectives."

"Glad to be of help. The fools didn't even go through the formality of seeking a warrant. A judge, unsympathetic to the Tammany machine, issued a writ immediately. But you do have a bit of a problem. They do actually have a case of assault against you that might stand up in court. We'll cross that bridge if it goes that far. Charles indicated that the Newspaper would provide you with legal resources."

"That's reassuring. I'll thank Charlie."

"One question I have, Mister Murphy. When I was looking at your booking record, it stated you were born in 1873. Is that correct? You seem much younger."

I paused, feeling a little trapped. No one had commented so directly on my youthful appearance. I knew I looked much younger than others my age. I had even taken to growing a mustache in the last several years. It gave me a look of a few more years. Apparently not enough.

"Yes. Just lucky I guess."

"Remarkable I should say. You could pass for twenty-five. Wished I had looked half as good when I was in my forties," Winslow said. "Surprised that Charles has not commented on it to you."

My boss might have except he had joined the paper only eight years previously. He never asked about my prior experience with the *Herald*. So he didn't know that in 1915 I had been a newspaper reporter for almost *twenty years*. Others at the Newspaper with the same longevity must have speculated about my youthful appearance, but no one ever commented to me directly. I was not sure this was a real problem at the time, but a subtle uneasiness had set in. Winslow's direct reference just confirmed the issue. The whole thing was inexplicable. It was not even something you could talk about to anyone. It wasn't even a problem, or so I thought.

The more immediate problem though was contending with the Keanes. I wasn't enough of a threat for Frank Keane to devote any real heavy play against me. On the other hand, his nephew Terry would be consumed with vengeance. Beyond that, I still had a criminal charge pending against me.

There was nothing I could do directly to counter a threat from Terry Keane. The best I could do was try to avoid situations that could expose me to violence. It was hard to anticipate what sort of situations might arise? To give myself a little protection, I was able to get a concealed weapons permit from a sympathetic police captain I had made look good in a story. I purchased a small Colt .25ACP automatic pistol. It wasn't much of weapon being such a small caliber and weighing less than one pound, but in a close-in situation it could do damage.

To really counter the threat from Terry Keane I had to bring down his uncle Frank. Terry Keane was only a ward boss because of powerful Uncle Frank.

The problem wasn't identifying the specifics of corruption ruled over by Frank Keane, but getting enough evidence to make a story. With Tammany Hall backing, Keane's control of City services in Manhattan was virtually absolute. Even though the New York City Council contracted for municipal services, Keane controlled what happened in Manhattan. The councilmen got their share so Frank Keane always got his way.

Everything carried a kickback or some other illicit benefit; garbage collecting, garbage disposal, repair contracts, building permits, zoning regulations, construction contracts, and purchase contracts for goods and services for everything a city uses. It went deeper than simple kickbacks. Contractors were forced to buy from certain suppliers with a Tammany Hall connection, or even Tammany Hall ownership through a straw man third party. Property intended for municipal projects was purchased through shell companies prior to public knowledge, then sold to the City at inflated profits. Money was often funneled through third parties through non-existent legal or consulting services. With political control of the Port Authority, Tammany Hall had its cut of profits of the massive commerce flowing through the port. Shipping paid kickbacks for berthing. If they resisted, there were labor problems with the longshoremen. The schemes were sophisticated and the audit trails obscure. Corruption had advanced considerably since the nineteenth century.

I needed something to grab the emotions of the public. Most of Keane's illicit dealings would not probably spark public outrage. People had come to expect political graft as just part of government. Only once in a while did something spur public outrage that led to change and the rolling of official heads. I needed something akin to Upton Sinclair's book *The Jungle* that caused public alarm about food safety when it was published ten years ago. Or the appalling working conditions at the Triangle Shirtwaist Factory that resulted in the tragic fire that killed 147 young women just a few years ago. Recalling these seminal events that captured the public's interest, I immediately knew where to start digging; the public health care system of New York City.

"Sounds like an idea to fit your personal objectives, Dillan," my boss Charlie Kendrick said when I broached the idea of investigating the health care system.

"Maybe. But I don't know if I'll even find anything that will implicate Frank Keane. At any rate it's an area that's never been probed. The Tammany Hall bosses must be getting something out of all the resources expended on the City's health care system. It still makes sense for the *Times* to investigate. If there's a story to be found, it'll make a big splash. Graft in the public health sector has a more immediate impact on the public."

CHAPTER 10

From *Time Travels* **by Dillan Murphy**
MANHATTAN, NEW YORK CITY – 1916

The New York City health care system was a gigantic municipal enterprise. There were all manner of different types of
hospitals spread throughout the City. It consumed major budget
resources of everything from supplies, maintenance, construction, repairs, and hundreds of city employees. I realized I had no
information on suspected graft associated with the healthcare
system. I also realized that with the pervasive corruption engen-
dered by Tammany Hall, Frank Keane must be siphoning money
from here as well. It was just a matter of finding where and how.
A scandal involving Manhattan's hospitals might provoke public
outrage if it directly affected people's lives. If big enough, it
could drive a stake in the heart of Frank Keane.

At least hospitals were a convenient place for a reporter to
ask questions. Since I was a crime reporter, I started first with
victims of violence as my reason to be in the various hospitals. I
was actually doing real crime investigative work often doing fol-
low-up stories to flesh out a story. After asking the obligatory

questions and gaining a rapport with staff, I ventured further afield with my inquiries to probe for sources of corruption within the system.

I realized a long time ago that I had a gift for drawing people out. People felt comfortable talking to me. I was a chameleon, able to change my persona to best fit the situation. I could talk the gutter language of lowlife criminals or be equally effective with the language of the upper tiers of society. That skill proved exceedingly productive in my quest to investigate corruption in the New York City health care system.

Most people like to talk about what they do. Many like to complain. Many like to criticize their bosses. Some have grudges. At the least, people like to gossip. The good reporter learns how to play on these tendencies.

I threw myself into the project non-stop for several weeks. I started first by doing old fashion research. That research gave me background for my story. There were more than 25 hospitals of all sorts in Manhattan in 1916. Manhattan municipal hospitals had a higher incidence of mortality than hospitals of most other major U.S. cities. Closer to home, Manhattan municipal hospitals were worse in all categories of care compared to privately operated hospitals, and worse than all of Brooklyn's hospitals.

A picture of pervasive graft soon emerged. I discovered that only a few suppliers of food serviced all Manhattan municipal hospitals. Not surprisingly, I was able to trace business connections with all these suppliers to the Borough president's office. Fewer yet were the number of firms holding contracts for services ranging from plumbing repair to transportation. Again, I discovered connections to the Borough's offices.

One food supplier was particularly suspect; Manhattan Institutional Distribution. Their offices were on the second floor of a building on Lower Broadway. It appeared to be nothing more than a two-room small office. The name was stenciled on the glass door. The woman receptionist acted slightly surprised when I walked into the office.

"Good day," I said and removed my hat. "My name is Stein, Joseph Stein. I represent the Jewish Memorial Hospital. I am in charge of procurement for the hospital. I would like to speak to whoever is charge on a matter of business."

"Well, sir. I am not sure.... Without an appointment, I ...."

A heavy set man came out of a second office and said, "My name is Dermot Flannery. Can I help you?" The man extended his hand but did not offer me to come into his office.

"Well, sir, I understand your firm sells a range of food products to the municipal hospitals of Manhattan. We are looking for new suppliers to bid on new contracts for Jewish Memorial for next year."

"How did you get our name?"

"Well, sir, it's a matter of public record. Might we sit down and I can provide you with the details for our upcoming solicitation of bids?"

"I'm sorry. We're not taking on any new customers at this time. Our supply sources are all fully committed," Flannery said.

"But you're a food distribution company aren't you? It would seem that you would have other producers that would be looking to expand."

"I believe I have answered your question. I'm very busy. Good day, sir," the man said then returned to his office and slammed the door.

Before I went there I knew Manhattan Institutional Distributors was a front. They held contracts for over 40% of all food products procured for all New York City municipal hospitals, including those in the other boroughs. I didn't realize they would be so brazen by locating it in an obscure office staffed by only two people. Some simple checking also revealed that Flannery was married to a cousin of Frank Keane.

While covering the aftermath of a Lower East Side gangland shooting, I found myself at Metropolitan Hospital following up on the fate of the victims. Two well known criminals were targeted for assassination presumably from some rival faction. Both men were killed in hail of bullets by four assailants. Unfortunately, an Italian grocer and his wife were also wounded in the attack.

I had pilfered a white orderly's smock in order to get closer to where the victims were being treated. I wanted to be the first to interview the attending surgeon when he left the operating room.

The door to the operating room swung open and slammed against the wall. Two men exited shouting.

"I'll not listen to your insults, Dr. Blair."

"Insults? I'll have you up before a medical review board. You're a fucking butcher, Jenkins! That patient is dead because of your incompetence!"

"Get away from me, Blair! I'll sue for slander if you keep that up."

"Slander?" Blair yelled. "You fucking asshole!" He grabbed Jenkins and threw him against the wall. Two orderlies separated the two and then hustled Dr. Jenkins away. Dr. Blair stood by himself gaining his composure when I approached him.

"What was that all about, Doctor?"

"Who the hell are you?"

"A newspaper reporter for the *Times*. Following up on the shooting victims."

"Well they're both dead. One had a chance until Jenkins bungled the surgery. You want a story? Come with me to the cafeteria. I'll give you something to write about."

What the good doctor related to me was a pervasive system of patronage at least at this hospital that endangered patients far more than kickbacks for goods and services.

"In 1910, the Carnegie Foundation commissioned a study of medical schools in the United States. At the time there were 155 medical schools in North America. Many of these schools were small trade schools unaffiliated with universities and run for profit by enterprising doctors. There was no real regulation of the medical profession up to the time of the report. There still isn't.

"The Carnegie appointed a guy named Abraham Flexner to study the quality of medical schools. Flexner visited every medical school and published his findings. The report excoriated many medical schools as little more than frauds as institutions of science. Schools that awarded medical degrees after only two years of listening to lectures, with very little or no laboratory work. Most trade professions have longer training periods."

"And your associate, Doctor Jenkins, is from one of those schools?" I asked.

"Of course. But the problem is much worse, at least here at this hospital. You see Jenkins came from the Hudson School of Medicine. So have maybe a third of the staff physicians working here. It's like an infestation of incompetence," Blair said.

"And it's one of those inferior schools Flexner exposed?"

"To be sure. One of the worst. It's still operating though. Want to know why? Because it's operated by the superintendent of this hospital, the eminent Dr. Frederick Snowdon. Prominent member of New York society. Friend of the Mayor. And an all around piece of shit. Runs this hospital like his personal fiefdom."

"Might you be getting into trouble for accosting one his protégés?" I asked.

"Probably. If I were staying, which I'm not. I'm a good physician, well trained. I'm not going to work in this warren of quacks any longer."

Dr. Blair gave me his address and agreed to a further interview. This was more compelling material about the damage caused to the City's health care system by Tammany Hall and Frank Keane in Manhattan. I had assembled enough material to start a sequence of stories. I still lacked a blockbuster exposé

though. I needed that punch to highlight the other material I had
unearthed. What I had painted the larger picture of pervasive
corruption that endangered the sick of the city. It needed only a
catalyst to spark the public's anger.

Two weeks later I found what I needed. In the middle of the
night, I received a telephone call from the disgruntled Dr. Blair.
He had taken a position at the Manhattan Maternity Hospital
and Dispensary on East 60th Street.

"Something terrible is going on, Mr. Murphy. Two infants
have died tonight. All the others in the ward are severely ill.
Seems like some type of virulent infection."

It was a terribly virulent infection. The death toll was eleven
newborn infants. Five others infants were affected but expected
to survive. Dr. Blair told me that the hospital administration was
circling the wagons. The medical staff suspected the cause was
tainted infant formula. No one was allowed to talk to the media.
Records were removed from the hospital. Blair told me the name
of the supplier of the formula. He also secreted some of the formula out of the hospital.

Manhattan Borough President Frank Keane held a press
conference at the hospital several days after the disaster. Terrible
loss. Unfortunate tragedy. The Health Department was conducting a full investigation. The cause of the deaths had not yet been
determined. The best medical technicians were conducting tests.
Keane opened the floor to questions.

"Mr. Keane. Isn't the cause of these infants deaths contaminated baby formula?" I asked.

"That has not been established. Such speculation is dangerous and irresponsible."

"I am in possession of a report from two different laborato-
ries that confirms a deadly bacterial presence in samples of the
formula fed to these infants."

"That is ridiculous. The best labs are still working on the
problem. You cannot be in possession of any of this formula. It

sounds like you are just looking for headlines, Mr. Murphy."

"Someone thought there might be a cover-up so they took the precaution of making sure there was a fair analysis. Want to see the reports?"

"Why would I? Who says they are even from Manhattan Maternity?" Keane yelled.

I waved a paper above the crowd. "I have an affidavit from a physician at the hospital. He's the person that provided the samples for independent testing."

The crowd of reporters now turned to face me and started to fire questions.

"There's more. I also have evidence that the suppliers of the baby formula, a company known as Quality Food Products is partly owned by Mr. Keane's son-in-law. They have exclusive contracts with all city-owned hospitals. Is there more contaminated formula out there, Mr. Keane?"

The crowd of reporters erupted with a blizzard of questions directed to Keane. Photographers let loose rounds of flashes.

"Officers, arrest that reporter for trying to incite a riot!" Keane screamed.

The few police officers had their hands full just trying to hold back what looked like a screaming mob of reporters surging forward as Keane exited the rear of the room.

The headlines from all the major New York as well as Eastern newspapers sprayed headlines of a corrupt New York City government responsible for the deaths of children. With my background work, the *New York Times* was able to pile on a continued attack against Frank Keane's administration day after day.

Within a week, the Mayor backed by others in Tammany Hall did damage control by throwing Frank Keane to the mob. Keane resigned. Investigations were initiated. His son-in-law and others at Quality Food Products were indicted on charges of manslaughter.

Tammany Hall would do its best to squelch any meaningful corruption investigations. I would keep the pressure on but I was a realist. The only real justice came a week later.

As he left his brownstone home, Frank Keane was gunned down. The assailant was the father of one of the dead infants at the hospital. His wife had hung herself in grief two days before. I wrote the front-page story.

The whole episode left me feeling empty and weary. I brought down a couple of miscreants but I was realistic about any broader effect. New York corruption continued as usual. No matter how many stories of official malfeasance got published, nothing structurally changed. There was no democratic process at work in New York City government. People had come to expect that was just the way things worked. It was like trying to exterminate the City's rat population. I took the view that major social changes would only come from some broader confluence of factors, not from crusading efforts of journalists like me. The term pissing into the wind aptly applied to my investigative journalism.

I needed a change. What better new challenge than the terrible conflict ranging in Europe. It was being inadequately reported in U.S. newspapers.

War had broken out in Europe over two years before. The United States was divided on the subject of entering the conflict. If it did, it would be on the side of Great Britain and France. President Wilson was determined that the Country remain officially neutral, although great amounts of goods and war materiel crossed the Atlantic in support of the war effort against Germany.

In America we heard the reports of the great numbers of casualties. However, that did not dampen enthusiasm for many American young men to join in the struggle. It was much the same feeling as I saw before the Spanish-American War even though this conflict was clearly something different.

I too was enticed by the call of this new adventure. The underbelly of the New York I knew so well often felt like a war zone. How could the real thing in Europe be that much worse for a reporter?

CHAPTER 11

PROVENCE, FRANCE – 2009

"My reporting career in New York had a fundamental impact on my life. I'd long ago left behind my rural roots. I was educated. I competed successfully in a difficult business. Rubbed shoulders with movers and shakers. Seen more than enough of society's seamier side. Successfully transformed my life from poor rural working class to urban professional in America's biggest and toughest city.

"But now I want to tell you about my experience during the Great War, World War One. That experience of less than two years transformed me. I want you to understand my life, and I want you to believe me, Allison. Recounting my experiences of World War One may help that process. Are you starting to accept my story as real?"

Allison looked down and responded, "I don't know, Elliot. I have to be honest. I can feel it's so real when you're telling me about the past, but it's just so preposterous .... just so .... I just don't know, Elliot."

"That's ok. That's why I wanted these few days to present

my story to you first hand. Couldn't expect to convince you simply by giving you the manuscript to read. How about we go back to the house. I want to tell you about World War One. Of all the things in my life, those experiences in the middle of that horror had the most profound impact on so many different levels. It changed me just like it changed the entire world."

The autumn day had turned cold. There was a hint of the Mistral, the cold, dry winter winds that blow across Provence from the north. Back at the house, Elliot started a fire in the hearth and set coffee to brewing. Allison joined him in the kitchen. They chatted about life in Provence; its unique culture, its love of cuisine and wine, its rhythms of daily life. Every day in Provence was a celebration of the moment, founded on centuries of tradition.

"Everything about this house is old and well-used, yet it has an elegance that is difficult to describe," Allison said. "I guess that's the difference between character and interior design."

"That's what attracts me to Europe. Life here seems more balanced. The architecture and culture are chronologically old, yet ageless. This house has permanence, almost its own personality. I feel part of this place."

They adjourned to the living area with their coffees and a good bottle of Sauterne. "Now I shall tell you what at the time was called the Great War. It was a war fought with nineteenth century military tactics and twentieth century weapons. It turned out to be a monumentally stupid contest of ego-centric politicians and incompetent generals. The carnage cannot be comprehended by later generations. The numbers of combat casualties were so staggering that it defies the ability to even imagine the scale of these events. Only those of us that experienced it can truly understand the horrors."

"Your novel, *Ypres*, was extraordinarily evocative. It continues to be critically acclaimed." Allison said referring to his novel of World War One set in the Belgian battlefield of Flanders.

"Evocative? Now there's a literary word. I think *Ypres* was a good piece of work too. Written from a first party perspective, I was able to develop compelling characters set against this nightmarish backdrop. So you're right, *Ypres* was more literary. But I'd like you to read my first novel, *Living Dead*, written in 1924 as Dillan Murphy. If you can find a copy that is. Where *Ypres* is more literary and better crafted, *Living Dead* is rawer, a more journalistic approach. I was attempting to relate the experience in the trenches by relating the dreadful details of life for the average soldier.

"I want to recount to you some of my personal experiences, but these too will still just be words. The trenches in Flanders wrought a change in my life that is difficult to articulate. I've read nothing that truly captures the horrors of that experience, my own words included. My brief combat experience in Cuba could not begin to prepare me for this incarnation of hell.

"World War One not only stands as a human catastrophe of colossal proportions, it also became an abrupt divide that shattered illusions. In its aftermath, definitions of patriotism, class, duty, honor, glory would become complex and subject to individual interpretation.

"After the Great War concluded through sheer exhaustion of the combatants, the world was forever changed. With almost ten million military deaths and another twenty-one million military wounded, Europe would feel the loss of a generation of young men throughout the remainder of the century. Beyond that physical reality, there was a deeper loss. It was something more basic than loss of innocence and naivety. Nothing could be hoped. Anything one believed in was fundamentally shattered. It was for me as well."

"You're not religious are you, Elliot?"

"No."

"Because of the War?"

"Not necessarily. As I said, my father felt harshly about the

Catholic Church. I was not mature enough to ask the more basic question as to his personal beliefs. I just assumed that he did not accept the concept of God. So naturally I did not gravitate in that direction. But the Great War made the most extreme argument against any concept of a benevolent God."

"What do you believe then, Elliot?"

"The short answer is I don't have a belief that I embrace, at least a belief in the larger question of being. I don't have a concept for *why* we exist. How do you answer that question for yourself, Allison?"

She paused for a moment to organize her thoughts. "I admit that I believe there is some larger entity responsible for this, for us. A God of some type I guess. I have trouble seeing how this vast complexity of life just came from chance chemical couplings."

"But that makes the case for God only as a default since there are no compelling alternative concepts."

"So you're ok with having no idea why we are? Seems with your gift of longevity that it would push you into believing in some form of God. Maybe even that you were specially blessed."

"Blessed?" he said with more edge than he intended. "I could easily make the case for being cursed. Always to be the outsider. Always having to hide a guilty secret. But I was not guilty of anything. How could I have relationships? Those close to me would grow old while I stand out in sharp contrast. Two hundred years earlier I would have been burned at the stake."

"Sorry, Elliot." Allison held her hand up signaling regret of her comment.

"No, no, Allison. I wasn't angry at you. Certainly not with you. I'm sorry. Suffice it to say that I have defined my own rationale for living my unusual life. It just doesn't include a god or some concept of a universal intelligence. Philosophically I might be labeled a pragmatic agnostic. No proof exists to support either the existence or nonexistence of a supreme being. But if there is a god, then he is clearly uninvolved in the welfare of mankind, so the question is academic. I simply live but am not troubled by the question of *why*."

"Ok. Enough of the metaphysics. Tell me about World War One," Allison said.

CHAPTER 12

From *Time Travels* by **Dillan Murphy**
PARIS, FRANCE – 1917

Although I had become a top reporter in New York with consistent front-page bylines, I was hungering to get my teeth into something different. Tilting at the windmills of crime and corruption no longer held the same enthusiasm.

It was a time of such great change, great hope. Technology advances and new social concepts burst forth. The electric light, the telephone, the automobile, the airplane came of age. Industrial automation was changing parts of the world from rural to urban societies. Advances in medicine and drugs changed life in the industrialized countries of the world. The great thinkers of theoretical physics Albert Einstein and Max Planck published their far reaching theories. All these great changes came about within the two decades since 1890.

The democratic process in the United States exerted its influence for the first time with a rising middle class. Women's suffrage and the organized labor movement pressed for rights with the weight of newly found power. There were the first stirrings of what would become the civil rights movements for African Americans. Against these hopeful factors mankind's uglier side responded with warfare and genocidal excesses. European nationalistic ambitions were to inflict horrors from the middle ages.

Those early years of the new century were a time of turmoil throughout the world. There was the Boxer Rebellion in China where radicals attempted to drive out foreigners. There was the Boer War in what today is South Africa between Dutch settlers rebelling against British rule. There was a war between Russia and Japan fought over territory. This was followed by an aborted revolution in Russia in 1905 as the peasantry attempted to throw off Tsarist feudalism. There were state sponsored atrocities perpetrated in colonial Belgian Congo. There was an impending revolution in Mexico. Then of course there was the run-up to World War One in Europe, the seminal event I believe of the twentieth century.

The question of America's entry into the War dominated the country in 1916. The *Times* had been getting its news from the British correspondents and an assortment of stringers. The news was stale and slanted. British journalism avoided reporting the uglier aspects of the war. Not good for morale back home. One only had to consider the casualty statistics to understand there was more to be reported. I convinced Charlie Kendrick to post me to France even before the United States formally joined in the War. I was the perfect choice. Kendrick knew I would produce newsworthy copy with an edge.

The Great War happened because everything that could go wrong did go wrong in European geopolitics. The assassination of the heir to the Austrian-Hungarian throne by a Serbian triggered a chain of events. The political and military leaders of the great European powers saw opportunity and threat into this singular event between two backwater nations. None had the vision or statesmanship to pull back from the course of events. It was the perfect convergence of volatile circumstances. Differing European cultures emerged from the last century with competing nationalistic aspirations fueled by historic hatreds. Every political decision only exacerbated events leading to all out war. Once the conflict erupted, every military move was met with a counter move that ended in continual stalemate throughout the War. It was this stalemate that bred the special horrors of trench warfare.

The War was only two years old by the end of 1916, yet the carnage was already something never before experienced. Germany's aggression westward across Belgium, thereby threatening Paris, had been stopped by the massive infusion of British armies since 1914. The warring countries had gone to war enthusiastically, each pursuing its own righteous justifications based on nationalistic culture and ideology. By early 1917 the War had evolved into a stalemate of appalling attrition of men and materiel. There were entire British regiments that had almost no original soldiers from 1914, having turned over manpower one hundred percent. The blood of a generation of young French manhood had been bled dry. By 1917, France was conscripting middle-aged men. The French Army was suffering epidemic mutinies. The German armies were starving and near exhaustion.

Opposing armies of over a million men each faced off in elaborate arrays of defensive trenches and concrete fortifications. The chessboard execution of the war by the generals belied the virtual hell for the soldiers in the trenches. For over two years the Western Front, as termed from the German perspective, had changed by only a matter of miles. Major battles were fought years apart over the same ground. In between these events was a constant attrition of casualties and men living in animal-like conditions of deprivation.

I only recount this background of circumstances to set the stage for my own experiences. Countless books have been written, my own included, and this is not intended to be another reexamination of that history. This is my personal recollection.

I arrived in Paris in late November of 1916. It was already cold as the city braced for winter. But Paris was still Paris. Except for an unusual amount of uniformed men about the Champs-Elysées, it was everything I had read about. Paris had a unique ambience that was only slightly altered by the war raging less than a hundred miles to the northeast. There were the beginnings of real food shortages, but generally, if you had money there was plenty of food, wine, and of course, plenty of women in the City of Light.

It would be a couple of months before I would able sort out how and where I wanted to report on the war. The troops at the front were settling in for winter. Even twentieth century warfare could not be waged effectively in winter conditions. I hated the cold so it was easy to rationalize the need to stay warm in Paris. I therefore spent the time probing and ingratiating myself with high-ranking officers. This was both to secure their assistance as well as to get meaningful material for my pieces sent back to the States until I actually got to the front lines.

From the perspective of Paris, the War seemed somewhat removed, yet it raged near enough to occasionally hear the distant drumming of large caliber artillery at the front. The most striking impression of war was the absence of young men unless in uniform. London and Berlin were probably the same. Would this be the harbinger of things in the United States when it entered the War?

The numbers of combatants and casualties were staggering, so much so that they became an abstraction. By the end of 1916 millions had died on both sides. But the remaining two years would push those numbers to unimaginable levels. By the end of the War in 1918, the carnage totaled 9.7 million military dead or missing, and 21 million wounded. Over one million men would fall as casualties in Flanders alone. The mind cannot conceive of violent death on this scale. Numbers simply could not convey the enormity of the conflict there. Nothing in prior history came close.

I dined with French and British officers that dressed in immaculate uniforms, often accompanied by well-dressed women. For these *gentlemen*, waging war was simply their profession. Later, having experienced the anguish and deprivations of the soldier in the trenches, I recalled these first experiences in Paris with disgust. The contrast added antidotal clarity as to how this debacle happened.

The better Parisian restaurants had no shortages for senior military officers. I suspected most of these officers had never even been to the Front, much less experienced anything of the average soldier's circumstances in the trenches. In retrospect, it was evident why the war was prosecuted so incompetently. I suspect the same problem existed for the Germans since they exhibited no better leadership than the Allies.

I will illustrate my point by way of an interesting personal footnote. I became acquainted with a French colonel of the Corps de L'Intendance, the equivalent to the quartermaster corps, responsible for supplying the Army with goods. A cushy job with many perks, not the least of which was being stationed in Paris. Having an avid interest in all things American, the Colonel and I became friendly.

One evening the Colonel invited me as his guest to a private party held in a suite at the elegant Hotel Meurice on the Rue de Rivoli. There were perhaps a dozen men, most in military uniform, all with young female escorts, myself included. Waiters served expensive wine and cigars on silver service. The host was a businessman, a major supplier to the French Army, my friend the colonel confided. After New York, I could smell the odor of corruption.

The Colonel said, "You are in store for a special treat my American friend."

I looked at the young woman accompanying me. The Colonel had arranged it. Perhaps just a young woman looking for fun to counter the strains of the War. Not likely. Probably just a newly minted prostitute by her lack of a coarse demeanor common to most in that profession.

"Oh, not her. But perhaps that too!" the colonel said and laughed. "I mean the entertainment this evening. We are to be treated to a performance by the famed exotic dancer, Mata Hari. An Oriental beauty. The toast of Paris for many years. She is truly a wonder. I have seen her once before. Her performance is not to be forgotten. It shall place you in the right mood for your later pleasures."

I learned much later that Mata Hari was actually Dutch. Her real name was Margaretha Zelle. True to the Colonel's billing, Mademoiselle Zelle put on quite a show. Although she was perhaps forty, she was still a great beauty.

I don't know about her dancing talents, but her costume and provocative movements were enticing. She was dark as a gypsy. She was barefoot and sported an exotic looking beaded headdress. Over her breasts she wore a bra of two cup-like affairs with her midriff bare and a loose-fitting slit skirt riding low on her hips. The skirt looked to be of silk with elaborate embroidery. As she whirled about, her skirt periodically parted to reveal she had nothing on underneath. Toward the end of her performance she pulled off her skirt and danced nude with only her breasts covered. It was a gloriously decadent evening.

CHAPTER 13

Provence, France – 2009

"Whoa. Wait a minute, Elliot. You're saying you knew Mata Hari?"

"No. I didn't know her. Just saw her perform. I mention her mostly to show how people and events become distorted over time."

"Still, that's amazing. Not sure I know her story. Some sort of spy?" Allison said. "Was that what she was? What happened to her?"

"Difficult to say if she actually was a spy. Probably not. But I'll tell you a little later in my story what happened to her."

"All right. Then tell me how you were coping with this age thing. In 1917, you were, let me see .... well into your forties? How old did you look?"

"Maybe thirty. Perhaps younger."

"So when did you suspect that you were .... ah, different?"

"I can't pin down a specific time. There was no sudden realization that I clearly looked a lot younger than my actual age. But I guess I could say that my time with the soldiers of World War

One made me confront the reality."

"Had anyone commented on your looking so young before that lawyer in New York?"

"Occasionally. But you see as a reporter I moved about. Saw different people all the time. Never part of any constant group. Didn't have a circle of friends. Most people had no reason to know my background, therefore my real age. I was just youthful looking, no more than thirty they thought. Even I thought that. But that changed in the trenches with the troops.

"I subconsciously knew I was different by this time. If I did give it thought, I was always confronted with the implausibility. There was no explanation. How could there be. It made no sense. It makes no sense now. I can't even speculate as to a reason for my condition.

"Most of those soldiers were in there twenties. I looked their age. When asked questions, I avoided revealing anything to suggest my actual age. I knew I was different. I also knew it would only provoke unwelcome inquiry. I might even be branded a liar. I invented a convenient history. In doing that, I was forced to admit to myself there was something very different about me."

"What did you feel when it was obvious that you were unnaturally younger looking?" Allison asked.

"That's complicated. Not easy to explain in words."

"But didn't you at least feel fortunate?"

Elliot reflected a moment before answering, "Actually it was the opposite. Even back that far when I first realized what was happening, it was more a feeling of anxiety."

"Anxiety? Doesn't everyone want to live a very long life, and better yet, to look young along the way?"

"You'd think so. But everyone just says that knowing it's only fantasy. What I begin to feel was alienation, albeit self-imposed. I had this terribly dark secret. I felt I must always remain an outsider. I must lie to guard my secret. How could I ever be part of anything?"

"But haven't you always been a loner? Even maybe a bit reclusive?"

"Probably I am a loner. But remember much of that is imposed by my problem. Who's to say how I might have been had I lived a normal life span, aging appropriately. At any rate, being individualistic doesn't mean one wants to be an outsider. At some level everyone needs some connection to his most personal environment. To be truly alone is a terrible curse.

"The unease started with having to lie about events in my life that wouldn't fit with the age suggested by my appearance. To illustrate, an incident occurred shortly after arriving in Paris. It was before I went up to the Front. It left no equivocation that my lack of normal aging was real. It also illustrates how cautious I had to be to live this lie because the truth was inexplicable. Let me read a passage from the manuscript."

From *Time Travels* by Dillan Murphy
PARIS, FRANCE - 1917

I had been in Paris several weeks. I was making the tour of visiting the various headquarters of the French, the British, and the newly arrived U.S. Expeditionary forces. I was scavenging for information to send back to the *New York Times*. The French colonel's cozy connection to suppliers of war materiel probably held some story of corrupt dealings, but it was still just filler. It would take a lot of work to develop. The real story was life and death at the Front.

Paris was full of reporters. We were all looking for something more than the military press releases. We rightly suspected that the information was at least censored and most was likely doctored to justify political positions. I realized that I had to get to the Front soon to get meaningful material. See things for myself. Experience the frontlines. Talk to real soldiers and officers.

I met a fellow American journalist. He was reporting for the

Herald Tribune, my old newspaper. One evening we were drinking wine, too much wine. The reporter is telling me about his exploits. As he became more intoxicated, his bragging reached a point of irritation. Having also had too much to drink, I forgot myself.

"Wait till you get up to the Front," he said. "Then you'll see what war is like. I've been here over a year. Seen the Frenchies massacred at Verdun last year. Killed and wounded by the thousands. Hell of a thing to see up close."

"Up close? You mean you were in the front line trenches?" I asked in a skeptical tone. This slightly overweight balding guy did not impress me as the type of reporter to risk himself in the thick of real fighting.

"You bet I was."

"You speak French?"

"No."

"Then how did you know what was going on?"

The *Herald* reporter looked angrily at me. "You suggesting I'm lying?"

"No. Just can't see you out there in the trenches. The cold food, the dirt, no water closet, artillery shells raining down, bullets flying."

"What the hell would you know? I was in this business when you were still at your mother's breast. You haven't done shit. Not sure I even believe that story about your run-in with Tammany Hall."

I had provoked the guy so what did I expect?

"Let me tell you what I know about war. I worked for the *Herald* before I went over to the *Times*. You weren't there at the time. Bennett himself sent me to Cuba in '98. Teddy Roosevelt got me posted as a correspondent with his Rough Rider regiment. I charged up San Juan Hill with his troopers. I've seen men shot and killed right next to me. Is that what you experienced at Verdun?"

The guy looked at me with a mixture of anger and bewilderment.

"Jesus Christ. You're the fucking liar here. And a stupid liar to boot. You expect anyone to believe you were in the Spanish American War? How old would you have been? Maybe ten?"

The guy reached into his pocket and pulled out some coins which he threw unto the table. He put on his bowler and got up to leave. "I'll do my drinking with other company. Fuck you, Murphy."

CHAPTER 14

From *Time Travels* by Dillan Murphy
YPRES, BELGIUM – 1917

I arrived at British General Sir Hubert Gough's Fifth Army headquarters the first week of July, 1917. We were thirty miles behind the front lines that faced the German trenches just beyond the town of Ypres in Flanders, Belgium.

Expressing my desire to go up to the Front, a junior officer thought with a name like Murphy that I should be assigned to the Irish Guards. I was therefore introduced to Major Horace Crawford of the Irish Guards First Battalion of the British Expeditionary Force. He was no rear-echelon staff officer. To the contrary he was hell-bent to be right in the thick of the fight.

"I'm returning to my regiment in two days, Mr. Murphy. If you wish to see what this war is really about, I shall take you up to the Front," Crawford said. "I've been in this fight since '14. Rough go back then. The Krauts almost pushed us back, but we held Flanders and therefore we held France. Now it's an ugly contest fought from muddy holes."

The British were the primary Allied forces fighting in Belgium. The bulk of the French forces were engaged to the south. The United States had not yet entered the War in early 1917.

The Major and I rode in an ambulance eastward from Fifth Army headquarters outside Amiens. A few miles west of Ypres, the ambulance deposited us outside the town of Poperinghe. A large tent had been erected over an excavated area to afford some protection from artillery. The Major informed me this was the Division's headquarters, several miles to the rear of the front line trenches. This far removed from the front lines seemed to me to limit command effectivity in the event of an enemy offensive. Seemed more a benefit for senior officers to remain in comparative safety.

Motioning to a soldier, the Major said to me, "This is Staff Sergeant Doyle. Follow his lead and you'll have as good a chance as any to survive up here. The Sergeant's a top soldier. Sergeant?"

"Sir!" the Sergeant braced to attention with the compliment. He looked like an old hand with a lean build that suggested a wiry strength, punctuated with a well-groomed large red mustache.

"This is Mr. Murphy, Sergeant. Newspaper correspondent from the States. He wants to go up to the front with us tomorrow. Give him what assistance you can."

The Major entered the tent and left me with the Sergeant.

The Sergeant offered his hand. "Glad to meet you, Sir. Are you Irish, Sir?"

"Irish descent. Both my mother and my father's parents came from Ireland."

"Well I'd say you're Irish then, Sir. We'll be relieving the Grenadier Guards Second Battalion who'll change places with us here in the rear. You see we've got two of the Brigade's battalions on the front line at any time, with two held in reserve. Theory is, if there's an attack, the reserve battalions can be directed to plug any breach in our lines. This your first time at the

Front, Sir?"

"Yes it is, Sergeant. That's not a problem is it?"

"No, Sir. Just that things can be pretty harsh in the trenches. Not many people who have a choice would want to venture out there. Fact is you'll be the first civilian I've known of."

"That's where the real news is, Sergeant. I won't get much hanging around with the brass back here."

"Right you are about that, Sir. So it's an early call, Sir - three AM. I'll show you to a place where you can a get a wee bit of rest. Do ya have plenty of socks, Sir?"

"I think so, but why's that so important?" I asked.

"Must keep your feet dry. Bloody wet in the trenches. You need to change at least three times a day otherwise you're apt to get trench foot. Trench foot is some mean shit, Sir. You'll want to be avoidin' it. I'll see about getting you some extra socks from the quartermaster. Can't have too many socks."

I picked up my gear, which was the typical conventional British Army issue. It was a heavy load that took some doing to hoist onto my back. Consisting of a large backpack, haversack, blanket, ground sheet, water bottle, eating tin, shovel, helmet, and gas mask, it weighed about fifty pounds. In place of a rifle, I carried a portable Corona typewriter in a leather case. It was a comparatively new invention within the last few years, weighing only five and a half pounds.

As we were walking, it started to rain so I broke out my waterproof cape. The Sergeant remarked, "Fuckin' rain, if you pardon my French. Freeze your arse off in the winter, then it rains almost every bloody day in the spring. Now it's summer and still raining."

Sergeant Doyle took me a short way to a ladder descending into a trench. He explained that though we were in the rear of the front lines, German artillery could still reach this far, so even here they lived in trenches. It was to be my first taste of trench life.

The trench was about eight feet deep. Rainwater ran down the sides filling the bottom. There were wooden planks, trench boards that you walked on to elevate you from the water. But that depended upon the amount of rain. I followed the Sergeant into a large room-type excavation covered with a wooded roof. The bunker was crowded with soldiers who all looked toward us as we entered.

"This here's Mr. Murphy, lads. He's a newspaperman from America, but he's Irish. Goin' up to the front line with us. He'll be making you famous back home 'less you'll be showin' him what a bunch of dumb arseholes you are," the Sergeant said.

The men were of good cheer and we shook hands all around. I unbuckled my gear and sat down on a long wooden bench. There were no bunks. At best I might find enough room to lie down on the wood planking. The floor was mud, getting worse as more rain water poured down the walls of the excavation. Sitting up, I dosed fitfully for a few hours until Sergeant Doyle rattled a mess tin with his bayonet to rouse the platoon. It seemed the middle of the night, which it was.

I fell out with the rest of the soldiers. Everyone was silent and grim. They had done this before. The fellow next to me said it would take two hours to cover the three kilometers to the front trenches. "Why so long?" I asked.

"It's tough going with all your gear. Especially in the dark. You'll see why when we're out there," he answered.

While still miles from the British lines, the terrain started to abruptly change as we marched east. From intact farm structures we moved to damaged farms and barns, then to no structures, then to no trees, then to no grass. We trudged through the once magnificent medieval town of Ypres. Its grand Cloth Hall, built in the thirteenth century, and its imposing cathedral, had been reduced to rubble by German artillery over the past years of constant shelling. Every building was destroyed or damaged. The civilian population had long since left.

Shell craters became increasing numerous until there was no direct route. We stumbled along in single file making a serpentine traverse through a field of gaping artillery craters filled with water. Our heavy packs made us prone to stumbling and falling. In places you sunk calf-deep into the mud. It was a cloying clay composition exceedingly slippery. Only where there were wooden *duckboards* was it possible to walk normally. And the rain continued.

"It's a good night to be on the march. Black as the Kaiser's soul," the soldier next to me whispered. "If they spot us, their artillery would do a bloody number on us out here in the open. That's why we move at night."

Sergeant Doyle kicked the soldier in the butt and whispered. "Shut your mouth you stupid bugger. If the Boche lob any artillery on us, I'll put a bullet through that empty fuckin' head of yours."

We arrived at the beginning of the front trench fortifications as dawn was breaking. The trenches were not mere holes, but rather a complex network of parallel and perpendicular excavations designed to anchor a defensive position. In the coming days I would learn that there were front line and secondary line traverse trenches, connected by perpendicular service and communication trenches. Underground bunkers were periodically spaced to store supplies and afford some soldiers shelter from the elements. It was a rat maze in more ways than one.

As dawn broke, I got my first glimpse of what was known as no-mans-land, the few hundred yards between the opposing forces trenches. Beyond the front lines was a surreal landscape starting with rows of barbed wire entanglements followed by ground so corrupted that the rims of shell craters literally joined each other. A few stumps of sheared-off trees jutted from the ground, otherwise the landscape was totally devoid of any vegetation. I glimpsed this through angled observation binoculars that allowed the viewer to stay below the trench rim. Exposing your head would invite a German sniper's bullet.

"Jesus, Sergeant, if that isn't a vision of Hell I don't know what is," I remarked as I surveyed the landscape through the glasses. The rain had lightened but the gray sky added to a sight so alien I knew I would have difficulty finding adequate descriptive words.

"Right you are, Sir. It is Hell," Sergeant Doyle said. "When you're out there you have to give up any hope of surviving. Bullets zipping by. Artillery rounds and grenades sending terrible shrapnel about. There's always the threat of poison gas. It's a stupid weapon, ugly as sin. Then there're the machine guns. Take out a whole platoon in a couple of minutes, they can. Seen it happen. All this as you're stumbling through this artillery-plowed field with its tangle of barbed wire, and always the endless mud. Seen many a soldier drown in a crater hole filled with water. Or you might just sink out of sight in some mud holes that are like quicksand. Better to die by a bullet I say."

"How long have you been here Sergeant?"

"Since '15. Survived the Battles of Loos and the Somme. Not many of us original regulars left. All these lads about you are fresh enlistees or conscripts. Good lads, but still don't have much training."

"How often do you attack?"

"Every time General Haig has a fart caught crosswise and thinks it's an original thought. Bloody too often if you ask me. And you know what happens if you're lucky enough to make it across no-man's land without being hit? You get to occupy the German's trenches. This shithole we're in right now used to be a German trench we took from them a year ago. That's all there is here in Flanders, endless trenches. Just trade one fuckin' hole for another, but only after you kill thousands on both sides."

It started to rain again.

"Fucking rain. That's all it's done since the start of spring. You see, Mr. Murphy, this is the worse place to be fighting a war from bloody trenches. I'm told Flanders has a delicate drainage problem. Now there's a stupid understatement. Can't even dig a hole without it filling with water. Then you plow up all the ground with years of artillery bombardment to make a real fucking mess. And if it ain't winter snow, it's rainin'.

"Newbury, front and center," the Sergeant said, signaling a soldier. "Newbury, this is Mr. Murphy, newspaper man from America. Be a good lad and help him get about."

"Peter Newbury. Pleased to meet you, Mister Murphy," the private said shaking my hand. He was a big-eared kid with a broad toothy grin. "Grab your gear and we'll find a place for you in the bunker."

I started to question the wisdom of wanting to be up here on the front lines as we sloshed down the trench. Rivulets of mud flowed down the sides of the trench. Boards lined the bottom of the trench so you could walk without sinking, but the water was still over the boards and up to your ankles in places. I could see why the extra socks. If the rain persisted, you were going to stand in water a good deal of the day.

By a *place*, Private Newbury meant a spot not otherwise occupied. There were no bunks, no chairs, no tables. These front line trenches were decidedly more miserable than those in the rear back at division headquarters. I put my waterproof ground sheet down and parked my gear. The bunker itself was a depressing place. It was nothing more than just a wider hole than the trench itself covered with a leaking wooden roof and duckboard floor. Kerosene lamps cast uneven light. It smelled of damp clothing and unwashed bodies.

Most of the men of the Second Platoon of Company A were in their early twenties. I couldn't imagine a crueler place, yet they were of surprisingly high spirits. In spite of being forced to live worse than an animal, with the strong likelihood of death or wounding that awaited their future, they joked and generally took care of each other. I believed it was a means to hold their individual terrors in check.

I intended to write about these brave men, to put a human face to this terrible conflict for my readers back in the States. By all indications, the United States would soon be entering the conflict. Americans needed to see beyond the lofty patriotic soundings by public figures and understand what it would mean for their young men. This was not to be a war of quick adventure like the Spanish-American War. The horrors would be worse than the American Civil War over fifty years ago.

After an evening of playing cards, smoking, and finishing off their daily rum ration, those not on guard duty found their spots to sleep for the night. I too wrapped myself with my blanket and attempted to try to sleep. It was not to be. The rain persisted with an even heavier downpour. Water flowed down the walls of the bunker raising the ground water level well above the duckboard floor. Everyone sought a way to not have to sit or lay in the water. The best I could do was lean against the sloping bunker wall with my feet in the rising water.

Bad as this was, there was worse. Once the lamps were extinguished I could hear noises of what sounded like the scurrying of small animals. Something touched my thigh. "Newbury? What's that noise?" I asked urgently in a harsh whisper.

"Rats. Big fuckin' rats. Won't bother you though. They're just scavenging for food. Everything always needs to be secured in crates or the nasty bastards will get into the rations."

I willed myself to suppress the panic, and then lit a match. Staring up between my feet was the ugliest looking rat I had ever seen, literally the size of a rabbit. "Sonofabitch!" I yelled and dropped the match. "Christ, did you see the size of that rat, Newbury?"

"Seen bigger I'm afraid. We call 'em corpse rats. They been feedin' off corpses. You see, there's a whole lot of dead out there from both sides that never got a proper burial. Lots of bodies you can't get to after a battle. Lots just sink into the mud. Everything freezes over in the winter, then come spring they start popping up. Rats have a feast."

"Wonderful. So what do you do about them?"

"Nothing you can do. They won't bite you. Some blokes kill 'em for sport. Some have been known to eat them. Meat rations are rare out here. As for me, no thanks. Not eatin' rat that's been feeding on a rottin' corpse," Newbury said.

The bile rose in my throat. Needless to say, my first night in the front line trenches was sleepless.

CHAPTER 15

From *Time Travels* by Dillan Murphy
YPRES, BELGIUM – 1917

As daylight broke, there were groans and curses as the platoon woke. Breakfast was a small ration of soggy bread, a bit of stale cheese, and a tin of tepid tea. The rain persisted in a steady downpour. I ventured outside the bunker with my rain cape and explored up and down the trench. Apart from the sentries stationed every twenty yards, the rest of the men did the best they could to keep dry. As I passed, gaunt unshaved faces looked out from bolt holes every few yards along the trench. Bolt holes were simply dugout areas in the wall of the trenches large enough for a man to squeeze himself into. It was a little drier there and afforded some added protection against shrapnel in the event of aerial artillery bursts.

With a horrid night spent with the rats and the privations of the soldiers I saw that first day, it took all my will to muster the courage to stay on at the Front. This was something out of medieval history. But I determined to stick it out. The day proved productive as I saw the battlefield from the soldier's eye.

I didn't relish nighttime, but knowledge is better than the unknown. I was exhausted but only dosed fitfully that second night. It was a short night. Around three in the morning the German shelling started. There is simply no way to adequately describe the terror of an artillery bombardment.

First of all there is nowhere to hide. My first instinct was to get out of the bunker. Its low roof made me claustrophobic. The unrelenting noise and the uncertainty if the round was going to land near could reduce even the strongest willed to paralysis. Close explosions hurt your ears and showered debris. The uncertainty was an unrelenting terror for sometimes hours on end.

I was huddled with a couple of soldiers sitting on the firing platform of the trench. No more than thirty feet away, a shell exploded directly within the trench, the concussion of its explosion knocking all of us into the water at the trench bottom. I didn't feel that I had been wounded, but my front was covered with blood and pieces of human tissue. The soldier next to me screamed and fought frantically to dislodge the severed hand in his lap.

The bombardment lasted four hours. The noise was virtually constant only increasing in magnitude when rounds exploded close by. Conversation was impossible even if anybody wanted to say anything. At seven o'clock, the bombardment abruptly ceased.

I made my way next to the young platoon lieutenant looking into no-man's land with the observation glasses. "Sergeant Doyle, get the platoon into firing position and fix bayonets," he shouted.

The rain had ceased but it was still a deeply overcast morning with a heavy fog hugging the ground. "Lieutenant, are you expecting an attack?" I asked.

"No question about it. That bombardment was across a several mile front. Anytime now they'll be advancing. We'll first hear firing from our forward observers, then they'll pull back to this line. Then our own artillery batteries will open up on the Germans. I must tell you Mister Murphy, that if the Jerries get into our trenches they'll take you for an enemy soldier. You being without a weapon won't stop them from killing you or taking you prisoner. I suggest you stay close to the Sergeant, Sir."

I thanked the Lieutenant and went to prepare my gear in the event that we retreated. I also pulled out a Colt M1911 .45 caliber semi-automatic in a leather shoulder holster. A friend from my Rough Rider days was still in the U.S. Army. We kept in contact and upon learning that I was going to France, he suggested I take along the U.S. Army officer's newest sidearm. I was officially a non-combatant but that distinction is lost on an enemy soldier faced with someone in the uniform of the other side.

I found myself next to Private Newbury. "What's going to happen, Peter? Have you been under attack before?" I asked.

"Many a time."

"Ever have to retreat?"

"Aye. Been in two retreats. But I tell you, Mr. Murphy, defendin' or even retreating is a damn site better than doin' the attacking. When you're to go over the top, the fear's enough to cause you to mess yourself. Better to be in the hole and have the other feller be runnin' about ducking bullets while crawlin' through barbed wire. And if you're wounded out there, well you're all but fucked for sure."

Made sense, but I can bear witness that defending was little better. Within minutes, British artillery batteries commenced their own barrage against the advancing German forces, although the fog prevented sighting the enemy. Soon, machine guns opened up. Put enough bullets out there and you'll hit some of the enemy. I guessed that the advancing Germans were visible as the entire platoon opened up with their Lee Enfield rifles.

For the next thirty minutes the fighting raged with the Brits firing and reloading as rapidly as possible. Then the first grenade came into the trench. A soldier standing next to me took the grenade's shrapnel and saved me. Then I heard other grenades exploding in the trenches. It meant that the Germans were gaining ground. Within minutes our section of trench turned to confusion.

Sergeant Doyle was rallying his men. The Lieutenant had been killed. Doyle sent a runner to the left to see what the Company's orders were. One soldier looked pleadingly to Doyle. "Sarge, we're bein' overrun! We've got to retreat!"

"Shut your fuckin' mouth, Soldier. We'll hold until we get orders otherwise."

Moments later, the runner returned. "Sergeant, the Captain says pull back to the secondary trenches and consolidate defenses."

"Retreat! Retreat!" Doyle yelled. At the same time, men came running down the trench from the right only to be cut down by Germans firing from behind them. The Germans had apparently overrun that portion of the trench. Several men fell from their standing firing positions and a German soldier jumped into the trench twenty feet from me. With no hesitation, I unholstered my .45 and shot him twice in the chest before he could discharge his Mauser. I grabbed by typewriter and satchel with my journals. As best I could, I ran through the standing water down the communication trench toward the rear trench line.

After a hundred yards I reached the secondary defensive trench, only to find that the entire Corps was falling back across a broad front. That meant leaving the relative protection of the rear trenches to navigate the crater-pocked landscape hoping not to be blown up by artillery or drowned in the mud. This was the same ground the platoon stumbled through the day before.

The German artillery started to land rounds into the rear of our lines to inflict casualties on our retreating forces. So the further you got from the front trenches, the worse it became. With every shell-burst men fell. Instinct wanted to force you to seek cover. I clearly expected not to escape the artillery. The fear of incoming rounds compelled me to slide down the side of a large shell crater filled with water to at least gain some moments of rest.

Within moments I regretted the move. As I slid down the side of the hole into the water, I collided with something. Fortunately there was only three feet of water in this shell hole. Turning to see what I had struck, I recoiled at the sight of the upper torso of a soldier. It was badly decomposed. The face was gone. It was disgusting beyond all description. A recent artillery shell had probably dislodged it. But to consummate my horror, a large rat emerged from the abdominal cavity, offal caked about its snout.

Retching, I scrambled out of the crater like a madman.

Hours later I reached the new defensive trench line. I was given a blanket and a ration of rum, and then fell asleep until the next dawn. After considerable searching, I found the Second Platoon, or what was left of it. Sergeant Doyle, Private Newbury, and eight others were all that remained of the fifty-seven men from the day before.

I slapped Private Newbury on the back. "Peter, it's good to see you."

Newbury barely acknowledged my presence. Both he and Sergeant Doyle had the *thousand-yard stare* of those that had been pushed to the limits of emotionally being able to function.

"Sergeant, I'm glad you made it. Seems you have nine lives," I said.

"More than nine. Should have died more times than I can count. God is just being cruel. He lets me see all these young lads torn apart. As a torment, he spares me to repeat it over and over. In the end, in the last battle, He will have me butchered too."

CHAPTER 16

From *Time Travels* by Dillan Murphy
YPRES, BELGIUM – 1917

I cannot fully explain how I willed myself to stay out there in the trenches as long as I did. It was emotionally shattering. The privations were disgusting beyond all comprehension. But I knew the value of the reporting I was doing. This was the real war from the perspective of the British soldier. I was able to bear witness to an experience that tested the boundaries of human endurance. If I returned to report from a rear position of safety, I would betray myself and these brave lads.

I seemed to be the only reporter at the true front. The British and French newspapers were full of politically correct or politically motivated commentary. My pieces sent back to New York portrayed the conflict in all its horror. This was what the soldier experienced. This was the real face of the War. This was what the American dough boys would be facing. There was no glory here, only death.

If I seemed one of the few correspondents willing to report critically on the War, the soldiers themselves avoided relating anything even remotely disturbing in their letters home. Many read their letters out loud to their mates. *'Weather a little bad. Much rain but it keeps the Germans in their trenches as well. Made many good friends. I'm with a swell bunch of blokes. Worse thing here is boredom. Not to worry, Mum. Maybe you could send more socks.'* The letters from home confirmed that their families had no appreciation for the hardship their sons and husbands faced. *'Are they feeding you well? Did you receive the chocolates I sent a few weeks ago? Good to hear you are making friends. Once the War ends you'll have to bring them around to the house. The Thompsons down the lane were informed their son fell in battle. We all feel terrible. Glad to hear there is little shooting in your sector. Keep well and out of danger, son.'*

Nor did their families understand the magnitude of the risk of becoming a casualty. There was no rotation once your tour of duty was up. The tour of duty was to the end of the War. The odds for one's survival diminished with each day.

These were young men facing death, living in wretched discomfort, yet to a man they wanted to shield their loved ones from worry. They faced death alone with only their comrades. Their bravery was only more poignant in view of the stubborn, unimaginative leadership prosecuting the War.

I sometimes felt guilty with my reporting of the true circumstances. Maybe my reports to the United States would not be read in the U.K. But then again, they should. The War was already stalemated. Winning could only be through attrition. Somehow the voice of reason should be heard over the chest-pounding of the politicians and the blundering of the generals.

Only the numbing fear of becoming a casualty distracts the poor soldier in the trench from more constant battle of just trying to live under conditions that defy description. Over the next couple of weeks I lived in conditions worse than domestic animals do. The rain never relented. Keeping dry was impossible. When the rain did stop, mud caked your clothing. Even without the rain, there was standing water in all the trenches due to the boggy terrain around Ypres. Keeping your feet dry was a constant endeavor. And the water itself was beyond disgust. Stagnant, full of urine, sometimes things worse than that, frequently populated with ugly fat slugs and a scum of algae.

I saw men with trench foot, their feet swollen and deformed to twice normal size. At best it was excruciatingly painful, at worse the feet were amputated. It is such a disgusting affliction that once when doing a piece about a field hospital I had to go outside to vomit.

Fierce looking beetles crawled in the bolt holes feeding on the body lice infestations breeding where the men would sleep. With no means of washing bodies or clothing, body lice was a chronic condition with every soldier. They fed on blood, creating a nasty, itching rash around your waist, underarms, and the groin area.

Decomposing corpses, both human and horse, open latrines, and unwashed bodies fueled a pervasively vile stench. There were no trees, no grass. Often there was no sky. There were no birds, no rabbits, no squirrels. The only living creatures were all manner of disgusting vermin and the poor soldiers.

The British Army regrouped. The Germans had insufficient troops to exploit the attack. A new Second Platoon was formed with survivors of other units. We were assigned to a position north of Ypres.

At 3:50am on the morning of July 31st, a British artillery bombardment of unprecedented intensity commenced along a broad front. The Irish Guards were in the first advance wave tasked with capturing what was called Pilckem Ridge. Calling it a ridge misconstrues what that implies. It was merely a slight rise of ground. There are no hills in Flanders. Nevertheless, the German defenses were well entrenched.

The Irish Guards went 'over the top' in the semi-darkness before dawn with a light rain and cloud shrouded sky. I felt a measure of guilt staying back in the cover of the trench. Through an observation periscope I witnessed a sight that made my combat experience in Cuba pale against this spectacle of men advancing into what they must regard as certain death.

The ground was so torn that the soldiers could only advance at a walk, even then frequently stumbling. Unbroken barbed wire entanglements blocked their path after a few hundred yards out. The realization that the artillery bombardment had failed to destroy the wire was a cruel blow. All these obstacles served to expose the British soldiers that much longer to murderous machine gun fire. The massive artillery bombardment had fallen far short of diminishing German defenses. By the afternoon, the rain increased.

This went on for three days. The British and their commonwealth country troops suffered thirty-two thousand casualties. That was the cost for advancing only 2000 yards. There are no words adequate to convey a true appreciation of what it meant to witness such an event.

CHAPTER 17

Elliot paused his story, and then seemed lost for a moment in the memories.

Allison had sat silently absorbed throughout Elliot's long World War One narrative. At this obvious break she said, "My God, Elliot. I read much of this in your novel *Ypres*, but hearing your own personal experience is emotionally jarring. You make my skin crawl with your descriptions."

"Probably was a bad place to break since we should be thinking about dinner."

"Dinner? After talk of rats and lice? Besides, I had a large lunch. Maybe something light later?"

"Sounds good to me. Perhaps some cheese and bread when we get hungry. How about more wine though?"

"Sure. You do like your wine, don't you?"

"Wine is such a sublime pleasure. It can never be considered a vice. I'm going to open a Bordeaux. Actually I prefer Bordeaux to the Rhone wines from here, but I do my best to exhibit local loyalty," Elliot said, then went to fetch a bottle from the cellar.

Returning, he commented, "One of my favorites. Left bank of the river that divides the Bordeaux region. The left bank wines are heavier on the Cabernet Sauvignon than the softer, less tannic Merlot based Bordeaux of the right bank. Personally I believe it's also the different *terroir*, the soil. Love them both actually. "

He opened the bottle and poured the wine into a decanter. "Adds air and helps to release the bouquet. Actually you should decant it a couple of hours before drinking, but we'll just have to rough it."

Elliot was clearly absorbed with the memories of his time in the trenches of World War One. He looked almost hypnotized as he recounted those memories. Allison studied him intently as he spoke but he seemed almost oblivious to her presence. The talk of wine was his own diversion to bring himself back to the present.

"Skip the talk about the wine, Elliot. I've been watching you. You've been going on for almost two hours. You weren't talking to me. You were reliving the events out loud. It's a little scary to watch you fall into your story."

Elliot reflected a moment before saying anything. "I've never recounted this to anyone since I lost Dominique. How could I, right? So, are you coming around to accept my story?"

"You mean about World War One?"

"I mean about my having actually lived these experiences."

"I don't know, Elliot. Listening to you I hear someone telling of being there. I ask a question about those events and you never hesitate. I'm convinced you believe it."

"But the logic of that says if you don't believe I'm that old, then I must be mentally ill."

"Goddamn it, Elliot, don't box me into making choices like that. I don't know. You're such a strong writer, maybe you just lapsed into adopting this research of events as real experiences."

"Then I'd be delusional then."

"Elliot, you brought me all the way here from New York to

convince me of your strange …. whatever you call it …. condition, affliction, I don't know. So I'm still here listening. You must see how difficult this is to suspend logic and accept that you're over 130 years old."

"You're absolute right, Allison. I'm sorry. For you to understand and accept this is just so important. I have no one else. I have little time remaining."

Allison started to tear-up. Elliot came over to her and hugged her.

"Damn it, Elliot, I don't want to cry."

He poured two glasses of wine and handed one to Allison. Settling back into his chair he said, "Then let's get back to the Great War."

CHAPTER 18

From *Time Travels* by Dillan Murphy
YPRES, BELGIUM – 1917

Just like the Germans, the British batteries delivered a barrage for several hours prior to an offensive attack. Once the infantry moved forward, the barrage was maintained progressively preceding the British advance to disrupt the Germans from consolidating an effective defense.

I followed slightly in the rear with the medical and supply personnel. By the end of the day the Irish Guards occupied the same trenches that we had been driven out of two weeks previously. The exchange of these few thousand yards of real estate came at a cost of many thousands of casualties on both sides.

I again linked up with Sergeant Doyle and the Second Platoon. Private Newbury had survived the assault, but clearly he had changed. Another private sitting next to Newbury said to me, "Peter'll be all right once we're relieved up here. Word has it we're due any time now. Just hope that Haig or Gough doesn't get ambitious with our lives," the soldier said referring to the two commanding British generals. "How the fuck does someone make general being so bloody fuckin' stupid? They just keep killing us then replacing the numbers with new boys from home. Soon there won't be any fellows left in Ireland or England."

The soldier nudged Newbury, "Peter. Ya know what I think? If we're to be surviving this war, there'll be a hell of lot more girls to go around. Could be we'll be in high demand. Could ya do with a fine piece of ass, Peter? Ah, I can smell that fine smell now."

Newbury made no response, only barely registering that he had even heard.

I asked the soldier, "You're Irish. Why are you here fighting for the British? Did you enlist or were you conscripted?"

"Well, it seemed like a good thing at the time. Don't hate the British like some Irish do. All that rubbish is old history. Seemed to me that the Germans would own the Continent if they weren't stopped. If that were to happen, Ireland and England would be in some deep shit. Germans are a warlike bunch of fuckers, ya know. Besides, my prospects were poor and the Army seemed like the best thing at the time. Didn't know about this fucking trench warfare though. Rather be scroungin' for a meal in Dublin right now than out here in this muddy hole in Belgium."

"Well put, Private. I could not have stated my thoughts any-more concisely, and I'm a writer. I'll use your insights in my next dispatch back to the States," I said.

Actually I probably would not. My old boss, Charlie Kendrick had suffered a heart attack and retired. The new managing editor at the *New York Times* admonished me for the slant to my recent copy. His words were: *'Too personal. You depict the horrors of the War admirably, but frankly they're a little lurid. I think our readers are looking for more balance that illustrates the larger strategic struggle. A struggle that will inevitably bring the United States into the War, with young Americans called upon to fight Germany. Need more uplifting reporting and details on the Allies' progress. What about a piece that shows America's contribution to arming and supply-*

ing the British and France?'

Utter bullshit from a self-serving asshole was my reaction. Rumor was that he intended to run for national office. Had ties to Tammany Hall. That said it all.

Unfortunately for the Platoon, rotation to the rear did not come before the unit was called on to resume the assault within two days. It's truly a frightful thing to wait before going over the top of the trench into the teeth of enemy fire. This time it would be worse. Because of the terrain with its shallow groundwater, the German Fourth Army had established a strong defensive line using concrete pillboxes, situated to provide an interlocking field of fire from machine guns.

British high command wanted to exploit their counter-offensive. After a couple of days for regrouping and re-supply, General Gough meant to try to dislodge the Germans from this reinforced defensive line. The British artillery barrage commenced at three o'clock in the morning. The men assembled at the edge of the trench. Sergeant Doyle called out down the line, "Time for makin' ready lads. Fix your bayonets."

No man spoke. All were consumed with their own thoughts. They all knew that unlike the attack that had just pushed back the German's, this one was going to be tougher, and bloodier. One man was shaking badly. Several appeared to be praying. One obviously had wet himself as a large stain spread down his leg. Private Newbury looked disoriented.

Minutes later the barrage stopped and whistles sounded up and down the line as officers signaled the men to leave the trenches and move forward. Newbury did not climb up the trench ladder. Instead, he turned and sat down.

The Lieutenant screamed at him from atop the trench, "Newbury, you get your fuckin' bloody arse movin' or I'll have you shot!"

Newbury did not budge, just staring into nowhere. The Lieutenant climbed back down into the trench. He came up to Newbury and pointed his Webley revolver at Newbury's head. "Last time I'll be tellin' you, Newbury."

The Lieutenant looked over at me apparently deciding not to shoot Newbury right there. "Mr. Murphy, you're a witness to this cowardice. I will have you stand to a firing squad, Newbury." With that, the Lieutenant climbed out of the trench to join his Platoon.

Through the observation glasses I watched the British forces advance on the German line. The lightly defended forward German positions were quickly overtaken. Once within range of the concrete machinegun emplacements however, the Irish Guards fell in increasing numbers. There was seemingly a point beyond which they could not advance as the dead and dying mounted under the withering fire. The attack seemed completely pointless. Forty minutes later, the remains of the Second Platoon stumbled back into the trench.

Sergeant Doyle was among the survivors. After barking orders to attend to his wounded, he came and sat next to me. "Seems I've survived yet another battle. I lost men today that I didn't even know what their names were. This is absolute madness. I will go on until I am killed. So will every man here. The war ended a long time ago with this idiotic stalemate, but the slaughter still goes on. This is now a place where men only die. Only the politicians and generals continue to talk about victory."

Several men were wounded, some badly. The Lieutenant was among those walking wounded with his left arm hanging limply and dripping blood. His face was contorted in rage as he walked down the trench. "Sergeant, come with me and find Private Newbury."

I followed them the short distance to a dugout hole where Newbury sat staring blankly.

"On your feet, Private!" the Lieutenant shouted. Sergeant Doyle grabbed Newbury by one arm and forced him to his feet. "Sergeant, arrest this man for cowardice in the face of the enemy and desertion. He refused my order to advance with the rest of the Platoon. He stayed behind like a sniveling coward while good men died in his stead. You'll be tried and shot, Newbury! See that he gets to the rear under guard, Sergeant."

Was Newbury a coward? Were the fellows that shook uncontrollably, that pissed themselves, braver because they still went out to die? Newbury had fought a good deal before this latest incident. Was this a conscious act on his part, or did he just emotionally shut down? In this crucible of horror nothing was that simple.

I stayed with the front-line British troops through August. To torment the poor soldier, the worst weather in 75 years reduced the entire battlefield to an impossible morass of mud. This bloodletting continued until early November. It became known as the Third Battle of Ypre, or Passchendaele after the name of another unfortunate town. The carnage for the Allies and the Germans was a combined 560,000 casualties. After the equally horrific Battle of the Somme one year earlier, it showed that the military commands of both sides lacked any semblance of imagination. They could only wage war with the brute force of numbers thrown against the enemy.

By the end of 1917, all the belligerents were exhausted. Millions had died. On their home fronts, deprivations were becoming severe. The outcome of the War was now a question to be resolved by the United States committing fresh troops.

Three weeks after returning from the Front at Ypres, I attended Private Newbury's court marshal. The details of the trial are not important. It was a formality. The result was predetermined. Private Newbury's circumstances were not even presented as evidence to the panel of British officers trying Newbury. He was defended, if it could be called that, by a young infantry lieutenant with no legal training. His cross-examination of Newbury's commanding lieutenant and one other soldier only made the prosecution's allegations stronger. The whole sham lasted thirty minutes. Found guilty of desertion in the face of the enemy, the presiding trial officer sentenced Newbury to death by firing squad. The sentence was to be carried out three weeks hence pending concurrence by the Commanding General.

I was allowed access to Newbury. He was held in a warehouse to the rear of the front lines in the city of Amiens. There were a dozen prisoners held there in a makeshift jail.

"How are you faring, Peter," I asked Newbury. "Do you need anything?"

Newbury barely acknowledged my presence. Still with that vacant stare he said, "I'm fine. Got my cigarettes. They give me all I want. Guess that's because they're goin' to shoot me."

"You are a veteran of many battles. Why did you refused to follow your unit in the attack that day, Peter. Didn't you know what would happen?"

"Don't know why I couldn't go. Just couldn't. Don't remember much about that day really. Do the other fellows in the Platoon think I'm a coward?"

"No, they don't think you're a coward. They feel badly about your .... your circumstance."

The truth was that those survivors of the disastrous attack had mixed feelings about Private Newbury's refusal. Characterizing the pervasive fatalism, one soldier simply said, 'Doesn't matter much, but the bloke should of gone over the top and died out there. Not shamed his family. We're all goin' to die anyway.'

With some pull from Major Crawford, the Chief of Staff for the Irish Guards who took me to the Front, I was allowed to attend Newbury's execution.

At 6:00 AM on a gray day with a slight drizzle of rain, Private Peter Newbury was marched outside. I was impressed with his composure as he was tied to a stake in front of the brick warehouse wall. A priest spoke to him and Newbury shook his head. I assumed this was in response to the offer of a last statement. The priest touched him on the face with the sign of the cross then backed away. An officer placed a black hood over Newbury's head. A medical officer pinned a white piece of cloth over his heart to act as a target.

Before the volley of rifle fire that extinguished his life, I could see the hood over Newbury's head sucking in and out as his final anxiety made him gulp for breath.

Newbury's execution was not an isolated event. After the war I learned that the British executed over 300 soldiers for desertion or cowardice.

Newbury was executed in September. In October I was present at another execution.

I had seen the exotic dancer Mata Hari perform in December, 1916. In February she was arrested on charges of espionage. Upon returning from the Front in the fall of 1917, I learned she had been sentenced to death. I contacted my old friend the French colonel.

"Are the charges true?" I asked him.

"Ah, who's to say. The War still goes badly. The morale of the *poilus* is still a factor."

The poilus were the average French soldiers. The *factor* the Colonel referred to was the continuing risk of mutiny. The first half of 1917 saw the French Army on the verge of collapse as whole units revolted. General Petain was elevated to chief of staff and brought stability through addressing basic grievances of the poilus. But with morale within the ranks still poor, the threat of mutiny was a continuing concern.

"Are you suggesting this might be political?" I asked.

"That will never be known. She was tried by a military tribunal in July. It was about the time that the mutiny problem was at its height. The court marshal was closed so it is not clear what evidence was offered. However, I have friends that say there was no real evidence. She was accused of sleeping with French officials to obtain information to sell to German officers. She said the money was for love not information."

"And when is this execution to take place?"

"In October, on the fifteenth at dawn. She will be taken from the Saint-Lazare Prison to a barracks in Vincennes. Want to attend? I could have it arranged since you are a member of the Press."

I agreed. Maybe I could write a real story that would be published in the United States. The French papers had to be careful to avoid government censorship. Even so, their stories implied a war hysteria with uneven reporting and a tendency to publish with an expedient political slant. I could speculate more directly in my piece that it was an incompetent French General Staff looking for a way to deflect their own shortcomings. An exotic dancer's execution should make for an interesting story in the United States.

The night that I saw her dance less than a year ago was perhaps her last performance. That evening seemed from another time after a few months in the trenches in Flanders.

I arrived by taxi at the Caserne de Vincennes, the barracks of an old fort. It was five in the morning, the sun not yet up. Along with several other journalists, we were escorted to an area of greenery backed by a tall hill.

Twelve Zouave soldiers, the execution squad, in their colorful blue and red uniforms were already in place. There was a chill in the air. The first hint of dawn was illuminating the sky.

"Name's Henry Wales. International News Service," the reporter next to me said and extended his hand.

"Dillan Murphy. *New York Times.*"

"This is some piece of murky business. Woman's a stripper not a bloody spy," Wales said. "Won't be able to say that. My own government wouldn't allow such criticism of the Entente. Been following this story ever since her arrest back in February. It's utter bullshit."

An automobile drove up and all conversation ceased among the reporters.

Margaretha Zelle was escorted by her lawyer, a priest, and two nuns to the appointed spot. She was wearing a black velvet cloak and a large black felt hat.

A French officer approached. Zelle's lawyer said something to the officer. Within moments, both backed away from Zelle.

"Good god. She refused a blindfold. Her hands aren't even bound," Wales said. "She's just standing there. That's one hell of a woman."

The officer yelled a sharp command. The soldiers raised their rifles and took aim on the left breast of Mata Hari. Another officer raised his sword. The sun having risen by now, reflected off the blade as it fell giving the signal to fire.

The volley of rifle fire dropped Margaretha Zelle to her knees. She then fell slowly backwards, bending at the waist.

A non-commissioned officer approached the fallen woman. Extracting his sidearm, he bent over, put the barrel to her temple and then delivered the coup de grace as was the practice to insure death.

"Fuck all! What a disgusting spectacle," Wales commented.

"Tell you what Mr. Wales; if you give me your background on the story, I'll see it gets published in the United States without censorship. Give you attribution of course."

Wales considered my offer for a moment. "I'll do that Mr. Murphy. Been covering this stupid war since it started. Damn thing started for stupid reasons. After that, the generals on both sides have made sure it continues with no end in sight. Unimaginative bunch of wankers. Can't publish anything critical in either the British or French press. So I'll do you one better. Besides this Mata Hari farce, I'll give you some other material you can maybe use."

Henry Wales' account of Mata Hari's execution is the standard reference for the event. It states the facts without wider editorial comment. True to his word, Wales gave me a wealth of information on the Mata Hari story as well as other material. My account of the Mata Hari affair was published in the *New York Times*. It pointedly accused the French Military of conspiracy by exposing the absurdity of the evidence, and all but accused them of sanctioned murder. Unfortunately, Mata Hari did not have celebrity status in the United States. The story was lost in the larger events of the American Expeditionary Force now committed to the conflict.

American troops had been in France for many months. The commander, General John Pershing had resisted French and British pleadings to commit the fresh American troops to fill gaps in the Allied positions. Pershing insisted that his green troops must first receive training. They would fight as an American Army not as reserve troops for the French and British. They were now ready to go into battle against the Germans. My editor wired me to join the Americans.

CHAPTER 19

PROVENCE, FRANCE – 2009

Allison sat transfixed as Elliot again paused his story. "You look as if you're physically reliving those experiences. You're transported back to that time. Whatever the cause of this time warp, you certainly have lived those events in your mind."

Elliot ignored Allison's vague reference that this was still a mental aberration.

"Whenever I think of that time, I can't quite put it into a category. It transcends logic. Words always seem to fall short. It was a war like no other. Nothing I've ever read adequately explains why this mass killing of young men went on for so long when for the last two years of the conflict there was no chance of anything approximating victory for either side. All wars kill soldiers. But this war had no movement. For years the Front moved back and forth only a matter of miles. Once the German initial attack was stopped in 1914 the great stalemate commenced.

"Every general and political leader had to know that at best their tactics could not achieve a victory. So all this death was only to bargain for better armistice terms. For this willfulness and stupidity, millions had to die. Instead of the Newburys, those that perpetuated the War should have been shot. My experiences left me with an abiding cynicism about governments, and a hatred for nationalism."

"What really started World War One?" Allison asked. "All I remember from high school was the Austrian Archduke being assassinated somewhere. Not even sure what an archduke is, or what Austria had to do with anything."

"It's complicated. Historians don't agree. The Austrian Archduke was the heir to the Austrian-Hungarian Empire. He was assassinated by a Serbian fanatic in Sarajevo. Two minor European powers yet it started a chain reaction."

"Chain reaction how? It was the Germans, the French, and English that did all of the fighting."

"You're forgetting the Russians and the Italians, and of course the Belgians. You see it was a complicated interconnection of alliances."

"So because of these alliances the whole world went to war?"

"That was the excuse for all the belligerents. They all had their own vested interests. It was more about nationalistic opportunity and controlling territory. It was about clashes of cultures."

"Isn't that what all wars are about?"

"Yes. It just seems that the run-up to the Great War was a unique tangle of factors; greed, blunders, old antagonisms, modern democracies versus monarchies. At some point the events took on an inertia that was beyond control."

"It's been said that the World lost its innocence in World War One. Is that how you feel, Elliot?"

"Innocence? The World lost more than that. It lost all faith in institutions. Cultures were shattered. Economies shattered. A whole generation of Europeans was almost destroyed. It was the most compelling argument against the concept of a benevolent God. Personally, it made me bitter. I became disillusioned. Yes, I was profoundly changed. Everyone of that time was."

Elliot looked at his watch and rose from his chair. "Didn't realize the time. It's late and we haven't had dinner. I'll fix us something simple if that's ok?"

He fixed a salad of tomatoes and fresh mozzarella cheese covered with a liberal serving of an excellent olive oil. Some cold ham with bread made a respectable light meal.

While they ate, Allison asked, "And after those executions, what did you do?"

"There was still more to my World War One experience. After witnessing the carnage in Flanders, my stories took on a bitter tone. They were political rants backed up by statistics with lurid antidotal depictions of combat. My editor had me transferred south to report on the American Expeditionary Force as it entered the conflict. I was admonished to avoid the kind of criticism that I had directed at the British and French General Staffs. These were now Americans I'd be reporting about. The telegram ended with *'It is your duty to reflect a patriotic tone in your copy.'* It infuriated me. I was not about to slant my reporting to suit nationalistic propaganda and a politically correct editor."

CHAPTER 20

From Time Travels by Dillan Murphy

Duty? It's a journalist's duty to report the truth. Had the venerable *New York Times* become a propaganda organ for the Wilson Administration? I certainly was not.

Combat operations in Europe ground to a halt as the winter of1917 set in. The conflict continued in the Middle East but the deciding contest in the east of France would have to wait for another spring to resume the bloodletting. I returned to Paris and took up the new task of reporting on the American effort.

Even though the United States had entered the War officially in April, 1917, by December of that year only four divisions of troops had reached France. The commander of the American forces, General John 'Black Jack' Pershing was under strict orders to maintain his command as a distinct national army. He was to resist any attempt to use the American Expeditionary Forces as reinforcements for weaken British and French positions. Pershing had been busy training his green troops, but avoiding participating in any combat operations in 1917.

It was clear that America would see its first taste of war in the coming year. I was in a unique position to give the American public first hand information on the upcoming events. The War was not finished. American boys would soon be fed into this caldron of death. I had a responsibility to give America a sense of what this war was like. What their sons and husbands would face.

Since I was on a kind of probation, I was careful in constructing my copy sent back to New York. I would criticize the prosecution of the War obliquely. The British and the French mistakes, and of course the Russian gross incompetence, would be reversed by the United States forces. I hoped that might be true, but sadly it was not to be.

So I spent the winter of 1917-18 ingratiating myself with the AEF. I found the same enthusiasm for the adventure of war among the Americans as I myself felt in 1898. This must have been the same the British and French troops felt in 1914 and 1915.

"Murphy! Come join us," A young American officer said.

I entered a café on the Left Bank where a young captain of the headquarters battalion of the U.S. 2nd Division said they would be dining. He was New York Irish and homesick so I was welcomed as a friend.

"Ah, Captain O'Connor," I said as I entered.

The captain jumped from his chair. "Sir, I'd like to introduce Mr. Dillan Murphy. He's a reporter with the *New York Times*. He's an old hand over here. Been in the front lines in Flanders last year. Murphy, this is Major Ellison, and Captain Brewster."

"Please join us, Mr. Murphy," the major said.

I shook hands all around and joined them at their table.

"Well, Mr. Murphy, do you speak French?" the Major asked.

"Enough to get by."

"Excellent. Then you can assist us in ordering dinner. The waiter is impossible. Gives us these menus, in French of course.

Then he can't translate anything."

I acted as translator and ordered dinner. I also added the most expensive wine on the menu. The waiter even asked if I knew how much that cost. I winked and told him the asshole Americans were paying. He smiled knowingly.

"So tell me, Murphy, what's your read on why the Brits and the frogs haven't defeated the Germans?" the Major said after dinner and a second bottle of wine.

"Well that's a question for military men and historians to answer maybe decades from now."

"Come on, Murphy. That's ducking the question. You've got to have an opinion," the Major said.

I instinctively didn't like the arrogant Major. Mid-thirties. Looking to move up. Wants to make lieutenant colonel sooner rather than later. Headquarters-type. Not the type to lead troops into combat.

"Saw a Japanese wrestling match in New York once. It's call sumo. Two big fat guys, 300-pounders, try to push each other out of a ring. They bang together something fierce. In sumo wrestling somebody gets pushed outside the ring and the match is done. In this war, each side just keeps pushing. It's apparently a wide ring because it just doesn't stop. Nobody wins, nobody loses. Soldiers just die."

"Interesting analogy, Murphy. But that's why the Americans are here. We'll not fall into the trap of trench warfare. Cap this whole thing in a matter of months. Bring down Germany and restore Europe to a civilized continent."

"And how do you intend to accomplish that, Major?"

The Major glared at me. My sarcasm was evident. "Well that would be confidential military intelligence, Mr. Murphy. Couldn't be telling you things like that. Could get you killed like that whore spy they executed last year."

I just smiled at the Major. "Certainly don't want that do we. So on that note, I should be leaving you gentlemen. Can I contribute to the bill?"

"No, not at all Mr. Murphy. We'll cover it," Captain O'Connor said.

I got up to leave then asked, "Major, can you arrange for me to be allowed to go to the front with our troops?"

"That should not be a problem, Mr. Murphy. See me tomorrow. I'll see you get a pass."

"Thank you. I appreciate that. Well then, good evening gentlemen," I said and shook hands all around. I saluted the waiter on the way out.

CHAPTER 21

From *Time Travels* by Dillan Murphy
BELLEAU WOOD, FRANCE – 1918

On June 1, 1918, I arrived at the American front lines 50 miles east of Paris. I hitched a ride on a supply truck heading for the 5th Regiment of U.S. Marines. They were dug in just north of the village of Lucy-le-Bocage. A mile beyond was a wooded area known as Belleau Wood.

I presented my papers to the unit's chief of staff, Major Waters. We were in a large tent that served as the regiment's headquarters.

"Know what you're getting into, Mr. Murphy?"

"Yes, Sir. I was with the Irish Guards in Flanders last year. Couldn't imagine anything could be worse than that." I doubted the Major had any idea what that experience was like.

"Suit yourself. I expect we will be in the thick of things any day now. The Germans have broken through the French lines north of here just days ago. The French Sixth Army is in retreat. We're here to support their right flank and stop the Germans from moving on Paris."

"Captain Jeffreys," the Major said to an officer on the other side of the tent. He motioned him over.

"Captain, this is Mr. Dillan Murphy. Correspondent for the *New York Times*. I want you to take him back with you to your unit."

"No offense to Mr. Murphy, but we can't be holding anybody's hand up there."

"I've been in combat before, Captain. I'll take care of myself."

"Sir, I must respectfully object," the Captain said.

"Sorry, Jeffreys, division headquarters says otherwise," the Major said.

"Very well, Sir. I'm leaving in five minutes, Mr. Murphy. I trust you're ready?"

"Right behind you, Captain."

An hour later we arrived at the Regiment's position. The Marines were secured into what appeared to be temporary trenches. Nothing like the elaborate British trench systems in Belgium.

"Looks like you don't intend this to be home, Captain."

"That's correct. My men can't wait to get into action. We'll not fall into the trap of this trench warfare like the Brits and French." Seemed to be the official American military position. At least they had learned from that failed strategy.

I spent the next two days mingling with the U.S. Marines. I got the feeling they were well trained, well motivated. But they had not yet seen combat. The next day the Germans attacked from the woods. In heavy fighting, the Marines turned back the assault. They were not yet seasoned veterans but they equipped themselves well.

"That was some real fighting, but these Germans are no match for U.S. Marines," a young corporal named Hobbs said. "Hope we get a few more chances to whip them before this here war ends."

"You'll get that chance, Corporal, but don't be wishing it," I said. "I've seen this now for a year. My guess is your generals will order a counterattack soon. The Germans are dug in the woods. It won't be easy to dislodge them."

"That's why we're here. The Colonel says we're the sharp end of the spear. That means the best. Better than the regular Army."

I shook my head slightly. I wondered if the young soldier would feel as confident after he went on the attack. After he saw his buddies killed. I remembered what Private Newbury had said about defending versus attacking.

The Marine counterattack occurred sooner than I expected, the next day after the German assault.

"What are your orders, Captain?" I asked Captain Jeffreys.

"At sunrise, we're to attack that hill to the west of the woods. Hill 142."

It appeared the Marines tactic was to dislodge the Germans from this hill in order to assault the main body of Germans entrenched in the wooded area.

The assault on Hill 142 was successful with the Marines suffering only modest casualties. Their mood was cocky. Twelve hours later they mounted a frontal assault on the woods itself. This proved to be a far grimmer task.

To attack the woods, the Marines had to cross a large open area. The Germans defended the ground with heavy machine-gun fire. Hunkered down in a shallow hole with two medical corpsmen, I watched the attack through my field glasses.

"What the hell!" I said. The Marines were advancing in massed formations almost shoulder to shoulder. It was something not seen since the early years of the War. These were tactics now abandoned by the British and French.

I turned to the medics, "What kind of stupid generals do you have? They're sacrificing their men! Stupid, criminal bastards!"

The medics did not respond. They had their own fears to contend with as they would soon venture onto the battleground to care for the casualties.

Brave Marines were cut down in terrible numbers. On this the first real day of U.S. action, the Marines lost 1100 men.

Two days later another American assault failed to make an advance. Two days after that, another assault was preceded by an artillery bombardment of the woods. Seemed the American military had not learned all that much about the tactical failures of the prior years of the War.

On June 11th, the Marines advanced into the woods itself. They expected much weakened German defenses. But unfortunately, artillery bombardments that should seemingly obliterate defensive positions and enemy troops rarely did. The Marines would learn this the hard way in Belleau Wood.

While not foolish enough to follow advancing troops across open terrain, I advanced much more closely once into the woods. I had placed myself next to Lance Corporal Hobbs, sharing the duty of digging a hole for the night.

"Wish I could have a smoke. Makes this waiting easier," Hobbs said.

"You boys did well. As good as the most seasoned combat veterans. It's still hell though isn't it?"

"Never could have imagined what it would be like. I'm afraid just like anybody, but it's seein' your friends tore up that's tough. Body parts missin', faces gone," Hobbs said in a whisper.

"Where you from, Hobbs?"

Before he could answer, we both heard a noise. A foot stepping on underbrush. Then someone exclaim in a whisper, "*Bumsen!*" Fuck in German.

We couldn't see anything in the absolute dark devoid of any moonlight. Hobbs brought his Springfield to his shoulder. It had a bayonet affixed. I unholstered my .45.

The German soldier nearly fell into our hole. Hobbs saw him only two feet in front and buried the bayonet fully into the German's abdomen. The German fired a round from his Mauser, and then all hell erupted.

Firing erupted all around. I fired two magazines from my .45. Didn't know if I was hitting anything. Just firing at the muzzle flashes out in front. The firefight lasted only a few minutes. It was an hour until the first light of dawn allowed us to see what had happened. That hour was made almost unbearable with the desperate cries of agony from the soldier bayoneted by Lance Corporal Hobbs.

The morning revealed four other dead German soldiers. At least we assumed they were dead. Probably a reconnaissance patrol. Then there was the wounded man lying just outside of our hole. With the daylight, the white pallor of his face showed his loss of blood. His eyes were pleading. We didn't understand German but we believe his cries were for his mother. He looked only sixteen or seventeen. There was nothing to be done for him. Mercifully he died a short time after sunrise.

By the end of June, Belleau Wood had exchanged hands between the Germans and the Americans six times. U.S. forces suffered 10,000 casualties. I had suffered as much as I could take of this war. My last telegraph dispatch to the *Times* read:

'Over the last two weeks the American Expeditionary Forces engaged in their first real combat test. The names of Chateau Thierry and Belleau Wood will go down into the annuals of American military as glowing examples of American resolve and courage. I was in the bloody trenches of Belgium last year with British Expeditionary Forces with the most seasoned combat troops fighting this war. American Army and Marine units proved every bit the equal of any fighting forces in the World.

I have been at the front lines with American Marines as part of the AEF's 2nd Division. The fighting was bloody. Almost 10,000 American boys were killed or wounded in the three weeks of fighting. Just 50 miles east of Paris, fighting in what was known as Belleau Wood sometimes became hand to hand with fists and bayonets. Even the French Military command has recognized the extraordinary valor of our fight-

ing units by bestowing the highest of citations.

With such a demonstration, it is unfortunate that the skills and courage of our soldiers and Marines are not equally matched by the military leadership skills of American commanders. I witnessed the same antiquated tactics that I witnessed in Flanders. General Pershing declared he would not get bogged down in trench warfare stalemate. Yet American tactics still send troops forward in massed formations, over open ground, against defended positions with machine guns. Men fall by the dozens before they can even fire a shot at the enemy. These are tactics from the last century. Do American commanders bring no new thinking to the modern battlefield? They achieved success at Belleau Wood only because American troops were fresh, well equipped, brave, and in superior numbers. Numbers sufficient to sustain horrific casualties. The 5th Marine Regiment that I followed lost two-thirds of its number in the Battle of Belleau Wood.

American entry into the conflict will most assuredly tip the scales in favor of the Allies. But is America prepared to pay the price in lives of its brave young men? At the least, the American Doughboy deserves the right to have a reasonable chance of surviving this War.'

CHAPTER 22

PROVENCE, FRANCE – 2009

"And if four years of carnage was not enough, the Spanish Flu pandemic took a terrible on both soldiers and civilians."

"That's right. I forgot that was also in 1918," Allison said.

"Ended up killing 50 million people by most estimates. Maybe as many as half the world's population got sick. It was just as devastating to humankind as the Black Death during the Middle Ages. In the last months of the War, more soldiers were dying of the flu than from battle injuries."

"Did people you knew die from the flu?"

"Several. I got sick myself. Laid me up for several days."

"So not everyone died. Why was it so much worse than what we experience with flu epidemics today?"

"This strain was more virulent than anything seen since. The Spanish Flu had an ugly twist to it. It caused a violent overreaction of the body's immune system. Younger adults were most vulnerable because of their stronger immune systems. The weaker immune systems of the very young or middle-aged adults resulted in fewer deaths among those age groups. The Flu infected rich and poor alike. Even the world leaders of the time contracted the disease; President Wilson, the German Kaiser, General Pershing. Of course they were middle-aged, so they survived. So was I."

"I'd never heard that. That's amazing," Allison said.

"More like tragic I would say. Following on all the millions killed in the War. It was a plague of truly biblical proportions. After two years, the infectious rampage abruptly ceased. As terrible as the Spanish Flu pandemic was, it was still the millions of casualties inflicted by the Great War that warped the fabric of the world.

"After accompanying the American forces at Belleau Wood in June, 1918, I had had enough of battling to write the truth. My editor was exceedingly unhappy with my copy. Much of it never reached print without rewrites that removed anything critical of American leadership. My last dispatch was too much. He cited the recently passed Sedition Act of 1918, passed in May. It was an amendment to the Espionage Act of 1917. The amendment prohibited not only criticism of the War, but criticism of even the Government of the United States. So much for the sanctity of the First Amendment. As for me, I was sick of the *Times* editorial demands and my own country's censorship. So I quit. The War ended anyway a few months later."

"So how old were you in 1918?"

"I was forty-five. Probably looked no more than thirty."

"Was your age and appearance issue becoming a problem?"

"Not necessarily. But I was aware it would become a problem eventually if I returned to New York."

"So what did you do then?"

"I was disillusioned with American war propaganda and censorship. Obviously it was no place to express free intellectual thought at that time. I was angry. Rather than return to the United States, I decided to stay on in Paris.

Amazingly, Paris seemed outwardly unchanged by the years of war. After the Armistice, the shortages of the War disappeared almost immediately. People were intoxicated with the end of the War. Women were plentiful and exuberant. I should probably have felt guilty for taking advantage of the situation during that atmosphere. Young men were scarce. All able bodied Frenchmen had been conscripted and their numbers decimated with the four years of war. The streets of Paris were testimony to how much the War had reduced the population of France's manhood."

"Did you ever feel guilty about not joining in the fight as a soldier?"

"Maybe at some level. At least at the time. Less in the years afterward. And now not at all. I respected those that bravely fought. They had feelings of patriotism. I simply did not have those feelings of loyalty to the United States, or any institution for that matter. Not loyalty to the extent that I would submit my life to the utter stupidity of a bunch of old men dictating war. The United States is the greatest country in terms of its laws, but things are still run by a privileged few, for reasons that are not always in the Country's best interest."

"Are you saying World War One was not in the United States' best interest?"

"Like most things, the answer is not that simple."

"Well if the United States hadn't joined Britain and France, wouldn't Germany have occupied Western Europe?"

"In World War Two, yes. In World War One, probably not. You see both sides were exhausted. Neither had anymore manpower they could expend. Only the very old and young were left. Both sides were stuck physically and mentally in opposing trenches that reinforced a stalemate. The difference was that Germany was more economically spent than the Allied countries. War materiel was in shorter supply. Food for the fighting troops as well as the civilian population was becoming desperate. Britain and France were in comparatively better shape, but only because of U.S. support."

"All right, so what might have been the outcome if the United States had not entered the War?" Allison asked.

"A clearly possible outcome would have been an armistice among exhausted equals. As it was, the weight of the United States tipped the balance. The armistice became punitive against the Germans. As we all know, that fuelled a nationalistic fervor that allowed Hitler and his aberrant Nazi Party to seize power and start World War Two."

"Didn't the Germans start World War One too?" Allison asked.

"Most definitely. Unilaterally invaded Belgium with the intent to sweep down into France all the way to Paris."

"So they got punished by the terms of the armistice. Isn't that justice?"

"And the World paid a terrible price later for grinding down Germany after 1918. Biblical type retribution does not serve mankind well. It just reinforces cultural hatreds."

"Not sure I see it that way. I would think that Germany simply got what they deserved," Allison said.

"But contrast that with the Marshal Plan that rebuilt Europe, including Germany after World War Two. This was Hitler's Germany. The cause of 50 million deaths. The perpetrator of the Holocaust. The United States did it for its own pragmatic reasons of course, namely to build a counter to the threat posed by the Soviet Union. The Allies could have taken a punitive approach like after World War One. I venture to say the World would be a much different place today had that happened.

"So much for the Great War. Like everyone else, I wanted to put it behind me. There was nothing drawing me to return to the United States. No family. No close friends. No job at the *Times* even if I was interested. I now spoke passable French. Had saved a modest amount of money. An American could live relatively inexpensively in Paris after the Great War because of the exchange rate. Now was a perfect time to try writing and decompress from the experiences of the last two years. And I could start a fresh life with an abbreviated history, at a younger age consistent with my appearance.

"I took up residence in a small fourth story flat on Rue Clément. A dormer window provided a view of the Left Bank rooftops and the towers of St. Sulpice church. There was enough light to feel comfortable writing there, although I spent a considerable amount of time writing at the cafes.

"For several years I attacked writing with an intense energy. Since I wrote in English, I was fortunate enough to get a couple of short stories published in England and the United States. Not much in the way of money, but it did establish modest writing credentials."

"What were the stories about, Elliot?" Allison asked. "War experiences?"

"Mostly. Fictional accounts based from the perspective of the common soldier. Some deeper material from the family perspective. One lighter essay about the similarities and contrasts of New York and Paris. Of course I was working on my novel, *Living Dead*.

"The war experiences still hung heavily, but I never felt freer. None of the drudgery of my former journalistic career. No digging about society's low and high born malignancies. I could now tell my own stories rather than the stories and the lies of others. No more deadlines, no more contesting with editors.

"I remembered meeting a wealthy patron of the arts in New York before the War. Her name was Mabel Dodge Luhan. She had a salon in a Greenwich Village apartment where she held informal gatherings attended by an eclectic range of intelligentsia. I was invited a couple of times. Very stimulating. It exposed me to the literary intelligentsia world. Mabel herself was the catalyst and the conduit for connecting people. I recalled she was very close to Gertrude Stein who hosted her own salon in Paris.

"So after a couple of years toiling away at making myself into a writer rather than a journalist, I was introduced to Gertrude Stein and invited to one of her Saturday evening gatherings."

"You're saying you frequented Gertrude Stein's salon in Paris?" Allison asked.

"I became a fairly frequent visitor."

"You must have met some of the great ex-patriot American literary giants that were hanging out in Paris then?" Allison asked with a tone of skepticism.

Elliot smiled. "Ernest Hemmingway got me my first invitation to the salon."

Allison looked at him with a stunned expression. She was torn between a flood of questions she had against the nagging issue that Elliot Gaston, or Dillan Murphy's life simply could not be real. "You're kidding aren't you, Elliot?"

"Not at all. I knew Hemmingway and Fitzgerald. Met Pablo Picasso once when he was visiting Gertrude."

"Wait a minute. You're saying you knew Hemmingway and Fitzgerald? And you frequented Gertrude Stein's famous salon?" Allison asked.

"Yes. Stein's house was also on the Left Bank at 27 Rue de Fleurus. Came to be called just '27'. Actually I didn't hang out there like some. Hard to understand when some of them did any work, and how they could work with as much drinking that went on. I was a working writer. It was stimulating to interact with other writers you respect, but writing was still something you did in a solitary environment. I was more like Hemmingway in my work habits. He worked hard at his craft. I disciplined myself to write every day as he said he did."

"Did you know Hemmingway well? What was he like?"

"Well we weren't real pals. Casual friends maybe. We shared the common experience of being in the War. He was in Italy of course. He clearly was more enthralled with the glory and adventure of war than I was. A big roaring bull of man, a lot like TR. His very persona was overtly masculine. Always doing larger than life masculine adventures. He wasn't as arrogant and full of himself as he became later on. Hell of a writer though. I loved his writing. His terse journalistic-styled prose. Guess most everyone did. But to your question, I'll tell you about one time that I spent a week in Spain with him."

"My God, you knew Hemmingway that well? When was this?" Allison asked barely able to conceal her enthusiasm even if she had to suspend belief that this could really be true.

"1924. Hemmingway was a bullfighting enthusiast, as everyone knows. To him the contest of the matador with the bull transcended the spectacle and even the danger aspects. It was an art form with metaphysical overtones.

"I'd never been to Spain. We took a train from Paris to Seville in the south of Spain. Long trip back in the twenties. Couple of days. His wife Hadley was going to stay in Seville with friends while he and I journeyed to the town of Ronda. I think he asked me along so he would have a drinking companion. Ronda is situated on this spectacular gorge in the hills of Andalusia. The journey was partly to see Ronda's magnificent Plaza de Toros bullring, partly to do some serious drinking."

"This is all in the manuscript?" Allison asked.

"Oh yes."

"Was this where Hemmingway acquired his interest in Spain?"

"Not sure about that. But Hemmingway experienced something more profound in Ronda than bullfighting. I certainly did. You see Spain was different than the rest of Europe at that time. Economically and socially it suffered arrested development. Its poor were more impoverished than any other country in Western Europe. Corruption dominated all public institutions. The peasants were brutalized under almost medieval circumstances. Spain was more like Russia than Europe at the time.

"Southern Spain, the Andalusia, was as bad as any area. Between our drinking adventures, we ventured out into the countryside and interacted with the people. Their miserable circumstances affected him deeply. I think that earlier experience in the twenties may have drawn him back to Spain in the late thirties to cover the Spanish Civil War as a journalist. His reporting was one-sided, always favoring the political leftist Popular Front."

"I'm dumbfounded, Elliot. Your story is .... I .... well I don't have the words."

Elliot and Allison chatted for sometime about his personal experiences with some of the other great ex-patriot literary figures of the early part of the century. Elliot was expansive on everything except his personal relationships with women.

"Elliot, you sound like a journalist. This is a personal account but without a lot of personal stuff. You're not telling me about your own life. You started to imply that there were lots of women in Paris in the twenties, but you never go beyond that. Why so guarded? What about your love life? At least tell me about your loves. With your life span there must have been many women."

Elliot smiled. "Oh yes. I have had a full love life. On reflection, I guess I feel a little guilty about all my sexual conquests in Paris. A continuation of my misspent youth in New York."

"Youth? In 1920 you're, let me see .... forty-seven?"

"Figure of speech. Relative in my case. But as an excuse, the roaring twenties is an apt name for those times. The Great War was history. Life could renew itself. Women were forging new life styles and freedoms. Sexual freedom was part of that change. Paris was in the vanguard. I didn't usually spend nights alone unless I chose it that way."

"What kind of women were they?" Allison asked.

"All types. They worked in shops. There was a teacher, a violinist, a journalist. Most were strong-willed. All were intelligent. That was my weakness, sometimes over physical charms. I learned to appreciate a wide range of new things from my romantic partners. On the subject of sex, I was taught new things there as well. The French were clearly not as repressed in sexual expression as American society. I wasn't exactly new to sexual experiences, but I was taught more than a thing or two, particularly how to pleasure women. That was a revolutionary concept for society at the time. Maybe because I gravitated to the type, these women were often assertive in bed."

"My, my. Now that's what I want to hear more about, Elliot, your sexual adventures in the twenties. A window into what life was about back then," Allison said.

"Well I don't want you to think I was just an adventurer. Among those Paris girls I did meet my future wife. Her name was Dominique. She was a student at the Sorbonne studying chemistry of all things. Dominique was the great love of my life. I'd like to tell you about her."

"You were married? I was getting sleepy but you now have my attention. How did you meet her?"

CHAPTER 23

From *Time Travels* by Dillan Murphy
PARIS, FRANCE – 1925

I met Dominique Bellamont at an outdoor café on the Rue du Vieux Colombier close to where I lived. It was May, 1925, a sunny, warm day late in the afternoon. This attractive young woman sat down at the table next to me. She was tall, wore no makeup, and was dressed like a shop girl in a white blouse and gray skirt. She carried a canvas satchel that appeared rather heavy.

The waiter approached her. "Mademoiselle?"

"Coffee please."

"Something to eat, Mademoiselle?"

She hesitated before answering, biting on her lip, "I think not."

Watching her I got the feeling she did want something to eat but was perhaps budgeting her money. I wanted to offer to buy her something but knew she would not accept. Then an elderly woman walking a large dog passed by on the sidewalk. The dog ducked under the young woman's table, wrapping the leash around the base of the table. In trying to extricate itself, the dog tilted the table, spilling the woman's coffee and dropping the satchel to the pavement, spilling books and papers.

I went to the aid of both women immediately, untangling the dog's leash to the thanks of the elderly woman. The woman apologized. More intent on verbally reprimanding the dog, she pulled the dog away and hurriedly continued down the street. The young woman bent down to pick up her books while I went about gathering her papers, which had blown about.

"*Merci beaucoup, Monsieur,*" the young woman said.

"My pleasure, Mademoiselle," I said in English and offered my hand. "My name is Dillan Murphy."

She took my hand and replied in English, "My name is Dominique Bellamont."

I motioned to a waiter, and ordered another coffee for both of us. "Perhaps a menu also, *garçon.*"

"I find I'm a little hungry. Would you join me?"

"Thank you, but you have already been too kind, Monsieur."

"But I would consider it a real pleasure, Mademoiselle Bellamont." She was hungry and apparently not offended by me, so she accepted and I joined her table.

She instantly struck me. Her eyes spoke of intelligence. Her hair was long, pinned up in careless fashion with errant strands falling over her ears. She was tall with an enticing figure of ample breasts and a slim waist. Apart from these noticeable assets, Mme. Bellamont's most captivating feature was the expressive form of her somewhat wide mouth as she spoke, smiled, or just listened.

"Are you a student, Mademoiselle?"

"*Oui.* At the Sorbonne."

"Ah, that explains why you're English is so good. And what are you studying at the University?"

"I am studying Chemistry."

"Chemistry? That is interesting. Are you going into some

scientific field?" I wanted to say that it was unusual for a woman but that would have been decidedly chauvinistic.

"In a way. You see I'm from Provence in the Rhone River Valley. It is wine country. Our family has been making wine there for generations. I am studying chemistry because I intend to make our wines the best possible. Good enough to compete with the wines of Bordeaux and Burgundy. Good enough to be served in the best Paris restaurants. I want to understand the real chemical mechanisms that affect the wine. Old men like my father just understand from experience. I believe our winery can do better if we employ modern techniques."

"And your father? What does he think?"

"My father is a sweet man, but he is old fashioned and not yet convinced. However, my mother convinced him that I should go to the university if that was what I wished. He thought I should get married. My mother argued that marriage could wait, intellectual curiosity could not. My mother is a very strong woman and she has a way of manipulating my father," Dominique said with a wry smile.

I smiled also and said, "So you will return to Provence when your studies are completed?"

"Oh yes. I am anxious to apply myself in the business. You see I have learned more than just science in the two years I have been studying. My father is satisfied to just make good wine. I want to make our business more prosperous as well. My father already listens to me more about those areas. He appreciates my mathematics skills. He understands I wish to help run our winery and there's less talk of marriage."

"You have brothers and sisters?" I asked.

She hesitated and her eyes moistened slightly. "I had two brothers. Both were killed in the War."

"I am so sorry. I can't imagine how difficult that must be for you and your family. As for myself, I was fortunate enough to survive my experiences in the War. I was a journalist not a soldier so I was not at the same risk."

"You are English?"

"No, American."

That led to a discussion about me. She was thrilled to learn that I was a writer and wanted to read the stories I had published. It was at that time that I fully confronted my lack of aging. I was explaining my life but was lying about details that would reveal my true age. I told her of my beginnings in the Pennsylvania coalfields, but with a later chronology. No mention of combat in Cuba. My tenure as a New York City reporter was abbreviated to just a few years. I felt guilty for concealing my real age. I still deluded myself as only being fortunate to look so young. I rationalized it as unusual, certainly inexplicable, but not the result of some unique abnormality. Who wouldn't want such a condition? But I was 51 in 1924 when I met Dominique. She was in her early twenties.

After the food, I convinced Dominique to have another glass of wine. This allowed me to turn the discussion back to wine-making. After two hours, the sun was setting. We both seemed a little surprised at how long we had been talking. Dominique agreed to meet again for lunch the next day.

We had lunch the next two days straight and dinner several times the following week. I was in love. After so many women, I knew my feelings for Dominique were different. Obviously she was attracted to me, but I had not yet gauged if she felt as strongly as I did.

She was a remarkable woman. Once past our first encounter, we were Dominique and Dillan. She rejected the forced politeness deemed proper between the sexes even in avant-garde Paris. She was animated in her conversation and confident in her views. She listened with interest to my opinions but didn't shy from challenging or disagreeing.

I knew it must be love since I had not tried to seduce Dominique into bed right away. I was cautious since I did not want to lose her by prematurely suggesting sex. It had been ten days since first meeting her when I worked up the courage.

We were walking back to Dominique's flat which she shared with three other young women. Throughout dinner I could think of nothing else than making love to her. Not far from the restaurant, I stopped walking and said, "Dominique, I love you. More than that, I want to make love to you. Tonight."

To my surprise she responded, "I love you too, Dillan." Than she kissed me passionately. "And it's about time you suggested that. I was beginning to think you were only fond of my intellect. Is your flat far?"

Dominique was not a virgin, but neither was she practiced in lovemaking. We spent glorious hours learning how to pleasure each other that first night. She never asked how I had acquired knowledge in certain techniques. For her part she was totally comfortable with her own sexuality. Even that first night, she walked about the apartment with nothing on except my unbuttoned shirt.

After a few weeks, she was spending most nights at my flat. Two months later I asked her to marry me. She said yes, but said that she wished to be married at home in Provence. So in the fall of 1925 we took the train to Avignon.

"How do you believe your parents will feel about me?"

"They shall love you as I do."

"No, I meant how are they going to feel about you marrying a foreigner?"

"Foreigner? Ah, because of your accent. They shall overlook that," she kidded.

"You know what I mean. Will that matter?"

"I never thought about it. But I don't think so. They will see how happy you make me. They are not overly protective as some parents would be of their daughter. They respect my judgment. Father may have to warm to the prospect more than

Mama. But that will quickly vanish because of what you do."

"What do you mean?"

"You are educated, worldly, and more importantly, you're a writer. Journalism as well as fiction. You see Papa is an avid reader. Loves to discuss ideas. Bores Momma sometimes with his monologues. Philosophy, history, passionate about literature too. My guess is that he will be anxious to engage you intellectually. So you must sound smart or he will not give you my hand," she said with a mischievous smile followed by a kiss.

Her parents met us at the train station in Avignon. Aimee and Pierre gave me a warm welcome. Aimee had tears in her eyes as she embraced me. I liked them instantly. I believe they liked me as well. Immediately I knew I would be accepted into the Bellamont family.

Things were falling into place. I felt as if everything previous in my life had lead me to this. It was a rebirth both metaphorically and even pragmatically. Before leaving Paris I had applied for French citizenship. It was relatively easy since I had good references. I gave my date of birth as 1898. A letter from the Catholic parish in Pennsylvania which gave the birth date and baptism of Dillan Murphy as 1873 was easily altered to '98'. Although I had never attended Mass, owing to my father's antagonism against the Church, the affirmation of my Catholic legitimacy avoided any obstacle with our union by the local priest.

We stayed at the home of Dominique's parents that summer. It was a small wedding at the local parish church. Local family friends and at least one of Dominique's old boyfriends attended.

In the fall of 1925 we returned to Paris to my now cramped apartment with the two of us. Two desks and piles of books took over our limited space. I was never happier. I continued to write while Dominique completed her university studies. Upon Dominique's matriculation from the Sorbonne in 1927, we left Paris for Provence.

Only for Dominique would I have made the move. I had become an urban creature. Paris was my adopted home. I was part of the literary community of Paris. Now I was going to the rural hinterlands. I would still write, but this was still a fundamental life change. What one does for love. I would miss my beloved Paris but at least it was to a picturesque place with a warmer climate. Fortunately Dominique was involved with winemaking not something truly rustic like sheep herding in the central highlands.

CHAPTER 24

From *Time Travels* by Dillan Murphy
PROVENCE, FRANCE – 1925

It did not take long to fall in love with my new family and Provence itself. Provence was food and wine. Magnificent natural scenery coupled with quaint old towns. It had its own special rhythms of life.

The Bellamonts owned about twenty acres of land. About half their land was vineyards, the rest mostly grazing for a few cows and a small herd of goats which provided milk for making cheese. The terrain was rolling with higher hills visible in the distance. The property consisted of a large stone house and a matching stone barn that housed the winery and cheese making. Not far from the barn was another semi-ruined stone building with a collapsed roof.

Once we married, we occupied a bedroom in her parent's house. My sense of lost privacy was soon replaced with a new sense of belonging. Aimee, Dominique's mother adopted me as if I were her son. Within days of my arrival, she said to me, "I see how you love my Dominique, how you make her happy. It is easy for me to love you too."

Dominique confided that she planned to renovate the ancient ruined old barn not far from the house. I think she sensed that sharing the house with her parents would not be a good long term arrangement for anyone.

After suggesting the idea, she took me to the old structure. It seemed in worse condition up close.

"You must be joking, Dominique. This can never be made habitable," I said gazing up at the sky through the collapsed roof. "It's nothing but some walls. From the look of it, it may have collapsed a hundred years ago. How old is this?"

"I believe maybe three hundred years. Older than our house and the winery building. But do not be dismayed. The walls are sturdy. They need little repair. That is the substance of solid architecture, not things like roofs and windows."

"I thought it was chemistry you studied, or was it architecture?"

"You are American. What would you know? You have no history. You build houses of wood that do not last," she said, but in a good natured tone. "Trust me, Dillan. With sound walls this will make a beautiful house. I have seen many such renovations of properties in worse condition."

I was skeptical, but Dominique was determined.

"We shall have our own house yet be close to the winery."

I quickly adapted to my new role as manual laborer alongside Dominique's father, Pierre Bellamont. He was a little more reserved in his affection toward me at the start, but we quickly bonded as friends. As Dominique said, he loved to discuss all manner of things; politics, philosophy, literature. He was equally enthusiastic in explaining the art of winemaking. Having someone to discuss ideas with daily was a major stroke of luck for Pierre. Dominique was delighted with how much her father was enjoying me being here. For my part, the manual labor was cathartic, the company stimulating. My French vocabulary expanded. My hard-to-place accent began to fall away. Unexpectedly, I did not miss the excitement of my beloved Paris. Café life was replaced with Provencal serenity.

Pierre had his own take on society and politics. One afternoon after a long day of trimming vines, we sat relaxing with a bottle of wine. It was May and a gloriously sunny day.

"I wished I would have had all girls, especially if they were like Dominique. Young women are not sent to war. You of course know that I lost two sons in the War. My oldest fell at Verdun, my youngest was gassed in Flanders."

"Dominique has told me. She loved them very much. She is still affected by the loss."

Pierre nodded. "I am a Frenchman. It was of course necessary to go to war against the Boche. They invaded. What could we do? Our very way of life was threatened. France had no choice. We are forever destined to warfare with the Germans I fear. But I blame not just the Germans for what the Great War cost France. Our own government and the generals I also blame. This was not a war that they tried to win. It was a futile exercise in attrition. Our generals were too incompetent to do anything other than send tens of thousands of young men to their deaths."

"Those are my thoughts as well, Pierre. And not only the French leadership, but the British too, and even the Americans. The Germans did the same, as did the Russians and Italians. Everywhere young men were thrown against terrible weapons of destruction to die by the thousands. There were no statesmen on either side. No thinkers, only plodders with no imagination. Worst of all, there seemed no regard for the losses. I'm certainly not a Communist but they make a persuasive argument that the working class died because the aristocrats of all the warring powers made the War."

I shared some of my experiences that reinforced our shared view. Told him I would show him some of my dispatches from the War. Told him that was the subject of much of my writing for several years. Trying to explain the War through my fictional accounts. Pierre wept as descriptions of my personal experiences caused him to conjure up thoughts of how his boys might have suffered.

"How long have you been making wine, Pierre?" I asked to change the subject.

"All my life. My father and grandfather made wines all their lives. My father bought this place in 1872, a year after I was born."

His comment stunned me for its implications. He was only two years older than me. There was no escaping the fact that I was profoundly different. But I still choose not to think of the implications of how Dominique and I would be affected sometime in the future. The problem seemed too remote.

"Wine making is still more art than science. Dominique perhaps thinks somewhat differently because of her education. But I tell you, there is no scientific test to determine the precise time to pick the grapes. You must *feel* the fruit as well as taste how the sugar has developed. In September as the fruit ripens, we shall check every few days to determine when to harvest.

"As you shall see, wine making is a yearlong endeavor. Right now we are preparing the vines to remove unwanted new shoots and define the density of fruit. That is key to developing the sugar content. Until harvest time in late September there is constant work. We will help nature to concentrate the energy into selected bunches of grapes by culling the vines. In August we will cut back the canopy of leaves on the east side to give our babies the gentle morning sun, yet keep the fruit shaded from the stronger afternoon sun from the west. After the harvest, there is continual work in the vineyard to prepare the vines for the next year. That is the viticulture process. It is said that good wine is made on the vine not in the barrel.

"But just as for good food where you must also have the best of ingredients, the making of wine still requires the art of the winemaker just like the chef. The whole process is controlled by taste. Just appreciating good wine is not enough. One must understand the most infinite subtleties of taste as the fermentation process progresses. The winemaker must understand the minutest differences of how to blend the different varietals to achieve the desired result. You see we might use any number of ten different varieties of grapes to make Châteauneuf-du-Pape AOC wines. I shall teach you all I know."

"And you learned your winemaking from your father?"

"Of course and even from my grandfather when I was very young."

"And did your grandfather learn it from his father as well? How far back does your winemaking linage go?"

"I don't know. *Grand-père* would never talk about his early years. My father suspected some family problem. All we know is that he came from the Burgundy region. Grand-père knew a lot about wine making. Wanted to make his own high quality wine. Good enough to compete with his native Burgundies."

"That is what Dominique has said she wants to do."

"And she may. She knows her wine. I have taught her well. And now of course she has the knowledge of science to explain what we old timers just know by our palate and nose," Pierre said and touched his nose with a smile.

"This AOC, what is that?" I asked.

"Ah, the AOC, the *appellation d'origine contrôlée*, is what shall allow us to make great wine. The law shall now protect us from the frauds that have plagued us by labeling inferior wine as Châteauneuf-du-Pape. It was passed only a few years ago. Ours is the first such area to be given that distinction. It is too early to tell, but we are hopeful. The Government has decreed that wine labeled as Châteauneuf-du-Pape, must be from specific grapes of the region, and be made according to specific traditional methods."

"That makes sense. And the local wine producers like the

idea?"

"Oh yes. You see we have a very long history of producing first rate wine here. Hundreds of years. Châteauneuf-du-Pape translates as the Pope's new castle. In 1308, Pope Clement V made Avignon the seat of the papacy for the Church. Clement new his wine since he was the former Archbishop of Bordeaux."

"I suspect Dominque has a strong appreciation for the art of winemaking by the way she talks about your skills as a wine-maker, Pierre. I believe she sees science as a way to enhance the art, not replace it," I said.

"I hope so. She is an exceedingly bright young woman, al-though exceedingly headstrong at times. It is good that you young people are possessed of so much confidence to conquer the world."

Another reference about age that brought a twinge of guilt.

"It's good that she has someone as intelligent and strong as yourself, Dillan. Dominique has her mother's spirit. She needs a strong hand. At least you only have Dominique to contend with. For all these years I have been manipulated by the two of them," Pierre said with a broad smile.

CHAPTER 25

"Sounds like this was a wonderful time of your life," Allison said.

"That it was. When I think of all that I've experienced, the years I spent with Dominique were enough of a reason to have lived. My life was so much poorer before Dominique. There has never been the same joy since."

"You're not happy now?"

"Perhaps content would be the better word. Perhaps just re-conciled to life, even to my unusual circumstances. Happy is a difficult state for me to define."

"How long were you with Dominique?"

"Eighteen years."

"That's a fairly long time. Did your age or lack of aging ever become an issue?"

"Only to me I think. When you are with someone every day, changes over time are so gradual you do not notice. If you took photographs it might be noticed, but we didn't have reason to have regular photographs. Photography at that time was still mostly by professionals. Dominique never raised any questions about my appearance. As for me, I looked for any sign of wrinkling in her face. I worried that she might then start to question why there was no discernable change in my appearance as the years passed."

"So what were you planning to do when your *condition* became obvious?"

"I thought about it constantly as the years progressed. It was like a set of worry beads. But I had no solution. Didn't know how I would begin to tell her even if I worked up the courage. She wouldn't believe me. You didn't, maybe still don't. What reason would I give to relate this preposterous story? So I continually avoided dealing with it."

"You never mentioned children, Elliot."

He said nothing for several moments.

"Well? Did you have any children?"

"No. We never had any children. We were careful not to for the first few years. That was not easy back then. None of the modern-day methods of contraception. Mostly a matter of avoiding the time of peak conception. Aimee and Pierre frequently brought up the subject of children. Dominique told them she wanted to complete her studies and become involved in the business before starting a family."

"And you, Elliot, what did you want?"

"I was conflicted. At some level the thought of having one's own child is maybe a primal urge. The complexity of having children in my case scared me to death. I knew there would come a time when Dominique would want to have children. How would life be when I might someday look the age of my own child? Long before then, Dominique would have aged and my lack of aging would be obvious. She would not understand why I never told her."

Allison nodded her understanding. She was wrestling with trying to understand this bizarre story that was becoming real.

"So what happened?"

"I abandoned the rational considerations that my longevity represented and after a few years we tried to have a child. However, Dominique could not conceive. No matter what and how much we tried, it never happened. Dominique was emotionally wounded for a time. As for me, I chastised myself with quilt over my sense of relief."

"Oh my. I never thought about that. But I actually meant what happened with Dominique?"

"That is a very sad story. The most painful event of my life. But let's postpone it until tomorrow. It needs some time for the telling and it's getting late. I suggest we call it a day and go to bed. I suspect this has been quite a day for you."

"Very well, Elliot. My head is spinning," Allison said. She kissed his cheek and climbed the stairs to her bedroom. "Good night, Elliot."

The next morning, Elliot was already outside drinking his coffee when Allison came down.

"You're up early, Elliot."

"My time is short, Allison. "Sleep is secondary to other things."

Allison started to argue about how doctors are consistently wrong, but Elliot declared that he had thoroughly dispelled any chance for error. Too many doctors agreed with the diagnosis.

"It's a bit chilly out here. Let's go inside and have some breakfast," he said.

After breakfast, Allison said, "I see you have a computer. Are you connected to the Internet?"

"Of course. Couldn't do research without it. I may be ancient but I'm still adaptive to technology. "

"Good. I need to check e-mails. I won't be long."

Thirty minutes later she came down the stairs from Elliot's loft office.

"All set?"

"Yes. Actually I googled Dillan Murphy. Pretty thin on material. Wikipedia has a short blurb as an American author living in Europe in the first half of the twentieth century. Your books are mentioned. No birth date. Speculates you were killed in World War Two. Another archive site had a 1910 *New York Times* article with a byline by Dillan Murphy on that Tammany Hall boss guy, Keane. I'd like to see the old archives from both the *Herald* and the *Times* from that period, but that's for another time."

"Good. Just more proof I hope. Unless you think I could have created such an elaborate false history."

"No, I don't suspect that. But it's still impossibly difficult to get my mind around the fact you are claiming to be the oldest man alive – and still not really *old*."

"I've never gotten my own mind around it. I've long since ceased to search for an explanation, either medically or philosophically. It just is. No matter how rare, I suspect there are others like me."

"Unimaginably rare I should say. No one has ever heard of such a condition. But we could discuss that endlessly. It's more important to me to hear about your personal life. That's what makes your story come alive within the context of all these historical events. So tell me what happened to Dominique?"

Elliot exhaled a deep sigh. "Dominique died. God I loved her. The best years of my very long life.

"In *Time Travels*, I tried to tell our love story without devoting an excessive amount of play to those circumstances important only to us. Our story was like thousands of others as the world moved once again toward conflict. Ominous thunderclouds were gathering in Europe between the world wars, but we were relatively untouched in our rural Provence. Dominique and I had an extraordinary life together until the onset of World War Two.

"The winery prospered during the thirties. Dominique slowly took control of the wine making, then eventually the business aspects as well. By some subtle understanding, Dominique replaced her father as head of the business. I participated, but more as a laborer when necessary. Most of my time was spent writing. My novel *Vintage Years* gained modest success. It was essentially a love story. Somewhat autobiographical except for the plot which I fabricated to give the story a skeleton. I became a minor celebrity locally."

"I've never heard of it. Have you ever read *A Year in Provence* by Peter Mayle?" she said.

"Certainly. About twenty years ago. I loved it. His was a lighter, more humorous treatment of Provencal life than *Vintage Years*. Just the same, I enjoyed how he painted a feeling for my adopted home. I have a copy of *Vintage Years* I'll give you. You'll enjoy it for the portrayal of the two central characters. That's Dominique and me."

"I'm sorry that I don't know your earlier work, Elliot, or should I say Dillan?"

"No reason you should. This was in the thirties. Unless you were Hemingway or Fitzgerald, authors of the time weren't in print by the seventies or eighties."

"What happened to the winery?" Allison asked.

"The Milice burned it down during the War. It's not far from here. I visit it regularly. Dominique is buried there."

"So how did she die?"

"Murdered. I'll get to that terrible event in a moment."

"By these Milice? Who were they?"

"The Milice were a police of sorts. French police of the puppet Vichy government of occupied southern France. They worked closely with the German Gestapo in France to give you some idea what kind of police they were."

"That was when?"

"1942. I'll get back to those events in a moment. Anyway, I'm very connected to Provence going back a long time. That's why I returned twenty years ago. Returned home. Enough time had passed to put those events of almost fifty years into a different perspective. I had someone I deeply loved. Her parents became mine. I had a family. The locals adopted me into their community. It was the first place that I could identify as a home in the sense of being part of a community. After New York and Paris, after reporting on crime and wars, the measured rural rhythms here were a tonic to my soul."

Elliot smiled as he recalled those memories. "You must read my other book from those times titled *Terroir*. Published in 1938. It's my only other work that doesn't deal with war or crime. Unlike *Vintage Years*, it wasn't commercially successful. It's about wine, and food, and Provencal life. Too much insider stuff to have a wide appeal. Didn't matter. I wrote it more for myself. I still reread it to take me back to those times."

Allison wanted Elliot to return to the story of what happened to Dominique. She could see he was reveling in the fonder memories of that time and chose not to interrupt. He was postponing revisiting the memory of Dominique's death,

"In the morning I would help in the fields or the winery. Dominique's father taught me the intricacies of viticulture. He was a marvelous guy, at peace with his world, saddened by the loss of his sons. Angry but not bitter. Dominique taught me the technical side of winemaking, gently corrected on occasion by her father's experience. Harvest season in was October. Long days of backbreaking labor but I loved every minute of it. In the middle of the day we relaxed over lunch prepared by Dominique's mother.

"It was Aimee Bellamont that taught me the basics of Provencal cooking. She made her own goat cheese, milking the goats herself. She marketed her cheese as *fromage de chèvre de Bellamont* to the same customers as the winery. I learned from her that cheese making was nearly as involved as winemaking. It was an ideal life. In the afternoon, I wrote. In the evening after dinner, Dominique taught me how to love.

"I clung to the illusion of my idyllic life in Provence even as I could see Europe descending into darkness. Hitler and his Nazi Party came to power in Germany in 1933. The Nazi's virulent anti-Semitism screamed on the radio even here in France. In 1936 events escalated that directly challenged France. German troops occupied the Rhineland. Mussolini invaded a backward Ethiopia in Italy's pathetic quest for colonial territory. In 1936 the Spanish Civil War broke out. Franco's Fascists moved to displace the republican government in power.

"Over the next couple of years the war in Spain took on greater significance as a conflict of political ideologies between Fascists and Leftists, and a contest of outside nationalistic interests. The Soviets and the Germans used it as a preliminary bout to the main event. Then with the coming of the Second World War, life changed abruptly for France with the German invasion in 1940."

CHAPTER 26

From *Time Travels* by Dillan Murphy
CHÂTEAUNEUF-DU-PAPE, PROVENCE, FRANCE – 1940

Dominique had no illusions about what was happening in Europe. The Sorbonne in Paris was the center of Leftist intellectualism in France. There was a significant population of Communists and Socialists among the student body. While she did not identify herself with any particular ideology, she still was decidedly very left-leaning.

The aggressions of the Fascists in Germany, Italy, and Spain, not to mention the heavily right-leaning factions in France and Britain, provoked Dominique to rants in her frustration. I certainly found the Fascist dictators reprehensible, but that did not mean I saw solutions in the extreme Left. I looked upon all ideologies as suspect. The Communists and Socialists promoted unrealistic social concepts. The Soviet Union was just another repressive regime. I frequently made the mistake of arguing the point with Dominique.

"All I'm saying is that Socialism doesn't define any real workable government, and that Communism is a dictatorship or oligarchy no better than the Fascists," I said.

"How can you make that absurd comparison?" Dominique responded. "The goddamn Fascists are the ones in power in Germany. They're in power in Italy and Spain. They're killing or suppressing anyone in their way. The Fascists could even take over France. We have our share of Fascists here too. Look at the anti-Semitic rhetoric."

"What about Stalin and the Soviets? How do you categorize that state? From what I read, Stalin kills more people than any-one else. Is he the alternative to Fascism?"

Dominique had her fight style up. "Hell no. I knew many Communists at the Sorbonne, and they would say that the Soviet Union does not practice true Communist concepts. Stalin is simply a dictator that has corrupted socialist ideology."

"Just like the Popular Front in Spain. From the reports, the real reports, not the bullshit which my friend Hemingway writes, the Leftists are committing the same atrocities as Franco's Fascists. Same old excuse that anything is acceptable if your cause is righteous."

"You know what you are, Dillan, you're an anarchist. Ac-cording to you, all ideologies are bad and no one should govern. You hate governments. You criticize France, the Brits, even the United States."

"No, no. I'm not an Anarchist. Anarchists are the silliest of the lot. They expect everyone to do things collectively with no leadership. I just don't trust government, no matter how it's structured. Power always corrupts.

"Government cannot have a collective moral aspect. It's simply there to make things work. If it's fair, it's only because of its laws and how those laws are executed. It's not the collective character of those in the government that make it good or bad. It's only the rule of just laws. The United States system is the fairest because of the foundation of its laws, not because of the people in government. Believe me, politicians in America are just as corrupt as anywhere. It's kept in check only because of its laws. And even then, only because a free press keeps a check on the politicians."

We were sitting outside on a warm summer evening. The bottle of wine was finished. Pierre and Aimee had long since retired. Dominique seemed to reflect a moment before countering my arguments. "You are either a political innocent or a complete cynic, *mon cheri*. But I did not marry you for your politics. Perhaps I married you for your skills at lovemaking. No?"

In 1939, Germany annexed Czechoslovakia, and then a few months later invaded Poland. In May 1940, Germany invaded France and the Low Countries of Belgium and the Netherlands. Within a couple of weeks the Germans had driven the Allied forces off the Continent at Dunkirk and swept over Belgium where they had bogged down in the First World War, twenty-five years earlier. This time was different. In another two weeks, the highly mechanized, fast-moving Panzer divisions had rolled across northern France and German troops entered Paris.

Everyone in France had known for some time that war with Germany was imminent. Because of Germany's and the Soviet Union's participation in the Spanish Civil War in the late 1930's, some naively assumed that war would be focused on the eastern front between Germany and the Soviet Union. Equally clear was the fact that Hitler had retooled Germany's military might in the twenty intervening years since the World War One Armistice. France had not. It therefore fell to Britain to help defend against Hitler's aggression on the Continent. But no one could believe how swiftly the German Panzer divisions brushed aside French and British resistance and occupied our beloved Paris in 1940.

The French government fell. The aged World War One General, Henri-Philippe Pétain who saved the French Army from mutinous collapse in the Great War, became the head of state. With no alternatives, he negotiated an armistice with Germany.

Under the agreement, France was divided into occupied and un-occupied zones. The Germans directly controlled the northern and western regions of France, and the entire Atlantic coastline. The semi-autonomous but essentially puppet Vichy Govern-ment, with Pétain at its head, controlled the central and southern portions of France. As a German ally, Italy was given control of the Rhone Alpes and Cote D'Azur regions bordering Italy.

The wooded and mountainous areas in the unoccupied Vichy zone of control became a haven for Communists and So-cialists, and for French soldiers that had escaped capture. Many organized into armed resistance cells, calling themselves the Maquis.

Until 1943, our life in Châteauneuf-du-Pape was relatively unchanged except for growing food shortages. Food rationing started even before the German invasion as the French Army was mobilizing in 1939. The war lasted only six weeks for France in 1940, but rationing continued as French agriculture was bled to feed the German war effort.

Ration cards provided for only 1800 calories per day for a French adult in 1940. That went down to 900 calories as shortag-es worsened before the Allied Liberation in 1944. But often there was not enough food available to fulfill even the meager ration quantities.

Residents of the larger urban centers had it worse than those in the agricultural producing areas. They might have to venture far outside their cities to seek even the most basic of food neces-sities. We survived better than most. We had cows and goats and land to raise vegetables. We had cheese and wine to trade. That was the key to survival during those war years. You had to be connected. Pierre and Aimee were well respected and knew people throughout the region so we had an effective support network. Even so, we often were hungry.

As part of the Vichy State, or the Unoccupied Zone, we did not initially suffer directly under the heel of German occupation as did the North. However, we soon realized that this puppet government of convenience looked no different than the Nazis. Henri Pétain, the hero of Verdun, the general that prevented the collapse of the French Army in the Great War, became the head of this French quasi-government, as much Fascist as the Nazis. From the onset, the Vichy Government embraced state anti-Semitism and anti-parliamentarianism. It rejected separation of powers. Worse of all, it vested power in a malignant group of French xenophobes.

In 1943 the situation began to change with the direct German occupation of southern France. Germany started to conscript Frenchmen for labor in Germany. Those of Jewish decent were being selected for deportation to different types of camps far to the East.

All across France pockets of organized resistance had formed. Well organized, they were actively resisting the occupation, or the equivalent in Vichy France. They gathered valuable intelligence which was forwarded to Britain. They were also increasingly active in perpetrating acts of sabotage.

While in the vineyard one morning in 1943, Pierre and I were approached by a man that emerged from an adjacent hedgerow into the vineyard. The man was carrying a weapon slung over his shoulder.

"Bonjour," the man said and extended his hand. "My name is Jacques Berry. Formerly Captain Berry of the French Army. Now, I once again fight the Germans. I am with the Maquis. I am here to request any help you might give us."

Like any insurgency, the Maquis could only survive with the active support of the populace.

"What manner of help?" Pierre asked.

"Food mostly. Any weapons you might be willing to spare."

"We have no weapons, but I think we can manage some food," Pierre said. He did not hesitate in his response. Pierre hated the German occupation and Pétain's puppet Vichy government. To him, Vichy was even worse than the invaders. They were traitors to France.

Jacques Berry waved his arm and two other men emerged from the shrubbery. Pierre and Aimee loaded up the men with as much provisions as we could spare. Aimee added a couple of blankets. "It's for the cold," she said to the two young men.

As they were leaving, Jacques Berry said. *"Merci.* If you ever have useful information, leave us a sign." Pointing toward the barn, he said, "Turn that wheelbarrow upside down and place a flower pot on top. Someone will contact you within a day. Vive la France!"

CHAPTER 27

From *Time Travels* by Dillan Murphy
CHÂTEAUNEUF-DU-PAPE, PROVENCE, FRANCE – 1943

A week after the Maquis visit, we were having our midday meal at the main house when a car and large lorry drove up. There was a loud pounding on the front door. Pierre answered the door.

Outside stood an officer of the Vichy police, the Milice Française, with two armed men in uniform behind him. Through the windows we could see additional armed Milice moving around to the back of the house. The officer pushed his way through the door of the house followed by his two men.

"Who lives here?" the officer commanded.

Pierre told him our names.

At this point I must explain about the Milice Française. *Milice* is French for militia. However, they did not act as a militia. They were formed in 1943 when the Germans demanded the French Vichy Government create a more reliable security force to counter increasing anti-government partisan activity. At the head of the Milice was a right-wing ex-soldier named Joseph Darnand.

After being captured in 1940 by the Germans, he escaped to Nice. Soon after he established a fascist-leaning paramilitary group. It fit the needs of the Germans and the puppet Vichy Government. Darnand transformed the Milice into a paramilitary police force. He wholeheartedly embraced Nazi social policies, particularly with respect to Jews. Darnand was actually given a German Waffen SS rank, which suggested where his real orders originated.

The Milice became the Vichy equivalent to the German Gestapo. More secret police than military, their mission was to hunt down partisans and roundup Jews for deportation to the East. Like the Gestapo, the Milice would use torture when it suited their needs.

"Papers," the officer barked. All of us handed over our identity documents.

"Monsieur Murphy. What kind of name is that?" the officer asked.

"Irish. I'm of Irish descent. But I'm a French citizen now," I answered.

"Irish. That is good. Ireland doesn't like Britain. However, Monsieur Murphy, I believe we have a problem. You say you are married to this woman?" The officer asked as he held the document up so as to let light come from behind to examine the document carefully. "It says here that you were born in 1898. That would make you forty-five. You look no more than thirty. How is that possible?"

"Perhaps good living?" I unwisely answered sarcastically.

The officer glared at me menacingly, intending to intimidate. "I think perhaps because this is not you. Who are you really, Monsieur Murphy? A Jew perhaps? We must get to the truth. Therefore, you will come with us."

Dominique yelled, "No! He is my husband. He is no Jew."

I tried to calm Dominique saying everything would be all right, while being more scared then I had ever been in the trenches in Flanders. There were stories of torture by the Milice to extract information. There were also stories of deportations to the East. This is what happened to Jews and others arrested as undesirable. Supposedly they were deported to labor camps in Germany, but rumors suggested a fate far more sinister.

Dominique brought me a jacket. Unfortunately she also brought my .45 pistol concealed underneath.

I took the jacket from her arm and was horrified to see her pointing the pistol at the officer, standing no more than five feet away. The Milice officer's mouth dropped open at the sight of the large caliber pistol pointed at him. Stupidly, he reached for his own sidearm. Events then unfolded with everyone in the room reacting.

Dominique shot the officer twice in the chest. One of the Miliciens reacted with a burst from his submachine gun. I lunged at him, striking him squarely on the jaw with my fist. The force plummeted him into the other Milicien and both went down. I viciously battered the faces of both men with my fists before they could mount an attack on me.

To my horror, I turned around to see both Dominique and her mother lying on the floor. Dominique had been hit twice in the abdomen. A large pool of blood was forming on the stone floor. I remember screaming.

Then there was the roar of a shotgun as Pierre shot a Milicien coming through the back door. In a rage, I picked up my .45 and shot the two Milice I had subdued both in the head. Picking up the submachine gun, I bolted out the front door. I crawled under the lorry assuming the remaining Miliciens would attempt to escape. Pierre would shoot anyone trying to enter the house. Within moments, three men came running around a corner of the house straight for the truck. A burst from the submachine gun dropped two of them. The third man retreated, but within seconds, I heard the report of Pierre's shotgun again.

Two of the men were not dead. I dispatched them with bul-

lets to the forehead. There was no mercy in me and every reason
to kill them.

When I entered the house, Pierre was on his knees cradling
his beloved Aimee and sobbing. I joined him on the floor, strok-
ing Dominique's hair, also weeping in my own black despair.

Both of us remained kneeling on the floor for some time, neither saying a word. Pierre finally said. "We will bury them my
son."

We buried Dominique and her mother in a corner of the vineyard. Finding the emotional strength was almost unbearable.
Pierre struggled to turn the earth with his shovel. More than
once he was overcome with fits of sobbing. I did most of the
digging, attacking the ground with a vengeance.

After a silent prayer, Pierre said. "Dillan, we must leave here
immediately. The Maquis will help us. I'll gather some provisions. You gather what weapons we can carry. We have only
perhaps a few hours to find refuge. We'll leave the signal for
Captain Berry, but we can't wait until they show up to contact
us."

In the Milicien officer's car I found a hunting rifle with a
scope in an oiled leather case. It was a British Lee Enfield .303
rifle with a custom-made sport-shooting stock of highly polished
wood. Undoubtedly it belonged to the officer. An expensive
hunting rifle probably stolen from some wealthy Brit living in
the south of France.

"I don't know where to find the Maquis, but we need to find
some refuge where we can hide. I have a cousin in Gordes. He'll
help us. It's to the southeast of here, maybe fifty kilometers,"
Pierre said. "We can make it in two days. It's hill country just
north of the Petit Luberon. We'll have to abandon the truck soon
or we'll be spotted. Don't want the Milice to know we went to
Gordes. There'll be places to stay out of sight once we are in
those hills."

I was in a daze and followed his instructions without thinking or caring. Pierre filled a satchel with some bread and a part of a cured ham shoulder. He packed another with some wine bottles filled with water. I was of little help. I must have seemed in much the same state as those shell-shocked soldiers I saw in the trenches of the First World War.

We headed south toward Avignon in Pierre's old truck. Outside the city we abandoned the truck to give the impression that Avignon was our destination. We headed east on foot, hiking well into the night until Pierre could go no further.

The next day we stayed under cover in a remote wooded area to avoid any Milice or German patrols. The following night we picked up our trek again. The terrain was getting more difficult and we made less than ten kilometers that night. At this rate our water would be gone within a day. We would have to approach a farm and risk being seen.

The third night we were exhausted and slept soundly enough that we did not hear the armed men approaching.

"Monsieur Bellamont? What are you doing here? What has happened?"

It was Captain Berry.

Pierre recounted what had happened. Berry told us it was fortunate they stumbled upon us. By now they would be hunted fugitives. It would be difficult to enter the hilltop town of Gordes without being noticed. Someone might easily pass the information onto the authorities. Had we even gotten through to Pierre's cousin we would have posed a danger for his family as well.

So my father-in-law and I joined the ranks of the French Resistance. Pierre proved too old to participate on missions. He was more than thirty years older than any of Berry's Maquis, except of course for me. He became the unit's father figure. I on the other hand was fit and fuelled by a rage to kill what was now a personal enemy.

CHAPTER 28

Elliot stopped his narrative and realized that tears were streaming down his face. "My life was destroyed," Elliot said. "But so were the lives of millions of others. This was war-time under an enemy occupation. I could either die or fight. There was no middle ground."

Allison came over and embraced Elliot. Tears flowed down his cheeks.

After some moments, Allison said, "I can't imagine what it would be like to see a loved one killed before my eyes. The events you've described, experienced …. they're overwhelming-ly sad, Elliot."

"You asked me about how I felt not participating in the Great War. Here is the difference. This was an enemy which I would destroy or willingly give my life trying to destroy. Maybe that's the definition of what motivates men to go to war. In my case it was simple vengeance."

Composing himself, Elliot continued. "I survived because of Pierre. His loss was double that of mine yet he was constantly concerned about my well-being. He was a wonderful old man. Throughout the days in the hills he stoically went about his tasks. At night, he went off to be by himself. I often found him weeping.

"Unfortunately, life exposed to the elements proved too hard on Pierre. He died of pneumonia in the winter of 1943. His companionship had saved me. He had become a second father. His death left me truly alone and empty."

"What did you do in the Resistance?"

Elliot looked at her intently. "I killed people. Mostly French Milice, some Germans."

Allison was slightly shocked by Elliot's matter of fact statement. "You mean like a soldier? The French Resistance was a guerrilla force wasn't it?"

"Sure. We were soldiers. Soldiers kill the enemy. I became a sniper."

"A sniper? You mean you shot people from a distance with a telescopic sight?"

"That's right."

"Did it bother you?"

"No, it didn't bother me, at least not until years later. Perhaps it should have, but I was in a blood rage. The Milice were not even enemy soldiers. Quasi-police. They weren't fighting a war. They were a tool of oppression. They were Fascist pigs, murderers. Fellow Frenchmen that brutalized other Frenchmen. They rounded up Jews to be sent east to the Camps. Gypsies, Freemasons, homosexuals. No different than the Nazis. They murdered and tortured people. The Milice deserved killing. I was not troubled about being that instrument." The bitterness was evident in his voice.

"You could see their faces before you shot them? Wasn't that …. I guess difficult?"

"During the stress of the moment, no. Afterward, it was difficult. There were disturbing dreams sometimes. I didn't feel guilty but the raw brutality of what I had done left deep scars. I can see those faces vividly, bisected by the cross-hairs of my scope moments before I extinguished their lives."

"What about the Germans? You said you killed them too. Weren't they just enemy soldiers doing what they had to?"

"The German soldier was the instrument of the Gestapo. German troops were guilty of massacres. In 1944, they murdered over 600 men, women, and children of a village in the Limousin region as a reprisal for Resistance attacks. Ours were military targets. They used civilians as a tactic. But regardless of that distinction, I was simply killing an enemy soldier. That's what a soldier is expected to do."

"This is where you got the material for *Le Resistance?*" Were you the protagonist Henri in the book?"

"Yes. *Le Resistance* grew out of that experience. The story was fiction but most of the events came from personal experience. I found that I had a skill that was uniquely suited to my new circumstances. Didn't know that until I actually used the hunting rifle in my first kill. There was no opportunity to practice so I was just thrust into the assignment. Eventually my comrades remarked on my aptitude with the rifle as I achieved several successes. Jacques Berry made me his long-range assassin. Most of my targets were officers. Best trophy was a German Waffen SS colonel. Head shot at over 250 meters."

Allison starred at him trying to gauge the measure of his comments. *Trophy?* The anger of almost seventy years ago was still hot. "Wow. Did you kill as many as your protagonist in *Le Resistance?*"

"More."

CHAPTER 29

From *Time Travels* by Dillan Murphy
Provence, France – 1943

"Can you use that fine rifle Monsieur Murphy?" Captain Berry asked.

"I believe so. I hunted in my youth," I said. I actually didn't know how proficient I might be with the weapon. I had not fired a rifle since I was a teenager.

"You shall get an opportunity soon enough. Unfortunately there is no opportunity for practice. It would bring unwanted attention. And ammunition must be conserved."

"What are you planning?"

"We shall move north tonight to Carpentras. The Milice have detained a number of Jews that they intend to transport to Orange tomorrow. From there they will be deported to the East by train. We intend to free them."

"Are you and your men Jewish, Captain?"

"Two are, but the rest of us are not. So you are wondering why we risk our lives to save Jews?"

I nodded without responding.

"It's because we are soldiers. For us the war has not ended. We still fight the Boche and their Vichy collaborators. These Milice are dogs. Frenchmen that have sold their souls. We fight for France."

"Many of the Maquis groups are Communists. What are your politics, Captain?"

"My politics are to see a free France. The Communists are a disease. All one has to consider is Stalin's Russia to see how corrupt that flawed concept is. We fight for France not politics. I have refused to join with Guingouin."

"Guingouin? Who is that?"

"Georges Guingouin. Leads the Maquis operating in the Limousin to the west. He's a Communist. Wants to see a Communist France after the Germans are defeated. After the surrender in 1940 my men and I went south and joined with Guingouin. We fought with him for a year, but I did not agree with his politics so I left. Most of my men chose to go with me.

"Someday the Guingouins may be the enemy of France. So this unit fights its own war. Most of us served together fighting the Boche. Our generals surrendered, we didn't."

"Pierre and I are not soldiers. Can we be of service in your unit?" I asked.

Pierre sat next to me. I realized he was an old man. This hard life would be difficult. Could he contribute?

The Captain looked at both of us. "I hope so. We all must pull our weight. What else am I to do with you? If you are captured you will be executed for what you did. Our existence will be hard on someone of your age," he said looking at Pierre.

"I shall keep up. I can cook."

"Excellent. None of us are good cooks. And you, Monsieur Murphy, you shall become a sniper with your fine hunting rifle. Tomorrow you may have an opportunity to use it."

We were camped just north of the town of I'Isle-Sur-La-Sorgue next to the river. Berry had a lorry and car that would transport us north the ten kilometers to Carpentras. We departed well before dawn. I had been to Carpentras often with Pierre. It was a market town. Berry explained the plan.

"The prisoners are being held at the Milice barracks. Our information says they will be taken by lorry to Orange. We will position ourselves a few kilometers out of town. It will appear as if our lorry has broken down. At the last moment it will pull out to block the road. We shall then attack."

As dawn broke, Berry's dozen men were hidden on both sides of the road. One man sat behind the wheel of the lorry, another looking at the engine with the hood raised. I was positioned on a slight rise, concealed by a thick bush. I had fashioned a clear view through the foliage and secured my rifle in the "V" of a stout branch.

I practiced sighting through the 4x power scope. From 100 meters, the head of the man standing next to the lorry filled the viewing area of the scope. I had never fired this weapon. I had to trust that it was well sighted-in being an expensive, well cared for weapon. The only thing I ever shot were squirrels and rabbits with a .22 caliber single shot rifle. Would I make a head shot or aim for the larger area of the torso? I never wondered if I would be able to take the shot however. My blood was up. I was anxious to exact revenge.

Within the hour, a single car approached. It stopped behind the lorry. Two uniformed men got out and approached the lorry. Through my scope I could see they were Milice. Our two men produced documents but something was apparently amiss. The two Miliciens backed away. One pointed his submachine gun at our men, the other drew his sidearm.

I took my eyes away to glance over at Captain Berry. He nodded affirmatively and pointed in the direction of the lorry. I was to take the shot.

I sighted the rifle to the back of the Milicien with the submachine gun. He wore a helmet. A true head shot was not feasible. I sighted instead at a point on his neck just below the helmet. Taking a deep breath, I expelled the air in my lungs slowly then applied a steady pressure on the trigger.

The rifle recoiled up. I ejected the spent round and worked the bolt to chamber another. Re-sighting, I saw that I had hit my target. I had to pan around to find the second Milicien in the scope. He was running back to his car. I took aim on his torso with a slight lead to compensate for his running, and then squeezed off my second shot.

Berry motioned me to stay put. Several men emerged from hiding. They piled the two bodies into the boot of the car and drove off. Twenty minutes later they returned on foot. Obviously Berry intended to resume his original mission.

Two hours later a small convoy consisting of a car followed by two lorries came down the road. When only a short distance away, the driver of our lorry wrenched the wheel to the left and positioned our lorry to block the road. The Milice convoy slammed to a halt. Miliciens poured out of the second lorry only to be met with withering fire from both sides of the road.

"Murphy, the car!" Berry yelled.

I took a sight on the officer exiting the car. The crosshairs fixed on a point on the man's right temple as he turned in profile. He wore a soft officer's cap rather than a helmet.

The shot took the officer down. I worked the bolt chambering another round. Within seconds I got off two more rounds. The second Milice exiting the car went down.

The entire ambush lasted only a couple of minutes. The remaining five Miliciens not wounded dropped their weapons and surrendered.

I sprinted down to the officer I shot. Captain Berry joined me at my side.

"That was extraordinary shooting, Monsieur Murphy."

I looked at the Milice officer's ruined head. The round had struck over the right ear. The exit wound on the left side of the head was an ugly hole. Blood had soaked into the road gravel. The rifle was obviously sighted in with precision.

"Perhaps it was just this fine rifle. Perhaps I missed but the man just moved into the path of the bullet. Perhaps just the short range. Perhaps just luck."

The sight made me nauseous. Revenge was bitter medicine. When I killed the men after Dominique's murder, I was in a blind range. This was different. The reality was wrenching.

"I believe not, Monsieur Murphy. Not with that many kills. It is clear that you have a real skill with a rifle. You shall be very useful."

Berry's men released the deportees from the second lorry. There were ten men and four women. All but two jumped down. These two were in a bad way requiring assistance to be lifted down from the bed of the lorry.

The woman's condition was a disturbing sight. Her face had been horribly battered with her eyes swollen shut and teeth missing. Her arms and legs were black from massive bruising. Dried blood streaked her blouse. She was carefully lifted down and placed on a blanket in the grass.

The other injured deportee was a man with his hands and feet wrapped in bandages. The bandages were rags torn from clothing. They were discolored with dried blood. The man was barely conscious, continually groaning in agony. The man cried out as one of Berry's men bumped a bandaged hand only so slightly. They laid him next to the woman.

After issuing orders to his men, Captain Berry went over to talk to the injured detainees. Only the woman could speak. After a few minutes he returned to where the surviving Miliciens were being held. They were kneeling while the Maquis trained guns on them.

"Stand," Berry said. There was a sharp edge to his voice.

The Miliciens stood. All were young men. Captain Berry grabbed a submachine gun from one of his men. All of us stood transfixed as Berry executed the five Milice troops with two bursts of fire.

Berry looked around at us. Our faces revealed a collective horror.

Berry said, "These are not soldiers. They are barbarians, torturers. The woman told me she was beaten with an electrical cable. When she passed out, she was revived and the beating continued. Her husband had his hands and feet burned with a welding torch. To do what they have done to these Jews makes them outside of humanity. We shall have the same fate if we are ever captured. This is no longer a war against soldiers. Killing these animals is an act of honor."

Berry's comments didn't appease my unease of what had just taken place. There was no honor in execution. Yet was this different than what I had done after Dominique's murder? It seemed so but I wondered if that was just my own rationalization.

On a practical level we were now saddled with the liberated prisoners, two of which needed medical attention. One of the deportees suggested they go north to his small town where he formerly owned a market. There was a doctor there who could be trusted. There were also farmers he knew that might be persuaded to hide the deportees. It sounded like a desperate plan to me.

It was the best we could do but still disappointing. It was unlikely that the deportees would be able to evade eventual recapture. Four of the men sensed this and asked to join our resistance group. Berry agreed after polling all of us.

We moved south into the hills just north of the ancient hilltop fortress town of Les Baux. Two weeks after the attack to free the Jews, Berry discussed our next mission.

"Our next mission will be to attack the Milice barracks in Arles. Gather around and commit this map to memory," Berry said, spreading a large hand-drawn map on butcher paper on the ground.

Using a stick as a pointer he explained the plan of attack. "Our information suggests there are approximately twenty Milice attached to this barracks. By nightfall, the majority of the troops return to the barracks. That is when we shall attack. Hopefully catch some of them in the open. We shall press the attack against those within the building. Unfortunately we have no grenades but we shall make do."

"How will we know when to commence the attack?" I asked.

Berry smiled at me. "Why you will signal the start of the attack, Monsieur Murphy. The officer in charge is a captain. When he arrives you will shoot him. That will start the attack."

"But what if this officer returns ahead of most of the other Milice? We would expose ourselves and lose the advantage of surprise."

"Yes, that could happen. However, this is how we will deploy to protect against that eventuality," Berry said. He used the stick to outline the plan. "Pay attention men. Four of you will be placed here, another four here, and four down here. These four will cover our withdrawal. Pierre, you will drive the lorry. As the Milice patrols return to barracks, these two groups will pull back to here to give us a concentration of forces to attack the building. If the captain returns sooner, Monsieur Murphy will kill him. You men in these locations will be well positioned to counter the Milice troops if they press toward the barracks.

"Robert and Maurice will conduct reconnaissance tomorrow. Robert is from Arles so he knows his way around. It's through him that we have this intelligence on the Milice. We shall attack them two days from now."

After our nightly meal, Pierre asked me, "This sounds like a very risky plan. What do you think, Dillan?"

"Risky? More like stupid. The barracks are right on the river. I'm not a soldier but it seems that will leave us limited options for escape. Sounds like the same nonsense I witnessed in the

Great War. Berry has no subtleties. He's a soldier that knows only to attack his enemy. Casualties are just a price to pay. Besides, killing the local Milice commander will be a success in itself to Berry. The important thing is that we all get away alive."

"And you will be able to shoot this officer like you did before, Dillan?" Pierre asked with his question meaning did Dillan have the will for such an act, not necessarily the skill.

"Maybe. Still not sure those shots weren't just luck. I would like to practice but that is out of the question."

"I have only shot a shotgun at birds so I am no authority on shooting," Pierre said. He did not acknowledge his own killing of the Milice at the house. "But I saw how Berry and the other men regarded what you did with some respect, Dillan. You are a soldier now."

Berry's group now consisted of eighteen men. The original twelve were all ex-soldiers. All were well armed with the captured weapons from the prior engagement to free the Jewish deportees. Berry was a soldier. His idea of making war against the Germans and their Vichy collaborators was more that of a soldier rather than the tactics of a guerrilla unit. He wanted to inflict damage on the enemy, not simply harass. He commented on his disdain for the tactics of some other Maquis units.

"We are soldiers, Monsieur Murphy. Those Communists in the Limousin act like bandits with their acts of sabotage. They avoid fighting the enemy like a soldier. That is because most were never soldiers themselves."

"I'm not a soldier, Captain."

"Ah, but you are wrong, Monsieur Murphy. You are proven under fire. And you are my special weapon, my sniper."

I shook my head and only nodded. Hardly a special weapon, but war creates such absurdities.

Two days later Berry moved us just outside Arles. Robert reported back that two hundred meters north from the Milice barracks they could park the lorry and pretend to be working on repairs to a dock.

Mid-afternoon, the lorry loaded with most of the men approached from the south. Several men were dropped off near the Pont de Trinquetaille. The bridge across the Rhone River would be our principle escape route. The lorry proceeded to a dock just north of the Milice barracks. Several men posed as workmen on the dock. Others moved across the road to a parallel street to set up a position from a different angle on the barracks.

I was in the car with Captain Berry. Pierre drove. We parked the car in front of an apartment building.

Berry's plan required a bunch of men with weapons to seek out hiding places in a busy town and stay concealed or inconspicuous for perhaps a couple of hours. It seemed like a recipe for disaster.

It turned out to be just that.

Within an hour of arriving in Arles and placing ourselves in position, large numbers of Milice troops moved against our positions in a coordinated maneuver. From the north a lorry pulled across the river road to block an escape in that direction. Miliciens poured out and took up position training their weapons toward our colleagues posing as workmen repairing the dock.

Two cars came up the river road from the south and blocked that route. From across the Rhone, an armored personnel carrier blocked the Pont de Trinquetaille.

Within moments of the Miliciens encircling us, firing broke out from our men on the dock. Gunfire soon could be heard from the streets parallel to the river road as our other forces came under attack from a fourth direction.

"This is an ambush!" Berry yelled in frustration. All three of us were out of our car. "Our only chance is try to fight our way back through the city."

While Berry was accessing the situation, I knelt down and trained my rifle on the Milice cars blocking the road to the south. They had exited their vehicles. Through my scope, I could see two officers. Both wore captain rank insignia. One was French Milice, the other German, Waffen SS by the lightning bolt insignia on his collar.

I chose the German as my first target.

Once I brought the scope back on target after the shot, I saw the German lying crumpled over on the road. The others had sought cover behind the automobiles so I had no second target.

"Dillan, get in the car!" Pierre yelled.

Pierre turned the car onto the street leading east away from the river. Within moments, rifle fire blew out the front windscreen but none of us were hit. Pierre accelerated the sedan to at least eighty kilometers per hour though Arles' narrow streets. Shots came from behind us but none found their mark.

We disposed of the car in a wooded area well off the road. The trek to our rendezvous east of Arles in the hills close to Les Baux took four hours. It was a difficult hike in the dark.

Once there, we collapsed in exhaustion. Pierre was in a bad way.

"It appears we were expected, Captain. How is that possible?" I asked.

The Captain took another drink of water before answering. "We were betrayed. Perhaps by the Jews we set free."

"How would they have known of our plans to attack the Milice in Arles?"

"The men knew that was a target under consideration. Maybe someone said something and one of the Jews overheard."

"Come on, Captain. That's not what happened. Someone within our group is an informer."

"I refuse to believe that. Except for the Jews and you, these are men I have fought with. Besides, where was there an opportunity?"

Berry knew the answer even before I said, "What about Robert and Maurice? They were in Arles for two days."

"Robert and Maurice are good soldiers. I just can't believe either would betray us."

"If you're wrong, Captain, we're in danger as well. They may have also told of the location of our camp here."

The Captain knew I was being practical, but said, "If any of the men escape from Arles, they will return here. We must stay. If we have been betrayed, then all is lost at any rate. I prefer to make my stand here."

Berry's was the soldier's view. I wasn't sure that was how I felt but I had no good alternative option either. Pierre could travel no further. He had fallen asleep after eating a little bread and cheese. I would not leave him to save myself.

"Very well. Shall we take turns standing watch?" I said.

Nothing eventful happened that night. We suffered with the cold not wanting to risk a fire. Winter was approaching. No one had yet approached our camp. I had the second watch as dawn broke.

Pierre came down the trail to my advanced position. He handed me a bottle of brandy. The fiery liquor took the edge off my chill. We chatted for an hour. Neither of us held much hope that any of the men would return. But later that morning five of our unit did returned. There were hugs and tears all around.

Berry's former sergeant told us what happened. "The Milice knew we were going to attack, Captain. I fear all those on the dock were killed or captured. From my group, Fournier and Bocher were killed, and the Jew Morceaux. But Laroche has something to tell you, Sir."

Maurice Laroche had accompanied Robert Renard into Arles two days before. "Robert disappeared yesterday after the shooting started. He told me to move forward to a new position. He would cover me. That's the last I saw of him."

"So what does that mean, Maurice?" Berry asked.

"When Robert and I scouted the town, it was really Robert. I spent most of the time hidden down under one of the docks. Robert said he could best do the reconnaissance alone since he was from Arles. He left his weapon with me. He was gone almost the entire day."

"You're accusing Robert of being an informer?" Berry asked.

"I don't know, Sir. I'm just telling you what happened," Laroche said.

"Renard's the only one that had an opportunity, Sir" the Sergeant said. "He had family still living there. That may be the reason."

The logic seemed obvious. Ultimately it did not matter if Renard had betrayed us. Our Maquis unit was decimated. We no longer represented a fighting force.

CHAPTER 30

From *Time Travels* by Dillan Murphy
PROVENCE, FRANCE – 1944

The debacle in Arles had an even worse consequence than the loss of our comrades. The enemy retaliated with reprisals.

Captain Berry took us east into the high country north of Aix. The eight of us sheltered in a barn of a sympathetic farmer who fed us. On the first morning which was only three days from the incident at Arles, the farmer brought us a Marseille newspaper.

Berry read it, then repeated it out loud for all of us.

'Yesterday in Arles, ten citizens of that town were executed by firing squad for complicity in the murder of Captain Rolf Blucher of the German Army. Captain Blucher was killed by a band of partisans that launched an unsuccessful attack against government forces in that city. The ten citizens were all suspected of providing illegal support to criminal bands operating in the unoccupied zone. The local commander of Vichy forces in the region, Colonel Broussard, has issued a warning that those providing material support for these criminals risk a similar fate. He cited that officers of the German Wehrmacht were here to sup-

port the French Government in Vichy. Any further acts of lawlessness would be met with the most severe reprisal against those providing assistance to criminal elements operating in the region."

It was a reprisal execution for the Arles attack and the previous attack that freed the Jewish deportees. Everyone knew that. The victims were not under prior arrest. The message was intended to challenge the Maquis by directly punishing the population which was necessary to our support. It would become a chilling test of wills.

"What was the purpose of our attack at Arles, Captain?" I asked.

"Because we fight for France. Would you have us give in to the Boche?"

"It wasn't the Germans that took reprisals. It was Frenchmen."

"But a German officer was killed. Vichy is nothing more than German puppets."

"The Milice are willing puppets. They don't need the Germans," I said. "What did we achieve for such a terrible loss?"

"All of us have only two choices; live under Vichy rule which is nothing more than German occupation, or resist. There is no third option. I choose to resist. I am a soldier. Resisting means fighting the enemy. There will always be casualties."

"If our attacks result in innocent people being executed, are you willing to continue, Captain?"

"We must. If we let their terror win out, then we are lost."

"Are you willing, Monsieur Murphy?"

"It's troubling to know that I am the cause of innocents being murdered."

"And you, Monsieur Bellamont?" Berry asked.

"I am an old man. Whether I help you or not will make no difference. I have nowhere to go. My family has been murdered. Seeking revenge on the murderers is all I have left."

"Monsieur Murphy, will you continue to fight also?" Berry

asked.

What else was there to do? Slink away to hide until the Americans someday beat back the Germans? I could not live with myself if I ceased to resist. My own revenge still burned strongly but the choices were no longer that simple.

"Yes. I will continue to fight," I answered with resignation.

So our decimated group continued to fight. Our existence was hard and always precarious. We moved at night and slept outside. We were dirty and always hungry. The rural French people that supported us gave up meager supplies of food and risked deportation or death if suspected of helping the Resistance.

As the Germans forced conscription for labor resources to be sent east increased, recruitment into Maquis units increased. Our own unit was soon larger than before the Arles losses.

After a number of successful shootings, Jacques Berry decided to make selected assassinations their own set of missions. Up to that time, I usually took my sniper shot as just part of a broader mission. If we were going to attack, typically I would take the first shot at a target of opportunity, making my kill and signaling the start of the attack.

"You have become very effective with that rifle, Monsieur Murphy. How many have you killed so far?" Captain Berry asked.

"Fifteen."

"And many of those were officers. We are going to increase such targeted killings. They shall be the principle reasons for a new series of missions. Let every German and Milice officer fear for their own safety. Make them fear every time they venture out. Let them feel the terror of never knowing if they'll take a bullet in the head."

Captain Berry created a special assassination team consisting of three others and myself. Two of the others were women, the other an older man of sixty. One woman was in her late twenties, the other old enough to pass as the wife of the older man. Seeking out high value targets to kill required infiltrating towns and cities. Intelligence was essential not only to execute the mission but to successfully escape. A young man would be suspect since the Germans had implemented obligatory labor service on young Frenchmen. The Maquis gained recruits from those refusing to go to Germany and work in factories to support the Nazis war machine. The Milice knew this, so any young man would be a target of suspicion.

I got around the problem by wrapping my left knee in a makeshift brace under my trousers, simulating a bad leg. A war wound if questioned. Our papers were first-rate forgeries.

Perhaps my greatest success was a mission in the city of Avignon in early 1944. The magnificent old walled city on the Rhone River was now the sector headquarters of the Milice with a German Gestapo liaison office. Our mission was to kill the Milice commander. The purpose being to terrorize the Milice command and to show them there was no safe refuge even at the highest level.

The older man and woman team had reconnoitered the vicinity surrounding the Milice police barracks. They found rooms available in an apartment building a short distance down the street from the Milice headquarters.

The younger woman of the team, known as Marie, was a musician, a cellist. She was from Lyon, and she was Jewish. She had been away when the Milice came to their house. Her entire family however was deported east to the camps. Marie was perpetually withdrawn and said little when we were alone. When called upon to play her role however, she was able to retrieve her true personality with an occasional engaging smile.

Posing as man and wife, we rented the room located by the older members of the team. It could not have been better for a sniper position. It was on the second floor and since the street took a slight bend, the view from the room looked directly onto the front entrance of the police headquarters.

Once inside the room, Marie opened the cello case. Removing the cello, she loosened the strings and removed the bridge that elevates the strings. She then separated the neck of the cello that had been modified for quick removal with a thumbscrew. The cello body had been modified to house my dismantled rifle components. It was a clever concealment but ruined the cello acoustics.

I set up one of the chairs to use the chair back as a rest for my rifle. I would sit in the other chair. Once assembled, I sighted the rifle onto the target, the chair set back from the window within the darkness of the room so as not to expose the weapon from the street. The range was 250 meters plus. It would be a fairly long shot, but within my range.

The hard part was the waiting. We might be here for days. Unfortunately Marie was reclusive and poor company. She harbored her own demons. I did not intrude. So we ate our bread and cheese mostly in silence with me sitting in the chair watching out the window and her on the bed. There was no relaxing. Once I took the shot, we would have to leave immediately.

A German staff car drove up to the Milice Headquarters the next morning. Through the scope I watched an officer exit the car and enter the building. The black uniform was that of a full colonel in the German Waffen SS. For the next hour, I stared intently through the scope waiting for either the Colonel or the Milice Sector Commandant to appear. The Milice Commandant was my assigned mission, but a high-ranking German officer was an attractive target of opportunity.

The question of which target was answered when both came out the front door of the building. As if finding their marks on stage, they stopped to say something to each other.

My first shot caught the Milice commander in the right temple. I ejected the spent round and chambered another with the bolt action. It was a maneuver I practiced at length to maximize the ability to get off successive shots. The stupid German colonel helped by turning from the fallen man to look in the apparent direction of the shot. He was looking face-on when my second shot hit him below his right eye.

I dismantled the rifle and helped Marie secure it inside the cello. Several long minutes passed before we could exit the building. Our other team members had detonated a small bomb under a police lorry behind the barracks as a diversion once they heard the crack of my rifle. Our chances for escape were still probably only fifty-fifty.

Rather than try to immediately escape the city, we exited at the back of the building and circled back around the end of the block to the street in front. The ploy was intended to appear as if we were returning home. Our story was that Marie had been to a fellow musician's house practicing. The story would not hold up under much scrutiny but at least we were not fleeing the scene. In fact, we were approaching toward the scene.

"Halt!" A Milice soldier yelled. Two others accompanied him with weapons leveled. "Papers!"

We produced our documents and asked what all the commotion was about. The soldier asked what we were doing. Marie answered calmly using our cover story.

"Open the case." The soldier ordered. Marie unfastened the hinges and opened the cover. She pulled the cello and bow out of the case. "Play something," he ordered.

Marie played a few bars of a classical piece. The rifle concealed inside badly degraded the sound of the instrument, but the soldier did not seem to notice. As for me, I was not as calm as Marie. I could not stop thinking about the same circumstances when Dominique was killed. In the back of my waistband was the .45 pistol. I had no intention of being arrested in this situation. The Milice soldiers let us go however.

CHAPTER 31

PROVENCE, FRANCE – 2009

"Were you like the Russian sniper in Stalingrad in that book, *Enemy at the Gates*?" Allison asked.

"Yes, I read it. In some ways I guess," Elliot answered.

"How many would you say you killed?" Allison asked.

"Twenty-six. I can remember each one vividly. Killing people is not something you forget, especially when their faces are seen through the lens of a riflescope. That makes it very personal."

"My god, twenty-six? I can't imagine all of the emotions that must suggest." Changing the subject, she asked, "What happened to your father-in-law, Pierre?"

Elliot's face saddened. "Pierre died of natural causes. His heart gave out. The physical demands of our existence eventually took their toll. I was with him at the last. He told me he loved me. Said he loved me as much as he had his own sons. Thanked me for the years of love I gave his daughter. Wrote out a will naming me as his beneficiary to his land."

"After Pierre's death I became truly lonely. Hatred makes a

poor companion. Pierre had been my attachment to humanity. You see there is something slightly troubling about being a sniper even to one's own colleagues. Even they saw it as an exceptionally ugly part of war. So I kept to myself and nobody usually tried to draw me out.

"In the end, I came to realize that I suffered from the same perspective that fuels all hatreds; justifying the brutalities inflicted upon one's enemies as just consequences for what was done to you. In my mind, those that I killed were deserving of the worst death. I tried to acknowledge that in the ending of *Le Resistance*. Tried to explain the toll it takes on one's own humanity."

"It was perhaps my favorite of your books, Elliot. Was this killing of the two colonels the last for you?"

"No. There were more. Especially during the few months leading up to the Normandy invasion by the Allies in June, 1944. Captain Berry's Maquis group had grown. We were fairly well armed with captured weapons because of Berry's bent on attacking German military units. We continued operations even after the invasion, moving north to harass the Germans. At the urging of Allied agents, Berry coordinated our efforts with other Maquis units."

Allison shook her head. "Amazing. The things you've done. All those wars. Amazing that you haven't been killed somewhere along this extraordinary long life. You certainly have been in harm's way enough. You seem to have always gravitated to danger. It's now 1945. The War's over. *Le Resistance* was your first book, at least as Elliot Gaston. But it came out around 1982. It was one of my first editing jobs at the agency. You didn't write during those intervening years?"

"*Le Resistance* was not my first book as Elliot Gaston. Just my first to be publish in the United States. I had a couple of books published in Europe before that."

"I didn't know that. What were they about?"

"Based upon some other experiences after the War. I'll tell you about that later. At any rate, they were not commercially successful so I decided to try marketing *Le Resistance* in America."

"It was a great adventure story with wonderfully drawn characters. Apparently it was autobiographical. Your protagonist wasn't as conflicted as you portrayed in your own experiences."

"That's why *Le Resistance* is fiction. Author's prerogative to play God and shape things as he sees fit. I liked my character better than myself."

"So what did you do those intervening years? And when did you become Elliot Gaston?"

"It's late my dear. Tomorrow I'll relate the next chapters of my life following the Second World War. And I'll explain how I became Elliot Gaston."

CHAPTER 32

PROVENCE, FRANCE – 2009

Elliot was already up with a cup of coffee when Allison came down to the kitchen the following morning.

"Don't you ever sleep?" Allison asked.

"Seems like there's so little time left. Funny to say that when I've lived longer than perhaps anyone."

"For someone with a supposedly terminal disease, you look remarkably healthy, Elliot. Seems so odd and all the more tragic."

"That's what makes this cancer so deceptive. The doctors said there may be periods when I feel fine. Right now I do feel fine. Omelet?"

After breakfast, Elliot suggested a walk. The weather had turned unseasonably warm. The sun was bright in a clear sky. Elliot led them down a tractor path between rows of grapevines. The leaves of the vines had turned colorful hews.

"My god, Elliot, Provence is a spectacularly beautiful place. I can see why you returned here after the War."

"Well I didn't exactly return after the War. That didn't happen until the late seventies."

"I became your agent in what '80 or '81? I always thought you were just this Frenchman living in idyllic Provence. Apparently not?"

"No. There's lots of personal history since the War ended. My intention was to return to Provence. By August, 1944, the Allies had pushed the Germans out of Paris. The War would not officially end until the spring of 1945, but the end was in sight. It was still before the final German counteroffensive that we remember as the Battle of the Bulge. But most of France was essentially liberated by that time and the War was over for us in the south. The Resistance ceased to have a mission."

"Must have been an emotional time with all you went through."

"Yes, it was an emotional time. Hard to explain all the things going on. It was an unusual relief to be able to come out in the open. No hiding. No sleeping in the wild with your weapon at the ready. The killing was now ended. The ability to sustain myself through revenge was suddenly gone. I felt utterly lost."

"That's understandable. You'd lost Dominique and her family."

"Deeper than just the grief. Revenge had sustained me for two years. It was a solitary journey of violence, very focused with little opportunity for reflection. Pierre was the last attachment to that part of my life that once held the promise of happiness. I can't begin to explain in words what Dominique meant to me. I filled the last two years with killing. So the end of the War meant no return to anything, including my own peace."

Elliot said nothing for several moments. He stopped walking, lost in thought. Allison just looked at him without saying anything. There was still a skeptical aspect to her buying into his story. It was still just too preposterous but she was carried by his narrative. He now seemed lost to a previous time. This was either real or he was suffering the most unusual of mental disorders.

Elliot returned to the present. "On the larger level, we beat the Germans. Instantly the whole basis for the French Resistance ceased to exist. So like my comrades, we all returned to our homes. Of course many of us had no homes, or at least no loved ones to return to. I was not unique in my loss of family.

"I returned to Châteauneuf du Pape. Took me two days to make the journey from Lyon where I was when the War ended. I was blindly returning to home."

"It must have been at least a time of great relief after fighting all those years," Allison said.

"It was a relief for sure. For me though, the reality of the end of the War was a sense of hopelessness. I also had to face up to my lack of appearing to age. I was 71 in 1944 and looked to be in my thirties."

"But you thought your aging condition could somehow be accommodated or resolved when Dominique was alive, didn't you? Wasn't that always a looming issue?"

"Of course. But I had a reason to delude myself. We were together over eighteen years. Small signs of Dominique's own aging were appearing. Some lines around her eyes, the discovery of the first gray hairs. Of course nothing seemed to change with my appearance. I continually constructed scenarios of how I would tell her. How would she react? Look at how you reacted. But at least I had a reason to hope for a solution then. Not so in 1944. I could never resume my life here."

Not wanting Elliot to retreat back to the depressive recounting of the loss of Dominique, Allison asked, "Not sure I can imagine how tough a time that must have been. So sad that you had even lost the place you came to love. What happened when you returned to Châteauneuf-du-Pape?"

"It was a terrible shock. The Bellamont property was destroyed. Fire gutted the main house and barn as well as our house. Only the stone walls still stood. The weeds suggested the property was probably burned right after we left."

"The graves …. were they still there?"

"Yes."

"Are they still there now?"

Elliot looked at Allison. This of course was another opportunity to convince her of his story. Relating his personal history by building it with enough complexity, detail, emotion, and conviction might win Allison's acceptance. "Yes of course. Would you like to visit? It's only a twenty-minute drive."

"Yes I would, Elliot."

"Very good. Afterwards we'll go to lunch in town."

The visit was emotional for both. They walked past the destroyed buildings as Elliot had described. Well cared for vineyards surrounded the building ruins, but around the buildings themselves were tangles of weeds. The gravesite itself was hidden by unattended tall grass.

"You placed the headstones?" Allison asked. She parted the overgrowth to read the inscriptions.

"Soon after the War. I arranged for Pierre's body to be interned here next to Aimee and Dominique. The land, the vineyards I sold. All except the buildings. These will be left as they were along with the graves."

Allison was surprised at the depth of her own reaction. Beyond witnessing Elliot at the gravesite, she felt her own wave of unsettling emotion wash over her. Looking at the graves she experienced a decidedly visceral acceptance of Elliot's strange tale of longevity.

Lunch was at a remote restaurant north of Châteauneuf du Pape on the highway north to Orange. It was well off the highway, a place favored by locals. Elliot knew the proprietor. Allison was treated as a visiting celebrity.

After a protracted lunch with solicitous service, Allison said, "You are certainly well respected here, Elliot. What service."

Elliot laughed. "I believe it's more you than me, my dear.

Paul likes the ladies and someone with your looks is bound to attract his attentions."

"Well the food is extraordinary also," Allison said. "But you must continue your story. We're only up to 1945. There's decades more to tell me about."

"That there is. But I will try to be selective otherwise my story could stretch into weeks. Everything of course is in the manuscript. When we return to the house I'll fill in those years after the War."

It was late afternoon when they left the restaurant and returned to the house. Darkening clouds suggested rain. Elliot built a fire.

"Wine?" he asked.

"Absolutely not. I'll fall asleep with any more wine. You French do drink a lot of wine. I'll make us some coffee instead."

After setting the coffee to brew, she returned to the living room. Elliot lit a fire and then sat down in his favorite chair.

Allison sat down across from him. "Elliot. I must tell you that I do now believe you. No matter how preposterous this story of your life, I've watched you relive it. I guess it could still be some sort of psychosis that causes you to believe history as your own experiences, but I don't believe that. I've seen how you literally relive the details, how you feel the emotions of these events. Never once have you been confused in the chronology. Visiting the graves today was unnerving. It's all so amazing but still troubling."

"Thank you, Allison. Think about how troubling it's been for me. Think about how difficult it was for me to come to grips with what was happening with me."

Allison leaned forward and clasped his hands in hers. There were tears in her eyes. "Elliot, you can't give up. You can't die."

"I'm not giving up. I'm taking my therapy. But I'm still realistic. Besides, everyone dies. Wouldn't you say my mortality is long overdue?"

"Shit. It's just such a waste."

"Decades ago I would have agreed. But it's time I think. You must understand there's a certain relief. There's normality to a natural death after a long life. But let's not dwell on that. Let me pick up my story from 1945."

CHAPTER 33

From *Time Travels* by Dillan Murphy
NUREMBERG, GERMANY - 1945-1946

The years following World War Two were a time of continuing upheaval throughout the world. The War would unleash
nationalistic aspirations that could not be denied. The Cold War
was born as the Soviet Union refused to return Eastern European
territories that were seized as their armies thrust westward
against Nazi Germany. These puppet states became the Soviet's
equivalent to colonies. It was anything but a time of peace.

France was broken. Economically raped by Nazi Germany
during the years of war, it was also broken in spirit. The French
Army suffered total defeat and surrendered in a matter of weeks
to the Germans in 1940. It was a terrible reversal to World War
One where France and its allies brought Germany to defeat.
Practically speaking, the French military debacle did spare
France the terrible loss of life experienced in the First World
War. However, coupled with the years of occupation, it was a
debilitating blow to the French psyche.

The puppet Vichy government with its control of Southern

France only left a deeper divide once the War ended in 1945. France continued to convulse with antagonisms from the War, particularly over the issue of collaboration with the Germans. Immediately following the Allied liberation, there was a wave of executions of accused collaborators. Woman suspected of fraternizing with Germans were publicly humiliated by having their heads shaved. Within a matter of months, the newly formed Provisional Government brought order but the scars of the occupation still ran deeply through French society. The excesses of the Vichy government against its own citizenry would leave lasting hatreds for decades.

I returned to Châteauneuf du Pape to settle my affairs there. The probate of Pierre's will bequeathing the vineyard property to me would take some time to process within the post-war legal structure.

I found an old solicitor that Pierre had mentioned using well before the War who was still practicing law. He remembered hearing at the time that Pierre and Aimee Bellamont had vanished along with their daughter and her husband. Rumors spoke of a police matter. I told him my story. It was no worse than the tragedies suffered by so many others, but he was noticeably saddened.

Never once did I consider staying on in Châteauneuf-du-Pape. I loved the people and the place, but only with Dominique. It held nothing now except ghosts. I was a writer not a farmer, nor skilled at making wine. Memories would forever haunt me if I stayed.

Eventually I would have to leave anyway. At some not too distant time, my lack of aging would become an issue in the small community. Being fundamentally an urban creature, I would return to Paris. I executed a power of attorney so the old solicitor could sell the vineyard property once the probate was settled. I arranged for Pierre's body to be brought home and buried with Aimee and Dominique. Before leaving for Paris, I arranged for headstones.

All of Europe was in ruins, but quiet for the first time in six years. Not so for the rest of the world. Changes to the geopolitical landscape wrought by World War Two unleashed new struggles for power and independence from colonial domination.

After settling things in Provence, I headed for Paris seeking a job. Fiction writing had provided a modest savings before the War. However, since I was known to be fighting with the Resistance my bank account was confiscated by the Vichy Government. The Bellamont property would yield something but no telling how much in the economic uncertainty following the War. My best option was to return to journalism for a regular paying job.

I arrived in Paris in July of 1945. Germany had surrendered. Charles de Gaulle had established a Provisional French Government. My first try at employment was a newly formed newspaper. The founder had fought with the Resistance. I hoped that connection might give me an edge.

Hubert Beuve-Méry granted me an interview. After swapping war stories, he said, "I believe I heard of you in '43. The Germans and the Milice called you the *Irishman*. They wanted your head badly. You were with Jacques Berry's group in Provence I believe?"

"That's right." I was surprised that I had that notoriety.

"Some say you were an extraordinary shot. Known for targeting enemy officers. That true?"

"Not sure how great a shot I was. My rifle was fitted with a telescopic sight. Most shots were not at a great distance. Like all of us, we did what we could. Captain Berry was keen on taking the fight directly to the enemy so we frequently found ourselves in shooting situations. I had many opportunities."

"Nonetheless, your exploits speak for themselves. So you speak and write English fluently. But you don't really have a journalism background. You're a novelist. Journalism is wholly different. It is not something you can just jump into and produce good work."

"However, Monsieur, I do have a degree in journalism from Columbia University in New York. Beyond that, I think you would agree that at the least I can write. In fact my published novel based on the First World War came about after exhaustive interviews with veterans."

I was stepping lightly regarding chronology. I guessed that Beuve-Méry would probably not check when I actually went to Columbia. Of course I could not cite my actual journalistic experience with the New York newspapers given my age appearance.

"You seemed to have accomplished much for someone so young, Monsieur Murphy. Might I inquire as to your age?"

"Forty-six next year."

Beuve-Méry's eyes widened in some surprise. "That's amazing. One would guess not much more than thirty. What is your secret?"

"Just lucky I guess. People have remarked about it before."

"Very well, Monsieur Murphy. I will give you a chance. I trust you can remember those things they taught at university. And remember this is reporting not fiction writing."

And so I joined *Le Monde*. My early assignments covered the reconstruction efforts not only in France but the Low Countries, Italy, and of course Germany. My English skills gave me the ability to interact with the ubiquitous Americans that were in the vanguard of everything going on in post-war Europe. That was how I landed my first major assignment, the war crimes trials at Nuremberg, Germany.

The centerpiece of the Nuremberg war crimes trials was the Trial of the Major War Criminals. The defendants consisted of twenty-one of the remaining ranking political, economic, and military leadership of the Nazi Third Reich. Justice was cheated by the suicides of the most reprehensible of the Nazi hierarchy;

Hitler himself, Goebbels, Himmler, and eventually Goering before he could go to the gallows.

The trial lasted almost a year from November, 1945 until October, 1946. It was an emotionally wrenching event but still a mind-numbing endurance of endless testimony.

I was selected to represent the French press as a witness to the executions of the ten Nazis receiving the death sentence only two weeks previously. As deserving of death as these Nazis were, it was still a difficult ritual to experience. I had witnessed the executions of Private Newbury and Margaretha Zelle, aka Mata Hari. These were probably terrible miscarriages of justice, but the actual act of taking their lives still seemed more in keeping with civilized society. Death by firing squad had some dignity both for the victim as well as the executioner. Perhaps just an emotional response on my part, but the gothic theater surrounding hanging felt like a barbaric throwback.

The place of execution was a small gymnasium at the Nuremberg Gaol. Three wooden scaffolds stood in a line. They were eight feet square and stood eight feet high, accessed by thirteen steps. The rope was suspended from a crossbeam between two vertical posts. Below the trap from which the condemned man dropped, three sides of the scaffolding were boarded up while the fourth was covered by a canvas curtain. For no apparent reason the scaffolds were painted black. It was almost claustrophobic once all the functionaries and witnesses crowded in. We were all too close to the actual executions for my liking. Perhaps it was befitting the magnitude of the crimes of these defendants, but it was still a stage of horror. Adding to the depressing theatrics of the venue, it was one o'clock in the morning, chilly and damp.

Only two of the scaffolds would be used, alternating every other condemned man while the prior victim hung for a sufficient time to allow a physician to pronounce death. The ugly reality of hanging was that death was often not immediate. Some victims strangled to death in a disturbing spectacle. The third scaffold was a spare. Why a spare was required was never explained.

A British correspondent stood next to me. "Too bad fat Hermann will not be among the guests. I was hoping to see how they would manage his considerable heft. Looking at the gallows that might have been a problem."

Hermann Goering had been convicted and sentenced to death with the other ten. He cheated the hangman by committing suicide with a concealed cyanide capsule only two hours before his appointment with the gallows.

"He wasn't so fat at the end," I said.

"Still too bad we can't see him dance on the end of the rope."

"Ever seen anybody hanged?" I asked.

"Can't say that I have. How 'bout you?"

"No. I've seen executions by firing squad. Those were disturbing enough. I suspect this will be worse."

"Christ, these buggers deserve worse than hanging. I'll not be having bad feelings about these bastards' deaths."

"Neither will I. I'll just be having bad feelings about this barbaric event."

Our debate terminated as the first condemned man entered the room. It was Joachim von Ribbentrop, the former Nazi foreign minister. Stoically he ascended the stairs escorted by two U.S. Army sergeants. On the platform he was turned to face the witnesses. Asked by an interpreter if he wished to make a final statement, he said 'God protect Germany', followed by a few more words expressing his wish for peace in the world.

A black hood was drawn over his head. As prescribed in the U.S. Army manual, a large diameter manila hemp rope was used. It was boiled to take out stretch, waxed or greased, with the noose formed into six coils. It was fixed under Ribbentrop's left ear. The hangman cinched the noose snug then immediately stepped back and pulled the release lever.

Ribbentrop fell out of sight beneath the scaffold and the rope jerked taunt.

Two minutes later, Field Marshall Kieitel entered the chamber. His execution proceeded on the second scaffold. Ribbentrop still hung from the first scaffold.

The proceedings paused while an American and Russian doctor examined Ribbentrop's body to confirm death. In a bizarre move, everyone was permitted to smoke during the lull in the executions.

Once the doctors emerged from under the scaffold, the hangman cut the rope and prepared the gallows with a new rope for the next man. Cigarettes were ordered extinguished and the grisly business resumed.

The seventh condemned man was Julius Streicher, the vicious Jew-baiting propagandist of the Third Reich. His was not a good hanging in the sense of an efficient death. As he approach the steps he yelled, 'Heil Hitler!', startling everyone. Still defiant, his last words before the hood was placed over his head were 'The Bolsheviks will hang you one day.'

As Streicher passed through the trap door, the rope snapped taunt but his body was obviously swinging wildly as evidenced by the rope's excessive twisting movements. Groans could be heard from the interior of the scaffold.

After looking down into the scaffold, the hangman finally descended the platform and entered the enclosed area underneath. Within moments, the groans ceased and the rope stayed still. Perhaps because of Streicher's small stature his neck did not snap?

"Bloody hell. What's that about?" my British colleague whispered.

"My guess is the hangman put some weight on Streicher's body to finish the job. Told you this was an ugly business."

The ten executions took two hours. In a bizarre conclusion to the grisly proceedings, the body of the recently deceased

Hermann Goering was brought into the gymnasium to take its place alongside the bodies of the other condemned. It was a fitting conclusion to the disgusting spectacle.

My editor liked the piece I wrote about the executions. I thought it was a thinly veiled editorial comment on the barbarity of executions, even for the most egregious criminal acts. The editor thought it painted a real mood of the historic proceedings. He commented that it served as a further form of retribution for the condemned to die in such a despicable way, absent of any dignity. I took some criticism from the public however who saw my position but held the view that no punishment could be base enough for these Nazis. Everyone missed my point. I was lamenting the effects on society engaging in these barbaric executions, not any sympathy for the condemned.

CHAPTER 34

PROVENCE, FRANCE – 2009

"I couldn't wait to leave Nuremberg," Elliot said. "The year there felt like a prison sentence. There was no respite from the continual weight of the War Crimes Trial. The Germans were a beaten people. The gloom was cloying. The town was full of non-Germans but it didn't matter. All talk at the bars was dominated by conversation related to the Trial. There was no escape. The emotional scars of the War still affected me. I became severely depressed. I came damn near to going over the edge."

"What do you mean? Like thoughts of suicide?" Allison asked.

"Probably not suicide. At least not directly. More in the form of destructive behavior. Probably more emotionally destructive than physical. However, I was less than cautious on subsequent reporting assignments. I may have subconsciously harbored a death wish."

"The Nuremberg Trials had that effect?"

"Not entirely. The year in Nuremberg was a just a difficult ordeal at the wrong time. It was a difficult year at a vulnerable time. First the loss of Dominique, then all that I suffered in the War. I had nothing to emotionally sustain me. What future was there?"

"Today they'd diagnose your condition as post traumatic stress disorder. You lost your wife to murder then fought a brutal war as a combatant. Of course you'd be depressed. Must have been an epidemic of that at the time."

"Absolutely. But we tend to focus on our own problems. Even if others are suffering, it's no consolation."

"So how did you get through it, Elliot?"

"Not sure. How does anyone get through emotional crisis? The human condition adapts. At least I was back in my beloved Paris. Even as disrupted as life was just after the War, Paris was still Paris. Lots of wonderful memories of Paris. But the memories were part of a different time, a different life. I was starting over. I was still not over the loss of Dominique. The pain was still pervasive. No amount of intellectualizing gave relief."

"The intensity of the War years postponed the grieving process," Allison said.

"Not sure if that isn't just psycho-babble, Allison. If the wound ever heals it just scabs over at best, or leaves you crippled at worse."

"Well that's what's meant by the term *process*. Everyone deals with it differently. Some might not ever get through it. Some might be so emotionally scarred that their lives are fundamentally altered. How did you fare, Elliot?"

"Ok. I'll bend to your psychoanalyzing. I obviously got through it. Scarred but not crippled. Altered most assuredly. At any rate, Paris didn't work as a balm. My reporting assignments focused on the dysfunctional Fourth Republic that was the government of France following the War. I was disinterested in the boring debates of petty government functionaries, pathetically wrestling with great problems beyond their collective intellect. I jumped at the chance to go to Palestine to report on the flow of

European Jews into the British Protectorate."

"Wait a minute, Elliot. Before you skip to your next war, tell me more about this personally difficult time in Paris. You do tend to avoid those personal details. You're too much the reporter. After all, your book is about your strange life not a history of the twentieth century. So when was this return to Paris, 1947?"

"Yes. I left Nuremberg right after the executions in October of '46. But my book is more about the history of the twentieth century. I've just told it from my firsthand experiences. It's the unique perspective of one man's experience spanning over ten decades. The sights, the sounds, the changes in the human condition spanning those times. I report firsthand on the awful sameness of mankind's continual barbarity. It's not intended to be an autobiography."

"But it is, Elliot, the most engaging of autobiographies. It's you as a person that gives the story its power. That's what will engage the reader. That's what engages me. I'm your literary agent after all. I know something about this. Christ, Elliot, you're a damn fine fiction author. Your characters are real and complex. It may be the plot and the actual historical context that's the strength of your work, but it's your characters that breathe life into your stories. It is you that breathes life in this memoir."

"Ok, I concede. Those personal revelations are all in the manuscript of course. I was just trying to give you the abridged version. But since you insist, I'll tell you about those difficult years following World War Two."

CHAPTER 35

From *Time Travels* by Dillan Murphy
PARIS, FRANCE – 1947

I found an apartment on the Left Bank only a few blocks away from where I lived in the 1920's. A better place, larger, with more light. It looked over a quiet street not far from the Jardin du Luxembourg and the Sorbonne. The apartment was furnished with reasonably good furniture. Book shelves lined one wall of the living area. The only thing I changed was the pictures on the wall.

The apartment had been occupied by a ranking Gestapo officer. Prior to the German occupation, it was the residence of a deported Jewish professor at the Sorbonne. I was not sure of the origin of the oil paintings but I presumed they were the legacy of the professor not the Nazi tenant. They were pretty pastoral landscapes but not to my taste. The landlord told me that photographs of the former Gestapo tenant with Hitler and Himmler had occupied the empty wall spaces. I repopulated the walls with inexpensive paintings purchased from antique shops and street artists of Paris.

Unfortunately, there was no way to reprise better times. Dominique was dead. I had suffered the continual stress of combat for two years. I had killed many men. The violence was often revisited in my dreams. I was not the same nor were the Parisians. They had suffered the deprivations and indignities of the German occupation. In many ways it was more emotionally crippling than the terrible loss of French lives suffered on the battlefields of World War One.

The contrast of post World War One Paris compared to World War Two was striking. Even with the loss of hundreds of thousands of Frenchmen, Paris was aflame with life in the early 1920's just a few years after the Armistice. Not so with Paris in 1947. Life still struggled to escape some general shroud of collective malaise. The four years of German occupation heaped a collective violation on the French that was more difficult to expel. Much as a woman might not recover the scarring of a rape, Parisians had still not recovered even two years after the Germans were driven out.

Everyone else's problems didn't make me feel any better. All it did was to allow me to justify my own depression as perfectly consistent with the general condition. Getting through those times was a difficult journey.

I didn't have any friends in Paris. Being naturally gregarious that should have been easily remedied. Unfortunately I found myself all too frequently getting into arguments. Stupid intellectual disagreements usually fuelled by too much liquor. Looking back on that time, drinking became a disruptive influence on my life. It never affected my work but certainly damaged relationships.

As to my journalistic work, there was little to damage. It was boring, tedious work. My assignments were the government affairs of the newly formed post-war French government. Admittedly it was a tough job for newly elected bureaucrats to form a functioning government after years of occupation. And of course they didn't. The Fourth Republic was just as weak as their pre-war predecessor the Third Republic. The scope of reestablishing institutions, rebuilding the economy, dealing with alleged colla-borators, particularly with the former Vichy government that governed the south of France during the German occupation, all of this and more proved overwhelming. When faced with great issues, political bodies most often revert to inaction or focus on small peripheral issues. The Fourth Republic was no exception.

Only upon looking back to that time did I realize how anti-social I was. Good people that should have become friends be-came distant with my argumentative outbursts. After work, drinks turned into rants and drunkenness into arguments. Asso-ciates began to make excuses to avoid socializing with me. While I understood it was my attitude that was putting people off, I didn't give a damn.

To hell with them. What did they know? Everyone had their own demons but nobody had my problem. Which was what? A protracted lifespan? Something everyone would envy. What sort of perversity was this? How could I explain witnessing all I have without the ability to share that experience with others? There could be no life partner, no enduring friends. I would outlive all of them. Watch them grow old while I remain unchanged. Had Dominique not been killed, what would have become of us? Mine was the life of an outcast.

Self-pity became my refuge. That and alcohol. My daily rou-tine took on a consistent rhythm. While my personal life may have been going downhill, professionally I was still effective. Covering government affairs was boring and to my thinking largely irrelevant. The world had just suffered an immense upheaval yet the politicians debated minor issues. While I held the view that those in the Government were small thinkers, they nonetheless still represented potentially good copy. No matter my personal issues, I always delivered good work to the news-paper.

My earlier skills honed in turn-of-the-century New York City still proved effective. It was effective in the sense that it gave me a perverse raison d'être and at the same time generated good copy for *Le Monde*. I could adopt a wide range of personal styles to extract comments from my subjects. I was even better at this manipulation now since I had no regard for the value of any of those that confided in me. I had no friends, just targets of opportunity. Dredging up controversy and scandal became a specialty.

Evenings were spent largely alone. Since I didn't cook at the time, eating at home was limited to cold meats, cheese, and bread. Dining out alone became a utilitarian requirement since I had to eat a better variety. Walking the streets of the Left Bank held none of the magic of those days in the 1920's. I was emotionally shaken at that time following World War One, but it was different from this time in the late 1940's. Perhaps it was the exuberant times of Paris in the 1920's. I was part of the great literary environment of that time. The implications of my abnormal longevity were brushed aside when I met Dominique. Now that was all gone. The future held nothing.

The singular redeeming aspect of this difficult time in Paris was the discovery of photography. Quite by an accident of circumstances, I fell into photography. It became a new creative outlet to replace my non-existent creative writing.

While in Nuremberg, my editor suggested I take photographs to augment my reporting of the War Crimes Trials. The Trials were a protracted event with not enough photographic opportunity to warrant the expense of a staff photographer.

I knew nothing about photography. From past observation, cameras were bulky, complicated affairs with a totally alien technology. In postwar Germany, there were few functioning shops but there was always the ubiquitous pawn shop. Fortunately, I found a pawn broker that was himself an amateur photographer. His shop had a good collection of cameras to offer and seemingly expert advice. He could have simply been praying upon my ignorance, but his recommendations were instructive and the selected camera proved sound.

I bought a 35mm Leica model lllc manufactured during the Second World War. It was smaller than the box-like cameras of the earlier half of the century. According to the pawn broker, it was the latest in German technology. I paid 35 francs and another 5 for a light meter. He enthusiastically provided twenty minutes of bewildering instructions. As I left the shop, I assumed my venture as a photographer would come to frustration.

Surprisingly, that was not the case. There was a learning curve of course, but it was not long before I was taking respectable photographs. Sufficient for the Newspaper, but more importantly I was exposed to the possibilities for artistic expression. Everything about photography is light. In my early efforts I learned not only the technical aspects of simply taking properly exposed photographs, but the effects light has on shaping the artistic expression of the result. With my mistakes, I often saw art instead of a poor photograph.

My photographic services were not required by Le Monde once I returned to Paris after the War Crimes Trial. But I did begin my artistic photography if that is not too grand a label. These early works conveyed a deep melancholy, dark in mood as well as texture. The tone changed over the decades, but the strong influences of light remained my style.

I had few romantic associations during that long year in Paris. Women can sense a troubled spirit and mostly kept their distance. While some may gravitate to a wounded soul that was not the aura I gave off. I was antagonistic. My declarative pronouncements invited argument not romance. My few sexual liaisons usually were with bar-flies satisfied with dinner and a few drinks in exchange for disappointing sex.

I could not remake Paris into my vision of twenty-five years ago. Everything was changed about the city. Of course memories are inherently flawed and reshaped to fit our prejudices. Everything about me was changed as well. I was looking through a different lens.

While my personal life was sliding increasing downward, professionally I was forging a reputation for delivering hard-hitting pieces. The editor of *Le Monde*, Hubert Beuve-Méry, called me into his office in early, 1948. "What do you know about Palestine, Dillan?"

"Palestine? Not much. The British control the area. Violence between the Jews and the Arabs."

"And violence against the British by the Jews," Beuve-Méry said. "They want their own Jewish state not a supervised partition from the Arab population. The British got control of the region after the defeat of the Ottoman Empire in the First World War. Their mandate, sanctioned by the League of Nations, was to establish a homeland for the Jewish people while doing nothing to disturb the existing non-Jewish population of Palestine. Only naïve politicians could think such an unrealistic concept would ever be workable."

"And now you have these new Jewish refugees that survived the Nazi concentration camps wanting to emigrate there," I added.

"Exactly. That European exodus is tipping the region toward war. Britain is attempting to limit these Jewish refugees entering Palestine. Since the War ended, Jewish extremists have been committing acts of terror against the British military there. They want them out even if they must contend with the Arabs by themselves."

"So if a Jewish state is declared, the British can get themselves out from under the problem by simply leaving," I said.

"Eventually that will probably happen. Right now they're stuck with an untenable problem. And there's the added tragedy of Europeans fighting Europeans again, this time Holocaust survivors and the British military. You've got these death camp survivor émigrés facing Palestinian Arabs bent on destroying them, with the British caught in the middle.

"For centuries, Muslim Arabs have coexisted with Jews in the region. The Arabs resent Europe displacing them from their ancestral lands with Jewish Holocaust refugees. There are already the beginnings of a religious war. Whatever happens, this promises to be the newest flash point in the world. I'd like you to go there and cover this for *Le Monde*. Claude Donay has been reporting from there for the last several months. Frankly his pieces have been boring. I'm bringing him back. Maybe he's just getting old. Anyway, I hope your more aggressive style can give us better copy. This United Nations vote last week to partition Palestine will inevitably lead to war between the Arabs and Jews."

"Why's that inevitable?"

"Because partition gives the Jews a defacto state of their own. Something the Arab states of the region cannot abide."

"What sort of material are you looking for, Hubert?"

"Palestine is starting to look like a war zone. The violence will only get worse. I need it reported as such. This is not salon journalism. You're good at pulling people out, Dillan. I want stories that will give our readers the sense of what this conflict is about. Something more than just the statistics of the violence and the political rhetoric. The world views the Jews as victims. Those in Palestine are taking an aggressive stance. Just who are these Jews?"

I wasn't sure I relished the idea of going to Palestine. Biblical depictions of desert scenes came to mind. But anything that would extricate me from the boredom of political reporting in Paris would be welcome. I was self-destructing here in Paris.

CHAPTER 36

From *Time Travels* by Dillan Murphy
TEL AVIV, PALESTINE – 1948

I arrived in Tel Aviv in January, 1948. It was my first ever flight. I stepped off the DC-8 arriving from Athens into a sunny Mediterranean day close to 20 degrees centigrade. From the air, Tel Aviv was a spectacular sight. The pervasive white buildings were of modern design standing in contrast to the emerald green of the Mediterranean. It was as inviting as any resort on the French Riviera.

The good beginning was dispelled with the bus ride into the city. The bus looked and rode like a relic of WWII, perhaps of an even earlier era. Cars and trucks we passed on the highway looked no better. This was a hard scrabble place in spite of its modern architecture.

I was booked into a modest hotel on Ibn Gvirol Street. It was fairly new as was Tel Aviv itself. The city was only founded in 1909. The Hotel Abraham was part of the great master plan that became known as "The White City". Beginning in the 1930's, thousands of buildings were constructed in what was known as the International Style of the early twentieth century. It was a shock to the senses for someone more accustomed to centuries-old European architecture. This International Style was based upon form following function, and devoid of any ornamentation. Personally I found it utilitarian and sterile. Tel Aviv did not match my envisioned idea of the exotic Middle East.

The Abraham was a compact small hotel, no-frills, but with clean small rooms. I selected it because it was home to a number of foreign journalists. Proximity to these professionals was the quickest way to get the lay of the land. Those same journalists selected the Abraham for both its reasonable rates and its well stocked bar.

On my first day I ventured into the Abraham's bar. Inquiring about foreign journalists, the concierge told me that the well known *Times of London* correspondent, Geoffrey Williamson was staying at the hotel. He walked me toward the bar and pointed out a short balding man. Williamson had a face of burst capillaries from years of too much whiskey and chain smoking by the look of the cigarette butts in front of him.

"Mr. Williamson. Might I buy you a drink?" I asked.

Williamson turned around. "And who might you be?" It was said as a mere question with neither warmth nor hostility.

"I'm Dillan Murphy. I'm a correspondent with *Le Monde*."

Williamson shook my hand. "Murphy? What kind of French name is that?"

"Irish obviously. My father was Irish. Hope you don't resent the Irish, especially a French one."

"Don't give a rat's ass about the Irish actually. A violent bunch of fuckers that Britain would be better off without. But I won't hold those intemperate opinions against you, especially since you're a Frenchie."

"I appreciate that. Just been here a day. Thought I could pick your brain to get the lay of land. Buy you a drink?"

Williamson downed the first whiskey and I ordered another

round. After some small talk about my background, he got down to his take on what was going on in Palestine. No fear of balanced journalistic opinion from Williamson.

"It's a bloody fucking mess is what it is. Britain's got its hands full with all these rag heads in the Middle East and India. You add the fucking kikes to the mix and it's hopeless."

"So why don't the British leave Palestine, and for that matter India? The days of empire with colonies has long since past."

"I agree with the letting go of India. Just a poverty ridden place with beggars and no natural resources. That's just His Majesty's Victorian stubbornness. Now as for the Middle East, that's something different. It's all about oil. Palestine doesn't have oil, but British control here gives it a reason for a military presence in the region with the great oil reserves to the east."

Williamson's empty glass prompted me to order him another whisky. The man was a prodigious drinker.

"The Jews have been in Palestine for some time and the British since World War One. What's behind the current conflict?" I asked.

"Simple. The place is being flooded with Jews. Refugees from the Nazi camps and Stalin's persecution of Jews in the Soviet Union. The Arabs see themselves marginalized with an increasing Jewish population driven by immigration. It's also a natural reaction to foreigners, especially foreigners of a different culture. The Arabs wouldn't admit it, but deep down they fear the Jews taking over everything of importance. The Arabs are disorganized and backward. The Jews are organized, educated, and driven."

"Don't think much of either side do you?"

"You're right I don't. I hate this place and all the buggers here. The Arabs don't contribute shit to the world. Did you know they were the most technologically advanced culture in the world a thousand years ago. Then they slid into decline ever since. Now they're just a bunch of tribes scattered across the

Middle East. No technology, no industry, primitive agriculture. Cover up their women, stop and pray all day with rugs they carry around. Don't drink alcohol. Just a bunch of goat-fucking ragheads. Here's to Allah."

Williamson took another pull of his drink.

"And your opinion of the Jews?" I asked.

"Don't get me wrong; what the Nazis did was an abomination. But why should the Arabs have to pay for European excesses? Christian excesses mind you. I agree with the Arabs on that. The rest of the world has a guilty conscience and like I said, the Arabs haven't got their shit together so they can't stop it.

"The Jews make this bullshit case that God promised them this land, therefore they have some special right to be here. Now the Jews lay claim to this pile of sand and rocks as compensation for what happen in Europe. Like everywhere the Jews go, they eventually take over things."

"Tell me this, Williamson; you seem pretty anti-Semitic but I just don't get why the world hates Jews. They've never made war on anyone. They don't control lands. What's your reasoning for this persecution throughout history?" I was baiting him. I had never understood why the Jews stirred such visceral hatred. I was interested in the view of an avowed anti-Semite.

"The fact is that Jews are parasitic. They worm their way into a society then end up controlling the money by controlling the banking and the commerce. From their wealth they gain political power. If not checked, the Jews eventually control everything."

"Sounds like envy to me," I said. "The Jews are successful so others are envious. Since the Jews act differently, it's easy for others to condemn them as a group. That's why Jews have been forced to live in segregated groups. Even then they seem to excel in business."

Williamson glared at me for a moment. "I see you're one of those that see the Jews as some poor persecuted people unjustly abused by others. Look at history. The Jews have corrupted so-cieties throughout history. That's why they were forced into ghettos in the Middle Ages."

Williamson's diatribe and my arguing continued through a couple more drinks. Among the anti-Semitic and anti-Islamic remarks, I did get a feel for the underlying antagonisms pushing Palestine toward war.

"And you British; what's your take on your government's role here?"

"Typically British. Try to run things in a civilized manner but make a cock-up of it we always do. These blighters here in Pales-tine are not up to it. The Arabs are too stupid and the Jews are too bloody self-righteous. Oil and water.

"The lines of partition separating the Arabs and the Jews is bloody ridiculous, the product of political compromise. Then of course you have Jerusalem. Both sides claim Jerusalem as their holy city. Even the goddamn Christians hold it as a holy place. So you have this narrow corridor from the sea stretching to Jeru-salem that gives access to the Jews to their portion of a divided city. Right now you have a civil war going on. If the British Ar-my leaves then there'll be a regional war. All the surrounding Arab states will come to the aid of the Palestinian Arabs. The Jews will lose Jerusalem and be forced to make a stand on the territory bordering the sea. The British military won't be able to stop it."

"So what do you think will be the outcome?"

"A lot of fucking blood will flow. The Jews won't give up. The United Nations won't let the Jews be annihilated. So the British Army will eventually be called on to re-establish order. I might venture to speculate that His Majesty's Government is planning on that scenario. We'll let these blighters sort it out by killing each other, and then we'll take charge again. There'll be a new set of boundaries between the Arabs and the Jews. The Arabs will kick the Jews out of Jerusalem which will settle that major source of contention. The British will retain a presence here indefinitely which will serve our strategic objectives nice-ly."

It was an interesting theory worthy of Machiavelli. If that was to be the future, my guess would be it would result from some sequence of events rather than political design.

After listening to Williamson, I determined that I would start working the Jewish side first. At least they were more organized. The Arabs were more fractionalized, and if there was to be war, the real players were the surrounding Arab states of Egypt, Sy-ria, Iraq, Lebanon, and the British puppet state of Transjordan. That would be a tougher slog to dig out the kind of pieces my editor wanted.

"I'd like to interview someone in authority in the Haganah. That's the Jews unofficial military arm isn't it?"

"Right. At least one of them. The main one. It'll be tough to get to anyone high up in the Haganah. Secretive bunch for un-derstandable reasons. Ever since the bombing of the King David Hotel a couple of years ago, the British have been wary of the Haganah. The Haganah claims the attack was perpetrated by a group of terrorists calling themselves the Irgun. For my opinion, that was a convenient excuse. All the fucking Jews are organized together."

"Just the same, how do you suggest I go about trying to get some interviews?"

"Good luck. None of us have gotten very far. You'll have to start with the *Bitch*. Her name is Julienne Bontoux. Information officer for the Haganah. Got to go through her. Arrogant bitch with a sharp tongue. Usually information officers what to culti-vate the Press. Not her. Information is limited, usually just Jew-ish propaganda. The fuckers talk like they have a real army."

"Got to start somewhere. So where do I find this Julienne Bontoux?" I asked, confident I would be more successful than someone with Williamson's attitude.

Williamson gave me an address. "Could be you might have better success than I've had."

"Why's that?"

"Because she's French like you."

I departed the bar and left a particularly drunk Geoffrey Williamson well after dark. I pleaded too much alcohol. Actually I needed dinner and an excuse to get away from Williamson. Tomorrow I'd contact Mademoiselle Bontoux and begin to sort out what was going on in Palestine, at least from the Jewish perspective.

CHAPTER 37

From *Time Travels* by Dillan Murphy
TEL AVIV, PALESTINE – 1948

Even though this was the desert and on the Mediterranean, it was still cold. January might normally be close to 20 degrees Celsius as a high, but this day was nowhere near that warm.

The office where I was to meet Mlle. Bontoux of the Haganah would have been just a nondescript shop front on a Tel Aviv side street had it not been for the barricades and sandbags. Three armed men with Sten machine guns stood guard. Their civilian dress and choice of weapons was a vivid reminder of my days with the French Resistance during the War.

Once my press credentials were checked, I was given a thorough pat-down for weapons before being allowed to enter the building.

The office was a small cramped affair. Two women sat at a long table scattered with papers and four telephones. There were no file cabinets. Obviously this was not a headquarters. Understandably with the mounting tensions with the British Army, Haganah operations would be secret.

The two women wore pseudo-uniforms of kaki shirts and dark trousers. They were young, mid-twenties, with their hair pulled back in a utilitarian style. Neither wore any makeup. These were Jewish soldiers.

One woman asked something in what I assumed was Hebrew.

"Perhaps you speak English or French?" I asked.

She responded in English, "Yes?"

"I am Dillan Murphy, correspondent for the French newspaper *Le Monde*. I'm new here to Palestine. I wonder if I might have a few moments with Miss Julienne Bontoux? I understand she is the Information Officer."

"Do you have an appointment?"

"No. But I promise to be brief."

The woman glared at me and then got up without saying a word and went through a door into a rear office. Within a few moments she returned and ushered me into the office.

Seated at a desk was another young woman. She was dressed in the same style as the other two but there the similarity ended. She was attractive, the other two were plain. Her naturally curly hair was pulled back into a bun. There was clearly a command in her bearing although she was probably not yet thirty. She wore lipstick. Perhaps a touch of vanity in this soldier?

After introductions she curtly asked, "What can I do for you, Mr. Murphy?"

"I just arrived in Palestine. My assignment is to interview as many people as possible to give our readers a sense of what is going on here. I hoped you could perhaps arrange some interviews with Haganah officials."

She glared at me for a moment before saying, "That's pretty arrogant on your part, Mr. Murphy. *Get a sense of what is going on here?* Think you'll be able to do that in a couple of days? Explain the whole thing in a couple of newspaper articles. Make the fucking French people understand? Make the French perhaps less anti-Semitic?"

"I thought your job as Information Officer would be to make sure the Jews got the best possible press. Seems you're more like the guard to make sure there's no information. I guess they were right about you."

"Which is what?" she asked.

"They call you the *Bitch*."

My remark caused only a slight reaction, maybe a quick hint of a grin.

"And who's *they*?"

"The foreign press corps. Not smart to wage war against the international press. They're not the enemy of the Jews."

"Whatever. The answer is still no regarding interviews. Now if you'll excuse me."

Not a good start on this assignment. Thirty years ago in New York I was much better at manipulating sources. Picking a fight was foolish and unproductive. Besides that, I really didn't want to offend this interesting woman.

"I'm sorry. I put that rather badly. I'm really just looking for some help, Miss Bontoux. Perhaps I should address you as Mademoiselle Bontoux? By your accent you are clearly French speaking," I said in French.

"As you prefer," she replied in French with a hint of surprise.

"I'm not sure I understand your anger at the French. You are French are you not?"

"Obviously I was once French. But that is in the past," she said switching back to English. "My own countrymen condemned my family simply because we were Jews. Not even practicing Jews, but Jews nevertheless. Both my parents died in Nazi concentration camps. I fought in the Resistance but was captured by the Germans. I too spent time in a concentration camp. However, back to your request, I'm sorry but ...."

"You were in the Maquis? Where?"

"I was from Lyon. Our unit operated within the city."

"I am also French even though I was born in America. I too suffered a great personal loss. My wife was murdered by the Vichy Milice. Like you, I fought with the Maquis just further to the south in Provence. I was with Captain Jacques Berry. Perhaps you heard of his Maquis unit?"

Bontoux was stunned for a moment. "Yes. We knew of Captain Berry's group. You were known as assassins. My god, with your name, *Murphy* .... were you the one they called the *Irishman*? The one who killed so many?"

I nodded.

She said nothing for several moments, just biting on her lower lip. Her demeanor softened. "Well. Maybe that changes things. I'll see what I can arrange, but I can make no promises. I assume you'll also be interviewing Arabs and the British as well?"

"Of course. My job is to try to explain the issues, not draw conclusions or take sides. But I'll tell you this; from the basics I've learned, Palestine is not only a complicated mix of circumstances but there are legitimate arguments from both the Jewish and Arab perspectives. There might never be a resolution to the differences."

"I cannot agree. Jews have a clear right to exist and defend ourselves. The world has driven us back here. This was our original homeland. We shall not leave again. The Arabs of course have rights, but not the right to drive us out or kill us. But I will still see what I can do to get you some interviews. You may return tomorrow afternoon. I shall advise you then if I have been successful in your request."

She rose from her chair and offered her hand. I took her hand and held eye and hand contact long enough that she broke away when it became uncomfortable. I felt an attraction that I had not experienced for many years. Perhaps she did as well? It did seem that I was unusually successful in view of her reputation.

I returned the following afternoon.

"Good news, Monsieur Murphy. Surprisingly Commander Shaltiel himself has agreed to give you a brief amount of time. This is very rare. I believe you were granted this time because of your wartime exploits in the Resistance. You see, although David Shaltiel is originally from Germany, he got his military training in the French Foreign Legion. For security reasons, you will meet me here tomorrow at one o'clock. From here we will drive to the place of the meeting."

"That is good news. That is even more than I expected. I thank you for your personal efforts."

"I believe it was the French connection that the Commander found intriguing," she said.

"I'm sure it was your good word that did it. There's something else I'd like to ask. I can't stop thinking about the coincidence of both of us having fought with the Maquis and then meeting here in Tel Aviv. I would like to hear more of your wartime experiences. Might I be so bold as to ask you to dinner?"

Bontoux recoiled as if slapped. "I'm sorry, that would be out of the question."

"I apologize. Strictly professional of course, but I apologize if that might be personally awkward."

More composed and to my surprise, she said, "What if I was married?"

"Well I didn't think you were married. No ring."

She seemed a little flustered. Flirting was alien to her. "At any rate, I avoid professional entanglements."

"It's just dinner and conversation, Mlle. Bontoux. Those bad times during the War were not that long ago. I don't know about you, but I still have a lot of emotional scars. Having such an unusual shared experience just seemed like a way to …. perhaps just help deal with those difficult memories. But I understand. I will see you here tomorrow then."

I turned to leave, but she surprised me again by saying,

"Wait. Perhaps I was too hasty. I've not been out to dinner in a long time. It should be the season to celebrate. I would like to have dinner. What about tomorrow after we return from your interview with the Commander?"

"That would be excellent. You decide where. Somewhere very good. I have an expense account."

I was delighted she accepted. Maybe I was reading too much into her acceptance. I would need to make sure she understood this was personal, not a way to exploit a source. It had been some time since I was emotionally attracted to a woman. For that matter, it had been some time since I cared how a woman felt about me. Maybe the wounds were healing. The woman Williamson called the *Bitch,* clearly had another side.

The following afternoon Julienne Bontoux herself drove me to a synagogue in a twenty year old black Mercedes Benz sedan with a bad second gear. Everything here in Palestine appeared second hand or makeshift. My guess was that the Jewish army, the Haganah, was probably makeshift as well.

Bontoux told me that I was to meet David Shaltiel in the office of the senior rabbi. She would wait for me in the car.

Shaltiel gave me an hour. It was a captivating hour. He briefly chronicled his life. As remarkable as that life had been, I concluded that the Jewish cause in Palestine was even more fragile than I had imagined. If the military experience of the commander of your army extended only to the rank of sergeant in the French Foreign Legion, then what must constitute the caliber of the army itself?

When I returned to the car, Julienne Bontoux asked just a few questions about the interview saying I could tell her more over dinner. She dropped me at my hotel saying she had work to complete and she would come by the hotel at seven o'clock.

It felt like this would be a real date. I spent the rest of the afternoon writing an article I would wire to Paris the next day about my interview with the commander of the Haganah.

Around six I shaved and put on a clean shirt. Then I headed to the bar for a whisky before Julienne arrived. Unfortunately, Geoffrey Williamson was at the bar. He saw me before I could retreat.

"Murphy. Join me for a drink."

Reluctantly I sat down on the bar stool next to him.

"How'd you make out with the wicked witch of the Haganah?"

"Fine actually. Don't find her that off-putting as you apparently do. Helpful actually."

"Well that's bloody fucking interesting. Bloody fucking irritating it is too. You're here one day and she's *helpful*. Maybe she's just hot for you. For the rest of us it's shit all. Fucking bitch I say."

"Enough." I put my hand firmly on his shoulder. "Listen, Williamson, because I'm only going to tell you this once. Call her a bitch around me again and you'll find yourself looking up from the floor. Understood?"

"Who the fuck do you ...."

My grip tightened on his shoulder with sufficient pressure to cut him off mid-sentence. "Thanks for the drink." I took a seat in the hotel lobby.

Julienne Bontoux walked into the lobby a moment later. I was a little dismayed to see she was still dressed as she was earlier, hoping for something more feminine. I got up and walked over to meet her. Looking over my back, I was amused to see Williamson coughing as he swallowed his drink wrong after seeing the *Bitch* greet me.

"You have already made my evening, Mlle. Bontoux. I assume you know of a British reporter named Williamson?"

"Of course. Miserable excuse for a journalist. A total asshole."

"Well put. I would agree. Doesn't think much of you either. At any rate he just choked on his drink after seeing you leave with me."

Getting into the car, she said, "I thought we might try a res-taurant that I heard was very good. It's French. Might be pricey. I've never been. Shall we chance it?"

"By all means. Who recommended it?"

"Well, as I said, I do not dine out often, at least at nice restau-rants. So I called a British information officer I know and asked him where senior British officers might dine. Since the British are the only people that have money here, that's the best source of recommendation."

The restaurant was a delight. The rear was open to the Medi-terranean. They had a decent wine list, heavy on Bordeaux fa-vored by the British and me as well.

"Your interview with David Shaltiel went well?"

"Oh yes. Your commander is a remarkable man. We ex-changed war stories. He talked of the justifications for the Jewish struggle here. Not any argument that I haven't already heard. Coming from him though it gave me a sense of the determina-tion of the Jewish community in Palestine. More than determina-tion. It's the very fabric of the Jewish existence here that says we might die, but we will not be driven from this place. He makes one feel that you Jews will fight to the death, even to the death of your women and children."

"The Commander has that sort of impact on people. His own story is like so many of us. He probably did not tell you that he was tortured by the Gestapo after being captured in 1936. He was trying to smuggle currency out of Germany to buy arms for Palestinian Jews. I was told he was horribly tortured in over twenty different Gestapo headquarters for weeks. After that, he was sent to Dachau. That's where he gained his spiritual strength. That's where he became a leader under impossible conditions. After that, you can see that no matter how difficult our ambitions are in Palestine, nothing compares to the horrors of the Nazi camps."

"You mentioned his spiritual strength. From our brief meeting, I got the impression that David Shaltiel is not very religious."

Julienne Bontoux smiled broadly. "That's an understatement. I meant spiritual in a broader, philosophical sense. David Shaltiel is not religious at all. As I understand it, he's from a rigorously orthodox Sephardic family. At an early age, he rebelled against the faith of his parents. You should hear him when he is angered by some religious position. Your meeting was as close as he would get to a rabbi or synagogue. That is a misconception when people refer to Jews, here or anywhere. I'm a perfect example."

"You're saying you're not religious either, but you would still call yourself a Jew?"

They were interrupted as the wine arrived. The waiter made a show of decanting the 1929 Latour.

Bontoux said, "I do not know Bordeaux all that well but I do know that Latour is a famous label. This must be expensive."

"Well I like good wine. Latour is known as a first growth Bordeaux, meaning one of the historical best. The newspaper indulges my expense account."

After taking a sip she said, "Oh my. This is magnificent wine, Monsieur Murphy."

"Yes it is," I said after taking a sip myself. "I wonder if you would consent to calling me Dillan. Monsieur Murphy sounds like my father."

Bontoux smiled then took a more serious look for a moment. Clearly she was gauging the implications. "Yes. Dillan does sound more comfortable. And I am Julienne. Now where were we?"

"The Jews and religion. You were going to explain."

"What religion are you, Dillan?"

"Ah, well, I'm not religious either. Never been to church actually."

"Neither have I. My parents were not religious, and neither were their parents. Yet we are still called Jews. Somewhere back in your family history, there was an identification with some religion. Go back far enough and everyone had to declare even if you did not believe. It was a social imperative."

"I guess I'd be considered Roman Catholic by that association."

"See what I mean. So you're Catholic and I'm Jewish, yet neither of us is remotely religious. It's a way of culturally labeling people. If that label is *Jew*, then other cultures will persecute you."

"That certainly seems to be the case throughout history. Why do you think that is, Julienne?"

"I don't know really. The Jews of every country have usually been successful. But that may have been by force of necessity. My theory is that the stereotypical Jewish attributes are evolutionary. You see if Jews were forced to live in segregated communities, ghettos, and prohibited from things like the medieval guilds, then they had to improvise. In these closed communities they were forced to be creative. So they became merchants and bankers since they couldn't be craftsmen and farmers. They invented or developed services other communities needed. When they became successful, those other communities resented that success."

"Ok. That's an explanation for success in business, but what about other endeavors where there seems to be a disproportionate number of Jews; like science, medicine, law? Jews are from all over the world. It can't be genetic," I said.

"I would agree. What exactly makes someone a Jew? It just seems to be a cultural identification. The only ones with long noses are the Slavs. My theory is simply that being forced to live under difficult conditions, those limited avenues open to Jews are culturally exploited. All those endeavors that are heavily populated with Jews are education intensive. Every Jewish household places an extraordinary emphasis on education."

"So you're saying that Jews as a group seem to be dispropor-
tionately more successful in commerce and intellectual pursuits
out of historical circumstances? That seems a little too simplistic.
Interesting hypothesis though."

"How do you explain it then?" she said.

"Don't think I have a theory. Never thought about it really.
Jews have certainly suffered unreasonable persecution over the
centuries. But enough of history. Tell me about yourself. What
did you do before the war?"

"Medical school. I also play classical violin."

"And your parents?"

"My father was a physician. My mother taught literature at a
university."

"Tell me this; since you're not Jewish in terms of religious
faith, do you resent being classified a Jew? It has cost you so
much."

"Yes. At least I did. My bad luck. Being Jewish caused my
family to be killed and for my own suffering at the hands of the
Nazis. So being considered Jewish is a reason to be angry. Angry
at the world. Angry at other Jews even. But I am stuck with who
I am. This new state we fight for is the last refuge. Never again
will we be persecuted and scattered."

"But you may be destroyed," I said.

"Perhaps."

"You said before that you were in a Nazi concentration
camp. How did you manage to survive?"

"That is something I do not talk about."

"I'm sorry. I didn't mean to be inquisitive."

"Of course you did. You're a reporter. But I forgive you." She
smiled to make sure that I was not too wounded. "Let's order
dinner."

CHAPTER 38

PROVENCE, FRANCE – 2009

"And does this Jewish woman become a lover?" Allison asked.

"You are incorrigible, my dear. Your prurient interests need to be curtailed." Elliot said, but was smiling.

"Nonsense. I'm a literary agent. I know what sells. Based on what I skimmed so far in the manuscript, you've still made it read more like a history book."

"I disagree. It reads more like a historical novel."

"Maybe, but one without much sex. Your novels have major romances and a fair amount of sex so why not this work? Perhaps it's easier to write fiction than write about your own romances?"

"No. Just artistic license to frame the work more as a witness to history, not a memoir."

"Look, Elliot. Your story takes you through the death of your wife then the horrors of the war years. Then you struggle to regain your balance. You write about your depression, your anger. Relationships were difficult. In your own words you were spiraling downward. Now this Jewish woman comes along. Even your first words about meeting her suggest a romantic attraction. So was she a lover?"

"Yes. Briefly. I'll relate the whole story to you, but first let's get some lunch. We'll go into the village to get the necessary items."

"Ok. You can tell me about Mlle. Bontoux on the way.

"No. We shall take a break from talking business and enjoy ourselves. That is the Provencal way. Work is secondary to the pleasures of life."

In the village, Elliot went to the butcher shop which also had a good selection of fresh seafood. Elliot greeted the butcher and introduced Allison. The butcher then proceeded into a long commentary over the merits of each of his selections. This was not New York style market shopping.

After twenty minutes in the butcher shop, they set out down the street to the green grocer. The same ritual took another fifteen minutes. On to the bakery, where Elliot introduced Allison to the owner. He was delighted to try his limited English with the pretty American. The ritual concluded with the purchase of two baguettes.

"You French spend more time buying food then cooking it. And you do this most every day," Allison remarked.

"But it's part of the enjoyment of food. Part of the ritual. The French are fussy about the quality of their food. And since ninety percent of the taste of the food is the quality of the ingredients, selection is as important as the preparation. I quite enjoy the whole process actually."

Lunch was simple and quickly prepared. A green salad with tomatoes and crumbled Roquefort cheese was followed by scallops sautéed in butter. The day was sunny and warm enough to eat outside. Elliot served a Côte de Beaune appellation Burgundy wine.

"Burgundy's are lighter in body with less tannins than Bordeaux. Pinot noir grape, more difficult to grow. But the joy of Burgundy is in its unique complexity," Elliot said. "It's perfect for foods where you do not want the wine to overpower the food. I often substitute it for foods typically paired with white wines."

Allison took a sip and savored it on her palate. "I see what you mean about complex tastes. But you're still a wine snob, Elliot."

"I prefer the label of cultured country gentleman."

"That too. But this is so incongruous. You're smiling, enjoying yourself yet you're dying of cancer. You've had this unimaginably long life that's now coming to a close. You must be the oldest person living."

"Oh I wouldn't be so sure about that. There's no reason to think that I'm singularly unique."

"If there were others there would be some written references, or legends."

"There are. There are Biblical references like the patriarch Methuselah in the Book of Genesis."

"That's fairy tale or metaphorical stuff. Nobody takes those references as actually applying to real people."

"My point is there is no reason to believe I am unique and every reason to believe I am not. Rare, even exceedingly rare, but probably not unique. Statistics favor that there is other intelligent life in the Universe, but equally favors we will probably never encounter it."

"But it just shouldn't end like this for you."

"You're looking at it only from what you see as negatives."

"And dying of cancer isn't a goddamn negative?"

"I grant you that dying of cancer would be no one's preferred way to go. Ultimately it's just a detail though. On the larger scale of what my life has been, turn your perspective to a different angle. I've lived perhaps longer than anyone, well beyond a century. Isn't it time for this to end? The idea of no perspective when that end might be has often been a torment. I hope people see that in my story.

"Imagine having to hide such a secret from everyone around you. Imagine how the passing of time is like the ticking of a bomb that will destroy those you love. Imagine loving someone with the absolute knowledge you will outlive them. Watching them age as you stay the same. The subtle differences becoming ever more pronounced. The ultimate questioning. The impossible truth.

"That's why I wrote the book, Allison. That's why I'm sharing this with you. Not only to get it published but for the first time to be able to share with another person what my life has meant. You're the closest I have to family, Allison."

Tears ran down Allison's cheeks. Once back in control, she said, "I'm sorry to be so emotional. It's just so damn hard to understand all this, Elliot. And it hurts to know you're dying. You're a friend not just a client. Oh, hell. So get back to your story. Make me feel good by telling me that Mlle. Bontoux turned your life around."

"What Julienne Bontoux did do was bring me back from a dark place. For whatever reason, we deeply connected."

"So tell me about Julienne Bontoux."

"Very well. I'll tell you about my brief romance with Julienne."

"Oh no. Brief? Did this end badly too? Not another tragedy I hope."

"Life is full of losses. With my longevity I have experienced more than my share of losing those close to me. But it's those relationships that shape one's life. Without them there would be no tragedies but neither would there be any real happiness. Julienne Bontoux made me realize that. I hope I have been able to impart that view of my life in *Time Travels*. Even though our time together was short, Julienne Bontoux resurrected me. Because of her, the remainder of my life has had value.

CHAPTER 39

From *Time Travels* by Dillan Murphy
TEL AVIV, PALESTINE – 1948

That first dinner date with Julienne Bontoux was unusual. I was the reporter yet I found myself answering her questions, mostly about my war experiences. She was guarded about her own past. I thought it was perhaps a way to deflect my questions but after a time I could see she was genuinely interested in my past, but equally not willing to open up about her own history.

We parted that evening with a chaste handshake but a promise of another dinner two days hence. It was my first pursuit of a relationship of any meaning since Dominique's death. It had only been a few years but so much had happened in those years. I found myself excited about seeing Julienne again.

Our second date was different. First of all, Julienne dressed differently. Not Parisian chic but what passed for Palestinian chic. After all she was a Jewish soldier. But an ankle-length dark skirt, heels, and a white blouse, with her carefully applied make-up made a striking impression. Her naturally curly hair was worn down with some attention to style.

Julienne had selected a different restaurant. This one was not populated by transient foreigners. It was Russian, complete with its name spelled in Cyrillic letters. It was modestly furnished, a place for eating and drinking not show. The clientele was Jewish, ethnically Russian.

Julienne had been here before. She gave me a brief tour of the menu which was in five languages. We started off with chilled vodka.

While my war experiences were difficult, Julienne's must have been markedly more harrowing with her previous reference to being in a concentration camp.

"I have told you everything and you have told me nothing," I said. "I had seen war before. This must have been worse for you. Will you tell me what happened?"

Julienne looked at me for a moment and then nodded. "You are right. But your exploits in the Resistance were so much more interesting."

"No, Julienne. I want to hear about how you fought as well, but tell me first what happened to your family. How did they die?"

She chewed on her lip a couple of times.

"We lived in Lyon. It was 1943. As Jews, we eventually had to register as such with the Gestapo. We wore the armbands with the Star of David. My father was a physician, my mother a professor at the university. I was in graduate school studying medicine. My younger brother was in his first year as an undergraduate student. Ours was a cultured life with privilege. All that ended with the German occupation of the Free Zone."

"After the German occupation I was forced to leave the university because I was Jewish. So were my mother and brother. Soon after that, my father was prohibited from practicing medicine to non-Jews.

"The family adapted by serving the Jewish community in Lyon. My father's services were in even greater demand with only a couple of other Jewish doctors to serve the Jewish community. My mother taught Jewish students in a makeshift school. I'm afraid my brother and I were an added burden. We were both angry and hostile."

"Understandably. All French people hated the German invaders."

"We of course hated the Germans. But I hated the Jews too. I wasn't a Jew. I didn't go to synagogue. I had no education whatsoever in Judaism, no religious feelings. Neither did my parents. So why were we being identified as a Jews and our lives being destroyed?

"I reluctantly helped my father at his clinic. It was for my father, not for the Jews. Since we were not practicing Jews, my friends and my parents friends were mostly non-Jews. Once of course you wore the armband of a Jew, you had no non-Jewish friends. I resisted making Jewish friends out of spite.

"One night I was away from home. I was a violinist. I think I told you that before. I studied music for a couple of years before turning to medicine. Music was my passion and a great solace during those terrible times. Anyway, I was playing with my chamber music group to a small gathering. Our audiences had dwindled with the German occupation.

"When I returned home, the front door was open. My parents and brother were gone. There was an overturned table and lamp in the living room, but no other evidence of a disturbance.

"A neighbor came to the open doorway. We were not close but she was kind enough to tell me what happened. She simply said that the Gestapo had taken my parents and brother. My brother struggled she said. The men in the black leather coats beat him and dragged him away. She said my parents left with each carrying a suitcase as if for a trip.

"Deported to a German concentration camp?"

"Extermination camp. Auschwitz. Well to the East, in Poland. Actually known as Auschwitz-Birkenau. After the War I learned that my parents died in the gas chambers. My brother's fate I never learned. He probably died under the forced labor brutality or disease."

Death by murder is always hideous. But death in the Nazi camps was a medieval horror. The endless photographic records and testimony of witnesses at the Nuremberg trials recounted human cruelty on a scale never before documented. My hardships and losses during the War paled in comparison.

"I covered the War Crimes trial of the Nazi leadership in Nuremberg over a year ago. The evidence presented was almost beyond comprehension. Hard to believe evil existed on such a collective scale," I said.

"While you were listening to the crimes of the Nazis, I was in yet another camp. A British camp now. A displaced persons camp. Full of former concentration camp inmates. The food was better but it was still confinement behind barbed wire."

"This was after you were in a Nazi camp?"

"Yes. Bergen-Belsen. I was sent there by the Germans in late 1944 after our Maquis group was captured. The British used the same site as the Nazi concentration camp after they liberated us. The British burned the barracks to try to control the typhus, but they kept the barbed wire fences. I never understood why as victims it was still necessary to confine us behind wire."

"I know of Bergen-Belsen from the war crimes trials. So many died there of disease," I said.

"Yes. Thousands. Mostly from typhus. There was severe overcrowding, not enough food, no medicine, and no sanitation. Thousands died even after the camp was liberated. The Nazis intended for all those there to die."

"But you survived. How did you manage that? Your medical training?"

Julienne Bontoux noticeably struggled with her emotions. She poured another vodka and belted it back in the Russian style.

"I survived because the Boche liked music. There were a number of us that performed several times a week for the pleasure of the camp commandant and his officers. The commandant was named Josef Kramer. He became known as the *Beast of Belsen* for his brutality and all the death he caused. His previous assignment had been at Birkenau. All of that got him convicted of war crimes and hanged.

"Kramer was a Nazi pig but he liked music. When we played for the SS officers we were fed first. Without that extra food, I would have died. As it was, I was there only five months and still weighed only 44 kilos when the British liberated the camp in April, 1945."

"You're saying the British converted this same facility into a displaced persons camp housing the former inmates?"

"That's right. I spent almost another year there. The Jews wanted to go to Palestine. There was talk of a Jewish state. For most of us, there was nothing to return to of their former homes. But the British were not allowing any mass immigration to Palestine. That's why they kept us locked up."

"Did you want to come here to Palestine? Being French you could have returned home," I asked.

"Let's have some dinner and I will tell you how I came here."

We dined on braised chicken in prune sauce and a strange assortment of accompanying ethnic Russian dishes. The food was interspersed with periodic shots of vodka.

"You drink vodka like a Russian."

"Learned that from some Russian fellow inmates at Bergen-Belsen. Smuggled vodka. The British minders didn't want to allow alcohol but we managed around them. The camp was still run like a prison."

"So you're still at Bergen-Belsen. How was it that you got to Palestine? The British have been pretty effective restricting Jewish immigration to Palestine? I recall that incident with the ship called the *Exodus* a few months ago."

"The British sent those refugees back to Europe. People like me from Hitler's concentration camps. After all we suffered, we were denied a place to live."

"Wait a minute. Go back. Tell me why you even wanted to come here. You didn't even identify yourself as Jewish."

"Hard to say what I identify myself as. I am French by birth but I can never live in France again. To the French I am a Jew. Doesn't matter that I am French as well. So I can be a Jew. Being a Jew is a state of being more than a religion. I had few options. Circumstances often determine much of one's destiny.

"The British have limited Jewish immigration to Palestine for their own political reasons. The British also harbor a lot of anti-Semitic feelings. They want to control things. They still think in terms of empire. I hate the arrogant bastards. The sooner we drive them out of Palestine the better.

"Europe is still full of Jewish survivors of the Nazi camps with no place to go other than Palestine. Whole communities were destroyed in the Holocaust. No homes or possessions remained. Our non-Jewish neighbors had turned against us. I became Jewish because I was nothing else."

"Were you treated well by the British?"

"To the extent we were properly fed and received medical treatment. But we were still confined. Not allowed to go to British controlled Palestine. Bergen-Belsen is still full of thousands of Jews that want to come to Palestine. There are other displaced persons camps all over Europe. These people have no countries to return to."

"So how did you manage to get here?"

"The Haganah sent agents into Bergen-Belsen. They actually conducted training clandestinely to prepare some of us to come to Palestine to fight. Periodically they smuggled people out. I was selected early on because of my experience in the Resistance. The Haganah provided false papers to get us into Palestine. My papers were those of a Red Cross worker. Since I spoke French it was easy."

"Why did that make it easier?"

"First of all, my papers didn't make me an immigrant. Secondly, most Jews trying to get here were from Eastern Europe, Poland, Russia, Ukraine. So I fit the part of a French Red Cross worker."

"What did you do in the Resistance? In fact how did you even connect with them after the Gestapo took your family?"

"I grabbed some clothes and left our apartment immediately. I was in shock with the loss of my family. We had heard the rumors about these German relocation camps being terrible places at best, people dying at worse. With how Jews were treated in occupied France, it was easy to believe these dire rumors. I was determined not to be taken."

Enough of the vodka, I ordered coffees and some Port wine. Julienne ordered some sort of ethnic sweet cake for dessert. Absorbed in her story, she resumed before we had even finished eating.

"The only person I could think to ask for help was a former fellow student in medical school. Jules Guignard. An intense young man. He had a crush on me but I had no romantic feelings toward him. He was very left leaning in his politics, maybe even a Communist. For some reason I still had his address.

"Anyway, I went to his apartment. He lived with his parents too. There was a slight scene since I still was wearing my armband identifying me as a Jew, so we left hurriedly. The short version is that Jules knew someone that knew someone which eventually led me to a Maquis cell operating in Lyon. These people were all committed Communists. Only one other was a Jew."

"What sort of things did your group do?" I asked.

"Blew up things mostly. Passed information on to the Allies. We had a wireless radio provided by a British spy. That was my job. I was the communications person. I learned ciphers. I passed information between groups. Had several sets of false papers when I moved about. Real spy stuff. I spoke some English which helped. I also looked after the medical needs of the group."

"What happened?"

"I never found out how the Gestapo rounded up our entire group. One by one. They had all of our names, knew where to find us. Someone within our group obviously gave them the information. Someone was captured then tortured I assumed. Could have been some other reason for betrayal. Doesn't matter really. I was lucky again though."

"What do you mean *lucky*? You were captured by the Gestapo and sent to a concentration camp. How's that lucky?"

"I was lucky not to have been tortured. At least not too badly. I was beaten, but at least with just fists. Others were beaten with rubber hoses to inflict terrible bruising. Worse were the pipes to break bones. Finger nails were pulled out. They burned some. So many fell prey to the head of the Gestapo in Lyon, a psychopath named Klaus Barbie. You didn't survive his personal interrogations.

"So yes I was lucky. Lucky to have survived where a good many did not. I was beaten shortly after my arrest. Before it was my turn to be interrogated, the entire lot of us was shipped out to Bergen-Belsen. Being lucky was therefore relative."

I was numbed by listening to her tell of her wartime ordeals. Hearing Julienne relate the brutality she suffered and witnessed penetrated more deeply than listening to the witnesses testifying at Nuremberg.

That night we made love for the first time. It was un-expected, at least on my part. I was still emotionally off balance hearing of Julienne's ordeal under the Nazis. To my delight she simply said she wanted to be with me that night.

After retrieving my room key at the front desk, I met Julienne at the back delivery door of the hotel. She wanted to avoid being seen by any of the other reports probably in the bar.

Once in my room, we desperately wanted each other.

Julienne undressed and stood in front of me. Perhaps she wanted the reassurance that she was sexually desirable. She was.

"I haven't been with a man since .... since .... I don't even remember."

CHAPTER 40

From *Time Travels* by Dillan Murphy
TEL AVIV, PALESTINE – 1948

Portraying our intimacy might seem to run counter to Julienne Bontoux's reputation as the Haganah *bitch*. For those first several weeks together in early 1948 we were lovers, both vulnerable from the events of the recent past. But the other side of Julienne was equally true. We connected and fell in love so she was different with me. To others she was every bit the tough face of the Haganah. Like others in the Haganah, she saw the Palestinian Jews standing against the world. Everyone else was viewed with hostility – the Arab Palestinians, the surrounding Arab states, and of course the British. Julienne carried a real chip on her shoulder.

Even our romance fell prey to politics during these last months of the British Mandate in Palestine. As I learned more and heard from a range of other voices in Palestine, Julienne and I frequently fell into heated arguments. She accused me of naivety at best, anti-Jewish views at worse. I accused her of being a fanatic, blinded to seeing countering views, rejecting logic. Sometimes we reconciled by making love, other times we parted with harsh words.

Our worse argument came in April. We had been together for over three months. Not living together but seeing each other several times a week. Through Julienne, I connected with a range of those influential in the Jewish community and its unofficial government. Discussions after my interviews with Palestinian Arabs and the British were often the catalyst for disagreements. Julienne could not be objective on any view counter to establishing a Jewish state.

The unofficial Jewish government had their unofficial army the Haganah. The Haganah came about in the 1920's to protect Jews in Palestine after the League of Nations gave Great Britain a mandate to govern the region. In the 1930's a more militant Zionist faction split from the Haganah, calling themselves the Irgun.

The Irgun progressively engaged in more violent attacks, particularly directed at the British. In 1946 they bombed the King David Hotel in Tel Aviv. And yet another more virulent splinter group, the Lehi, established itself from the most extreme element of the Irgun. This came about in 1940 when the Irgun suspended attacks against the British at the onset of World War Two. The Lehi wanted no truce from attacking the British. They became more commonly known as the Stern Gang after their founder.

The event in April, 1948 that caused the world to gasp in shock was the massacre of over one hundred Arabs of the village of Deir Yassin. The attack was perpetrated by over one hundred fighters from both the Irgun and the Stern Gang. Woman, children, old men, and even babies were brutally slaughtered. Here were Nazi death camp survivors perpetrating their own version of crimes against defenseless civilians.

Julienne was the first Jew I questioned. "How is the Jewish community going to respond?" I said with some anger.

"It was the act of criminals. Even the Haganah disavows the

acts of the Irgun. The Stern Gang is the worse of the lot. All they know is killing," she said.

"Maybe so, but the world will not parse out their affiliations. They'll only see that Jewish fighters committed a terrible atrocity."

"And the world will not attempt to balance that with the millions of Jews killed by Hitler and Stalin."

"This is not a score card. The Jews make their claim as victims of the greatest act of genocide ever perpetrated. They lose that moral high ground if they're seen to retaliate using the same methods."

"Fuck the world. They'll get over it. They'll accept this was an isolated act of criminals, or they won't. Our fight will still go on."

"The Jews here need the rest of the world's support. You can't ignore that. Can you get me interviews with any top officials?"

"Not likely. This is a sensitive subject."

"That's why the Jews must explain to the world."

"There's a more pressing issue now - Jerusalem. That's why this village was attacked. They were trying to relieve the pressure on the only supply route to Jerusalem."

"So the Haganah is going to shrug this off as part of greater military campaign? This was not collateral damage. It was collective murder."

"What the hell are we supposed to do? The Haganah has no control over the Irgun or Lehi. It even worked actively against them a couple of years ago."

"But now the Haganah needs them? Is that why the Haganah leadership doesn't speak out?"

"Is this you asking or are you just being a reporter?"

"It's me. You people are so assured of your right to this place that you rationalize the end justifying the means."

"You people? Fuck you, Dillan!"

"Yes, you people. You identify yourself as a Jew. You speak for them."

"You still don't understand. The world doesn't understand. We will not be moved from this place. We may die, but we will not again be driven out and scattered. Throughout history we have been the outcasts. We understand what it means to be alone. If the rest of the world turns its back on us, then so be it."

"The Irgun and the Lehi have been bombing and assassinating British soldiers for a long time. I think the Haganah finds that convenient. They disavow involvement yet get the benefit of harassing the British. No wonder the British favor the Arabs over the Jews."

"Get the hell away from me!" Julienne shouted.

We parted angrily that night, not seeing each other for days. Not until Julienne told me a week later that she was going to Jerusalem in one of the supply convoys. That brought me out of my martyr mood of being unfairly wronged. Nothing could be more dangerous than supply convoys trying to get through to Jerusalem.

The partition of Palestine was a last desperate attempt by the United Nations to control the civil war. It was too late and ill-conceived. Partition relegated the Jews to the coastal areas and the Arabs to the east. The source of ignition to this tinderbox was Jerusalem.

Jerusalem was the spiritual wellspring of the three great western religions, Judaism, Islam, and Christianity. In the partition of Palestine, Jerusalem was declared an international city. Geographically, Jerusalem stuck out onto the end of an artificially defined peninsula deep into the Arab sector. Jerusalem became accessible to Jews only by a single road through this narrow corridor. The 60 kilometers from Tel Aviv to Jerusalem were beset with increasing attacks by Arabs on Jewish supply convoys. Jewish Jerusalem was being straggled. The British made no effort to assist the besieged Jews of Jerusalem.

At best, they only kept the Arabs and Jews apart. War was coming to Palestine and Jerusalem would be the strategic objective.

The ever increasing conflict in Palestine was a mix of an unusually broad cast of antagonists. The ambitions were so complex and layered that no objective person could see any peaceful resolution. Conflict had been escalating for years. It could only get worse. The Jews best hope was the disunity of the Arabs arrayed against them.

The populist Grand Mufti of Jerusalem, the leader of the Palestinian Arabs, was not supported by the surrounding states of Egypt, Syria, Iraq, Lebanon, and Transjordan. All these state players had their own competing interests in driving the Jews out of Palestine. With the exception of the British trained Arab Legion from Transjordan, the military capabilities of the other Arab states were relatively poor. Their only advantage was overwhelming numbers compared to the Jews.

Julienne had come to my hotel early in the morning. We had not spoken for days. I was surprised and overjoyed to see her. I realized how much she meant to me.

She walked into my room and closed the door. "I'm sorry we fought, Dillan. I care for you."

I put my arms around her and kissed her, flooded with the joy of having her back. She responded but then gently pushed me back.

"I came here to tell you that I'm going to Jerusalem, Dillan. I am needed there."

Her pronouncement stunned me. Nothing could be more dangerous. Convoys attempting to supply food and medicine via the only road to Jerusalem came under regular attack from Arab irregular military forces.

"Why? Why do you have to go?"

"Because I was asked. They need medical help in Jerusalem. There are only a handful of doctors for a hundred thousand

Jews. People are suffering with the shortages. Now there are casualties from the constant fighting."

I knew I could not dissuade her. Not my place to be selfish either.

"I think it's a bad idea, but I understand. I'll go with you then, Julienne."

"Dillan, this is dangerous. This is my cause not yours."

"You're my cause. I couldn't bear staying behind and worrying about you. Not sure I could even communicate with you in Jerusalem. What would you have me do? Besides, I'm a reporter. I should report on what is happening in Jerusalem."

She nodded her understanding. "I love you, Dillan. I've missed you. Make love to me right now."

I did. Fearing the loss of the other, we were both tender and desperate. Tears flowed as we held each other tightly.

"We leave tonight after dark," Julienne said an hour after she arrived. "I shall pick you up here at nine o'clock. Take only bare essentials. There is no room for luggage."

I put a clean shirt and underwear in a shoulder bag along with a toothbrush, razor, and a bottle of Scotch. My portable typewriter was equipped with a shoulder strap. I might be stranded in Jerusalem for a time and didn't want to rely on making handwritten notes with my terrible hand writing.

On the top of the satchel contents I placed my old .45 and two spare clips. Once again I ignored the rule of going unarmed as a non-combatant. That was not realistic. Geneva Convention protocols did not prevail in the heat of a firefight. I might put myself in harm's way but I would not die like a sheep.

That evening I stood outside the hotel waiting for Julienne. Promptly at nine, a small lorry stopped for me. The load bed had a canvas cover. Julienne jumped down from the rear. She was armed with a Sten submachine gun.

She and I rode sitting on crates facing each other. The rest of the truck was loaded with medical supplies. There was a driver and another armed man in the front. Within fifteen minutes we arrived at the convoy staging area just outside Tel Aviv.

The convoy consisted of a motley collection of trucks of various sizes. Several had been crudely armored with steel plates welded to protect the engine and the driver. Julienne explained that these would act as defensive vehicles populated with the few heavier caliber machine guns the Haganah could scrape together.

Thirty minutes after we arrived, the convoy departed. It took us an hour to reach Latrun close to the mid-point of the journey. Julienne told me this is where Joshua commanded a Jewish army thousands of years ago. We could expect to be attacked by Arabs somewhere over the remaining thirty kilometers.

The lights were extinguished on all of the vehicles. The rear lights were taped over to darken the brake lights. Our fifty-truck convoy crawled along at barely twenty kilometers an hour. It was a cloudy, half-moon night so each vehicle was separated by only a small distance to maintain continuity. I could feel we were climbing a slight grade.

"We're coming near to the hills of Castel," Julienne said. "I am told that this is the most dangerous place for attack because the Arabs control the high ground overlooking the road."

"Are there no soldiers screening our convoy?" I asked.

Julienne looked at me in puzzlement. "Screening?"

"Covering our flanks, our sides."

"No. That is not possible. We do not have enough fighting men to cover such a distance. The only soldiers are those on the convoy. There are about forty of us that are armed."

"And if we are attacked, what is the plan?"

"We shall rely on the armored trucks in front to provide the main firepower. If the convoy can keep moving we will fire from the trucks. Notice how these crates are stacked to give us a firing position with some cover. We will throw back the canvas."

"And if the convoy stops?"

"We listen for the command to jump to the ground and take up defensive positions."

"Then what? We'd just be stuck here. Can't turn around. Do we back down the road in the dark?"

"Obviously that would not be possible. We will mount a counterattack."

I was dumbfounded. A counterattack? With only forty fighters against an attacking force of undetermined size? At night? This was no military plan. It was either naïve or desperate, probably both. These Jews were no ordinary fighters.

An hour later, all hell erupted. Small arms fire raked the convoy. Within minutes, two mortar rounds landed fifty meters to the south of the road. The attacking Arabs would make the correction for the next rounds.

Julienne threw back the canvas truck cover and took up a firing position shielded by a stack of crates. The incoming fire was from the north side of the road. I took out my .45 and crouched next to Julienne.

Our truck ground to a halt then started to roll backwards. Within seconds we smashed into the truck behind us. Both Julienne and I were thrown out onto the hood of that truck.

"You ok?" I yelled.

"Yes."

We both scrabbled to the south side and took up positions after crawling under the truck. We were joined by the soldier from the passenger seat of our truck. Even in the dark we could see he was wounded in the face. His right eye seemed a dark hole, but hard to tell in the weak light.

"Driver was killed," he said. "I can't see well. Think I was hit too."

Julienne examined his wound but there was nothing she could do to help. Her hands came away wet with blood from the young man's face.

"Look for the muzzle flashes then fire short bursts," I said to her. "Conserve your ammunition."

Our wounded colleague passed into unconsciousness so I took up his German made bolt action Mauser. It was of little use in this situation with only muzzle flashes to indicate targets. I decided to save the few rounds in the magazine for a real target rather than shooting blindly.

As expected, several more mortar rounds came in. The flashes of the explosions along the convoy suggested the Arabs were quickly making the trajectory adjustment. Since were stationary, they would soon be zeroed on our position. We would not survive if we stayed here.

"Julienne, we must get out of here. Back down the road the way we came. We'll all be killed by the mortars if we stay here."

"Our orders are to protect the supplies. Headquarters will send help."

In the pale moonlight now appearing with some parting of the cloud cover, I could see the determination as well as the fear in Julienne's face. She was a soldier and a Jew. She would do whatever was necessary.

"All we can do is hope that a mortar round doesn't score a direct hit. How much ammunition do you have left?"

"One spare magazine and whatever's left in the gun," she said.

"Ok. Don't shoot anymore. Only if you can see somebody fully and right in front of us." I shook my head in disbelief at the lack of military planning sending the convoy out with so little protection and insufficient ammunition.

A short time later the mortar barrage ceased. Puzzling since the Arabs had us exposed. They may have run out of mortar rounds. Or they might just be waiting for daylight. Once dawn broke we would be exposed and unable to escape under the only cover out here – darkness.

A man came down the line of trucks with a jerry can of water and a cup.

"Half a cup only. Don't know how long it will need to last," he said in Hebrew. Julienne asked him what the commander was planning.

After the man left I asked, "Well? What's happening."

"Headquarters radioed that a relief force was moving up the road. Unfortunately, they were attacked ten kilometers behind us. The fighting is heavy. Even if reinforced, we're told no help will arrive before dawn. So at dawn, the commander has ordered an attempt at breaking through. We will leave the damaged trucks."

"Breaking through in which direction?"

"Toward Jerusalem of course."

That seemed like suicide. "The British won't help?" I asked.

"No. They do not involve themselves with the sectarian conflict. They no longer play any role in the matter."

Julienne and I had entwined our bodies to keep warm against the chill of the desert night. As the first hint of light appeared upon the horizon, orders were relayed to mobilize. I tried to rouse the wounded man next to us. Julienne pronounced him dead after I pulled him from under the truck.

"I'll drive. Get to the passenger side," I said. The truck was British-made with the driver on the right. That was also the direction of the Arab attack. Plus I knew I could handle the truck assuming it was still in running order.

Our dead driver was still slumped against the steering wheel. There was no time to delicately remove his body while standing exposed to the Arab attackers. Climbing into the seat, my trousers soaked from the pooled blood of the dead driver. Julienne climbed in through the other door. The windshield was shattered.

"Break out the broken glass," I shouted at Julienne.

She worked on clearing the windshield with the stock of her submachine gun while I attempted to start the engine. I carefully worked the choke mindful that if I flooded the engine we would have to abandon the vehicle. After a couple of tries the engine caught. The truck in front did not move. I couldn't tell if it was waiting or disabled. Moments later someone came running down the stalled convoy shouting commands.

"Pull around the truck," Julienne said to me.

I put the truck in gear and pulled to the left. In the weak light of dawn I could see the other functioning trucks moving up the road ahead. As many as a third of the vehicles had been disabled by Arab mortar rounds.

Then the attack renewed. I could hear small arms fire ahead. We were ridiculously exposed driving at no more than twenty kilometers per hour. Some of the trucks were crudely armored. Ours was not.

I heard the impact of two mortar rounds before the third scored a direct hit on the truck directly in front of us. The blast force punched me in the face. I instinctively yanked the steering wheel to the left to avoid the wreckage ahead. Unfortunately, my wheel left the road and dipped into a depression. The truck angled beyond its center of gravity and slowly fell over on its left side.

I landed hard on top of Julienne. Hoping I had not injured her, I scrambled out through the open windshield. Turning back to help her I realized she was unconscious. Worse yet was the profusion of blood. I grabbed her wrists and pulled her through the windshield opening.

Laying there in the sand I yelled out in anguish. The source of the blood was evident. Something had torn a gaping wound in the side of Julienne's neck. Her heart was still pumping out her remaining blood in spasms. In a moment the disgorging of blood stopped. I knew she was dead.

I sat at her side as the convoy passed. More mortar rounds descended. Small arms fire intensified. As the last truck past, my survival instincts took over. The fighting moved up the road following the convoy. I suspected the Arabs would soon descend upon the damaged trucks to plunder the supplies. I grabbed a canteen of water and Julienne's Sten gun. The Arabs attacked from the right side of the road so I moved off to the left seeking cover.

A hundred meters away I found a cluster of large rocks. I spent the day there listening to the Arabs strip the trucks of goods. There was sporadic gunfire. I speculated that the Arabs were dispatching wounded Jews. I had no intention of being captured. At least the daytime temperature in the desert this time of year was moderate.

By nightfall, all was quiet. I planned to set off back down the road to Tel Aviv after first locating another couple of canteens of water. I had a long trek ahead of me. Fortunately the chilly desert night would help.

I remember little of my journey that night. My burden was not Arabs or water, but the loss of Julienne. To have been resurrected only to be plunged back into despair so soon was a cruel twist of fate.

I may have been eventually able to make the journey back to Jewish controlled territory by foot if my water held out and I wasn't spotted by some Arab. But that proved unnecessary. My survival luck held once again. As dawn broke the following day, a British patrol with armored vehicles was proceeding up the road to Jerusalem.

Once I determined they were British not Jordanian Arab Legion, I ran toward the road and hailed them down. A British Army captain in the lead jeep brought his convoy to a halt.

"Who the hell are you?" the captain yelled. A British soldier jumped from the jeep and trained this rifle on me.

"Journalist. French. The newspaper *Le Monde*." I answered. I was holding Julienne's machine gun and wearing my .45 in a holster on my waist.

"Journalist? Why are you armed? The Press is supposed to be neutral. You take a side? Jews I assume?"

"Just protecting myself. I was with a Jewish convoy attempting to reach Jerusalem with food and medicine. Arabs ambushed us. Mortars did a lot of damage."

"Fucking Jews. Trouble makers all of them. They even attack British troops."

"Is that why the British don't protect them? Thought the mandate meant keeping the peace. Jerusalem is under siege by the Arabs. Shouldn't you at least protect movement of food and medicine?"

"Smartass are you mister reporter? Corporal, take this noncombatant's weapons."

After disarming me, I took a seat in the back of the jeep.

Traveling toward Jerusalem, we arrived at the scene of the Arab ambush. There was a string of damaged trucks stretching over a kilometer. Debris was scattered from the looted cargo. The bodies of dead Jews were scattered where they fell. I snapped photographs with my Leica.

As the convoy passed by slowly, I spotted Julienne. When I left her I had placed her jacket over her face. It was now gone. Her face was grotesque with the eyes and mouth open. I leaped from the jeep and ran to her, falling on my knees.

"Corporal, get that sonofabitch back here!" the British captain yelled.

I felt a hand on my shoulder. "You'll have to be getting back to the vehicle, Sir." The young soldier said with some compassion seeing my grief.

I turned and looked at the soldier. "What's to be done with these bodies?"

"You'll have to be asking the Captain about that. Let's go."

I took off my jacket and covered Julienne's face once more, then turned back toward the jeep.

"What are you going to do with the dead, Captain?"

"Do? Why nothing. My orders are to proceed to Jerusalem and report on conditions along the road. Not our job to bury

Jews."

"You can't just leave them here, Captain."

"Sure I can. No way to transport them anyway.

"You're no better than the fucking Nazis."

"Watch your mouth reporter."

Standing in front of the officer, I spit in his face. He was dumbfounded for a moment, but then struck my face with the back of his hand.

CHAPTER 41

Allison took a deep breath before saying anything. "I had hoped for a brighter episode, Elliot. A new love. An episode of your life like that with Dominique. What a cruel blow. Weren't you bitter?"

"For a time. Not sure I can explain how I felt. Much more complex than grief. I grieved of course over losing Julienne. But there was something that didn't totally sadden me. It was more about what she gave me than what I lost."

"Well you only knew her for a short time. Not like the years with Dominique."

"No, I don't think it's that simple. Maybe it was where I was in my life. More mature, coming to terms with my *condition*. Surviving the War. Maybe it was her sharing her life experiences. She wasn't Dominique. Julienne was different in so many ways. While Dominique was fine wine with a myriad of subtleties, Julienne had the sharp edge of whiskey. I loved them both. I truly loved Julienne even though for such a brief time. Certainly the many years I had with Dominique made for a profound depth in that relationship. Not sure it's possible to compare one love to another. Most people only experience one real love in their lives. I had two."

"This was only 1948. You mean there have been no others since then?"

Elliot laughed. "You are forever the romantic, Allison. There have certainly been others since then. But Dominique and Julienne were uniquely special to my life."

"So what happened after your altercation with the British officer?"

"I stayed on in Jerusalem until the end of July, 1948, reporting on the war. David Ben Gurion declared the State of Israel in May. The surrounding Arab states then immediately launched attacks. The British stood on the sidelines while they prepared to leave Palestine all together as their mandate expired in June.

"But the war was short-lived. The Arabs were poorly trained, poorly lead, and the various Arab states were not united in a common effort. The Jews were not only better organized but collectively committed to die if necessary. The war continued into 1949 interrupted by several cease fires. By the end of this round of Arab and Jewish conflict there was a mass exodus of Palestinian Arab refugees. Displaced European Jews immigrated in the thousands. The struggle for control of Jerusalem was not resolved. The result left the city divided. The State of Israel was now a reality, but the seeds of future conflicts were assured."

"I feel as if I'm listening to a newsreel. You seem to have been at the center of all the great events of the first half of the twentieth century, Elliot," Allison said.

"Not all, but certainly more than most people. Being a reporter naturally involved me with events of significance. Most everyone was involved in some way with the two world wars. Many experienced both eras just like me. My life just spanned well before and beyond."

"Don't you regret that you won't be able to continue for decades more? To see what the world will become in the twenty-first century?"

"In a word, no. The twenty-first century will be the same as the past - full of wars. Look at the wars going on right now. I've had the equivalent of two normal lifetimes and I saw no change in how the world functions. I don't want to die, much less by cancer, but I'm not expecting to see some brighter future just around the corner. I've only covered my life to 1948. The rest of the twentieth century was hardly peaceful."

"Ok. I've not read the manuscript on purpose. I want to hear the entire narrative verbally first from you. I'm still trying to get my head around the fact that you are well over a hundred years old. To buy that is like being asked to believe in aliens."

"I can imagine how difficult that must be. But emotionally you now accept by story, even if you're still having intellectual doubts?"

"Yes. I've come around to accepting it. You're not an alien are you?"

Elliot laughed. "Hardly. But before you leave Provence, I hope you will have no lasting doubts. More than that, I can give you some tangible evidence that will confirm my age."

"What evidence?"

"I promise, before you leave. Right now I want to tell you about Algiers. It was 1956. It was another milestone event in my life."

"Elliot, you can't just skip from 1948 to 1956. Aren't those eight years noteworthy? Besides that, what about the loss of Julienne? How'd you deal with that?"

"As to Julienne, like I said, I felt the loss but not the deep grief and rage that persisted after Dominique's murder. Maybe because Julienne died as a soldier. Maybe because we were together for such as short time. Julienne renewed my life. Perhaps selfishly, I would not give that up to plunge back into the dark despair of before."

"But you were very much in love with Julienne."

"Yes. Perhaps differently than with Dominique though. As I said, they were different women, I was different, the circumstances very different. The many years with Dominique created an emotional depth understandably different from the brief time with Julienne. For a time I experienced feelings of guilt about why I was not more devastated with Julienne's death. Those thoughts passed. What her death did do was force me to come to grips that I was different and long term relationships were to be avoided."

"How's that? She died violently just like Dominique. Nothing to do with your longevity," Allison said.

"True. But it brought the realization that had they not both died prematurely, I would have faced a terrible dilemma at some point years later. Any relationship would end badly. Julienne's death just forced me to reconsider future relationships. I needed to avoid lasting emotional entanglements."

"That's a terrible sentence to impose on yourself. And did you?"

"Not entirely."

"You mean like the woman you're currently seeing?"

Elliot paused before answering. "That's somewhat complicated."

"Complicated? How's it complicated. Do you love her?"

Elliot was uncomfortable. "I have a great affection for her. But it's not the same as it was with Dominique or Julienne. So who's to say? Maybe it's our ages."

Allison decided not to pry further.

Elliot took her pause to return to his narrative. "To your question about those years leading up to 1956, I returned to Paris after leaving Palestine. I continued reporting from Paris for *Le Monde* during this time of world-changing events.

"The world should have experienced some respite from the devastating effects of World War Two. Sadly this was not to be.

Instead, the world continued to convulse. The Soviets blockaded access to Berlin, landlocked within East Germany. South Africa institutionalized Apartheid. McCarthyism threatened the constitutional foundations of the United States. East European countries became Soviet Union puppet states. Mao Zedong solidified China into a Marxist state. North Korea invaded South Korea. The U.S. and other allies invaded Korea. Chinese troops invaded North Korea to counter allied successes setting off a miniature world war three. The Soviets exploded a nuclear bomb. The United States upped the ante by detonating the first thermal nuclear bomb. And the list could go on. The wounds of World War Two had not yet even healed into scars while a fresh round of conflicts inflicted new wounds.

"Fortunately I avoided going to Korea. Palestine was bad enough, but Korea looked much uglier. My next foreign assignment was the conflict in British controlled Kenya, labeled by the British as the Mau Mau Uprising. The British again. I still had a grudge against them after Palestine. Partly personal I admit. My stint in Kenya was short. Threatened with prison by the British, I was deported out of Kenya for a piece I wrote."

"What did you do to warrant that?" Allison asked.

"Talked to the wrong people. The story to be told was of the native black people, not the British government or the white farmers. You see Kenya was the last vestige of British colonialism. This was colonialism in its most rank and degenerate form. It was vintage British colonial excess."

Allison said, "I recall from some college history reading that the Mau Mau uprising was about blacks butchering white farmers. Some real savagery. People killed with machetes? Was that how it was?"

"Oh, there was certainly brutal violence committed by the black rebels, but it was more than matched by the British and their colonial police. Never really amounted to much bloodshed by the rebels but what did occur was portrayed in the West as this barbaric revolt by rampaging blacks against peaceful white farmers. The reality was sporadic acts of violence committed by a few black extremists. It was enough however to justify British repression of a growing nationalist movement with its own brutality. The whole problem was caused by British colonialism. Inevitably this became subjugation of the native people.

"The British indiscriminately arrested suspected rebel sympathizers. They hanged over one thousand in trials that mocked western judicial norms. The detention camps were little better than Nazi-like forced labor camps. The British were good at this having given the world the concept of concentration camps during the Boer War in South Africa at the turn of the century. These Kenyan camps suffered shortages of food with the inmates overworked and brutalized. Sanitation and medical care were non-existent. Thousands died of reported *natural* causes in these camps. It was a story about the camps that got me into trouble. That and the pictures."

"Pictures of what?" Allison asked.

"Incriminating photos from inside a particularly notorious detention camp. I bribed a guard, a black man, a Kenyan. He took the photos for me from inside."

"How did know who to approach?"

"You forget that I was very good at this thing back a long time ago in turn of the century New York. Of course I didn't do it directly. Someone who knew someone that had a relative that was in the colonial police. He was either sympathetic to the rebels or just greedy. Money changed hands. The photographs were remarkably telling. Couldn't have done better myself. They turned out to be internationally sensational. My man captured a prisoner being flogged. There was a photo of a row of emaciated men standing in a food line clearly suffering from malnutrition. An open ditch ran with raw sewage. An overcrowded barracks with men in filthy rags reminiscent of Nazi concentration camps or a Soviet Gulag."

"How did you get caught?"

"The photos were published in *Le Monde*. I was their man down in Kenya so I was immediately implicated. I knew the British would react strongly. I expected to be expelled from Kenya but didn't think I would be jailed. Dragged before this stereotypical, cartoonish Colonel Blimp army officer, I endured a verbal tirade that left the guy red in the face and gasping for breath. The photos probably were a personal embarrassment. He didn't seem to like the French much either. So I was thrown into a filthy cell. Rats, insects. Tropical heat. Did four days there. Limited water. One daily ration of a piece of stale bread and a watery soup. No sanitation facilities, just a bucket. The bucket was never emptied during those four days."

"You must have been some hard-assed journalist in your day, Elliot. How'd you get out of that mess?"

"My editor pulled some strings with the French government who in turn applied pressure on London. Got support from some British newspapers that didn't like the idea of a fellow journalist being imprisoned for getting a story. My name was even brought up at the Prime Minister's weekly appearance before Parliament by the opposition party. In the end I wasn't worth the trouble to the British. I was kicked out of Kenya, not that I would have stayed anyway."

"Your survival escapades are as amazing as your longevity, Elliot."

"Remember, I was a reporter sent to places where there was already much trouble so I was bound to get caught up in bad situations. But I concede that I've had more than my share of good luck getting out with my skin intact."

"Was your editor upset that you were deported from Kenya?"

"Oh, certainly not. Quite the contrary in fact. Besides, it was the British government I embarrassed. Well worth the story that was made by the photos. I became somewhat of a celebrity at *Le*

Monde. On other stories, my photographs were compelling front page caliber that boosted my story's impact. I discovered I had a talent for capturing dramatic photographs. I had an eye for the telling photo, frequently peripheral to the central event, something to frame my copy. The photo often was a story in itself. Let me show you."

Elliot went to a file cabinet next to his desk and removed a number of envelops. Allison opened the envelope marked *Kenya 1953*. Thumbing through the black and white photos, she came to those that Elliot had described.

"Jesus Christ. These are horrible. I mean they're extraordinary photos, just like you said, but the subject material is unsettlingly brutal. I can see why the British were unhappy with you. What's this envelope marked *Indochina 1953-54*?"

"Modern-day Vietnam, Laos, and Cambodia. Like the British in Palestine, the French inherited responsibility for the region after World War Two. Like the British, they too treated it as a colony with all the expected problems."

"These are interesting by contrast," Allison commented as she looked at the Indochina photos. "Not so much of the war here. These depict a place of real beauty. The French preceded the Americans in fighting a losing war there didn't they? What was the great battle they lost to the Vietcong?"

"The Viet Minh actually. The battle was Dien Bien Phu. It was the debilitating defeat of French elite forces that soon lead to the 1954 Geneva Conference that resulted in the partitioning Vietnam. That of course would lay the ground work for the United States great disaster there a decade later."

"So this is another harrowing tale of adventure you are going to recount?"

"Not really. I didn't witness any fighting except some artillery barrages. Most of the fighting was in the north. My assignment was to cover the conflict from the broader political perspective, not the front lines. Could France win this war?

What would define winning? Sound familiar today? So I spent most of my time in Saigon. That's where these photos were from. Exotic, elegant, decadent Saigon. The Paris of the Far East. Very French."

"That sounds interesting. So is there a decadent story in your Saigon tour of duty?"

"No. I brought up that episode only as an introduction to a much larger personal saga of my life - Algeria. The loss of Indochina by France created a political mindset that impacted events in Algeria in North Africa. You see Algeria was a French colony for over a hundred years, with generations of French settlers. An independence movement was becoming a very real threat. The success of Ho Chi Minh in Vietnam against the French served to bolstered Algerian independence aspirations.

"While in Indochina I re-established a connection with my old Maquis commander, Captain Berry. Only now it was Lieutenant Colonel Berry, French military intelligence. After the French defeat in Indochina, Berry was reassigned to Algeria. Through Jacques Berry I gained an understanding how the French experience in Indochina affected the French Army. Their demoralizing defeat at the hands of the Viet Minh would profoundly contribute to events in Algeria.

"Let's go into Avignon for dinner. There's a wonderful restaurant inside the walls of the old city. The food is outstanding. Over dinner I'll pick up my story in Algiers in 1956. I'll also explain how I became Elliot Gaston."

CHAPTER 42

From *Time Travels* by Dillan Murphy
ALGIERS, ALGERIA – 1956-1957

The French seized control of the vast territories of Algeria in 1830 from a loose Turkish military rule. Amid decades of fighting indigenous Algerian resistance for nearly twenty years, Algeria was subdued. It was not unlike the westward movement in the United States during the same period. The native peoples were driven from the best land by the encroaching European settlers. And just like the western expansion of the United States, Algeria became an integral part of France.

Four times the geographic size of metropolitan France itself, Algeria was partitioned into three French Departments, thereby incorporating it into the French political structure. It had greater status than other French colonial holdings. But that only meant it was more secure for the *colons*, or the *pieds noirs* as the white French settlers were called. As elsewhere, these settlers were in the substantial minority to the *indigenes*, the native Algerians. Tensions between the native Muslim population and the French settlers festered over the next hundred years as political and economic power always favored the minority ethnic European French.

A renewed period of insurrection started in earnest in 1954. *Le Monde* sent me there on assignment in 1956. By that time the situation in Algeria had escalated into a full blown independence rebellion.

France had recently suffered a staggering military defeat in Indochina. They had just granted independence to bordering Tunisia and Morocco. Algeria was another matter entirely. European Algerian *colons* and the military high command wielded considerable political influence in Paris. The eventual commitment of 400,000 French troops in Algeria clearly bore this out. Algeria was French soil and would stay French.

I arrived in the capital, Algiers, in February, 1956 by ship from Marseille. The dry heat of North Africa was a welcome change from the oppressive heat and the monsoon rains of Indochina. That would of course change once summer arrived with its blistering North African heat. In a way, Algeria felt more French than Indochina. Indochina felt truly a colony. The architecture, the vegetation, the very culture felt alien, certainly not European. In contrast, the city of Algiers looked European, not much different than a French coastal city on the opposite side of the Mediterranean. At least that was the impression coming into the harbor. I had not seen the old Casbah sector yet or I might have had a different impression.

I secured a taxi for the short ride to the L'Hotel des Poste. The hotel was a magnificent white structure of Moorish influence with the upper window openings reminiscent of Venetian design. It was located close to the port and close to government offices. The area was part of the modern city of Algiers. The old rat-warren of narrow streets known as the Casbah was a short distance to the north but culturally a hundred years distant.

A good many of the people on the street clearly were European. Even many ethnic Arabs dressed in Western attire, including most of the woman. There was little visible evidence of Islamic practice in the modern part of Algiers. In all respects it appeared more prosperous than Tel Aviv.

That of course was the illusion as well as the problem. Algeria had a western appearance in its coastal cities. But the majority of the population was indigenous and did not think themselves French. The people did not practice their Islamic faith with extreme fundamentalist views, but neither were they European. France was still an occupier.

France saw Indochina as a colony, but saw Algeria as part of France. But one only had to venture into the vast areas away from the major cities on the Mediterranean coast to see an entirely different culture from the westernized coastal cities. Once the Atlas Mountain range was crossed, the terrain fell away to the Sahara Desert. These locales were the romanticized outposts of the French Foreign Legion fighting Arab bandits in nineteenth century Algeria. To those Arabs of course, the fight was to drive out an invader.

On the day I arrived in Algiers, over 100 people had been killed in fighting throughout Algeria that day alone. The French now had over 200,000 troops stationed there. A seemingly large number but insufficient to police everywhere and still have resources to mount effective offensives against the insurgent FLN's guerrilla tactics.

I learned my old commander Jacques Berry had been assigned to Algeria. He was on the staff of General Jacques Massu commanding the 10th Parachute Division. These élite troops were dispatched to insure that the vital city of Algiers not only remained under French control, but that rebellion there would be crushed. Massu was aggressive and not afraid to apply extreme measures to complete his mission. Authoritatively he had carte blanche, with civil rights suspended under edicts of martial law. Lt. Colonel Berry was Massu's chief of staff.

The headquarters for the French Army in Algeria was in a

nondescript building on a corner of the Place Bugeaud, in the heart of Algiers only 400 meters from the harbor. It was secured with sand-bagged machine gun positions and barbed wire barriers. Paratroops were stationed about the parameter of the plaza. It was only a short walk from my hotel.

"Bonjour, Dillan," Berry greeted me, giving me a hug with genuine affection. "It is good to see you again, old friend."

Berry ushered me to a chair and ordered a clerk to bring us coffees.

"Glad to see you survived Indochina, Jacques. Will Algeria turn out differently?"

"*Merde!* That jungle shithole. Impossible terrain. Tenacious enemy, inadequate resources, and poorly commanded. We didn't understand the culture. Got drawn into what was really a civil war. We backed a stupid move to reestablish a monarchy. For all of Eisenhower's bluster about stopping Communist expansion, the fucking Americans did nothing to help us."

"Even so, how did the Dien Bien Phu debacle happen?" I asked.

"A stupid strategic position. We French still have a problem of promoting incompetence to the general staff. Dien Bien Phu was well within enemy territory way to the north. It had to be supplied by air. Worse yet, it was surrounded by high ground. General Giap was able to pound the base with heavy artillery positioned from there."

"Artillery the French Army didn't know he had. Wasn't that an intelligence failure?" I gave Berry an inquisitive expression knowing he was in army intelligence.

"Partly. We failed to infiltrate the Viet Minh. Yet they were effective in the South against us. That's what I mean about the culture. Didn't have enough people that spoke the language. We looked foreign. Had to rely on native Vietnamese for intelligence. Couldn't tell good intelligence from misinformation. It was a disaster waiting to happen."

"So why will Algeria be any different?"

"Because Algeria is France," Berry said. "We have been here over a hundred and twenty years. Generations of native Frenchmen have made Algeria prosper. Without them the region would be nothing more than a collection of backward tribes. Besides, the Algerian Muslim is not as alien as the Oriental."

"The Algerian Muslims don't seem to think of themselves as French. You have a real war going on here, Jacques. Seems no different than what's happening in colonies everywhere; India, Kenya, Malaysia, Indochina, even Palestine."

"It is different. Algeria is more like Northern Ireland is to the British, or the Basque area to the Spanish. These are not colonies. They are part of the very fabric of the Country. They cannot be given up. Like all of these places you've got a small number of committed terrorists causing the trouble. Here you can see the specter of Communist ideology at the root of the problem in Algeria. The ringleaders are all Marxists. They get support from Egypt, and through them, the Soviets."

"Those are not good examples, Jacques. But regardless of the arguments, I'm a reporter simply looking to report on what is happening and stay above political editorializing. Can you help me with access to good material?"

"Absolutely, *mon ami*. What about going out with a patrol into the rural areas outside of Algiers? I think that could be arranged."

"What are these patrols doing?"

"Doing what soldiers do - looking for the enemy. Armed rebels. Search and destroy missions."

Later that evening I had drinks with Jacques Berry. Too many drinks. Too much reminiscing about World War Two. Too much of Berry's demonizing the native Algerians and their pursuit of independence.

Berry's was the same elitist view of the colonizer as anywhere else. I saw no difference between a French Algeria and a

British Kenya. It seemed obvious to me that these colonial powers must eventually relinquish their hold. They were an anachronism. Those descendents from the colonizing Europeans held all the power and wealth. The native populations were little more than serfs. Algeria was no different. It made me uncomfortable to think of myself as French. There was a twinge of guilt in not revealing my true feelings to my old comrade.

The next day, Berry introduced me to Colonel Paul Ducournau, commanding the crack 18th Régiment de Chasseurs Parachutistes. Ducournau was a graduate of the French military academy, Saint-Cyr as were most of the senior officers in the French Army. Like most of the regimental commanders, he was a veteran of Indochina. I found it telling about the French Army command that senior officers that failed so badly in Indochina still held command positions. Subsequently I was introduced to a subordinate officer, Captain Edmond Perault.

"We leave before dawn the day after tomorrow Monsieur Murphy," Captain Perault said. "It is not usual for a journalist to accompany us on a mission. I cannot be responsible for your safety." He was obviously not happy with being saddled with me.

"I've been in combat before, Captain. I'll take care of myself."

"Where was that, Sir?"

"In France. I fought with the Maquis."

The young officer raised an eyebrow. "You look a bit young to have been in World War Two, Sir. How's that?"

"Just lucky. Good genes. People have commented before about it. I'm not as young as I look."

The officer did not seem convinced. "So what did you do in the Resistance?"

"Killed the enemy. Over twenty I know of. You see I was a sniper. I fought with Jacques Berry. It was Colonel Berry who arranged for me to accompany you on a mission. Do you have a problem with that?"

"No, Sir. I believe I understand. I will send someone to your hotel tomorrow. Best you spend the night with us in the field since we move out in the early morning hours the following day."

"What is your mission, Captain?"

"If by that you mean the Regiment, it's to destroy an FLN unit. As for me, I'm an intelligence officer. My mission is to get information."

The FLN was the acronym for the Front de Libération Nationale, the principle Algerian nationalist movement. Ever since the FLN killed over one hundred European *colons* near Philippeville six months ago, the French Army had pursued a campaign of their own retributive brutality.

The Captain explained they had intelligence that a senior FLN leader was holed up in a small village in the countryside of the Aurès Mountains. The area was in eastern Algeria over three hundred kilometers from Algiers. The paratroop regiment would travel by truck the next day. The raid on the village of Tiffelfel was scheduled for the following morning, supported by another infantry regiment stationed closer to the village.

The next morning I climbed into Captain Perault's jeep. I was armed with my camera which I decided to keep hidden. I also wore my .45 sidearm in a holster which I did not hide.

"We are looking for Belkacem Krim. Our intelligence reports he has infiltrated back into Algeria from Tunisia. We expect to encounter a sizeable group of FLN fighters with him in Tiffelfel."

"What's the plan, Captain?" I asked.

"The village has mountains to the west. Three companies of a Colonial Infantry Regiment will take up positions to the south and east to close off escape of the rebels. Four companies of our regiment will attack from the north. The dark troops are the anvil and we're the hammer."

"Dark troops? What do you mean?"

"Blacks. Mostly from Senegal. The noncoms and officers of course are French. For my part I don't trust them. Neither does the Colonel. We expect them just to hold their position and close off any rebel attempt to escape."

"Are there civilians in this village?"

"Civilians? They're all fucking Muslims. Not sure where the line is drawn. If they don't have a gun then we'll treat them as non-combatants. That's the best they get. They still give the rebels food and shelter. These villages are stinking shitholes that breed rebellion like garbage breeds rats."

I shared a tent with Captain Perault. We drank my Scotch to stave off the night chill but sleep still eluded me for hours. Perault was difficult company. I had a nagging anxiety that I could not expel. At four o'clock in the morning the Captain aroused me from a shallow sleep.

"We leave in fifteen minutes, Monsieur Murphy."

The jeeps and troop trucks crawled along the rutted road for thirty minutes. When we stopped, no one spoke. The men communicated with hand signals. There was some illumination with a half moon and a cloudless sky.

At the first light of dawn the French Paras moved out. Within minutes, small arms fire erupted. A sergeant reported to Perault that they were engaging rebel sentry positions.

Another captain in direct command of the French troops communicated by radio with the officer leading the attack on our left. "Move quickly through those houses to the east, Fournier. Clear them of any hostiles!"

Two companies attacked the western side of the village. I followed the advancing soldiers along with Perault, passing two bodies I assumed to be rebel sentries. Their weapons lay close by.

Two paratroopers entered a house, followed by a burst of submachine gun fire. The soldiers exited the house, stopping for a moment to cast a look at me before moving to another house. I entered the house. The sight sickened me.

It was dark in the house. I found a kerosene lantern on a table that probably served as the occupants' sole light. The poor light cast by the lantern only added to the horrific scene. Four dead. First was an old man in the front room. Blood pooled around his body. Probably trying to protect his family. In a back bedroom there was a young woman cradling two young boys in her arms. They were maybe ten and seven. Each had multiple bullet wounds. The woman's face was unrecognizable. Blood splattered the adobe mud walls of the room. I set the lantern in front of the bodies and then adjusted the camera settings for the poor light condition. I shot a roll of film.

When I emerged from the house and attempted to enter another, Perault barked an order to a soldier to prevent me. "It's not safe, Monsieur Murphy. We've killed a number of rebels so far. There could be bombs yet inside these houses."

Actually I didn't have to go into the houses. The French soldiers were dragging bodies out. There were no young men among the bodies. Mostly women and children. I snapped more photographs.

"Monsieur Murphy. I was not made aware that you would be taking photographs."

"Of course I take photographs, I'm a journalist. Is there a problem?"

"Perhaps. I must clear that with my superiors. I must request that you take no more photos."

"Concerned that photos of dead civilians, just women and children might be bad publicity?"

"Civilians? Yes there are few young men. For just that reason it's clear that this village is supporting the rebels. The young men fight with the rebels. Their women give them aid. So these are not civilians."

"That's fucking bullshit, Captain. You've just murdered these people for no reason other than they're Muslim."

Before the argument could progress, what had been only sporadic fire erupted in an intense exchange to the south of the village. The French had surrounded one house that was returning fire. Over the next ten minutes, French mortars destroyed the house and the gunfire ceased.

The French soldiers dragged out six bodies from the house. I could not tell, but I assumed they were FLN fighters since they had fired on the French.

Overhead, a single engine aircraft flew in ever widening circles looking for any FLN fighters in the bush.

I wandered among the ghastly scene. More bodies were being pulled from the houses. Many of the bodies were partly dressed or still in bedclothes. I counted over thirty dead. Occasionally a pistol shot rang out. I could not see firsthand but I guessed that the wounded were being dispatched by the French soldiers.

A short distance away was an equal number of live villagers sitting on the ground. They were the same mix of old men, women, and children. Captain Perault was addressing them through an interpreter.

"Sergeant, take that one and that one into the house over there. Lieutenant, keep the rest of them right here," Perault ordered.

As Perault followed the two prisoners being lead away, I attempted to follow. Perault turned. "Stay out here, Murphy."

"Why's that, Perault? Don't want me to see what you do to defenseless old men?"

"Keep this man under guard! He's not to go anywhere," Perault ordered one of the soldiers.

I went back to the group of detained villagers and sat down. Within a short time, terrible screams came from within the house. There were widespread rumors about the French Army using torture. It was obvious what was going on inside that house.

Sometime later Captain Perault emerged from the house and came to the group of villagers. Through the interpreter he said, "We know this village gives aid to rebels and terrorists. Your young men fight for the FLN. We want information. If we get that information we will leave here. If there is no cooperation, then many will suffer. Suffer terribly. I do not care if you die so you can understand there is no limit to the pain that I will inflict. So we will continue until I get information."

This time two women were selected. The screams resumed. The disgusting routine repeated for the next three hours.

The raid had netted eight dead rebel fighters but no Belkacem Krim. Enough for the French Army to claim partial success and inflate the number of reported rebel dead by including the slaughtered non-combatants. I wondered if my reporting would have any impact. I might be censored. If not, I might be expelled from Algeria by the Army Command if my reporting ran counter to the official position. I would have to be careful if this was not to end like my Kenyan assignment.

CHAPTER 43

From *Time Travels* by Dillan Murphy
ALGIERS, ALGERIA – 1957

A couple of days after returning to Algiers I was recounting my experience in the field with Jacques Berry. We were having drinks at my hotel.

"Do you know this sort of thing goes on, Jacques?"

Berry was noticeably uncomfortable. "Yes. It has unfortunately become accepted practice since Indochina. I disagree with these practices, but it sometimes yields important intelligence."

"It's not only stupid, Jacques, it's unproductive. Does the Army think they can crush these cultural aspirations for independence? How is Algeria to be governed – as a military state subjugating the population by force? Forever? Where are our French ideals?"

"I would agree with you, Dillan. My stomach turns with these reports. But there is nothing I can do."

"You're the chief of staff to the commanding general. Doesn't that give you some influence?"

"Not on the subject of brutal methods. Massu only commands Algiers not all of Algeria. Besides, Massu himself has no problem with these harsh methods. In fact he's bringing in an officer from Philippeville to intensify these brutal intelligence gathering methods. Massu only wants results. That's why he was assigned this command."

"Harsh? No, Jacques, this is torture and murder. These are the same crimes committed by the Gestapo, by the Milice. It's that sort of barbarity that you and I fought against in the Resistance."

"Damnit, Dillan, what would you have me do? I'm a career army officer. Should I resign in protest? What would that accomplish?"

"I'm not here to judge you old friend. You can only make your own decisions. As for me, I'm going to expose this. Expose this official secrecy. Make the rumors about the Army's use of torture and murder into headlines."

"Do that and you'll be thrown out of Algeria, Dillan. Or simply just killed. That could happen. Don't be foolish with your righteous indignation. This is a dangerous place."

"I understand, Jacques. But I'm never foolish. I've done this before. What I need is some inside help. If you're against this will you help me?"

Berry took several moments to consider what I was asking. He took a drink of whiskey before answering. "Very well. This is an ugly stain on French honor. The sooner it's exposed, the sooner it gets fixed. I'll do what I can, Dillan, but remember you're on your own. This could be dangerous. I'm not your confederate in whatever you're planning. I'll disavow any knowledge of what you're doing if I'm ever questioned."

"I won't drag you into anything, Jacques. I'll find other newspapers than *Le Monde* to publish. Careful of course to avoid the material identifying me as the source. If I'm found out, at worst it will be as if I betrayed an old friend. Still willing to help?"

"Reluctantly. Algeria is a nasty situation. Worse than Indochina. I fear it will end just as badly for France. The Algerian situation is tearing France apart. So I follow my conscience, not my duty as an army officer."

I wanted to deflect Jacques' thoughts from the philosophical to the practical. "Where do you suggest I start?"

"Well you might want to start with our newest staff addition. The reports from Philippeville frankly sicken me. I understand he is responsible for institutionalizing this brutality. We are soldiers not thugs. This officer is different."

"Could I see any of those reports?"

"Christ no! They're classified. That goes too far, Dillan."

"Of course. I understand. So you can introduce me to this monster?"

"Yes. As soon as he arrives. In about two weeks. He's to report here on the 8th of January. Not sure he'll talk to you though. Secretive bastard I'm told. His name is Aussaresses. Major Paul Aussaresses."

I embraced Jacques Berry as he departed the hotel bar. Sitting back down to finish my drink, I was approached by a man, a European by his looks.

"Monsieur Murphy, may I introduce myself. I am Elliot Gaston. I'm with *L'Express*. You know the magazine?"

"Yes. How do you know my name?"

"I was at Massu's headquarters a couple of days ago. Trying to get an audience with somebody, anybody for that matter. Then I see you ushered into Colonel Berry's office. I simply asked the clerk your name. I wondered how you got to see Berry when I'm treated like the plague. Then I see you two having drinks and acting like old pals."

"I know Colonel Berry from the War. As for you getting the cold shoulder I'd say it was probably the slant of *L'Express*' opposition to the conflict here in Algeria." I did not welcome the intrusion but Gaston was a reporter doing nothing I wouldn't do to work a potential networking angle.

Gaston replied, "I'm sure you're right. Personally, I think what the Army is doing in Algeria is a stain on France. It will never come to a good end. May I buy you a drink?"

"Very well." I didn't want another drink but then Gaston might be a resource for me as well. We obviously shared the same negative opinion of the French Army's conduct in Algeria, though it was premature to confide my opinions to Gaston.

"Been here in Algeria long, Monsieur Gaston?"

"A year. Right after the Philippeville Massacres. Things have degenerated since then. More French troops. Torture, executions. People just turn up missing. Difficult to get hard facts. The Army isn't talking about this dirty work. So you get what you can from the native Algerians and a few drunken soldiers talking too much."

"So where do you get your information?"

"Well I can't be specific about my sources. Let's just say they're mostly not sympathetic to the French Army."

"Some are perhaps wanted by the Army?"

"Some."

"Why are you telling me this, Monsieur Gaston?"

"Because we might be of mutual assistance, Monsieur Murphy. You with access to the Army, me with access to the other side shall we say."

Now this was interesting. I tried to gauge if Gaston was who and what he claimed. Maybe he was some agent working for French Intelligence. "Interesting proposition. I'll consider it. But I've just arrived a week ago. I'm just getting information you probably already have."

It was Gaston's turn to consider his thoughts before proceeding. "I am aware of what happened at Tiffelfel. I also know you were there."

"You seem to have excellent sources. Why are you so

interested in me?"

"How did you feel about what you witnessed at Tiffelfel, Monsieur Murphy?"

My face noticeably tensed.

"Let me guess, or let me hope that you were disgusted with the Army's tactics of murder and torture there. You have some measure of access which is denied to not only me but most other reporters. The Army wants to do things in secret. For whatever reason they've made an exception with you."

Not answering his question as to my sympathies, I said, "Exchanging information as you suggest could be dangerous. We could be accused of spying for the enemy. Could even be construed as treason. Don't relish going to the guillotine for a story."

"I know what you're saying but I'm not suggesting we provide the FLN with any intelligence. Just like you, I simply want to get the truth out there to the world, but more importantly to Frenchmen back home."

I was still wary. I needed to check out Elliot Gaston before exchanging any information. "I'll think about your proposal. Let's stay in touch. Now I'll say good night since I've had more than enough to drink."

During the next week, Jacques Berry secured permission for me to visit an internment camp. If I had any equivocations about what was going on in Algeria, that experience brought the circumstances into stark focus.

It was no different than the British treatment of suspected dissidents in Kenya. Squalor, inadequate food, no medical treatment was evident just by looking at the detainees. The facilities were filthy. Open sewage ran down makeshift channels. The barracks were not even buildings but more like boxes constructed out of corrugated metal. Upon entering one such building I gagged at the overpowering stench. I could not imagine how human beings survived under such conditions.

The inmates themselves were filthy. Their ragged clothing and emaciated appearance suggested that many had been incarcerated for some time. These were not defiant insurgents, at least not most of them. Too many women and old men. These were people caught in some broad net to get intelligence or for some larger political motive.

"Can I take photographs?" I asked my officer escort, a young lieutenant.

"No, Sir."

"The inmates here look like those in the Nazi concentration camps. Don't feed them much do you?"

The officer glared at me. "They're terrorists, Sir. They're treated humanely, but that's all they're entitled to."

"Terrorists? All of them? Have they been tried in a court, even a military court? Have they even been charged?"

"This is war. These Muslims understand nothing of the niceties of a civil society. These inmates are prisoners of war."

"Doesn't look like they're being treated to accepted standards for prisoners of war."

"You're a Frenchman are you not? You sound like a Muslim sympathizer. Is that the kind of shit you write in your newspaper?"

"I've seen too many of your kind. The blind following the stupid, or even the criminal. Frankly, Lieutenant, I don't give a fuck what you think. How do you think I got access into this *camp* as you call it? The answer to that it is way above your rank. Now, since you were ordered to show me about, get on with it."

It was a difficult piece to write. I tried to illustrate the terrible conditions imposed upon these detainees. I wished I had photographs like from Kenya. Words were inadequate to describe the degradation. I settled for working the argument of how this was contrary to French concepts of justice and the rule of law. I had to temper my outrage so as not to further compromise Jacques Berry's position since he provided me access to the camp.

What the experience did accomplish was to make me receptive to Elliot Gaston's proposition of cooperation.

"I've been catching hell over you, Dillan," Jacques Berry said. We were having drinks at my hotel again. "First the piece on that mess at Tiffelfel. Your piece in *Le Monde* condemning the Army for what amounts to accusations of murder was bad enough, but the photographs that appeared in *L'Express*. You don't know anything about that I suppose?"

"Not my pictures, Jacques. Captain Perault wouldn't allow any photos."

My photographs given to Elliot Gaston for publication by *L'Express* were attributed to a villager after the paratroopers had left the grisly scene.

Berry looked at me debating if he believed me. "Speaking of Perault, he bitched about you to his colonel who complained to Massu. Then your piece about the internment camp comes out. The General wanted to know why I was helping this unfriendly journalist."

"What did you say?"

"I told the General you were an old comrade. Told him what you did during the War. Told him I'd have a word with you."

"You in trouble over me, Jacques?"

"Not yet. After all, I'm Massu's chief of staff so he trusts me. But I'm afraid I'll need to distance myself from you. Can't help you anymore. Massu personally supports these extreme measures and will not tolerate more critical press."

"Any chance in getting me an interview with this major you told me about? The one rumored to be promoting torture?"

"Aussaresses? No way. Out of the question now. I'm afraid you're out in the cold just like any other journalist now, Dillan."

Not actually out in the cold. Just one line of source closed off. Digging out stories about bad things and bad people was my talent. Algeria was full of both. So I turned my attention from infiltrating the French Army to getting inside the rebels of the FLN.

Elliot Gaston was a good starting point. We became friendly. For a journalist he was surprisingly *not* cynical. I liked him. Although Gaston's leanings were well to the left, and he sympathized with the native Algerians, he didn't have the grit to burrow into the underbelly of the environment to get at real stories. I quickly learned that his contacts were largely known sympathizers, mostly intellectuals, with no access to much that was newsworthy. Gaston wrote lightweight crap for the most part. My photos of Tiffelfel where the best thing he ever got.

But Gaston's sources at least gave me a starting point. That is how I met a young Algerian lawyer named Fariza Sahnine. She was thirty. Unmarried, independent, French educated, and anything but the traditional Algerian Muslim woman.

I was introduced to Fariza in an arranged date. Elliot Gaston had arranged for a day at the beach. He wanted to introduce me to his girlfriend as well. It was she who suggested a date for me. I was assured that Fariza was very pretty.

"Dillan, there's something I must tell you about my girlfriend, Lucille."

"Don't tell me she's not pretty?"

He smiled. "Oh no, she's pretty all right. It's just that .... well, she's married."

"That's your business I guess, Elliot. Hope you know what you're doing though. Where's her husband?"

"Here in Algeria. He's an army officer."

"Jesus Christ, Elliot. That could be a risky adventure you're involved with. What if you're seen together?"

"We're careful. The husband is away on duty outside of Algiers most of the time. Lucille says the marriage is in name only now. She wants to leave him."

We went to the beaches at Tipasa to the east of Algiers.

Lucille was pretty. But I was soon distracted by Fariza who

was not only pretty but exotic. She had a café au lait completion with almost black eyes. Long black hair, left uncovered. Under her skirt and blouse she wore a white bathing suit that offset her coloring and a shapely figure. She was obviously not an observant Muslim.

Fariza and I spent the afternoon in endless conversation as we wandered around the Roman ruins. She was a passionate advocate for Algerian independence. Her work was defending Algerians arrested by the French. I told her about my experience at the village of Tiffelfel, and the internment camp. I made a pitch for her help in steering me to those in the independence movement for interviews. She was noncommittal but said she would make some inquiries.

We had a late dinner at a quiet seaside restaurant. All of us got a little drunk and lost track of time. It was too late to return to Algiers because of the curfew. Elliot and I might be all right, but not Fariza. Nor was it advisable for Lucille to have to identify herself at an army checkpoint.

Elliot suggested we get rooms at a local Tipasa hotel. For the sake of propriety, the girls shared a room as did Elliot and I. After breakfast we returned to Algiers in Elliot's rented car. We dropped Fariza outside the old Casbah quarter. She agreed to have dinner with me that night. She suggested a restaurant in the Casbah. She drew me a map to navigate the maze of narrow streets.

For the next several weeks, I saw Fariza frequently. It was both professional as well as personal. She energetically pursued setting up interviews for me with influential Algerians. From the personal perspective, we became lovers after that second night

.

CHAPTER 44

PROVENCE, FRANCE – 2009

"You have a decided attraction for beautiful, intelligent, strong-will women, Elliot …or Dillan. Now it's a little more confusing what to call you. There was a real Elliot Gaston then? So how did you come to adopt his identity?"

"I'm getting to that a little further along in my story."

"Ok. So tell me about this dark beauty, Fariza. My God, she doesn't get killed too does she?"

"No. She wasn't killed. Unfortunately we were not together long enough for it to develop into something larger. Not our choosing, just larger events. Part of the same events that led me to become Elliot Gaston."

"That's terrible, Elliot. I've decided to continue to call you Elliot not Dillan by the way. That's how I know you. I mean you keep having these serial relationships with interesting women who then leave your life. That's just so sad."

"I was with Dominique for lots of years so my relationships haven't all been abbreviated. Besides, you're forgetting my *problem*. – I was 83 in 1956. When you live that long and still look to be not yet forty, it might be expected that you'd had a number of romantic relationships over that time. Besides, look at the kind of life I've led. Wars are tough on relationships."

Allison looked at Elliot. He was pushing 140 years old. The thought was still absurd. He looked to be around sixty. A good looking sixty at that. That reality was still intellectually irreconcilable. "Still, it's very sad. To have loved so many women and have those relationships all end tragically."

"I've suffered more grief than I care to dwell on. But that aside, I still had the ever-present aging issue that would have brought its own grief. How could I have a sustained relationship when the other person aged twice as fast as I did? Just look at my situation in Algeria. I was 58 years old even based upon my documentation with the false birth date. I looked to be in my thirties. If anybody ever paid attention, like a soldier at a checkpoint, I might have been in serious difficulty."

They were sitting in front of the fireplace. A fire was ablaze. Dusk was descending. They were sipping wine and nibbling on cheese.

"The thought just struck me that you have loved women across all faiths."

"What do you mean?"

"Well, Dominique was Catholic, Julienne was Jewish, and now this Fariza was Muslim."

"Culturally speaking perhaps. You forget none of them were religious. Both Julienne and Fariza were nationalists. The religious affiliations were only cultural labels. As for Fariza, she was even anti-Islam. She demeaned Islam for relegating women to less than second class. She was very French but more Algerian. More than that, she was a Marxist."

"Marxist? You seemed to have covered the entire range of social and political experience of the twentieth century as well."

"Understandable since I lived the entire century."

"By this point in your life, I mean the 1950's, you seemed to have distanced yourself from the loss of Dominique and the trauma of the War. Is that true?"

"I wouldn't say distanced. More like found my balance. Found a new perspective. I wasn't made whole again. More like recovered from a severe wound to continue life impaired but functional. It was not just Dominique. It was not just the War itself. It was what I did during the War that left heavy scars."

"You mean those you killed?"

"Yes. But you see it's how I killed. Most soldiers never see the faces of those they kill. But I saw those faces. I imagined their lives just before I extinguished those lives. It was intensely intimate. I've read something on the subject. It's a common reaction for snipers. Even one's comrades sensed something was different if you were a sniper. Not to be shunned, but someone better left to their own introspective world. You were the messenger of death and the aura of death hung about you."

Elliot had been more matter of fact in recounting his War activities previously. Allison realized the experience of killing men at a distance with their faces up close in the crosshairs of a telescopic sight still profoundly affected him.

"So by this time you fully realized that this aging thing was something far more than just unusual. Were you completely convinced you were ….? I'm not sure what to call your condition."

"A freak?"

"No, Elliot. What I meant was how at this point did you see the rest of your life?"

"I guess I would say that I adopted a pragmatic view. No more dodging the issue. It was something I had to consciously manage, no different than having a serious medical condition. Of course that meant being extremely aware to frame my life within the confines of my appearance age. There were lapses.

"For example, I was recounting my life to Fariza. An abbreviated chronology, but still basically true. I spoke of Dominique and my experiences during the World War Two. The problem arose when Fariza worked the math and determined I must have been not much more than twenty when the Germans invaded France. How then my implied years of marriage, wine making in Provence, etcetera, all prior to the War? It was an awkward moment that I got out of with some contorted explanation. An explanation Fariza probably did not believe. Made me realize just how much an intimate relationship was fraught with risk, leading ultimately to a bad ending."

"Ok. So tell me what happened in Algeria. You found a new lover and you became someone else. My god, Elliot, your stories read like an old-time serialized adventure. They flow like those of Scheherazade. The climax to be anxiously anticipated, to then flow into a succeeding adventure. *Time Travels* will be a captivating read."

"I hope that's the case. True to that format, I'll tell you about what happened to me in Algiers in 1957."

CHAPTER 45

From *Time Travels* by Dillan Murphy
ALGIERS, ALGERIA – 1957

Fariza knocked on my hotel door. It was almost ten o'clock at night. She was late and I was starting to worry. We were to have had dinner at eight.

I opened the door and she rushed into my arms.

"Are you all right?" I asked. Her hair was somewhat mussed and her clothing disheveled.

"Yes. I'm fine. Sorry for being late."

"Did something happen?"

Fariza sat down in a chair and lit a cigarette. "Would you make me a drink?" She had taken a liking to my Scotch. "I was stopped at a checkpoint. Searched. A pig of a soldier just wanted to feel my body. When he grabbed my breast I slapped him. They detained me for over two hours."

"Shit. No more going about after dark by yourself. I don't want anything to happen to you." I handed her a drink and kissed her forehead. "Why were you late?"

"I was meeting someone. Arranging an interview for you.

An important interview with Kussil Boudiaf. You know who he is?"

"No."

"He's the editor of an underground anti-French newspaper called *La Voix du Soldat*. The French Army is the principle target of the newspaper's attacks. He was intrigued with the idea of talking to a fellow journalist, even a Frenchman. I told him you were sympathetic to the idea of Algerian independence."

"Excellent. I appreciate your efforts, Fariza. How is this interview to be arranged?"

"That is what I was discussing with Boudiaf's people before I was detained. It must be planned carefully. For Boudiaf's part, his people must insure that this is not a trap, or that you are not followed. He's high on the Army's wanted list. They will contact me tomorrow. You will not be told of the time or place until right before we leave for the meeting."

"We must celebrate then. Are you still up for dinner at this late hour?"

Fariza crushed out her cigarette and got up to stand in front of me. "I have a bad feeling about this, Dillan. This is dangerous. I wish you would not have this meeting."

I got up and put my hands on her shoulders. "It will be fine. This is what I do. Nothing will happen. I have friends in high places."

Fariza shook her head as if to say I did not understand. "I don't want dinner. Perhaps later."

She proceeded to remove her skirt. "I want you to make love to me, Dillan. I'm scared and I want to feel you inside me."

We never did have dinner that night. Fariza made no attempt to leave for her office until the following morning. I awoke to the glorious vision of her dusky nakedness next to me. Sun filled the room and a gentle breeze from the sea fluttered the curtains through the open window. We made love again. Later we bathed together and then had a large breakfast brought to the room.

Fariza went to her office at midday. I was to stay at the hotel all day to wait her return on the assumption that she would receive instructions for the meeting. When she finally called my room, it was late afternoon. I was to meet her at a bar near the docks close to the Casbah at seven o'clock.

I took a table outside on the sidewalk and ordered a coffee. Fariza arrived ten minutes later.

She kissed my cheek and sat down. "Are you ready?"

"Of course. What's the plan?"

"Shortly, we shall walk to a restaurant in the Casbah. Someone will meet us there. Someone I will recognize. After that, I am not told what is to happen. Meeting here at this bar was another precaution. I followed you from the hotel to make sure you weren't followed."

We left the bar for a twenty minute walk to the restaurant in the ancient Casbah quarter of Algiers. Fariza navigated the Byzantine warren of narrow streets remarkably well. I was totally lost after a few minutes of constant turns.

At the restaurant we ordered more coffee. Within a few minutes a young man approached and nodded to Fariza. She said to me, "You're to go with this man. Once your meeting with Boudiaf is concluded, he will return you here. I will be waiting for you."

I touched her hand and left with man. We walked for over thirty minutes, seemingly in circles. I suspected it was to spot anyone that might be following. The man probably had others helping to insure security. To my thinking, it would be absolutely impossible to follow anyone in these streets without being discovered.

Eventually the man stopped. Checking that no one was within sight, he quickly ushered me through a door. From there I followed him through what appeared to be someone's home, out a back door, down an alley and through another door into a different building.

The room we entered was full of boxes, paper, and a small printing press. Two young men looked at me then resumed their tasks. I was led through the clutter to a back office.

Seated behind a table acting as a desk was a small man of about sixty I guessed. He was balding. His face had a close-cropped, graying beard in the Islamic style. Kussil Boudiaf was dressed in a white shirt with suspenders.

"Monsieur Murphy, a pleasure to meet you," he said in excellent French, rising from his chair and shaking my hand. "Tea?"

As he poured tea into two glasses he said, "Although a Frenchman, I am told that you are troubled about what the French Army is doing here in Algeria."

"Yes. I do not believe any good Frenchman would condone torture and murder, no matter the professed justification," I said.

He handed me the glass of tea and sat down. "I am not so sure, Monsieur Murphy. I believe that any people might justify such methods if they believe the cause sufficiently worthy. That happens throughout the world."

"Even with native Algerians? The FLN has been guilty of some savage brutality and murder of Europeans also," I said.

"That is correct. To my point exactly. The FLN commits their atrocities to provoke a brutal response from the Army. It's innate in humankind to rationalize the acceptability of any action to support their particular group. All it takes is a claimed righteous cause and the demonizing of the enemy. That's what Hitler did to the Jews. The French treat the Algerian as an inferior people, uneducated, dirty, with an alien religion. The Algerian views the French as an arrogant, greedy colonial occupier, raping Algeria."

"Can I quote you?"

"Most certainly."

"Why did you grant me an interview, Monsieur Boudiaf?"

"You write for *Le Monde*. Frenchmen read *Le Monde*, not my underground newspaper. A Frenchmen writing of the excesses of the Army in Algeria has much greater weight."

"I must be guarded in what I write or I will simply be expelled from Algeria. I have already experienced events that I could not report in detail."

"I am aware of that. I am also aware that you have gone to lengths to get that information published through different channels. I believe you are ….."

Our conversation was interrupted by a loud crash from the outer room and a single gunshot. Within moments the door to Boudiaf's office was kicked in. Four army paratroopers in camouflage uniform with weapons crowded into the small room. Boudiaf and I were forced against the wall. An officer told them to handcuff us.

"So it is you, Murphy. Consorting with the enemy now?"

I recognized the officer. It was Captain Perault.

In the outer room, I passed the man who had guided me here. He was lying on the floor with blood pooling about his body. We were marched out of the Casbah under a heavy contingent of paratroopers. Once out of the ancient alleyways to a wide street, we were placed into the back of a truck with a canvas cover. Made to lie face down with our hands cuffed behind our backs, the soldiers placed their feet on our backs to prevent any attempt at resistance. It was only a short ride before I heard heavy doors being opened, and then shutting once the truck had passed through.

Boudiaf and I, along with the two workers I had seen in the printing room, were pushed to an area in the building stacked with wooden crates. I assumed this was a military warehouse near the water by the smell of the air. The warehouse was illuminated by weak lights hanging from the ceiling casting shadows in places.

We were told to sit on the floor. I whispered to Boudiaf, "How did they discover your location?"

Boudiaf looked at me as if I might be the cause of his betrayal. "Someone informed the French. That is always the way. Unless it has something to do with you? We will find out shortly if you are friend or enemy. If you are a friend then you are in for a very bad time as I shall be. If you have betrayed us, then may you suffer damnation in hell."

Perault entered the warehouse ahead of another officer, a major. They were followed by two soldiers carrying a wooden chair. The chair was set in the middle of the open area in front of the truck.

Perault said something to the major and pointed toward me. The more senior officer was an ugly fellow with a large nose and an expression of distain.

He approached to where I was sitting on the floor. "So you are Dillan Murphy. I have heard much about you. All of it bad. Friend of Colonel Berry I understand. The Colonel should choose his friends better. You are obviously not a friend of the French Army. Perhaps you're even a traitor to France."

"And who are you?" I said.

"Major Aussaresses. Colonel Berry was naïve enough to suggest I should grant you an interview. Tried to tell me how important your newspaper was. Seems I'll now be *interviewing* you, Monsieur Murphy."

Shit. This was the guy that orchestrated the atrocities at Philippeville. Massu's butcher. I was suitably terrified. There is no way to prepare for being tortured.

"Captain. Proceed with your interrogations," Aussaresses said to Perault.

"Bring me that one," Perault ordered, pointing to one of the two men. It was the one looking defiant in contrast to the other who was physically shaking with fear.

The man was seated in the chair with his handcuffs re-fixed behind the chair back, effectively securing him to the chair. The truck's headlights were directed into the man's eyes.

Captain Perault began asking questions. The man responded in what I assumed to be Arabic. Perault responded, "Bullshit. You speak French. Now answer my question or I'm going to shoot you in the foot. Then the other foot."

The man blinked then uttered something again in Arabic.

Perault withdrew his revolver and pointed it at the man's right foot. The man looked wide-eyed but said nothing. Perault fired.

I had seen all manner of terrible things in combat, but being a witness to such torture twisted my guts. I vomited.

"Monsieur Murphy, this disturbs you? We have only just started," Aussaresses said. "You shall have your own turn in good time. Think about that."

The wounded man screamed in agony. The muscles of his neck went taut as he dealt with the agony of his wound. Sweat glistened his face. Still he refused to answer Perault's questions.

Perault shot the man in the other foot.

The chair bucked as the man reacted, tipping over on its side. The two soldiers righted the man and chair. The wounded man maintained a constant animal-like groan. His chin rested on his chest. Perault motioned to one of the soldiers. The soldier pulled the man's head upright to stare into the truck headlights and Perault.

"For the last time. Give me some names or you're a dead man."

Whether bravery or simply defiance, the man said nothing. Perault shot him in the forehead.

The soldiers removed the body. Perault motioned to the soldiers, pointing to the other man. Incapacitated with fear, the poor man could not stand without assistance. He urinated as the two soldiers dragged him to the chair.

Boudiaf and I were taken away to a dingy office in the warehouse. Ten minutes later there was a single gunshot.

"Whether Hakim told them anything useful or remained

silent we will never know," Boudiaf said. "Either way, the end is always a bullet. It's only a matter of how much pain one decides to endure. I believe he probably told them everything he knew. That is why we were brought in here. My presence might have given him enough courage to resist."

Boudiaf and I were brought back out into the warehouse. Boudiaf was taken to the chair this time. I was returned to sitting on the floor to watch.

"Do you know what this is, Monsieur Murphy? I am sure Boudiaf here does. Is that not so, Boudiaf? Well to enlighten you, Monsieur Murphy, we call it the *gégène*."

The *gégène* was a portable army signals magneto that produced electrical current when cranked. It was a simple, insidious means of torture. Delivering terrible pain depended upon the intensity of the applied current. It left no outward physical traces.

Boudiaf was a brave man, or maybe just so defiant that he appeared brave. Who can say what goes through the mind under such duress. I watched a sickening spectacle as he was tortured with the *gégène* for half an hour.

He was tied to the chair, including his legs. One electrode was attached to an ear, the other to his penis. As the current was applied, his entire body went rigid. The most disturbing aspect of the torture was that Perault asked no questions until Boudiaf was only barely conscious. The torture continued until Boudiaf could not be revived to a state of consciousness where he could even talk. Boudiaf never give up any information.

"It will soon be your turn, Monsieur Murphy. This is a rare experience for a journalist to actually experience interrogation. I hope you appreciate the opportunity," Major Aussaresses said. "As you can see, the Captain relishes his work. I also believe he dislikes you. I suggest you tell us everything about your association with these terrorists."

My heart was pounding wildly. The thought of being

inflicted with excruciating pain with no hope of cessation was terrifying. That of course was the torturer's premise – suffering with no hope unless you told everything. Assuming the torturer wanted information not just gratification of a sadistic bent.

Boudiaf looked about to die. He was barely conscious. His eyes were rolled back. Blood flowed from his mouth and nose.

There was a commotion somewhere within the warehouse shadows. A voice said, "Stand aside sergeant." I recognized the voice. It was Jacques Berry.

"What the fuck is going on sergeant!" Perault yelled.

Berry entered the area accompanied by two large sergeants, Foreign Legionaires by their uniforms. "Major Aussaresses. What is going on here?"

"Doing my job, Colonel. Gathering intelligence," Aussaresses said.

"Killing and torturing prisoners. That's not the job of a soldier."

"Colonel, if you have a complaint about my work I suggest you take it up with the General."

"Does your work extend to torturing accredited French journalists?"

Aussaresses did not answer. He stood there with an impassive expression.

"I asked you a question, Major," Berry said, standing close to Aussaresses.

"Murphy's working with these terrorists, Colonel. We caught him …." Perault almost spit out the words until Berry cut him off.

"Shut the fuck up, Captain. I'm addressing the Major." Turning back toward Aussaresses, "I said, does that include French journalists from influential newspapers, Major?"

Aussaresses said, "Colonel, this man was arrested with a known wanted man. He therefore has potentially valuable information. It's essential that we question him."

"Torture him you mean. I know what you do. You're a

disgrace to the Army, Aussaresses. And Captain Perault here is a fucking sadist. I'm taking custody of Murphy. You will take that other man into custody," Berry said to his own two sergeants while pointing to the barely conscious Kussil Boudiaf.

"Murphy is my prisoner, Colonel," Aussaresses said on protest.

"I'm pulling rank on you, Major. I'm taking custody of Murphy."

"My orders come directly from General Massu," Aussaresses said.

"So do mine, Major. I suggest you cease being an insubordinate bastard and do as I ordered. Don't cross swords with me, Aussaresses. You're not some protected species. "

Jacques Berry and his two Legionnaire sergeants bundled me away from the warehouse.

Once alone, Berry yelled at me, "Goddamn you, Murphy! Now you've done it. Do you know what you've done? Probably not. Kussil Boudiaf has been at the top of the Army's list of people to silence. They want him dead, not in a prison to become another martyr. Even Paris knows of him with his agitation against the French Army. What the hell were you doing with him?"

"Didn't mean to do this to you, Jacques. Can't begin to tell you how grateful I am for the rescue. That was looking pretty bad. How'd you find out that I was being held by the Major?"

"Because I'm in intelligence and I'm goddamn good at it. How did you think I became Massu's chief of staff? I have my own network of sources. Massu relies on me. He isn't going to like this though."

"Have I got you in trouble, Jacques?"

"Yes, for Christ sakes! But I'll talk my way out of it with Massu. I'll tell him that I rescued Aussaresses from killing you and creating a worse problem. But two things you've got to do. First, you can't write about this. Second, you must leave Algeria immediately. You've got three days at most. I suggest you leave sooner than that. Understood?"

"I understand. What about Boudiaf?"

"What about him? You expect me to rescue him too? My reach has its limits. Boudaif has been a pain in the ass to the Army for some time. It's out of my hands."

That meant that Boudaif would disappear. There was nothing I could do to intervene and I was too shaken to argue further. Berry dropped me at my hotel. It was one o'clock in the morning. I did not sleep. I consumed the better part of a bottle of Scotch while sitting by my room window with my .45 in hand. If Captain Perault should return, I was ready.

At dawn there was a knock on my door. I tensed and moved to the side of the door, ready to shoot whoever might kick in the door. It was Fariza.

We hugged and kissed. After I assured her I was all right, she said, "I waited at the restaurant for three hours. It was becoming awkward being alone there as a woman. So I waited until midnight outside the restaurant. Eventually I had to leave. I knew that something had gone wrong. I waited until the curfew lifted this morning to come here to the hotel. Now tell me what happened, Dillan."

After recounting the events of last night, we got down to pragmatic issues. "I must leave Algeria, Fariza. I have no choice. Ordered out by the Army. Back to Paris. I think you should come with me. It's too dangerous for you in Algiers now. What about it?"

Fariza closed her eyes and sighed. "I would like to be with you, Dillan, but it would not work. What would I do there?"

Neither of us had made declarations of love. We were lovers but I hadn't intimated anything more permanent. Even now my offer sounded more from concern than from love.

"You're a lawyer. There should be opportunities," I said.

"For an Algerian? In the professional ranks? I don't think so. Paris is not that cosmopolitan, or tolerant. I'd be just another North African immigrant."

"Fariza, you can't stay here. You may already be on the

Army's arrest list. You made the connection for me to Boudiaf. Now all of that is blown. Boudiaf thinks there was probably an informer. You could be in danger from either side. I can't bear the thought of you wasting away in one of those camps, or maybe even worse."

Fariza hugged me. "I went to school in France, Dillan. I know what it's like for someone like me to live there. I would never be accepted. How could I live like that? Do you ...." She paused. I knew what she wanted to ask but instead she said, "I must stay, Dillan, and you must leave."

I didn't have an argument. If she did come with me I would be responsible for her. I would take her from this danger but to an alien place. Eventually we would confront my aging problem. In making the offer I had ignored my own resolution to avoid such entanglements. So it was easy to agree with her reasoning for my own self-serving reasons.

We made love for a long time. Both knew it might be for the last time. Afterwards I could hear Fariza sobbing in the bathroom. Once composed and dressed, she shared the last of my Scotch. But soon after, her tears started to flow again. She got up from her chair and quickly kissed me, turning then to leave. "I love you, Dillan, but we were not meant to be together. Remember me."

She pulled away from my grasp and hurriedly left my room. It was the last time I saw Fariza Sahnine.

Elliot Gaston was still in his hotel room when he received my message to join me in the hotel restaurant for lunch. My message conveyed alarm. Gaston was perhaps also in danger so I had to warn him.

"Dillan, what's happened? Your message suggested some urgency," Gaston said as he sat down at my table.

I told him about the previous night's events. He sat quietly trying to absorb the implications.

"Elliot, the Army already sees you and your magazine as unsympathetic to the Army's mission here," I said. "If they connect you directly to the independence movement you could be in real danger of simply disappearing. Had Colonel Berry not arrived to rescue me, I expect I would have been killed last night."

Gaston shook his head and rubbed his face. "Jesus, Dillan. Hearing your firsthand account sends chills up my spine."

"It should, Elliot. Leave here, just like I'm doing. It's not safe. I told Fariza she may be in danger as well. The Army has gone amuck. General Massu knows what goes on and encourages it. This is not a place where an honest journalist can survive."

A waiter came to take our order. My stomach was in knots but I was suddenly very hungry. After ordering omelets, I excused myself to go to the toilet. Two well dressed young women sat down at the table next to us as I walked away. They carried shopping bags.

I was washing my hands in the toilet when the explosion blew in the toilet door and sent me flying against the wall. It was a few moments before I recovered. I struggled to my feet. Touching the side of my head, my hand came away with blood. I grabbed a towel to stem the bleeding.

The scene in the dining room was chaos. Cries and moans came from the wounded. The air was choked with dust. Furniture and bodies covered the entire room. No one was standing. Blood was splashed everywhere. There were body parts and human tissue on the floor and clinging to objects. Hard to tell where our table had been.

After some groping about I discovered Elliot. Or a body I thought was Elliot. Much of the left side of his body was missing. Most of the face was missing. Close by, there was a large hole in the floor. Gaston was apparently close to ground-zero when the bomb exploded. This would have been about the location of the table with the two women and their shopping bags. I couldn't be sure, but I didn't see bodies that looked to be them. So they were perhaps the bombers.

To be sure it was Gaston, I searched the pockets. The passport and wallet confirmed this was Elliot Gaston. I stuffed them into my pocket. I searched to see if he had any other personal effects. Nothing except his hotel room key.

I made my way out of the carnage. Pushing past hotel employees trying to lead me outside, I headed up the stairs to my room on the third floor. Everyone else was coming down the stairs to exit the hotel. I intended to recover my personal belongings and get the hell out of Algeria immediately.

Once in my room, I sat for a time on the bed. I was dizzy, probably from shock. After recovering, I changed clothes and hurriedly packed. When I was ready, I wondered what to do about Gaston's personal effects. I should see if there was anything of importance that I should recover from his room. I had his key. No point in leaving it to the hotel staff to steal.

Gaston had some notes that might prove useful. Some letters. One to someone about taking care of his apartment in Paris. Correspondence to his editor. Nothing to family. Gaston told me he was an orphan raised by an aunt and uncle. They too were killed in an Allied bombing during the War. Not married. This married woman here in Algiers seemed the only person close to him.

The thought struck me with a brilliant flash of clarity. Gaston was my solution. I pulled his passport from my pocket. It was caked with blood. The photograph was damaged. There was a fair resemblance generally to me. Elliot Gaston's year of birth was 1926. That was 28 years younger than my fabricated 1898 birth date. I could become a part of another generation. I could start over. Very soon my documented age would raise unanswerable questions forcing me to move on. I could reinvent myself right now.

Could this be pulled off? Of course. Dillan Murphy just *died* in the bombing. I would leave my personal effects in my room and vacate Elliot Gaston's room. No need to check out with all the chaos going on. What identifies the faceless corpse in the dining room? A process of elimination starting with a checking of hotel guests. Dillan Murphy's passport would be found in his room with his belongings. The destroyed body *could be* Dillan Murphy. Elliot Gaston's room would be empty. There would be a record of Elliot Gaston leaving Algiers by plane to Paris.

It was audacious. It could work. Elliot Gaston had no family. His only known romantic attachment was the woman in Algiers. She was married so no expected complications there. More than that, he was also a journalist. As Gaston, I would *resign* from *L'Express* where he was known. But I would still have a journalistic resume to work elsewhere. Was there a moral prohibition against doing this? Was I not entitled to survive with my strange affliction? I was not hurting anyone. Still, I was slightly uncomfortable with the ethical questions.

I was in a desperate hurry before someone showed up at my door. So for expediency, I simply left all my clothes, Murphy's clothes, and took Gaston's clothes and all his personal items. Except for picking out a few select personal items, I abandoned most of my personal effects and clothing.

So Dillan Murphy died in 1957, and Elliot Gaston was born again in a manner of speaking.

CHAPTER 46

"My God, that's extraordinary, Elliot," Allison said. "So there was a real Elliot Gaston. I guess you are Elliot Gaston now so that takes care of that name confusion. I can feel comfortable in calling you what I've always been used to. Your adventures are absolutely transfixing. Do you think this Major Aussaresses would really have subjected you to torture?"

"That I'm certain of. And Captain Perault would have relished inflicting it. Would they have killed me? Very possibly but I don't know for sure. Aussaresses was certainly capable of it. He would have had Perault kill Boudaif that night had Jacques Berry not intervened. It's likely Boudaif was killed anyway. He just vanished after that night. No body was ever found. Buried somewhere in an unmarked grave like so many others.

"More important people than me were murdered by the French Army in Algeria. That arrogant bastard Aussaresses was eventually promoted to general. In 2000, he went public detailing his use of torture and summary execution in Algeria.

Wrote a book. You should read it. He's unapologetic about his actions.

"It was unbelievably ugly. Algeria came close to destroying France as a democratic republic."

"How was Algeria that extreme?' Allison asked. "Why was it any worse than Indochina?"

"In Indochina, the French lost a war in a remote colony. Losing Algeria was like a piece of France seceding from the country. By 1962, 30,000 Frenchman had been killed and 500,000 Arabs. In desperation, the Army turned to terror tactics in an attempt to crush the insurgency. It didn't work of course. Never does. When it became clear Algeria would be granted independence, dissident army officers serving in Algeria came close to overthrowing the French government in a military coup d'état."

"So you left Algeria and returned to Paris – as Elliot Gaston. That must have certainly been strange. What did it feel like to now be someone else?"

"Lots of conflicting emotions. Sadness mostly. It was like giving up my past. Never to share those memories. Losing again all those people I had loved and lost before. The terrible uncertainty of starting what amounted to a new life. Now I would have another dimension of secrecy beyond just hiding my true age. Everything in my life was now false."

Elliot explained the details of escaping Algeria and entering his new identity. Before leaving Algiers, he sent a telegram to the editor of *L'Express* resigning. The stated reason was physical and emotional wounds sustained in the Algeria bombing. He would not be returning to Paris, but rather to Normandy to stay with relatives.

Dillan Murphy rented an apartment in Paris so there was no investment to be lost. As Elliot Gaston, a letter was sent to Murphy's landlady saying that he regretted to inform her that her tenant Dillan Murphy had been killed in a bombing in Algiers. A clipping from *Le Monde* about Murphy's death was enclosed. She could dispose of his belongs since there were no known relatives. He emptied his Dillan Murphy bank account immediately upon arriving in Paris. The thought struck him that he could now access any money Elliot Gaston had. Was that theft?

Next was to firmly establish documentation as Elliot Gaston. Gaston's passport was damaged with the photo torn and smeared with blood. While there was a resemblance, the damage helped, as well as to provide a perfect excuse to seek a replacement. The clerk was most solicitous after seeing his head wound and hearing the story of the bombing. He explained that another wound in his torso damaged the passport. A replacement passport was issued for Elliot Gaston with Dillan Murphy's photograph. The transition was official.

"Simple as that to get someone else's identity?" Allison asked.

"In 1957, it was. In today's world with electronic databases and threats of terrorism, it wouldn't be anywhere near that simple."

"Ok, so now you're Elliot Gaston. Did he have an apartment somewhere?"

"Yes. Also in Paris. North of the Seine, in the 3rd Arrondissement, the Marais district. My place had been in the 5th on the Left Bank, south of the river, so I would not be recognized in the same neighborhoods."

"Christ, this is confusing," Allison said. "But Gaston's neighbors would know you weren't Gaston. How did you get around that?"

"Simple. Gaston was away on assignment. I was an old friend. He was letting me use his apartment. That's the story I told a couple of neighbors that I ran into in the hallway. It was a good enough cover for a few weeks until I found somewhere else. At least that was my plan until something unexpected intervened."

Elliot paused and took a deep breath, seeming to organize

his thoughts before going on.

"Elliot, what's the matter? What happened back then?"

"Something terrible. It has always troubled me."

Allison said nothing as she watched Elliot wrestle with his thoughts.

"It happened within three weeks of my return to Paris. Although I was still mentally off balance as I grappled with adapting to my new identity, circumstances were going to plan. I had moved into Elliot's apartment. The neighbors bought my cover story. I had new identification papers. I was free to start a new life as someone born to the generation suggested by my appearance."

"What about all your personal belongings? Did you leave everything? Didn't you go back to your own apartment?"

"No I never went back. Too risky. Dillan Murphy was dead. But as far as personal things, there was nothing of real importance. Most anything of nostalgic value was lost during World War Two. Since the War, I traveled light. Never was much concerned about material things anyway. Sacrificed some clothing, but Gaston's shirts and suits fit pretty well. My journals and some writing notes I requested the landlady send to Elliot Gaston's address."

"Ok. So what happened that was so terrible, Elliot?"

"I killed someone."

"You mean you killed somebody in Paris?"

"Yes."

"An accident?

"Not exactly, though it was self-defense. Still, it was an ugly thing. I had no choice but to cover it up. If I went to the police it would be discovered that I wasn't Elliot Gaston. What happened to the real Elliot Gaston? Then my real identity would be examined. I suspect it would lead to more accusations about impersonating others because of my impossible life history. I would never escape the tangle of lies and the impossible truth."

For the next thirty minutes, Elliot explained what had happened.

From *Time Travels* by Dillan Murphy
PARIS, FRANCE - 1956

About a month after I had returned to Paris, I was returning to the apartment, Elliot's apartment remember. I unlocked the outer common entry door and entered the building. Someone else entered immediately behind me. I turned and recoiled as I recognized the man.

He was equally shocked. The heavy door slammed shut behind him.

"Murphy!" Captain Perault said. He was dressed in a civilian suit with a felt hat. A pistol with a silencer was pointed at me.

"Perault? What the hell are you doing here?"

"I have the same question of you, Murphy. You must know Gaston if you're here at his apartment."

I hesitated while trying to think of what to do. "What do you want with Gaston?"

"Shut up. Get upstairs," Perault ordered. "If you do anything sudden I will not hesitate to kill you."

Perault would know Gaston's apartment number from the post box label. We took the stairs to the third floor. Outside of Elliot's apartment, my apartment now, I turned to look at Perault.

"Knock," he said.

I knocked. Waited. Then repeated the futile exercise twice again.

"Where is he, Murphy?"

"I have no idea. He wasn't expecting me. I just decided to drop by and see if he was interested in a drink."

"You're friends with Gaston?"

"Acquaintances. Professional acquaintances. From our mutual work in Algiers."

"So you must have met Lucille?"

I was dumbfounded. The married woman Elliot Gaston was seeing was obviously Perault's wife. He was having an affair with the wife of a sadistic paratroop officer.

"We didn't socialize together in Algiers. I don't recall meeting any woman named Lucille. Who is she?"

"Never mind. We'll wait."

We waited outside the apartment door for close to two hours. All I could do was continue the charade. I had no idea where this was going, or what I could do to take control of the situation.

"Fuck this. Tell me what's going on, Murphy." Perault raised his pistol, pointing it at my face. "Where is he?"

"I told you, I don't know."

"Where do you live, Murphy?"

"Go to hell, Perault. I've no intention of letting you take me there."

Perault glared at me while weighing his options. Shooting me outside Elliot Gaston's apartment would thwart his revenge plans.

"Perhaps I'll shoot you in the arm. You know I am capable of doing that. No one will hear. Then the other arm if you don't cooperate. Want to reconsider and tell me where you live?"

Perault was losing control. His eyes confirmed that. He might very well shoot me. It was a terrifying prospect. He was prone to violence and maybe even psychotic. Adding revenge for being cuckolded made for an unstable mix.

"I might bleed enough to fall unconscious. Perhaps right here," I said. "Wouldn't be able to walk far probably. Blood all over the place. Then what do you do?"

Perault knew his threat to shoot me was hollow. I was now an obstacle preventing him getting to Gaston. He would need to get rid of me, but away from here. The clarity of that conclusion was unsettling. All I could do was stall for some time.

He ushered me out of the building and directed us south toward the River Seine.

"Why are you in Paris, Perault? You're not in uniform. Does the Army know you're here? Maybe you deserted?"

"Shut up, Murphy." The gun was pushed into my back.

I could not guess where we might be going other than for Perault to find a secure place to kill me. That became clear when we reached the river at Pont Sully. Perault pushed me down the stone stairway to the quay alongside the river. Once he was sure there was no one watching us he would simply shoot me and then push my body into the river.

Perault shoved me towards the shadowed area next to the wall under the stairway. With perhaps only moments before he shot me, I stopped abruptly. Perault pushed his weapon into my lower back as I hoped he would. Once the silencer touched me I knew where it was. Not hesitating, I swung around counter-clockwise catching his wrist holding the pistol with my left elbow. He did not drop the weapon, but it was forced away from me. Taking a step toward him, I threw my weight behind my right arm as I drove my fist into his nose.

The blow was on target. A sickening crunching sound confirmed I had done real damage. Perault went down on his back. The pistol dropped from his hand. Blood gushed from his face. He was unconscious.

I fell to my knees. My right hand hurt. The skin on two knuckles was split open. After a few moments to recover, I bent over Perault. His eyes were open but unresponsive. He was still unconscious. Blood continued to pour from his shattered nose. I felt for a pulse at his neck. Didn't think I felt one but it was hard to say. Adrenalin was causing my own heartbeats to pound in my ears.

I looked around. The quayside on both sides of the Seine was well lit but there were no people about on this chilly night. Perault's body was still in the shadows. Hard to say if any one might be looking down from the street level from the opposite side of the river. Hopefully it was too far away for anyone to really have seen what happened. I checked Perault's neck again. Definitely no pulse.

I wiped the blood from my hand on his coat and tucked the silenced pistol under his body, careful to avoid leaving any fingerprints. Might as well let the police puzzle over why the victim was armed with a silenced military issued weapon.

"Oh my God, Elliot," Allison said. "I can see why you needed to avoid going to the police. But you didn't feel guilty about it did you? Perault was a sadistic monster. You were only defending yourself."

"All of that's true. Days later I read in the newspapers about the body of an army officer being found by the Seine. It reported the officer, serving in Algeria, had been wanted for desertion and the murder of his wife. There were no details about his death, no name was given."

"See what I mean. The guy was a torturer and a murderer. He would have certainly murdered you too. No reason to feel guilty," Allison said.

"It wasn't really guilt. It was just one more thing to have to hide. What I thought was a resolution to my aging problem just added more secrecy and complexity. Even now the intricate web of realities, lies, dates, whose history I am living sometimes becomes overwhelming. Always being guarded about even the smallest personal detail adds a stress that makes it easier to simply avoid many social circumstances."

"It's hard to reconcile the two people you are, Elliot. For thirty years I thought you were this distinguished Frenchman. A literary figure. Sophisticated and urbane. Yet I've listened to your personal history that is laced with violence. You're someone entirely different. An Irish-American son of a coal miner who can be a very dangerous man when crossed.

"Was. I haven't killed anyone for years."

"Elliot, don't joke about that. You know what I mean."

"Yes I do. I've never thought about it that way. Guess I can see your point. Still, I think it's just the chance events created by dangerous circumstances. A journalist going in harm's way. Most of the violence has been in times of war."

"Not all though. What about New York in the early years? And this attack on you in Paris," Allison said.

"But those events were still bred of dangerous circumstances from my job." Elliot said.

"A fine point. Even granting your longevity, you've still experienced a considerable amount of violence. But returning to your story, did you go back to reporting after Algeria?"

"Not for a couple of years. I moved to an apartment in the 7th Arrondissement on a quiet street just off Rue du Bac. More upscale than the place in the 5th where I had lived in the 1920's and again after the War. Less students, less commotion. Well suited for writing which is what I did for the next several years."

"This is when you wrote your first books as Elliot Gaston?"

"Yes. The first was the novel *The Casbah*. Published in 1964. It was a not so thinly veiled story of my own time in Algeria. All the real players with the names changed of course. I followed that with *Lion Country* in 1967. It was about the Mau Mau rebellion in Kenya. That was not as much autobiographical."

"I don't know these titles, Elliot. At least I never read them. I do remember seeing references to your prior work when we took you on in 1981, but I never read them."

"They were published in Europe. Probably out of print by the time you knew me."

"Were they well received?"

"Not particularly. At least they weren't commercially successful. Neither the French nor the British wanted to be confronted with their colonial sins. After many rejections, *The Casbah* was finally picked up by the French publisher, Éditions

Gallimard. If not for the controversy it raised, sales might have even been worse.

"Read *Lion Country* if you can find a copy. It was some of my best work. I tried to give white people a sense of what is was like being on the wrong end of racism and colonialism. Racism and civil rights was a hot issue around the world in the 1960's. Some literary critics, especially in France and the United States, gave it good reviews. The British were not any more receptive to national criticism than the French. However, these works established me as a writer and got me accepted by your agency."

"So what was your lifestyle like while you were writing? Did you become reclusive after all that happened during the prior twenty years?"

"In some respects maybe. I had my routine. Wake late and then take a walk in the morning after coffee and reading the newspapers. Still the journalist at heart. Kept current on world events. I would make myself a light lunch and then write all afternoon, sometimes working well into the evening if the words flowed. I still went out for drinks and dinner occasionally."

"Women? After all your love affairs you didn't become a hermit I hope, Elliot. You had a lusty life up to then. Women were a part of your life. Tell me you were still fond of the ladies, even at …. my God, in your late eighties at the time!"

"I'm told that people even into their nineties continue to have sex," Elliot said with a smile.

"Especially if they look no more than forty. Which by the way, the real Elliot Gaston would have been what, in his thirties? Could you pass for that young?"

"I thought so. I looked no more than forty at any rate. I had the onset of a few gray hairs which I covered with hair dye for a few years. After that, letting some gray show added the appearance of normal aging."

"You're evading the question, Elliot. Were there more loves in your life?"

Elliot turned serious as he seemed to ponder the question. "There have been many women over these last decades. It's been fifty years since I became Elliot Gaston. There were a number of wonderful women over that long time. But I had learned my lesson. None of these affairs led to lasting relationships. A lot of hurt and disappointments, but in the end it has been a wise course."

Allison was taken with how sad Elliot looked with that pronouncement. For some reason, she suspected he was not telling her the entire truth.

CHAPTER 47

"But you did go back into journalism, right?" Allison asked. "Hard to see you giving up chasing real stories."

"Oh yes. It was in my nature I guess. I was drawn to being involved with world events. Remember this was the foundation of my fiction writing. So the next order of business was employment under my new identity as Elliot Gaston. But the more pressing reason was the fact that I would be an unpublished author as Elliot Gaston. I didn't get *The Casbah* published until 1964. I needed a more steady income until my fiction writing could prove sustaining.

"After hearing about what happened in Algeria, I'll have to read *The Casbah*," Allison said. "I was too focused on my job of editing your first work with us, *Le Resistance*, to bother with reading older material."

"Probably difficult to find a copy of it today. It was only published in French. Like I said, it wasn't commercially successful. Made a few enemies with *The Casbah*. I painted both sides in the Algerian War unsympathetically. The insurgents were a bunch of ideologues bent on forcing out the French at any cost. Their methods were murder and terror. That is typical to those without the means to wage conventional war. The French were committed to holding onto the last remaining territory of empire. This resulted in the Army degenerating into acts of torture and summary execution fully as bad as the insurgents. Remember, the OAS, the secret army organization, had just staged a failed coup so Algeria was still an open wound. It had only been a few years since the Paris Massacre. The public saw my book mostly as unpatriotic.

"The what?" Allison asked.

"The Paris Massacre happened in 1961. It was a perfect storm of factors that could only have ended in tragedy. The Algerian FLN had been committing killings and bombings targeted against police in France. Then 30,000 pro-FLN Algerians staged a demonstration, peaceful but still banned. Against them was the Parisian Police headed by Maurice Papon. Unfortunately, Papon had recently served as a prefect for one of the departments in Algeria. He was part of the repression going on in Algeria. Later evidence actually implicated Papon as personally instigating the firing on the Paris demonstrators."

"How many were killed?"

"Over a hundred, maybe as many as three hundred. Even that was covered up for a while. I was there. I took photos. It made me think of the village in Algeria. Yet this was Paris."

"I see what you mean about Algeria being such a big deal to France."

"Those photos and my copy were filed with a wire service as a freelancer. It helped land me a job with my old employer, the *New York Times*. I had Elliot Gaston's journalism credentials and I was fluent in English. At first I was just a stringer but as the Cold War progressed, the *Times* made me a correspondent in their Paris bureau. Fortunately, most of my work was centered in Paris so I traveled only infrequently, and then only within Eu-

rope. It was the time of the Cold War. That became my new reporting arena.

"Since I wanted to devote my real energies to fiction writing,
that work schedule worked well. *Lion Country*, set against the
Mau Mau Uprising in Kenya, was published in the U.K in 1967."

"You said that didn't sell well either? Why not? I see why
The Casbah would have had trouble in France. Did the Brits have
the same problem?"

"No it didn't sell well. My penchant for writing about unpo-
pular events was not good for marketing. The British still had
strong feelings about their own dwindling empire. But it's some
good work, one of my best. Also got me published in English."

"Did you cover any of the wars going on during the 60's,
Vietnam or the Israeli-Arab wars?" Allison asked.

"Only from the perspective of Europe. Only from the political perspective of the Cold War. Didn't go back to either place.
Glad to have missed those wars. Bad enough when I was in both
places twenty years earlier. The last war I covered from the field,
if you can call it a war, was the *troubles* in Northern Ireland. I
had a fleeting interest to explore my ethnic roots. But the experience didn't strike any feelings of ethnic ancestry in me. My father never pushed our Irishness. It had no real meaning to me."

"So how did you think of yourself? As American?"

"I suppose. But I'll confess, those feelings were not strong either. Even early on I had a critical view of nationalism whether
as a country or a culture. There are no good governments or cultures. Only individuals can be good."

"Ok. Sorry to have sidetracked from your story," Allison
said. "So you went to Northern Ireland. When was that?"

"1973. The start of a sectarian conflict that would go on for
twenty-five years. The Irish have been trying to drive the British
from the Island for centuries. Crack British paratroops had just
killed fourteen unarmed Catholic civilians the previous year in
Londonderry. As a journalist, you could always rely on the Brit-

ish or the French to be killing people in some other country. Anyway, the incident in Londonderry provided the basis for the Provisional Irish Republican Army to gain support among Catholics. The old IRA had almost collapsed as a cause. The British, stupid as always, gave life to a new bloody insurgency in Northern Ireland."

"And from that experience came *Belfast, A Novel of the Troubles*?" Allison asked. "That was the second book I marketed as your agent. I loved the older IRA gunman character."

"Me too. He was based on a real person. But Northern Ireland was just another conflict. It was personally more depressing than other conflicts I witnessed first-hand. Here was a western industrialized country consumed by the same social and political antagonisms as developing countries."

"Was that your last assignment? Were you getting too old for that type of thing?"

Elliot smiled. "If not physically, then at least emotionally. Northern Ireland was the last. You cannot continually see brutality and suffering without losing something in yourself. I hated war, yet was drawn to it for my own reasons. There's nothing more visceral to experience and to write about. For whatever reason, I got it out of my system. I had plenty enough experiences to sustain my writing. So I left professional journalism in 1975 to devote myself to writing."

"Your work has always been anti-war. For that matter, anti a lot of things. Some might suggest like Dominique did that at heart you're an anarchist," Allison said.

"I've developed some very strong feelings about war and the governments that wage war. War seems always the inevitable solution to social and economic differences. Its origin derives from ethnic and cultural tribalism that seems to exist in all societies. The social grouping becomes the principle body of identification for most peoples. People have a compelling need to identify with some group for security and validation of one's being.

Those that differ often become the enemy. All it takes is for someone seeking power to marshal the social group's jealousy, prejudice, greed, or fear. All of history is about that.

"Governments and societies always hold up the loftiest of principles as to why they must destroy the *enemy*. How else to convince young men to risk their lives? And in every war, young men are drawn to it for reasons of duty, glory, or simply adventure. The ideologues and politicians are only too happy to beat the drum of some corrupted policy to send young men to their death. Each side prays to their own god to help them kill the other."

Allison said, "I can see why you feel as you do by listening to you recount your life these past few days. But your books are about war, so it obviously holds a particular fascination for you."

"That's true. At the core, I'm a journalist. Because war shapes most of history, therefore war is the most compelling of events to write about. It's a perfect canvas to paint my stories. Stories about people caught up in these terrible events. I want the reader to experience my characters in these extremes. I want them to think about why these events happened, why they're not the simplistic black and white positions portrayed by the opposing sides. I want the reader to experience these histories through the eyes of real people not a dry history of facts. Fiction is the perfect way to express my opinions by illustrating rather than just telling."

"I love your characters, but I also delight in your unkind treatment of some of the major figures of this century. You clearly have contempt for most institutions, and you're not very generous to religion either."

"No argument there. If anyone reads history, you come away seeing war as a complex mix of factors. Although I've made war so much a part of my writing, I feel disgust with so much of the circumstances I have seen first-hand. It's never glorious, only ugly, and usually economically driven. Government and religion are often joined together in committing terrible damage on others, all in the name of some self-serving perversion. People see the First and Second World Wars as wars of combatants thrown at each other in epic military battles. There were collateral casualties, but still it was mostly one army against another. The conflicts I covered in the fifties and sixties were wars that seemed aimed at whole populations, not just at surrogate armies. They were largely civil wars even when they crossed political borders."

"I can feel that as you have recounted your experiences. As horrific as your telling of World War One is, Palestine, Kenya, and Algeria seemed worse in many respects," Allison said.

"As bad as the horrors of combat are, they shrink in comparison to the bestiality one ethnic group inflicts upon another in these nasty regional conflicts. History is not so much about heroes and villains as it is about people in power just doing the wrong things for the wrong reasons. I hope my writings convey those dark shades of history through my own experiences and through my characters.

"But enough of my harangue. I'll let my stories speak for themselves. That also brings us to lunch and the end of my narrative. *Time Travels* treats the rest of my life since the 1970's more briefly. That period is more a study of the challenges in contending with the consequences of advancing age without the commensurate advancing appearance. No interesting adventures."

"Your age, or lack of showing it, must have started to become a problem again," Allison said. "By your Gaston identity you were in your seventies by the year 2000. Couldn't travel out of France I'd guess. Your passport would raise potentially awkward questions in today's times. How have you managed that?"

"That's right. Last time I traveled out of Europe was in 1981. The time I went to New York to meet with your agency. The first time I met you, Allison."

"My god. That was almost thirty years ago. Doesn't seem that long ago."

"Beyond the inability to travel by air, there are other increasing difficulties. For example, my cancer treatments are paid by me. Using my French health card would be a problem. Couldn't exactly apply for private health insurance either. If I were not terminal I would be facing some eventual crisis around my documented age."

Allison just looked at him sadly.

"But to other things. There are some other materials I want to give you, Allison."

Elliot went to a file cabinet in his work area and extracted an envelope. He dumped out several black and white photographs onto the coffee table. Allison picked up the photographs. Their condition showed their age.

"All of these seem to be you. I can see that. You look to be in your early forties."

"Yes. They were taken since World War Two. Look at the dates and places noted on the back. I was actually 75 to 90 in these pictures."

Allison looked at each repeatedly. She was seeing her proof. These were unquestionably photos of Elliot Gaston/Dillan Murphy.

"And this item as well." He carefully removed a parchment document from the envelope. "This is my diploma from Columbia. Dated 1894. I was twenty-one. It's still in pretty good shape even though it's traveled a lot in the last hundred years. Of course that doesn't really prove that *I am* Dillan Murphy but it adds to the argument. And there is one final item. The only piece of real hard evidence I can offer."

Elliot brought out an ink stamp pad and proceeded to apply his right thumbprint to several sheets of paper. "You will find that my thumb print matches a passport record issued in 1917 prior to my going to France. I assume such archives must still exist. So what do you think, Allison? Do you now believe my story?"

Allison rose from her chair and put her arms around Elliot's neck as he was still seated. "I do, Elliot. As much as my intellect tells me not to, I do believe you. I've watched you tell me episodes of your life for several days. It could never be a fiction."

"No, but I could still just be a skilled delusional lunatic," Elliot offered.

"I don't think so. I've known you for thirty years. You're not delusional. But I'm still not sure why you felt compelled to write *Time Travels*."

"Too good a story not to write. Don't you agree? Some perversity in my makeup perhaps. Throwing my confounding condition of abnormal longevity out there, hoping to cause a controversy. And only after I'm gone. I certainly hope there's a controversy. Hope that the publicity will get my story read. Wish I could be around to observe it. More than that, *Time Travels* is my lasting imprint that I existed."

"I'd say you more than just existed. Your life has been about battling the bad guys. And you sure found your share. As cynical as you profess to be, your life has been a succession of triumphs. You've been a crusader all your life. So maybe you're not that cynical."

"Oh, but I am. Just contentious that's all. Not willing to accept things as they are. But I still think the world will never change for the better. Wars will never cease. Someone, some group will always want power at the expense of others. Can't get more cynical than that."

"Maybe you are cynical, or maybe just disillusioned with all that you've experienced. But there's another side of you, the side that still values people, the side that cares about rightness, the side that still loves. You may harbor a negative view of larger possibilities but you are more complex than what that implies."

"I'll agree with you that life is complex. My writings do not clarify anything. I never discovered any universal truth. Not sure I ever acquired any real wisdom. It's about seeing the complexities of life. Readers can draw their own conclusions from my work."

"And trying to publish *Time Travels* as non-fiction will make it more powerful," Allison said. "Still not sure I can make that happen. I'll be lucky just to get a publisher to take it without the label of a *novel*."

"I know you'll try. On a practical note, when you get back to New York, check on my earlier books authored as Dillan Murphy. Not sure if copies exist anywhere. And check out the old archives of the *Herald* and the *Times* with the Dillan Murphy by-line. You know my writing. Read them and see if they're me. You must also check out the fingerprint. That might take some doing. The records are so old. I would have no idea where they might be archived. But that's the only absolute evidence I can offer."

"I will, Elliot. But more importantly, I'd like you come back to New York with me. We'll get you to the best specialists on treating the leukemia. You can stay at my apartment. Please, Elliot?" Allison said.

Elliot embraced her. "Allison, I've been to the best oncologists in Paris. New York won't change the diagnosis. I know your offer to stay with you is genuine. But I won't have myself as an invalid. It might come to that near the end I'm told. I mean to stay right here as long as I can manage. Provence has been my home for a good deal of my life. The better times of my life were here. What better place to die?"

"I understand. I'd probably feel the same way. It's still so sad. Tell you what; I have to be in London in a couple of months. I'd like to come back down here to see how you're getting along," she said. She wondered if he would live that long.

"I'd love that," Elliot said and kissed her cheek. "Now let's open a very good bottle of Bordeaux and decide on where to go to dinner since this is your last night."

"That sounds wonderful, Elliot. But you haven't told me anything about your current life. I've never thought about it, but you've never mentioned any special woman in your life all the years I have known you. Let's see, I met you in 1981. You were ... you would have been over a hundred years old? Christ that sounds absurd to even say it. But anyway, you were ancient then. If you'll permit me an intimate question, are you, or were you, whatever indelicate way to ask it......still sexually active?"

Elliot laughed with genuine amusement. "The answer to your question is yes. The fact is I am the age you see, not the chronological age. I have had a few affairs over these last several decades. I have been in love more than once. Like I said before, I've learned to establish boundaries since inevitably these relationships could not last. "

Allison could not help a broad grin. "I'm sorry, Elliot, but the vision just struck me of someone over a hundred screwing." They both laughed almost to the point of tears.

"I'm sure I've disappointed several women. I know my own heart was broken a few times. I knew what it was like to be so in love and connected as I had been with Dominique. But I realized the insurmountable problems of my abnormal longevity in a permanent relationship. I was simply afraid to go there. I have lost so much and cost others so much with my strange existence."

"Is there someone at the moment?"

Elliot thought for a moment before answering, "There's a woman in Orange, just north of here that I see regularly. Her name is Claudette Dubois. A widow. Owns an art gallery. Loves classical music. Accomplished violinist herself."

"Ah, I knew it. Young and voluptuous I suppose?"

"You are obsessed with my love life," Elliot responded jokingly. "Yes, my lady friend is very attractive, however she is over fifty. Here, let me show you."

Elliot retrieved a photo album with 8x10 prints among several on a book shelf. He thumbed through to a particular photo and handed the album to Allison. "This is Claudette."

Allison took the album in her lap. "I should say she's attractive. More than that actually. Intriguing face. Or perhaps it's your photography. I can see the intelligence in her face. Obviously your type. Looks like this actress – can't think of her name. It's the eyes, Elliot. She has really special eyes. You've captured whatever it is."

"Of course it's the eyes. Every artist knows that. Capturing it is the challenge. But it has to exist first with the subject. The photographer can't paint it in like a painter might."

Allison flipped through the other photographs. "Elliot, these are extraordinary. Wonderful images of Europe."

Most of the pictures were of architectural subjects and scenes composed of something mundane. Some were of people, mostly captured in some state of doing something rather than posed. All had an art quality with their dramatic use of lighting. All were black and white. Claudette's photos were the only posed shots in the album, and the only photos where the woman was the sole subject.

"Just a hobby over the years. Most of these are from the 1980's on. Remember how I told you I picked up photography after my assignment in Nuremburg. It satisfies another artistic side. Good diversion during my low times. Always wished I could paint but never thought I had enough talent. I progressed beyond just pictures to real compositions. I was intrigued by the influence of light so I experimented. Never used a flash. Worked with the light I had and manipulated the camera settings to achieve what I wanted. Never have used color film. The black and white achieves a more dramatic effect with the influence of lighting. Learned how to develop my own work."

"These are really good, Elliot. Let me show them to some people I know in the art world. You could …."

"Could what, Allison? Get my photography exhibited? I'm dying remember. I don't need another career."

"Shit. It's such a waste," Allison said.

"No it's not. It's been a long and glorious life. I've experienced extraordinary events and met wonderful people. You're one of those wonderful people, Allison."

"You have been a special person in my life as well, Elliot." She felt tears coming on.

Elliot showed her his range of photographic work while they drank wine. Elliot's manuscript and illness were not discussed. With the wine and the emotional rollercoaster of his strange tale, Elliot was able to steer the remaining evening into a discussion of Allison's life. This was a special evening that turned out just right.

Elliot drove Allison to the Avignon TGV rail station early the next morning. A drizzling rain and gray sky added to the gloom. It was a tearful goodbye for both when she boarded the train to Paris. Allison kissed him on the lips.

That was the last time Allison Kryszka's was to see Elliot Gaston.

CHAPTER 48

MANHATTAN, NEW YORK CITY – 2009

Within a month after her return from Provence, Allison Kryszka was convinced that Elliot Gaston was absurdly, inexplicably Dillan Murphy born in 1873. She had tracked down obscure copies of Murphy's novels. The writing style she knew intimately as Elliot Gaston was evident in the voice of Dillan Murphy. Church records in Schuylkill County, Pennsylvania confirmed a Dillan Murphy's birth in 1873, as well as the death of his mother a few years later. It took a private investigator to secure the old finger print record of the young newspaper correspondent of World War One from old government archives. A lab confirmed the match to the finger prints she had witnessed Elliot making for her. The concurrence of a second expert opinion left no doubt. The technical jargon cited so many points of match, et cetera, both providing a 99.5% validity factor.

She was now convinced this preposterous circumstance of Dillan Murphy's longevity was real. It was now a question of how to proceed with handling *Time Travels*. Who could she get to edit the manuscript? Obviously it could only be her. How to go about getting it published? She couldn't just approach publishers as if it was non-fiction, a true account of the author's life. Perhaps just float the manuscript without saying anything as to perspective? Obviously it would be considered a novel. What else could it be? There was simply no way to convince anyone. She had only come to believe it herself after spending days listening to the person she knew as Elliot Gaston. The problem seemed intractable.

Communicating with Elliot was always cumbersome. He refused to get an e-mail address or a cell phone. Communication with Elliot was by snail mail or FedEx. She had discussed this with him on many occasions. His consistent response was that both forms of communication were intrusive. He saw no reason to give others immediate personal access to him. Yet here was someone who embraced using the technology of a personal computer for writing and the resources of the Internet for research. Even Elliot agreed it was a somewhat stubborn resistance to progress.

Two months after returning from France, Allison received a bulky envelope at her New York office. It was addressed from Aix-en-Provence, France. A number of lengthy legal documents were enclosed, all in French. The cover letter was in English.

Dear Mademoiselle Kryszka:

It is with regret that I must inform you of the apparent death of Monsieur Elliot Gaston. Monsieur Gaston regrettably appears to have died in a boating accident near Marseille approximately two weeks ago. The circumstances are not entirely clear, but it appears that Monsieur Gaston may have fallen overboard. A small power boat, rented by Monsieur Gaston, was found adrift several kilometers from shore in the Mediterranean. Monsieur Gaston had apparently rented the boat in the small coastal village of Cassis. Although, his body has not been recovered, the police feel that Monsieur Gaston may have fallen overboard while the engine was running. The boat was found without any fuel

remaining and the throttle in the power position. There was no indica-
tion of foul play, but there was some evidence that liquor may have
played a part.

Monsieur Gaston has not been officially declared dead, however
Monsieur Gaston left specific instructions with our law firm. Those
instructions state that in the event of his death, or reason to assume his
death based upon my personal assessment of the facts, I was to execute
certain transactions on his behalf in which he invested me with power
of attorney. Essentially, I am executing Monsieur Gaston's last will
and testament. Enclosed you will find an itemized list of assets that
Monsieur Gaston wished you to have. The necessary legal documents
to facilitate those transactions are enclosed. I have included copies of all
documents in both French and English. A certain portion of Monsieur
Gaston's estate will be placed in an escrow account to satisfy French
estate taxes. Several documents require your signature in the places
indicated on the French copies.

Monsieur Gaston has also included a sealed envelope addressed to
you personally.

Please do not hesitate to contact me if I may be of any assistance.
My sincerest condolences for your loss.

Respectfully,
Henri Randal
Attorney at Law

Allison cried out loud after reading the letter. When her secretary rushed in to see what was wrong, Allison was crying and
said, "I'm ok, just some personal bad news. Hold my calls and
shut the door please." It was several minutes before she opened
the sealed envelope from Elliot.

Dearest Allison,

When you read this, Allison, I will be gone. However, I had to leave
you with this before I left this very long life behind. There is something
important that you need to know. Forgive me if this hurts you, which I

fear it will. Nonetheless, I feel compelled to offer a confession. But first I must tell you a brief story. A story about your mother.

I met Marie Kryszka in 1957, in Paris after returning from Algeria. I was having dinner alone at a restaurant in the Latin Quarter. At an adjacent table, your Mother was dining alone. She obviously did not speak French, and her English was heavily accented by her native Polish. There was some difficulty communicating with the waiter, so I offered my assistance. Admittedly, I was attracted to your Mother. She was an elegant beauty. Engaging her in English, I was quickly captivated. Small talk revealed she wrote fiction so there was an immediate topic of mutual interest. The short version is that we connected on a much deeper level. We spent five days together in Paris. She never told me why she was in Paris.

Unfortunately, Marie left Paris. She was married and felt a deep remorse over our brief affair. I learned this from a note she left. She begged me not to try to find her. I couldn't at any rate since I knew only that she was going to the United States. I told you about how difficult that period was in my life. Your mother was a bright hope only to be extinguished before it could really begin. It was another terrible blow. Our brief Paris romance was like Bogart and Bergman in <u>Casablanca</u>.

With all that I have told you about my loves and affairs, you may think your mother was just another of those women that moved in and out of my life. It was only a few days but she had a deep effect on me. Maybe because she left me but I think it was much more.

It was twenty years later that I again heard from your mother. Again by a letter. It was posted from an attorney with instructions to locate me after her death. It was in that letter that she confessed that you were my daughter.

There is no delicate way to tell you that. She trusted me to decide if I would tell you or not. I decided that would not be fair to you. Your mother chose not to tell you so I decided to do the same. I was a complete stranger. You had your own life. And I had my 'special problem' that would eventually complicate any relationship. So I did the next best thing by creating a connection with you as my agent. It was opportune that you became involved with writing. Perhaps your mother's influence there. Glad your agency took me on. I have watched your career with pride. Now that your mother and father and I are all gone, I wanted to tell you for my own selfish reasons.

Several photographs I took of your mother are enclosed. They are yours now. No one other than your mother and I have ever seen these. The photos were gifts to each other during the short time we were together. For her it was the gift of making her look sensual and desirable. The degradation at Auschwitz left her feeling a loss of femininity. She cried the first time I showed her the prints right from the developing trays in the darkened closet I used for developing. I did not know of her terrible experiences at the time. She was a desirable woman. After that, she delighted posing nude for me. They were a gift to me to remember her, but I didn't know that at the time. Some of these photographs were possibly taken on the day you were conceived.

Don't be angry for keeping this from you. And don't grieve for me. I've lived two lifetimes. It has been my fortune to be able to define my life and live it on my terms. Most people cannot. I went out my own way, not wasting away in pain from some terrible disease. Imagine all the things I've seen and experienced. I don't think I wasted my opportunities. From a poor coal miner's son, to a modestly successful writer, to experiencing the great events of the twentieth century. That's more than a full life. I've acquired a measure of wisdom in that time. Not discovering some universal truth but having integrated my experiences into some larger understanding. My life has been rich. I've loved and been loved. The end is not something I dread.

Remember your mother fondly. She was an extraordinary woman. I knew she was Polish, but I learned only in her letter that she was also Jewish and survived Auschwitz-Birkenau concentration camp. It brought to mind Julienne Bontoux's recounting of her experiences in the camps. Your mother did not relate any details of her own experience, but the world knows the horrors inflicted on those that passed through those gates. She said your father, the real father that raised you all those years, had died a couple of years earlier. I assume he was a special man for her to have been that devoted, but she did not talk about him either. She gave only the brief explanation that he was also in Auschwitz-Birkenau, and she was indebted to him for saving her life.

On a practical note, you will find a copy of my will enclosed, properly witnessed and notarized. Go to my attorney in Aix-en-Provence as indicated. You are my sole heir. There's not a lot after French estate taxes; a very modest bank account, all rights to my copyrights and the property here in Provence. Consider keeping it. I believe you enjoyed your short time here. It's a marvelous refuge with rhythms from an earlier time, a different way of life.

I hope you find someone special in your life, Allison. You talk about John but somehow I sense that your relationship with him is more intellectual than emotional. Forgive me for being presumptuous and sounding fatherly.

And as a father, there is something else. Something that may not yet be obvious to you. With the revelation of my paternity, you must consider that you may also have my affliction. Not the cancer, but the abnormal longevity. You are fifty-one years old. When you look in the mirror, Allison, don't you ever wonder why you look to be in your thirties?

Perhaps I am wrong. Maybe you just have good genes from your mother. A few years ago I tried to trace my own ancestry to see if I was truly unique with this longevity, or if it ran in my ancestors. I subscribed to Internet genealogy sites. Found a parish birth record that could have been my mother's. Could not find my father, or at least any record that would definitively establish it was my father. It became more hopeless trying to trace my grandparents. I had too little information. The Murphys and my mother's name, O'Connor, are too common in Ireland. Add to this the inconsistent record keeping during the chaotic time of the 1840's during the Great Potato Famine. I could not confirm either of their births. Was either of them much older than they appeared? Who's to say? Obviously my longevity does not make me immortal. My own demise through cancer proves that. So my parents' deaths through disease proves nothing.

I regret that we could not have been father and daughter. I may have made a mistake by not telling you years ago, but I'm not going to dwell on that. I loved you remotely. I cherished those times we were together professionally.

Live your life fully, Allison. If that is to be an unusually long life, I hope that I may have given you some survival insights. Think fondly of me.

Love,
Your Father

Allison was overwhelmed. She cried inconsolably. After several minutes she recovered her control. Staring out her office window into the gray sky over the towering buildings of Manhattan, she did not move for some time, nor could she stop more tears.

CHAPTER 49

From *Time Travels Epilogue*, first draft by Dillan Murphy
PARIS, FRANCE – 1984

The title *Epilogue* is perhaps not entirely correct. While in a sense it is a concluding addition to *Time Travels*, it is as much a work in its own right. More like a sequel since it spans my later life which I only treated generally in *Time Travels* as my 'later writing years'. As the reader will understand, this conclusion to the story of the life of Dillan Murphy could not be made public until the real death, the fully mortal cessation of existence of Dillan Murphy. *Time Travels* concluded with the impending death of Dillan Murphy, aka Elliot Gaston. Obviously that did not happen. There was never cancer. The boating accident/suicide in the Mediterranean was a fabrication. All this was necessary to move to yet another identity.

Even as the new millennium approached, so did my increasing awareness of the jeopardy presented by my lack of aging. At a point in the not too distant future, the age reflected in my documentation would be untenable given my appearance. Even as early as the 1980's, it was obvious that one's identity was under much greater scrutiny than even just a decade earlier. The hijackings and terrorist attacks of the 1970's changed everything. The subterfuge to become Elliot Gaston and kill off Dillan Murphy would probably not work in the computer age.

I therefore embarked upon a pragmatic long range plan to establish another identity. It was not to be a sequential identity to that of Elliot Gaston, but rather a parallel identity. An identity in which I could develop a real history, my own history, which would evolve ultimately into an identity I could slip into when it became necessary.

Unfortunately, when that time came, I would have to terribly hurt those close to me at the time. Mostly through circumstances beyond my control, I had avoided that wrenching dilemma during most of my life. With the letter from Marie Kryszka informing me that I had fathered a daughter, that changed. Selfishly I remained connected to Allison Kryszka, albeit in a professional way, but nonetheless emotionally engaged. One day that future would arrive when I would cease to be Elliot Gaston. But I still had lots of years before confronting that problem.

So here begins the continuing story of my interminable life and trials. *Epilogue* is about the double, or more accurately, the triple existence that I kept in the shadows. I apologize for the confusion of once again introducing another of my names. I assure you, it was much more difficult for me.

CHAPTER 50

From *Time Travels Epilogue,* **first draft by Dillan Murphy**
PROVENCE, FRANCE – 1984

My identity as Elliot Gaston had served me well for twenty-five years. The transition from being Dillan Murphy was accomplished with no difficulties. Neither Gaston nor I had any family attachments. For that matter, there were few real personal attachments. That probably isn't being fair. Lucille would feel betrayed by Gaston. Fariza probably suffered some grief with the death of Dillan Murphy. But ours was such a short affair, and probably nothing more than just an affair. As for me, I was perhaps becoming used to losing lovers.

But I was approaching sixty by the dating on my passport. At some point in the next decade or two, that would become untenable. Acquiring Elliot Gaston's identity was an accidental opportunity. Acquiring another would take planning and creativity. So how to go about finding a new identity? A fellow author gave me the idea.

In Frederick Forsyth's *The Day of the Jackal,* the OAS assassin is a master of false identities. From a graveyard headstone, he would identify a person of the right date of birth and death. From there he obtained a copy of the birth certificate which led to obtaining other identity documents. It was not quite that simple in the 1980's.

I had purchased the house outside of Châteauneuf du Pape in Provence a year earlier. Splitting my time between the Paris apartment and Provence was a decided luxury. It afforded the opportunity to move north or south depending upon the season of year.

I chose to begin my graveyard search in Provence rather than Paris. Birth certificates were obtained from the local location where the birth was recorded. Better to deal with the small rural bureaucracy than with Paris. I started canvassing the cemeteries around Châteauneuf du Pape looking for headstones with the date of birth around 1960, and death at a young age. Not an infant's death, but not someone that would have left any significant imprint on society outside their immediate family. Certainly not someone old enough to have had a wife or a career. Contending with work records, or worse an unknown criminal record, could be troublesome. I would have to live with this identity for an indefinite length of time so I wished it to be defined by me, not a prior history. A 1960 date of birth would leap me ahead thirty-four years from Elliot Gaston.

It proved more difficult than expected. I tried the larger town of Orange to the north without success. Ultimately I had to go to a larger city to seek larger cemeteries or the task would take much too long. After several days in Marseille I found three possible candidates names. Before selecting one it was necessary to do some research and vetting. Not an easy task pre-Internet. The best public source was the local newspapers.

With my journalistic background I understood how to research newspaper archives and follow leads. At the time, there were two local Marseille newspapers, *Le Provencal* and *Le Meridional*. I might need both since I probably would find nothing more than brief obituaries. The newspaper staff treated me as one professional to another. I used my *Le Monde* business cards with the ploy about researching for a story I was working on. One name came closest to satisfying my requirements. The headstone read *Victor J. Laurent, Born 1961, Died 1983, Beloved Son.*

The first requisite was French citizenship. From the obituaries I learned that Victor Laurent's father was a French citizen. Victor was also born in Marseille, France thereby investing him with citizenship. Each French citizen receives at birth a national identification number called a social security number. This number is used for government provided social benefits, tax reporting, and anything else requiring personal identification. So Victor would have had a number at birth. It might take some doing to find it. It would take some sort of testing to determine if his death had nullified his social security number.

Victor Laurent's mother was Andorran. I knew little about Andorra other than it was a tiny principality in the Pyrenees bordering both France and Spain.

Before investing the effort in securing a copy of his birth certificate, I established that this Victor Laurent fit my other profile requirements. Fortunately the obituary was more expansive than just the basic facts and dates. His father was a criminal attorney, apparently prominent by the length of his son's obituary. The mother was also a former attorney in the Principality of Andorra. The story said the parents met professionally then married. Victor was born six years later. There was a sister three years older than Victor. That meant the parents were probably in their fifties and the sister twenty-six in 1984. Better if there was no family, but that would prove a difficult quest. To find such an ideal candidate could take months of work.

The death of Victor Laurent the prior year was the result of a skiing accident in the Pyrenees. The entire family was on holiday in the mother's home town of Canillo, Andorra. Laurent, an accomplished skier took a bad fall on an advanced slope, striking a rock, inflicting a fatal head injury. The skiing holiday was in celebration of his graduation from the University of Provence in Marseille where he majored in political science. Another useful piece of background.

So Victor Laurent met the basic elements I was looking for. A French citizen. No spouse or children. No career yet started. University degree was a plus. If ever required, it would provide some foundation history rather than materializing as a writer out of nowhere. Didn't suspect he had a criminal record coming from a prominent family of lawyers. There were of course the parents and sister, but I did not expect that to be an issue. I would be using a Paris address and the name was common. I took the pains to check the Paris telephone directory and found three Victor Laurents listed.

So began the tedious process of securing basic documentation. Not knowing what justification I might need, I took the precaution of having business cards printed as *Elliot Gaston, Attorney at Law, Ministry of the Economy, Industry and Employment*. Legal credentials of a government agency lawyer, even just the bluff of a business card, should insure cooperation.

The first item to acquire was Victor Laurent's birth certificate. Records of French births are kept at the Mayor's office of the place of birth. It was a public record and proved fairly easy to get a copy, even in Marseille. After completing the request, a certified copy arrived by post within a couple of weeks.

The French social security number was the essential identification I needed. It was the basic individual identification that all western countries use. I wasn't sure how to manage that. My best prospect was to obtain Victor's university records. That should contain a wealth of personal information including his social security number. Those records were not public information, but my sham official status got by that obstacle. The girl even made photo copies of his entire file including grade records and letters from his professors. Victor seemed a talented young man. Too bad he died so young. I hoped I would give him a surrogate life of some accomplishment.

The university records provided all I needed and more. Foremost, it contained Victor's social security number. During the eighties, the Carte Vitale, the French health card, did not have a photo so this would allow me to obtain a duplicate at some time in the future without raising questions. For some indefinite time, I needed the number only to report taxes on any earnings using the name Victor Laurent. I had no intention of using the identification for any medical services. I could not pass for a twenty-something young man.

The French social security number served as the individual identification number for all documentation. It would be necessary for eventually securing a passport. But that was premature. I first needed to test the validity of Victor Laurent's social security number. The foundation of identity was paying taxes. Eventually I would need to produce income as Victor Laurent. That would be the safest way. If the number was invalid, I would get some sort of official notification. In turn, I would resubmit as Elliot Gaston claiming an initial clerical error of the number, and the use of a pen name.

I had retired from professional journalism in 1975. For the ten years since then, I had devoted myself to writing. It had been tough getting my work published. I wasted several years on a non-fiction book chronicling my observations about the end of the European colonial era. It was boring and not sufficiently scholarly to be well recognized. Not until my third novel *Le Resistance*, published in 1982, did I establish myself as a writer. In 1984 I was still working on my WWI novel, *Ypres*. It would not be published until 1986.

So in 1984 I was setting myself two substantial goals. The first was to solidify my writing career as Elliot Gaston. The second was to begin a parallel career as a new, unpublished novelist. My retirement from newspaper journalism would not be a leisurely one.

For some time I had no idea how I would establish a new identity as a new writer. Before I could publish I had to write something. Write what? The same genre as Elliot Gaston? That was not possible. I couldn't develop another distinct writing voice. Victor Laurent must somehow coexist separately from the Elliot Gaston alter ego. Laurent needed to write distinctively different material.

Over a good bottle of wine listening to Vivaldi, the solution struck me. It was absolutely clear what Victor Laurent would write. My journalistic career with the *New York Times* from 1958 to 1975 spanned the time of greatest tensions of the Cold War. I had experienced both of the great world wars and wrote about those times as Murphy and Gaston. The Cold War was entirely something else. This was a war of rhetoric, of posturing, with the threat of mutually assured destruction preventing direct military confrontation. The only hot warfare was through surrogate regional conflicts. The Cold War was a war of gathering intelligence. Espionage was the front line. Spies were the soldiers.

This would be my new genre for Victor Laurent. Cold War political intrigue and espionage. The many years covering stories and developing relationships with those in the business of espionage gave me not only a wealth of material but a sense of the players. Their real stories were exciting, tragic, bizarre, and exotic. A perfect mixture for a novelist. I could still plot the stories to fit my own perspectives and biases. I could not alter my writing style that significantly, but this different genre would hopefully be enough to distinguish Victor Laurent from Elliot Gaston. It was a perfect solution. Elliot Gaston could continue to write of long past events. Victor Laurent would work in the present.

There was a plethora of spy-based novels out there so I had the challenge of bringing my own originality to the genre. The benchmark was David Cornwell's works writing under the pen-name as John Le Carré. While Le Carré was sometimes plodding,

he was unmatched in creating complex characters, but sometimes at the expense of plot. Le Carré was a Brit after all. I
thought I could breathe more life into my stories with equally
strong characterizations.

The plan became not only a duel identity existence, but a
duel writing task. The practical solution was self-evident once I
embraced the concept. I simply wrote two novels simultaneous-
ly. One might think this impossible. Quite the contrary. It was
liberating in the sense that I could withdraw from one work into
the other. Instead of conflicting, it allowed an escape from the
intense involvement in the other work. I wrote whichever story
suited my mood at the time. It was like having two lovers simul-
taneously.

I must digress briefly and relate how Allison Kryszka, became my literary agent. After receiving the letter from my former lover, Marie Kryszka in 1980, I set about trying to find out
something about my daughter. This was not easy pre-Internet. I
ended up hiring a private investigative firm in New York, arranged through my French solicitor.

Within a few weeks they located her. They sent me a brief
outline of her history. Born in 1958. Attended New York University, English literature major. Lives in Greenwich Village with a
lawyer, but not married. Employed by a literary agency as an
editor.

I was dumbfounded. A literary agent? Not that unusual I
suppose since her mother was a writer. The idea struck me immediately. Why not try to sign with this agency? Not only would
I potentially have contact with my daughter but switching from
my London agency to the U.S. might be professionally a good
move. I had just completed the *Le Résistance* manuscript.

The move proved right on all accounts. Not only did I establish contact with Allison, but she was assigned the editing task
for *Le Résistance*. A couple of years later she became my agent for
Ypres. This association with Allison's agency also proved benefi-

cial in getting Victor Laurent published.

Elliot Gaston simply recommended the agency look at a new author that had a novel of the cold war. He wrote with a literary style, rich with real-life characters set against a creative plot. The style was certainly more John Le Carré than Ian Fleming's flamboyant James Bond. I told Allison he wrote in a style similar to mine. That was what drew my attention. In the world of publishing, getting someone to just consider your work is a major hurdle. It seemed an acceptable deceit at the time.

My first book under the name of Victor Laurent was titled *The Red Apostles,* published in 1988. A different agent than Allison handled the book. Victor Laurent's author photo was not me. Not sure who it was. It just looked right. No need to ever meet face to face with the agency, especially since he also lived in France.

Red Apostles was a fictional work drawn from the real life British intelligence debacle of the Cambridge Five. These were the most senior of intelligence operatives in Britain's MI5 found to be spies for the Soviet KGB in the 1940's and 50's. Le Carré wrote two novels loosely based on these events. My novel was a variant that suggested there was a second group of British intelligence officers spying for the Soviets. They were unknown to the Cambridge Five. My fiction carried further by this British group successfully recruiting United States intelligence officers after World War Two. The speculation that this might be real was floated by more than one person I interviewed. It made for a good fictional read.

Seeking U.S. publication was also pragmatic. *Red Apostles* was about the failure of British intelligence. I remembered the poor response to Elliot Gaston's *Lion Country.* The British were not open to reading about their own shortcomings.

Red Apostles received some good reviews. '*Le Carré with more sex*' was my favorite comment. Sales were respectable. More importantly, it made Victor Laurent a published author. Getting my next novel published was much easier, and with a more respectable advance.

So with that first publishing success as Victor Laurent, I settled into what I considered would be my later years. Although in my case that might be a good many years. I embraced the thought of spending my days writing fiction. There was no desire to pursue more wars as a journalist. The Second World War and my assignments in the 1950's purged any need to experience further conflicts firsthand. The adventures of my youth at the turn of the last century held no allure in my maturity. Upon reflection, the peaceful years between the two world wars were the best of times. Times with Dominique. Writing, working the vineyards, enjoying family. What I did after World War Two came from habit.

For twenty-five years I did not write novels. From my last book as Dillan Murphy, *Terroir* in 1938 to *The Casbah* in 1964 as Elliot Gaston, I did no creative writing. Those were difficult years on an emotional level. For a writer however, the experiences of those years provided a wealth of material for later books.

With the task of maintaining two writing careers, I would need a lot of material. On a practical note, I also decided to adopt a truly duel life. As much as I loved Paris, the winters were too cold. Winter was to be endured. It was gray and depressing. The cold and snow forced you indoors. No sitting outside at a café or just enjoying a stroll. Rain was fine, even adding its own atmosphere, but snow was an uncomfortable inconvenience. So I decided that Victor Laurent would stay in Paris and Elliot Gaston would move to Provence.

I had always loved Provence. The fond memories of my years there eventually won out over the tragic times of World War Two. Those old scars had healed enough to return.

So Elliot Gaston *sold* the Paris apartment to Victor Laurent. I infrequently met my neighbors. It would not matter that they knew me as Elliot Gaston, if they even did. I removed my name from the buzzer plaque at the downstairs entrance, leaving only the apartment number.

As Elliot Gaston I purchased an 18th century farmhouse outside of the wine town of Châteauneuf du Pape. It was only fifteen kilometers from the old Bellamont property. Two years of renovation and modernization achieved the result of preserving the antiquity yet offering modern plumbing and electrical. I had returned home after forty years.

I would share residences for typically two or three months at a time between the two places, and between my two identities. I was free to cultivate friendships in both places with both identities under the guise of the need to retreat for periods of solitude to write. Both Paris and Provence felt like home.

By the early 1990's, Victor Laurent had established a real life. He paid taxes on income as a writer. He owned property and paid property taxes. It was still premature to use social security services, but it wasn't necessary since Elliot Gaston had a Carte Vitale for medical purposes. Perhaps in another ten years time my appearance age would be close enough to match my date of birth as Victor Laurent. At that time I would also seek a passport, completing the creation of the living Victor Laurent.

In a perverse way, harboring my terrible longevity secret seemed less of a burden. Living two identities, neither one being real, felt even more of a subterfuge. Everything was now a complex web of lies. Maybe I was now just used to lying. Maybe I just liked the variety of leading a double life. Maybe I was just getting old.

Not since my years with Dominique between the world wars, had my life been so content and ordered. Whether in Paris or Provence, my day typically started around eight o'clock. After coffee and reading the newspapers I took a walk. The walk ended late in the morning. I would typically have a late breakfast somewhere before returning home. After a shower I set to writing for the rest of the afternoon into the evening, usually putting in a good six hours work. I would sometimes make dinner if I was in the middle of work so I could get back to it for a couple of more hours. Often I dined out. This became my principle social connection. It is also where I became involved with two different women, one for each identity of course. Claudette in Provence and Suzanne in Paris.

CHAPTER 51

From *Time Travels Epilogue,* **first draft by Dillan Murphy**
MEDITERRANEAN, SOUTHERN FRANCE – 2010

My construction of a duel existence fell into place according to plan. Victor Laurent became a real person. All the foundations were in place to let that identity mature to a point when by necessity I would have to abandon my Elliot Gaston identity. Once again my appearance was betraying me. I had equally successful writing careers. I maintained two distinct places of residence, each with its own connections to neighborhood and social habits. Both identities had a small group of acquaintances. Genuine friends were still to be avoided. Intentionally avoiding close social interaction left a void. But intimacy with women was more difficult to avoid.

To have read the chronicles of my extended life, one can understand my attraction to women. Beyond the sexual attraction, a woman presents an emotional connection that may be as equally compelling. I like women. They think differently than men. As much as I intellectually tried to avoid these deeper emotional involvements, I was still all too human.

So inevitably I became involved with not one, but two women; one for each of my identities. One might also say for each of my lifestyles. Living in two distinctly different places allowed me to enjoy a range of experiences, love affairs included. I admit to a lifelong weakness for attractive, interesting women. I never saw a reason to sacrifice one trait over the other. I not only lived in vastly different places, from urbane Paris to rural Provence, but lived them as completely different individuals.

In Provence, there was Claudette Dubois. She was in her early fifties. Claudette had an exceptional intellect that was deceptively concealed with her low-key manner. She owned an art gallery in the city of Orange, a short distance north of Châteauneuf du Pape. Her husband died of cancer at a comparative early age leaving her enough money to indulge her artistic pursuits. She had studied art history and classical violin in her youth before raising two children.

At some point in our relationship she made it known that marriage was not her intention. The children did not live close. I never met the daughter. The son I met just twice. He seemed to take a dislike to me. Perhaps it was some sort of protective instinct for his mother. Claudette spoke only generally about her children. I suspected this might have been Claudette's way of keeping our romance at a controlled distance. Our relationship fit perfectly for both of us.

My periodic absences to Paris were explained as necessary to do research and work the business side of writing with editors at the publisher and my New York literary agent. Claudette only joined me a few of times in Paris over the years we were together. I rented an apartment each time in another arrondissement from that of Victor Laurent. Fortunately, Claudette was not fond of Paris so her stays were short.

In contrast to Claudette, my romantic connection in Paris was a successful business woman. Suzanne Neville was more than just attractive. She worked for the French bank, BNP Paribas. Her specialty was project financial analysis. She was exceedingly bright and was street-smart tough. Her style was more animated, more assertive than the calm demeanor of Claudette. Suzanne had a degree in economics from the Sorbonne and an MBA from Harvard. She spoke French, Italian, and English. At forty-two, she was hitting her stride professionally and relishing her success in a male dominated industry. Divorced twice, she was not interested in marrying again. She liked the fact that I was older and not in business. Suzanne was a beautiful shark with no conventional domestic aspirations. As with Claudette, it was a perfect fit for our respective lifestyles.

In contrast to Claudette, Suzanne was constantly suggesting she join me in Provence. My need to periodically spend protracted time away from Paris was explained as solitude to write. I did my research in Paris. The business side of writing consumed considerable time, also best conducted in Paris. But Suzanne was persuasive and never let a stint of my Provence visits go without at least one visit. Fortunately her professional demands made it difficult to spend more than a few days away from work. During her visits I rented an apartment just like the reverse with Claudette's visits to Paris. I varied those stays in other Provencal towns I enjoyed, usually cosmopolitan Aix, sometimes quaint Gordes, or St.-Tropez on the Mediterranean. All were far enough from Claudette in Orange to avoid running into people who knew me as Elliot Gaston.

Maintaining relationships with two women allowing each to think they were in a monogamous relationship was a deceit of which I am not proud. Both women deserved better treatment. The necessity of leading an imposed double life in order to establish my next identity was my rationalization. But it did not follow that I must maintain two long-running, parallel romantic relationships.

I was with Claudette for ten years and with Suzanne for the last five of those. The emotional trap was not only the freedom of two separate lives, but the charade of playing men of differing ages. With Claudette I implied I was sixty-two. A young-looking sixty-two she commented. With Suzanne, I professed to be fifty-four, only a slight stretch appearance-wise. There were a number of times that I made love to both Claudette and Suzanne within a span of a few days. Admittedly that was an erotic guilty pleasure.

"You hit the right notes, Elliot. You're an accomplished lover," Claudette said kissing me as she swung her legs out of bed. "I often wonder where you developed such skills. But that is your secret and my delight." We had just made love in the middle of the afternoon. "After we make love I often think we should see more of each other. But maybe that is why these weekend liaisons are so intense?"

Claudette had a well-toned body, not even qualified by reference to her age. She sat on the bed with the sheet pulled up to cover her breasts. Even with her hair disheveled, she gave the impression of self-assurance.

"I have those same thoughts, Claudette. But we both have demanding pursuits that define our lives. My writing is a solitary endeavor. You have your art and music. Besides, I fear I am not very domesticated."

"That is obvious. Never married. I suspect a host of lovers over the years. But you're not very expansive about your past, Elliot. Your talk of the past is rarely personally revealing. You have such a sense of history yet your own history is a mystery."

She got up from the bed and put on her robe. She said, "Let's shower and go out somewhere. I want to hear how your current project is coming along, particularly how you are shaping the central female character."

"Ok. But first take off your robe and let me see you, Claudette."

She did as I requested but still with a hint of shyness even though we had been lovers for years.

"Come here. I need to do some more character research."

I remembered that day very well. Everything was right except for one thing. It would be the last time I would see Claudette. Elliot Gaston would *die* within the week. I still feel guilty about deceiving her. I believe she loved me. She would first be concerned about my absence. Next would be the anxiety about what might have happened to me when she couldn't find me. Then there would be the grief over my *death*.

After leaving Claudette that day, I wrestled with the urge to postpone what I had planned. How could I give up such a woman? As always, the answer was the same. If we went on, it would soon become evident there was a problem with my lack of aging. How would Claudette react to a fate where she continued to age normally while I seemingly remained frozen in time? Why had I never attempted to tell her once so many years had past? But the reason was of course obvious.

I must also deceive Allison as well. If she bore the same unusual longevity, I had no wish to live as two furtive souls sharing a strange, conflicted life together. Easier to manage separately. And if she was just normal, then it would be the life I feared with someone close to me aging at a rate that would catch up to my appearance age.

I had constructed what I thought was a simple yet plausible plan for Elliot Gaston to *die*. I had set the tone with Allison that I had terminal cancer. Plausible reason enough to end a very long life as a suicide and avoid a painful ending under heavy medication. I carried no life insurance policy so suicide represented no financial loss to my heirs, or insurance fraud.

But casting off my identity as Elliot Gaston was itself a life-changing event. I *was* Elliot Gaston for over fifty years. I occupied the identity of Victor Laurent only half of that time. My Laurent identity did not have the same depth. I was Elliot Gaston with a part time masquerade as Victor Laurent. Now I would become that alternative solely.

I loved Paris, but I equally loved Provence. The memories here spanned most of my life. I would be leaving Provence perhaps for good. It was home for over thirty years, the longest permanence of my life.

Although in a terrible despair, I was still determined to go through with *killing off* Elliot Gaston. Preparations had been in the works for years. Once I determined to cultivate a new identity back in the 1980's, I embarked on a plan to fund that new identity. French estate taxes are oppressive. Over a period of many years, I found various mechanisms to divert money to Victor Laurent. With the discovery that Victor Laurent's mother was Andorran, I learned that the tiny principality was also a tax haven. This meant that they did not tax earnings outside Andorra. Nor did they tax capital gains on interest earned from deposits with Andorran banks. Bad enough to pay the high French income tax on my earnings, I would at least be able to shelter the interest on the savings and avoid the estate taxes.

When the time arrived, Victor Laurent had a respectable net worth, much of it hidden away in Andorra, while Elliot Gaston would leave only a modest estate. This consisted of the Provence property and enough cash for Allison to pay the estate taxes so she could keep the property. I hoped she would.

The mechanism of my demise was simple. I drove my car to the small seaside village of Cassis on the Mediterranean just east of Marseille. I booked a room at a hotel and had the hotel park my car. The following day I took a bus to Marseille which was only 25 kilometers. A taxi might leave some trace in the small resort town. In Marseille I rented a car and returned to Cassis. The following day I would execute my *accident*. In the two days spent in Cassis I made sure that I had conversations with the hotel staff so that I would be remembered. I made it known that I was going to do some diving.

I was a reasonably good swimmer but knew nothing about diving. I read enough to sound knowledgeable to the dive shop where I rented a wet suit, tank, regulator, and the other gear. The dive shop directed me to a boat rental. Before setting out, I bought a bottle of Scotch at a liquor store. The bag was imprinted with the store logo.

Making sure the forecast was for calm weather, I set out in the early afternoon. The boat was a twenty-footer with an outboard engine. Along with the rented diving gear I brought along a second wetsuit and my own lifejacket. I had purchased these in Marseille along with a waterproof bag. The orange canvas lifejacket was modified with a black wood stain purchased at a hardware store.

I powered the boat out of Cassis to a distance of perhaps four miles. Research had determined that there were no currents that would inhibit me from swimming back to shore. The blackened life vest and black wetsuit should make me invisible from any reasonable distance. I calculated I should be able to swim back within three hours, arriving close to dusk but with a margin so it wouldn't be totally dark. There was some anxiety about being caught out in the water after dark.

The diving gear and rented wetsuit were left in the bottom of the boat. They were only intended to suggest why I had rented a boat and to point to an accident rather than a faked disappearance. If it was thought to be suicide, that did not matter. I emptied most of the Scotch in the water leaving the bottle in the boat. Donning my own wetsuit and black life vest, I jumped into the water with the waterproof bag tied to my waist. The throttle was in neutral. It was an old boat with a basic dead man control consisting of a spring holding the throttle lever attached to the cable running back to the motor. I removed the spring and bent the end as if it had come off. The throttle would stay in the open position. Reaching into the boat, I pushed the throttle forward. The boat powered away, heading out to sea. It was a terribly lonely feeling.

I made it to shore in a little over two hours. I was exhausted more from the anxiety than the physical exertion. I purposely navigated my return to the west of the harbor of Cassis, to the rugged coast known as Les Calanques. Although rugged, there was a walking trail not far from the water that I could hike the couple of kilometers back to Cassis.

Exiting the water at a place where the rocky cliff was low, I climbed the ten meter rock wall. The sun was setting. No one was within sight. From the waterproof bag I took out regular clothes and dressed. Within the bag was another folded back-pack large enough for the wetsuit and the black lifejacket.

With the backpack, I looked like any other hiker as I walked back to Cassis. I drove off in the rental car leaving traces of Elliot Gaston to be found.

CHAPTER 52

From *Time Travels Epilogue,* **first draft by Dillan Murphy**
MARTINIQUE, FRENCH ANTILLES – 2010

It was a gray February afternoon in Paris. Suzanne Neville had arrived at my apartment on Rue du Bac after calling to say she was coming over. She had just arrived on the high-speed TGV train from a business trip to Toulouse in the south of France.

There was little preamble to our lovemaking when she arrived. To say Suzanne was sexually aggressive was an understatement. Where Claudette exuded a refinement even in her approach to lovemaking, Suzanne made love with rapacious lust.

"You like the way I look don't you, Victor?"

She knelt on the bed totally naked. Her breasts were perfect, and she knew it. She leaned back to thrust out her pubic region and make sure I had an enticing view.

"Of course. You look outstanding, Suzanne. Your body is a work of art. You could be a model." Suzanne could also have been a porn star.

Suzanne bounded off the bed. "I'm tired of winter. The weather was a lot nicer in Toulouse. Why don't you let me come see you more often when you go to Provence?"

"Because, just like you, I have to work. I need the solitude to write. You're traveling half the time anyway, the other half you need to be working here in Paris. Besides, you're a distraction, delightful, but still a distraction. Exhausting as well."

Suzanne smiled, taking that as a compliment. "Ok. Then why don't we go somewhere warm for a couple weeks holiday? I'll make the time. We can distract and exhaust each other."

"Like where, Provence?"

"No. It's not that warm right now in Provence. You know that. Some place warmer. The tropics for example. I saw this ad for Martinique in the rail station. Perfect time to go there. We could lie on the beach, make love, and just relax in the sun. It's French, so it'll be easy to get along there. Do you good to get away too."

Looking at Suzanne naked with the prospects of spending a couple of hedonistic weeks in the Caribbean was an enticing thought. "Perhaps you could persuade me."

It was March. Martinique weather in March was typically around a high of 80 degrees F, with little rainfall. It was actually a department of the French republic. Although the locals might speak a Creole dialect, French was the official language. It was a lush green paradise lorded over my Mount Pelée on the north end of the island. Its fame was the volcanic eruption in 1902, destroying the island's principle city and killing tens of thousands. The mountain had been quiet since then and of no concern according to the tourist bureau. The tourist bureau also did not comment on the racial and class tensions that had escalated in the last couple of years. Just like a beautiful woman, every paradise has its flaws.

Suzanne made all of the arrangements. She traveled extensively and knew how to research locales and hotels. The upscale Hotel La Bateliere was a good choice. The hotel was situated on the beach just north of the main city of Fort de France. Suzanne pointed out that it was an ideal location to explore the island by car. Centrally located, we could drive north to the old city of Saint Pierre, destroyed by the 1902 eruption. Or we could drive northeast around Mount Pelée, climbing through lush rain forests to the rugged east coast. To the south were secluded beaches.

The first day we lounged around the hotel swimming pool. The next two days we explored the island which was only 20 by 40 kilometers in size. With that out of our system, we settled into an easy routine of sleeping late then spending the day reading and maybe a little work on our notebook computers. Making love became a late afternoon ritual. We usually drove the short distance into Fort de France for dinner favoring the local color over our hotel restaurant.

Whereas I chose to be unconnected electronically, Suzanne was never far removed from her job. After we had been in Martinique for almost a week, she received a cell phone call from her boss in Paris. We were reading on the beach, sipping pina coladas.

"Paul wants me to pay a visit to the local BNP Paribas manager here in Fort de France," she said. "Seems they have a major project pending. Wants me to go to a dinner the day after tomorrow with some local big shots. He thinks I might be able to help push things along." Paul was her boss.

"Because of your looks probably," I said. I was mildly irritated for her job intruding on our time.

"Don't be a prick, Victor. It's because I'm corporate. Adds weight and prestige to the local manager's stature. Besides, it will give me a chance to see what the local investors are like and give Paul my impressions."

"I'd like to ask their opinion about all these protest signs we see," I said. "And that demonstration we passed yesterday in Fort de France. They've apparently got some problems here. And who or what are the *bekes*?"

"Oh shit. Don't be getting into political debates at this dinner, Victor. I'm supposed to be helping this business deal not sabotaging it."

"And what is this deal?"

"Paul says it's a large scale combined agricultural and industrial development project. Large at least for Martinique. Lots of pieces. Intended partly as an economic stimulus. Martinique has suffered during the recent recession. Prospects for a recovery are bleak. BNP is involved at the request of the Government. There's public funding that will flow through BNP as well as government guaranteed loans we'll provide to private investors for the project."

"How does this help the local workers? More jobs, better jobs?" I asked.

"I don't know. It's not my project. I suppose it will."

"Like most of these deals, the investors will benefit the most," I said.

"Christ. Are you a socialist or something, Victor? Don't pick a fight and fuck up things. This is my job you know."

I held her shoulders and kissed her. "I'll be on my best behavior. I won't make you look bad. I'll pretend I'm doing research and listen rather than argue. Even if the dinner guests turn out to be assholes."

Civil unrest in potentially violent form was closer than I imagined. I vaguely recalled reading about some rioting in early 2009. It never got much play in France. What had been festering since then was a continually eroding economic situation for the poor. Of course the poor were the native black majority. The wealth was held by the whites of European ancestry with the derogatory label of *bekes*. The racial tensions made the situation volatile. Added to this mix was the steadily growing influence of an independence movement. I could see the parallels with Algeria fifty years ago.

Suzanne had not researched our island paradise deep

enough. But such issues are always downplayed to avoid loss of tourist revenue. There was little coverage in the press, and nothing about any further threat of violence. While we stayed mostly at the sequestered hotel during the day, we missed the increasingly boisterous demonstrations of the last few days. We did not learn until later that the power outage two nights previous was the result of a labor strike. This was not the place to come for a holiday but we did not realize that yet. Until the night of the business dinner we had no idea that the potential for widespread violence was a serious threat.

The dinner was to be held at a restaurant in the affluent suburb of Didier. Suzanne and I took a taxi not wanting to navigate the residential streets at night with our rental car with perhaps too much to drink. The elevation of the road steadily increased as the taxi drove north out of Fort de France. Progressively the houses became grander as the elevation increased. This was where the wealthy of Martinique lived.

La Belle Epoque restaurant was a turn-of-the-20th century colonial style mansion. It had a commanding view over the city. The dining room was elegant with the service of crystal and silver. The room opened onto an expansive paved terrace surrounded by a garden, with the city of Fort de France spread below. The entire restaurant had been reserved for the evening for this event. There were about forty guests standing about the terrace sipping drinks. The men were dressed in tropical tuxedos, the women in designer dresses. It was a perfect tropical night. Waiters served hors d'oeuvres of seafood, pâtés, and cheeses. A piano player supplied background music. The atmosphere was decidedly more French than Caribbean. Most of the guests were white. The restaurant staff was black.

Suzanne made her rounds of the wealthy of Martinique. I could see why she was effective. She looked stunning in a cream dress revealing a good amount of cleavage. The dress was set off by her dark hair and a new tan. But once she engaged in business talk it was clear she was no mere beauty. When the topic turned to finance or banking, she was in her element. I was introduced as her *companion,* a novelist. Most of the men preferred to discuss business with Suzanne rather than literature with me. Given how Suzanne looked, that was understandable. Prospects suggested a long, dull evening of business conversation.

Unfortunately, that was not to be. Sounds erupted in the distance. It was gunfire. Everyone went out onto the terrace to look down toward the city. A number of fires could be seen. The head of the Martinique police and the Mayor of Fort de France hurriedly left taking the small contingent of police from the front of the restaurant with them.

"What's going on, Victor?" Suzanne asked. More fires seemed to ignite. Gunfire continued in the distance.

"I don't know. Rioting it would seem. Apparently Martinique's business elite are out of touch with the real situation here."

"What should we do?" she said.

"Don't know yet," I said. "I think we stay put for right now. We don't have a car. A taxi is out of the question."

Suzanne went back into the dining room to speak to her colleague from BNP.

I turned at the sound of shouting. Already on edge with the specter of potential violence, I knew from experience that something was wrong inside the dining room. Instinctively I jumped from the terrace and hid behind a bush. Within moments several armed men appeared on the terrace. They ushered the guests back into the dining room.

I crept to the wall of the restaurant next to an open French window.

A voice in heavily creole-accented French said, "You will not be hurt if you obey. You are now prisoners of the Martinique Liberation Front. You will be held in exchange for the release of our comrades being held by the French police."

"What if the government will not bargain?" a man asked.

The leader of the armed men answered, "They will. Or you will be killed. One at a time. I believe the government will bargain once Frenchmen, or perhaps even women, start to die."

I snuck a quick look inside the dining room. There were seven men I could see. All were armed with handguns, except for one man with a pump-action shotgun. At least there were no assault rifles. Poorly armed, I figured them for some rag-tag separatist group looking to gain from the economic turmoil. Probably Marxist leaning from their name.

I worked my way around to the front of the building. In front were three more men. Unfortunately, they did have assault rifles. Two cars had been parked cross-wise blocking the driveway from the entrance to the restaurant. They were prepared for a police assault. At least there was no threatening mob.

Once the gunmen communicated with the authorities, police would arrive. Maybe French police if there were any on the island. Whatever provincial Martinique police forces existed, they probably would not be equipped to deal with a hostage situation. When that happened, it could become a dangerous standoff. No telling the outcome. Suzanne might endure a terrible ordeal even if she escaped unharmed.

While the situation remained fluid, I would at least try to formulate a plan to rescue her. First I had to determine where Suzanne was. Was she exposed if I tried to do something and there was shooting?

"I want the women to separate from the men. Women on this side," the gunmen leader ordered. The women were grouped into a corner of the dining room.

Looking to the men, he said, "Tell us your name and what you do." Reluctantly, the men stated their names and professions. One man refused and was struck hard in the face with the leader's gun. One of the gunmen took notes. They assumed the men were of importance, the women just wives or mistresses. Better for Suzanne that she was not identified as *important*. But then the thought occurred to me that she might therefore be considered more expendable as leverage.

Taking short glances into the dining room, I located Suzanne toward the back of the group of women. She was somewhat out of the way of the gunmen.

After a half an hour, the leader placed a call on a cell phone. He spoke loud enough for everyone to hear. "This is the Martinique Liberation Front, inspector. We have occupied the La Belle Epoque restaurant in Didier. There are many of us, all well armed. We have hostages. Many prominent people. Let me read you their names."

After reading the names of Martinique's ruling elite, along with several mainland Frenchmen, including the Deputy Minister of Economics of the French Republic, he resumed reciting his demands. "Our demands are simple. First, we demand the release of all Martinique political prisoners now held by the French government. Secondly, we demand safe passage for ourselves by aircraft to a neutral country of our choice. In exchange we shall return these *bekes* unharmed. However, if the Government refuses, we are prepared to start killing hostages. You have two hours until midnight to reply. After that, we shall kill one hostage every thirty minutes."

Rhetoric or just bombastic threat? No way to tell. The Government would not grant their demands. At the least, the situation would soon escalate into something dangerously unstable.

My plan was simple. Two gunmen stood outside on the terrace facing inward to guard against anyone trying to escape into the surrounding garden from the terrace. One was the man carrying the shotgun. He was closest to me. He was the key. If I could overpower him and get hold of the shotgun, I would be a formidable counter to the other men armed only with handguns inside the dining room.

For a weapon, I found a shovel and pick where workman had been constructing a new planter. I choose the pick.

If I could approach the twenty feet without being heard, I would incapacitate the man and take the shotgun. With a pick I would most likely kill him. So be it. If he heard me in time, he'd turn and kill me with the shotgun. Either way, one of us would die badly. A lifetime of being in life-threatening situations taught me to develop a course of action and then execute it quickly. Debate and hesitation could cost you your life.

The other gunman outside was at the far end of the terrace. He could still shoot me before I recovered the shotgun. Nothing I could do about that.

I removed my shoes to quiet my steps on the terrace pavement. With short, quick steps, I covered the twenty feet to the man closest with the shotgun. The pick was poised over my left shoulder as I advanced.

The man never heard me. The sharp point of the pick sunk into the upper part of his back several inches with a sickening sound. The man let out a load grunt and exhale of breath. He went down hard with the shotgun clattering to the stone tiles of the terrace.

In a matter of seconds the other gunman turned and fired wildly at me. My attack took him completely by surprise and his shots were not aimed. I retrieved the shotgun as he fired. He was fifteen meters away, easy to miss with a handgun especially if panicked. I focused narrowly on the need to get the shotgun, holding down my own instinctive reaction to try to avoid being shot.

I brought the shotgun to my shoulder and took the time necessary to bring the man into my sights. It was an act of will not to rush my shot. The man took another shot that again missed. The shotgun was a twelve-gauge. Not sure what type of shot it was loaded with but it did not matter at this range. The shotgun bucked up and to the left as I pulled the trigger. My shot took the man in the upper abdomen.

All this happened in only a few seconds. Turning abruptly to the dining room, I chambered another shell then picked my next target; the leader. He went down as well with a terrible spattering of blood. My shot was high, catching him in the face. I racked another round and turned my sight on anther gunman. The man leveled his handgun toward me and fired. Another miss. I exhaled and fired. Moving to the next target felt like shooting pheasants back in Provence with Pierre. Like the birds, the remaining gunmen fled the restaurant.

"Stay down!" I shouted. "There are more gunmen outside."

After several minutes of silence, I moved cautiously toward the front door of the restaurant. I cracked the door slightly to look outside. I saw no one. Only the normal night sounds could be heard.

Things remained that way until police sirens could be heard coming up the road. The quests clamored around me shaking my hand and slapping my back. One of the guests was a doctor. He pronounced three of the men dead. The fourth was still alive.

Suzanne wrapped me in her arms and cried uncontrollably. She was aghast at the carnage. Death by shotgun left an ugly aftermath. Some of the guests gawked at the dead men and the pooling blood. Others averted their looks. It was gruesome, especially the man I shot in the face and the other with the pick still imbedded in his back.

From the look of the wounds, the shotgun had been loaded with double 00 buckshot, a police load, not a sporting load of smaller sized birdshot.

"My God, Victor, what have you done?"

She meant it as a comment about the enormity of what happened but I reacted to the literal question.

"Done? I killed the bastards and saved you from whatever."

"No. I mean that's wonderful. Not wonderful with the bloodshed, but so …. I don't know the words. You saved us all. And you could have escaped. It was horrible to watch. I'll never get the images out of my mind. What possessed you to do what you did?"

I couldn't actually say why I did it. More rage than courage. To protect Suzanne? Unfortunately, everyone else saw my rescue of the hostages as spectacularly heroic. How could such a circumstance intrude upon me? What were the odds? Greater than being struck by lightning. Yet here I was, thrust into the spotlight. Doing the right thing was a catastrophe that could now cost me everything. I did the right thing only to have it potentially destroy me.

I was questioned for hours about the details of the event. The French Deputy Minister of Economics, one of the hostages, was profuse in his thanks. Over my protestations, he vowed to bring my heroic actions to the attention of the President. He apparently did since the French President mentioned my name in comments about the violence in Martinique early the following morning at a news conference.

My hopes of downplaying publicity were further dashed as news photographers snapped pictures as Suzanne and I left police headquarters in the morning. It had been less than a year since the *death* of Elliot Gaston. My face displayed prominently as front-page news would be seen by those that knew me.

Suzanne was enthralled with my hero status. Once she recovered from the emotions of the event, she had endless questions about the mechanics of the killings. Why did I do it? How was I so calm with the bad guys shooting at me? How did I feel about having killed these men? What about sinking a pick into the one man? She visibly shuddered at that thought.

It was mid-morning before were got back to our hotel. During the night the police reestablished control. A curfew was set for that night. Paris was sending 200 special riot police to reinforce the situation. Once back at the hotel, we made preparations to leave Martinique immediately.

Suzanne was continuously on her cell phone recounting

events to everyone she knew back in France. I deflected multiple calls from the hotel desk about reporters seeking interviews. Once we secured a flight, I arranged to leave the hotel by a service entrance to avoid reporters and photographers.

Suzanne had pulled strings to get us the last two first-class seats on a 7:00pm Air France flight to Paris-Orly. My escape from the hotel worked effectively until we arrived at Martinique's small Aimé Césaire International Airport. The place was clogged with passengers. Every flight was booked full. Reporters and photographers were capturing the chaos. Unfortunately, one reporter from outside the police station recognized me.

"Monsieur Laurent. Can you tell us what happened last night? The police say you single-handedly rescued a number of people being held hostage by armed gunmen," the reporter asked. The microphone was thrust in my face. Worse yet, the reporter's photographer was capturing my image on digital video. I was trapped among the throng of people surrounding the ticket counter. Other photographers joined in the frenzy.

"I have no comment. It was a difficult situation. I simply reacted. Nothing more to say."

"The police say you killed three men and wounded another. The President is even calling you a hero. How were you able to overpower these gunmen? Do you have a military background?"

"I'm sorry. We have a plane to catch."

"Was your companion among those you rescued?" the reporter said referring to Suzanne who was clutching my arm."

"Yes I was," Suzanne said. "Victor saved me and everyone else. It was a terrible thing to live through. Victor Laurent probably saved many lives."

I pulled her along toward the boarding gate while holding my hand in front of the camera lens. But I knew I was too late to avoid the photographs that would probably appear the next day throughout the world.

As expected, I not only made the front page of *Le Monde* but the inside pages of the *Times of London* and the *New York Times*. Unfortunately, they all carried pictures of me. I made the broadcast news as well. Several reporters called seeking interviews. The video tape showing Suzanne and I leaving the hotel was played by all news networks. There were two messages from the French President's office.

Worse yet, three days later, the French tabloid *Le Parisien* did a story. My photo was front page. Inside were grisly closeup photos of the dead gunmen, including the pickaxe sticking from the back of the one man. The day after, the British tabloid, *The Sun* did their own story.

'Writer Kills Gunmen: In a bizarre episode during recent rioting in Martinique, a novelist brutally killed three gunmen to rescue his girlfriend and other hostages. A militant separatist group had taken a gathering of influential guests hostage at a restaurant. A published novelist, Victor Laurent, was able to miraculously kill several of the gunmen singlehandedly and chase off the others. France has hailed him a national hero.

Inexplicably, Laurent was able to approach one of the gunmen from behind and then kill him by sinking a pickaxe into his back. Taking the man's shotgun, Laurent proceeded to shoot three of the other gunmen. All this took place while the gunmen were firing back at Laurent. One witness remarked on how calm and measured Laurent was as he took aim while being shot at. Laurent's ability to execute such a brutally efficient counterattack on the hostage takers suggests some sort of professional military or police background. Available background information on Laurent does not indicate any prior experience or training that would explain his heroic actions. Many feel that Victor Laurent ....'

We were discussing the newspaper report while having dinner at one of our favorite Left Bank restaurants in the 6th Arrondissement on Rue Christine. "I don't understand why you are shunning the spotlight," Suzanne said. "You're a ligitimite hero. You saved lives. It will boost your book sales. Look at all of the free publicity. And I certainly can't understand your refusal to be honored by the President. You won't even return their calls."

"I'm not a celebrity. I simply did what I had to, Suzanne. It was a terrible ordeal. I killed three men. I don't need to relive the event any more than I already do. So no interviews. No honors from the Government. I don't even want it to be the topic of conversation with our friends. I want to put the whole event behind me. I want my life back."

Within a week, the killing of the gunmen in Martinique was no longer news. The troubles in Martinique continued but large scale violence seemed to have been avoided. The militant separatist group that engineered the hostage taking faded from the scene. I thought I may have escaped my likeness being recognized as that of Elliot Gaston. I was mistaken.

CHAPTER 53

From *Time Travels Epilogue,* first draft by Dillan Murphy
PARIS, FRANCE – TODAY

My door buzzer in the downstairs building entry sounded on an afternoon two weeks after returning from Martinique.

"Yes?" I said into the intercom.

"Monsieur Laurent?"

"Yes. Who are you?

"My name is Henri Thomas. I'm a reporter with *Le Parisien.* May I have a brief word with you?"

"I do not give interviews about what happened in Martinique. Goodbye."

"A moment, monsieur. It is not about Martinique. It is something else."

"What then?"

"Perhaps we could talk in your apartment. I think you'll find what I have to say interesting."

What was this about? I had little choice. I needed to know what this reporter was pursuing. Worse yet was the fact that *Le*

Parisien was a tabloid publication.

I buzzed him in and waited at my open door. He was a short man in his forties in a bad suit. I refused his hand shake to set the tone that this was not to be an invited exchange.

"I'm busy. What's this about?" I asked, closing the door but not inviting him to sit down.

"I'm not at all sure. You see we were contacted by someone who claims you are someone else."

"What the hell does that mean? You came here because someone has mistaken me for someone else? Haven't you got better material to work with?"

"Well, it's a little more than that, Monsieur Laurent. I said the very same thing. So this person sends me photos. They're either you or your identical twin. See for yourself."

My heart sank as I took the photos from him. They were me. Several were taken by Claudette. Another was of Claudette and me. Foolish perhaps in retrospect but how could I have anticipated these events.

"I admit this person has a likeness to me, but it's certainly not me. So why are you interested?" I said.

"Likeness? I would say much more than that. Do you know a Charles Dubois?"

Shit. That was Claudette's son.

"No."

"How about a Claudette Dubois?"

"No. So who are these people?"

"Claudette Dubois is the woman in the picture. She lives in Provence. Her son came to us after his mother recognized you in the recent news photographs and broadcasts about what happened in Martinique. He claims you were romantically connected with his mother for a number of years."

"Well it's not me. I don't know these people. And that still doesn't explain why any of this is of interest to *Le Parisien*."

"Well, Monsieur Laurent, it seems the man Madame Dubois

knew was named Elliot Gaston. Interestingly, Monsieur Gaston was also a writer like you. A novelist even. Here are several photos from dustjackets of his books. They appear to be you as well."

He handed me the Elliot Gaston photos.

"Even more curious was Elliot Gaston's accidental death less than a year ago. No body was ever found. A boating accident in the Mediterranean. The police in Marseille have not ruled out suicide. Perhaps it is neither."

I handed the photographs back to the reporter feigning no interest.

"Listen, I've told you I don't know these people. I can't imagine where you see a story in any of this speculation that I am this Elliot Gaston. I'm sure you've checked my background. I've published several books over the last twenty years. Why would I be this Gaston person? These people have an uncontrolled imagination. Because I bear a resemblance to this person, this woman saw my picture in the news and jumped to a ridiculous conclusion. She's probably suffering from grief over her loss. Perhaps she and her son are trying to perpetrate some hoax on the newspaper."

"Possibly, but I don't think so. Perhaps there isn't a story here. Perhaps it's some odd coincidence. But that's the way investigative reporting works. Your instincts suggest there is something newsworthy so you pursue it. Sometimes it leads nowhere, but other times they develop into real stories. We'll see where your story leads, Monsieur Laurent. By the way, weren't you born in Provence? Are you sure there's nothing you want to add to explain this strange set of circumstances?"

"Goodbye, Monsieur Thomas," I said as I opened the door suggesting he leave.

That visit changed everything. I was a good investigative reporter myself and I knew this guy would probe further. It wouldn't take long to track down Victor Laurent's parents. They would be in their seventies if they were still living. They would confirm their son died in a skiing accident in 1983. That would lead to his French INSEE number which would be the same as mine. If this involved the Government, they would discover that the passport fingerprints of Gaston and Laurent were from the same person. The apartment sale by Elliot Gaston to Victor Laurent would eventually be uncovered.

All this would clearly point to a fraudulent conspiracy demanding a criminal investigation. I had committed any number of crimes. I might even be suspected of some involvement with the death of Elliot Gaston. Whatever the outcome, I would be subject to arrest. There would be no way to extricate myself from the tangle of lies and the unbelievable truth that would never be believed.

The life I had created was ruined. Everything had come undone. The day after the reporter's visit, I packed my bags with a good deal of my clothing and a few personal items. My old notebooks from World War One were the most bulky. Dominique's and my wedding rings were the most precious possessions. Much of my life I would have to leave behind. Fortunately in the digital age I was able to commit all my writing and photographs to electronic files backed up on USB drives. Most of my life I could carry on my notebook computer.

Depending upon how events unfolded, there was a distinct possibility I would not be returning. I also might not see Suzanne again. After abandoning Allison and Claudette a year ago, I would now lose the last person connected to my life. Suzanne and I had many years ahead of us. Now that was gone. I was leaving my home and my life to go into hiding as a fugitive.

Before leaving the apartment, I sent an e-mail to Suzanne reading, *'Leaving Paris for awhile. Hounded by more reporters about what happened in Martinique. They even got my cell phone number. I broke it in anger so you can't call me. I'll call you in a couple of days. Not sure where I'll be, just away from here. Love you, Victor.'*

The cell phone was gone, purposely discarded not broken. No telling where this was going. Cell phone calls left digital tracks. Perhaps that was being paranoid. Besides, I never liked cell phones. Handy for your own use but it gave others far too much immediate access to you. I would have to be cautious about using my e-mail account. Technology had it's drawbacks for someone wishing to hide.

I took a taxi to the Paris Montparnasse rail station. Using cash, I purchased a first class ticket to Toulouse in the south of France on the high-speed TGV train. The seemingly odd choice of choosing the industrial city of Toulouse as a place to hold up temporarily had a practical reason. It had the most direct rail connection to the Principality of Andorra. That was my potential refuge if everything went wrong. I owned property in Andorra. A small chalet I rented out. Even though closely aligned with France, Andorra was just as much connected to Spain and ultimately was its own miniature sovereign state. Besides, Victor Laurent's mother was Andorran. That might offer some future citizenship possibilities.

From the internet, I found a small boutique hotel in Toulouse. It wasn't a particularly interesting hotel but it did have a view over the Garonne River running through the city. The old town section of Toulouse was a short walking distance. Not exactly Provence, but I didn't plan on staying that long. So I hunkered down to observe events.

Using the Internet, I kept an eye on *Le Parisien's* on-line site. Nothing about me appeared since the reporter had paid me a visit a week ago. Nothing appeared in any of the other French publications either. Could be that the *Le Parisien* reporter wasn't able to expand his story. Maybe his editor just killed it. Tabloids don't usually work a story very long so maybe I would be lucky.

I called Suzanne at her apartment from a public telephone in Toulouse.

"Where the hell are you? And why haven't you called?" she

said. "I've been back just two days and the police visited. I want to know what's going on, Victor. This is not about Martinique."

"Easy, Suzanne. I'll explain later. You need to trust me."

"Trust you? The police asked me all sorts of questions about someone named Gaston. Who the hell is he? And some woman, a Claudette something in Provence? Who is she, Victor?

"I don't know either one of them."

"Bullshit. Your lying, Victor. I saw the photographs. I thought I meant more than that to you."

"Come on, Suzanne, you've not being fair."

"Then tell me how it was that you bought your apartment from this Elliot Gaston. That's what the police told me."

I paused for a moment to gather my thoughts and fabricate another lie. "A solicitor did the deal. I never paid attention to the seller's name. This whole affair must have something to do with this Gaston person."

"I don't believe you, Victor. This Gaston person and the woman live in Provence. You go to Provence every couple of months. That's too much coincidence. First you go off without warning without any way to contact you. No cell phone. You don't answer my e-mails. All this on the pretext that it's about what happened in Martinique. Now the police want to talk to you. That's the real reason why you left and that's what you're not telling me. Call me when you want to tell me what's really going on, Victor."

She disconnected.

Now I was wanted by the police. Suzanne didn't give me a chance to find out what the police questions were about. It didn't matter really. If arrested, they would eventually discover that I was Elliot Gaston. Hard enough to explain being in my eighties. They would of course contact Allison as Elliot Gaston's literary agent. How would she react? They might discover the yet un-published manuscript for *Time Travels*. No telling where that would lead. Whatever happened, I would never again own my life. I regretted most how my deceit would affect Allison.

The following day I was having a coffee at a café. On the empty table next to me was today's edition of *Le Parisien*. My photo was on the front page.

The headline read: *'Hero of Martinique a Fraud?* The article read: *'Victor Laurent, the novelist who single-handedly killed three terrorists and rescued a group of hostages is being sought by French police. Laurent who lives in Paris has not been seen for over a week. His girlfriend, Suzanne Neville, a BNP Parabas executive, has told police she has no idea where Laurent might be.*

Why Laurent fled is not clear. The police are not charging him with any crimes at the present. He is currently wanted only for questioning as a result of a bizarre set of circumstances that might lead to criminal charges. The most intriguing circumstance is that Victor Laurent was apparently leading a double life as another published novelist, Elliot Gaston, for perhaps twenty years. Photographs of Gaston and Laurent are clearly the same person. The police have also confirmed that passport fingerprints for both Laurent and Gaston are identical.

To add to the mystery, Gaston's year of birth was 1926 making him in his mid-eighties. Current photographs are clearly of someone much younger. Laurent purchased his Paris apartment from Gaston over ten years ago. Then last year, Elliot Gaston supposedly died in what was ruled either a boating accident or possible suicide in the Mediterranean. Authorities have no theories as to what might be behind this Gaston and Laurent connection.

Laurent/Gaston appears to have led a completely double life for many years. Laurent lived in Paris, Gaston lived in Provence, dividing his time every couple of months. In Paris, Laurent maintained a romantic relationship with Mlle. Neville. In Provence as Gaston, he was romantically involved with an art gallery owner, Claudette Dubois. It was through Claudette Dubois that this entire affair became public. Upon seeing the photographs of Monsieur Laurent in the news after his heroic rescue of hostages from armed gunmen in Martinique, she recognized him as her lover of many years, Elliot Gaston.

An unnamed senior police official made the observation that Victor Laurent's books were Cold War espionage novels yet Laurent did not have any apparent experience in intelligence work. He speculated about the possibility that Laurent might be a spy with his double identity architected by some foreign intelligence service. The same police official commented that Laurent's brutal retaliation against the gunmen in Martinique suggested some sort of professional training.

The police are still investigating the background of both the Laurent and Gaston identities to determine ....'

CHAPTER 54

From *Time Travels Epilogue,* **first draft by Dillan Murphy**
PRINCIPALITY OF ANDORRA – TODAY

It was clear what happened. Claudette saw my photograph splashed everywhere in the media after what happened in Martinique. She told her son. Outraged that I had duped his mother, Claudette's son contacted *Le Parisien* since they ran a major front page article of me and photos of the dead gunmen. He probably contacted the police as well. Claudette would feel doubly betrayed with my alter-identity photographed with the younger Suzanne. She probably cooperated fully. A woman betrayed. She certainly had every right to feel that way.

I thought about calling Suzanne to explain everything. Explain how I aged at a rate of only half of the normal human process? Considering the effort in convincing Allison, that would be rejected as ridiculous. And how did that justify deceiving her with another life, with another woman, for years? It was hopeless. There was no explanation possible. I was simply a liar for my own venal purposes.

What about Allison? I could contact her eventually. Would

she understand? Would she forgive me for cruelly abandoning her when she knew the truth of my life? Why in fact did I abandon her? Afraid to admit to the deceit of my Victor Laurent identity all these years? Afraid of a relationship that might endure even with my longevity?

Time Travels Epilogue will be published only after my real corporeal death. At least I hope it will. It will be a remarkable sequel to *Time Travels*. Until then, I will continue to write my interminable saga that is not yet ended. I am now just looking for some measure of peace in my remaining years. I might never find that now. Perhaps I should just let events unfold. Not sure I cared anymore.

I was not at all confident about what to do next. The life I had so elaborately constructed had come apart in a matter of weeks. I lost everything. I was a fugitive, yet I had not committed a crime, at least none of any consequence, and certainly not with any malice. With a heavy heart I made plans to go to Andorra. That prospect further depressed my spirits. It was an exile.

I had been to Andorra only twice, both times in the summer. The first time was to see the place first-hand, and a second time to conclude the purchase of a small chalet as an investment. A management company rented the property and took care of cleaning and maintenance. It proved a good investment with just the revenue from the four months of the ski season alone. It was approaching May now.

Paris was as cold a climate as I could manage. I tried to be in Provence for the better part of winter each year. Even there it was often uncomfortable in the winter. Now I was going into exile to a ski resort in the Pyrenees. I did not ski. Was this justice, bad luck, or some divine retribution?

The only way to get to Andorra was by motor vehicle. There was no airport. You could only get close by train to a point just outside the border with France. Andorra had an area of less than

500 square kilometers, all mountains, and about 90,000 people. To call it a backwater would be an understatement. It was not a Monaco.

It was not clear how much of a refuge the Principality of Andorra might provide. If I was wanted in France, then Andorra's unusual status might not prove all that helpful. Andorra had most of the trappings of a sovereign state with its own parliament. Andorrans had their own passports. But technically Andorra recognizes the President of France and the Bishop of Urgell, Catalonia, in northern Spain as joint heads-of-state. That unique arrangement was over 700 years old.

I had no idea what that meant in practical terms. At least French was widely spoken along with the native Catalan. I owned property here. Victor Laurent's mother was Andorran. I could only hope that I was not important enough for the French authorities to cast their search for me into Andorra. Technically I was not a fugitive since I was not charged with any crime, at least not yet. The problem was chiefly that I could no longer live in France without fear of being detained for questioning by the police.

The train arrived at the small isolated Gare de l'Hospitalet-près-l'Andorre. This is where you took the bus into Andorra. The small rail station was an isolated and depressing place. A few vehicles with ski gear mounted on roof racks were parked in the lot. A bus was parked in the dirty slush of melted snow.

I looked like a tourist that had over-packed with my two suitcases and notebook computer. For me it was everything that I possessed. The bus was full of young skiers. My spirits lifted a little as the bus made its way through breathtaking mountain scenery still shrouded in snow.

I was able to book a hotel in the center of the village of Ordino until my own chalet became available after the last scheduled rental concluded for the season. Ordino was at least a picturesque village in the northwest of Andorra. However, besides skiing in the winter and mountain hiking in the summer, little else went on. For an outsider, this would be a cultural wasteland. Spending my remaining years here was a depressing thought. Certainly nothing would distract from my writing. It was a beautiful prison, but still a prison nonetheless.

Covering ones tracks in the twenty-first century was a complicated affair. In the age of databases a person existed everywhere and everything they did was recorded somewhere. Difficult enough that I had to use my French passport for identification but at least my passport was not electronically scanned when I entered Andorra. Even though Andorra was not a member of the EU, it still observed no formal immigration control for EU citizens. Since it was a tax haven, customs inspection had little purpose.

However, other identity essentials needed replacement. The most problematic was not being able to use my credit cards. To get new cards, I would still need to provide my French INSEE number for credit checking. I would need a new form of identification to get credit. Obtaining Andorra citizenship would be the only way to pursue constructing a new identification. I had no idea if that was even possible, much less how long it would take. In the mean time I would resort to cash. At least that was not a problem since I had long ago established an Andorran bank account for tax shelter purposes. My bank debit card was almost as good as a credit card. I closed my French bank accounts in Paris and left with a sizeable amount of cash from there as well.

As I was returning to the hotel from lunch one day, the desk clerk called to me. "Monsieur Laurent. Someone called asking if you were a guest here. They did not give a name. We are of course discreet and do not give out our guests information. Thought you might wish to know."

I tipped him generously and told him to let me know if anyone called again. Unfortunately it was becoming a messy divorce I told him. He understood completely.

According to the desk clerk, it was a man that called. Who or what was he? How did he track me here in only a couple of weeks? A reporter? The French police?

A week later as I walked through the lobby, I made eye contact with a man in his fifties. He averted his glaze immediately. Not sure why it piqued my interest. Probably because I was on edge. Maybe because the guy looked a little out of place. He was older than most of the ski crowd, balding, reading a magazine in the lobby in the afternoon. Just didn't look right.

The next evening after returning to my room from dinner down the street, I had the sensation that someone had been in my room. Sitting down to make some notes in the computer, I noticed a stack of pages I left on the desk. The papers seemed too neatly aligned. At least it seemed that way. Just paranoid? The housekeeper perhaps. But I realized that if it was something more, it didn't really matter. I had nowhere to go.

The last rental on my chalet expired with the ending of the ski season. I had been holed up in the hotel for four weeks. Canceling the rental arrangement with the management company, I took possession of my own place. It would be cheaper than living at the hotel but I would be even more isolated unless I got a car. It was several kilometers outside of Ordino. For the time being I would walk. It would be a good daily exercise regime to walk into town each day. At least it would soon be summer.

I arranged for a taxi, giving the driver the address to the chalet only a couple of kilometers outside of town promising him a decent fare for the short ride.

"Do you come to visit Andorra?" the driver asked in heavily accented French in response to my French.

"Perhaps to live here. I was here a very long time ago," I answered.

"Ah, Andorra does that to those who visit. And what is your business if I might ask, Monsieur?"

"I write books mostly."

"You are French?"

"Yes, I guess you'd consider me French."

"*Parla català?*" the driver asked in Catalan.

I recognized the phrase. "No, only English and French. I will have to learn Catalan."

"Ah, it is *dificil* to learn a new language. Once you are older it takes a long time. I had to learn English to drive taxi. Took many years."

"Well, I have a lot of time."

I settled into the chalet. An open loft with a large window afforded a perfect writing place. The view was spectacular even for someone who didn't like snow. Spring had arrived with mountain flowers blooming. Nothing newly suspicious had happened. What I felt back at the hotel was probably only imagined. I was not wanted for any serious crime. French police would have an interest only if I were detained for some unrelated reason. And that would only happen if I committed some blunder. There was no reason French authorities would be actively searching for me, least of all outside France. At least I didn't think so.

My anxiety was simply in being caught and being robbed of living out my life on my own terms. The scenario would involve the police investigating an identity theft. I was guilty of passport forgery and social security fraud. I wouldn't go to jail. But this would lead to some sort of public revelation. My remaining life would be one of hounding by a curious press. I would not be able to write. I would have no friends or loved ones. I betrayed all those close to me. Life would be reduced to mere existence, not worth living.

Andorra was not the location I would have chosen for exile but I was starting to adjust. I resolved myself to live this life of forced austerity. I would remain hunkered down in this exile. Better to immerse myself in writing than become an object of public curiosity. Unfortunately even my writing was wrecked. I would have to adopt a new pen name. That meant starting all over as an author.

Working in the loft a week after moving in, the doorbell rang. It was the middle of the afternoon. I had no neighbors close by. No one had come around to the chalet since I moved in. With some trepidation I went downstairs. I might as well face up to whatever impending fate this might be. I opened the door.

"Hello, Father," Allison Kryszka said. "I think you have some explaining to do."

Photograph acknowledgements:

Cover – top photograph: Battle of the Somme, 1916; Source: Imperial War Museum; Author: Ivor Castle; Permission: public domain
Cover – bottom photograph: Tour Eiffel; Source: Dillan Murphy archive; Original author: Douglas Clark
Page 8: Anthracite coal mine near Scranton, PA, 1905; Source: Keystone View Co.; Permission: public domain
Page 18: 1895 vintage erotica; Source: vintagepics.com; Original author: unknown; Permission: public domain
Page 23: Mulberry Street, NYC, c. 1900; Source: Wikimedia Commons; Original author: unknown; Permission: public domain
Page 32: Col. Theo. Roosevelt with "Rough Riders" on San Juan Hill, 1898: Source: en.wikipedia; Original author: unknown; Permission: public domain
Page 45: Fifth Avenue, New York City, Easter Sunday, 1900; Source: Bureau of Public Roads; Author: U.S. Bureau of Public Roads; Permission: public domain
Page 54: Flatiron Building, Manhattan, NYC, c. 1903; Source: Library of Congress; Original author: unknown; Permission: public domain
Page 68: Tour Eiffel; Source: Dillan Murphy archive; Original author: Douglas Clark
Page 79: Stretcher bearers, Battle of Pilckem Ridge, Passchendaele, 1917; Source: Imperial War Museum; Author: Lt. J. W. Brooke; Permission: public domain
Page 88: Second Battle of Passchendaele, 1917; Original source: unknown; Original author: unknown; Permission: public domain
Page 93: British Mark I tank, Somme, 1916; Source: Imperial War Museum; Author: Lt. Ernest Brooks; Permission: public domain
Page 100: Derelict tank and exploding artillery shell, WWI, 1917; Source: Library & Archives Canada; Author: Canada Dept. of National Defense; Permission: public domain
Page 113: French 37mm gun; Source: U.S. National Archives; Author: U.S. Department of the Army; Original author: unknown; Permission: public domain
Page 117: Battle of St. Mihiel, 1918: Source: U.S. National Archives: Original author: unknown; Permission: public domain
Page 132: Rue Lepic, Paris Montmartre, 1925; Source: Post card 1925; Permission: public domain
Page 139: Vineyard near Castillion-du-Gard, Provence, France; Source: Dillan Murphy archive; Original author: Douglas Clark
Page 152: Châteauneuf-du-Pape, Provence, France; Source: Dillan Murphy archive; Original author: Douglas Clark
Page 158: Vineyard near Châteauneuf-du-Pape, Provence, France; Source: Dillan Murphy archive; Original author: Douglas Clark
Page 166: French partisans, Paris, 1944; Source: Le Comite de Liberation du Cinema Francais; Permission: public domain

Photograph acknowledgements (continued):

Page 178: Gordes, Provence, France; Source: Dillan Murphy archive; Original author: Douglas Clark

Page 193: Nuremberg War Crimes Trials, 1945-1946; Source: U.S. National Archives; Permission: public domain

Page 204: Palais de Luxembourg, Paris, 1922; Author: Eugène Atget; Permission: public domain

Page 211: Hurva Synagogue, Jerusalem, before 1948; Source 1939 JNF photo archives; Permission: public domain

Page 218: British checkpoint Tel Aviv, 1948; Source: *To the Promised Land* by Uri Dan, Doubleday, 1988 p.115: Original author: unknown; Permission: public domain

Page 235: Arab volunteer fighters, Palestine, 1947; Source: interet-general.info; Original author: unknown; Permission: public domain

Page 244: Irgun's ship Altalena on fire near Tel Aviv, 1948; Source; Slater, Elinor & Robert, *Great Moments in Jewish History*, Jonathan David Publishers, 1988; Author: Israel Government Press Office; Permission: public domain

Page 267: French 13th DBLE, Roman ruins, Lambaesis, Algeria, 1958; Source: private collection of Lt. Col. Paul Paschal; Author: Richard Bareford; Permission: public domain

Page 278: Algiers, Algeria, 1921; Source: Colliers New Encyclopedia; Author: Publishers' Photo Service; Permission: public domain

Page 291: Algiers' Casbah, 1900; Source: *Architectures Françaises: Outre-Mer*, Pierre Mardaga éditeur, Collection Villes, 1992 ISBN 2-87009-475-2; Author Viollet; Permission: public domain

Page 336: Louvre Museum & Pont Royal, Paris; Source: Dillan Murphy archive; Original author: Douglas Clark

Page 338: Cimetière du Père Lachase, Paris; Source: Dillan Murphy archive; Original author: Douglas Clark

Page 349: Cassis, Southern France; Source: Dillan Murphy archive; Original author: Douglas Clark

Page 357: La plage des Salines, Martinique, 2006; Source: Barbacha/Nicolas Bouthors; Permission: public domain

Page 371: Paris Left Bank, 6th arrondissement; Source: Dillan Murphy archive; Original author: Douglas Clark

Page 379: Grau Roig, Andorra, 2006; Source: Wikimedia Commons: Original author: unknown; Permission: public domain

www.ingramcontent.com/pod-product-compliance
Lightning Source LLC
Chambersburg PA
CBHW030353030726
47497CB00002B/325